DEATH & GLORY

A BURNINGSOUL NOVEL

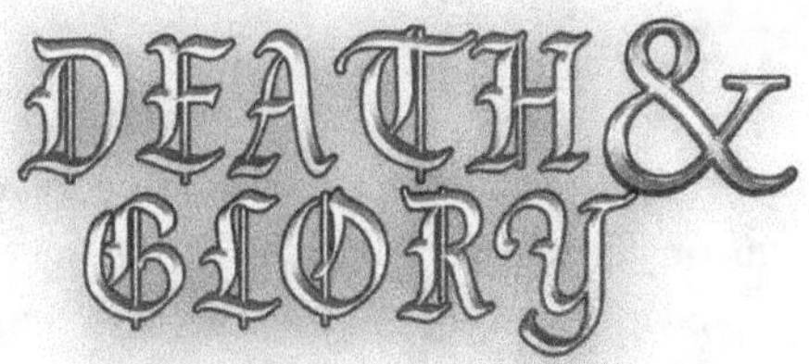

DEATH & GLORY

A BURNINGSOUL NOVEL

REGINA WATTS

Burningsoul Saga Book IV: Death & Glory
© 2025 Regina Watts
ISBN: 978-1-957469-18-8

Text: Regina Watts
Typesetting: M. F. Sullivan
Cover Painting: Vanette Kosman

http://www.hrhdegenetrix.com
http://www.paintedblindpublishing.com
publicity@paintedblindpublishing.com

*For you,
my patient readers.*

VISITATION

I DID NOT recognize Weltyr right away: that was how old he looked.

In some strange manner, I was aware I dreamed; yet, I was also aware I could have done nothing to awaken from the dream of my own volition, which made it as static as any day of human life. Perhaps it was the scenery of Dunnun's island, where I found myself, that provoked the lucidity of my dreaming state—but, more likely, it was my flagging master's will. Indeed, I was so aware of the island and the wrongness of its presence around me that I forgot my own existence. I was preoccupied by the bluff upon which rested a solitary figure, hunched with age, cloaked in black, a broken walking stick in the embrace of his arm.

Only as he raised his eye to me did I remember myself, and by this context make sense of his presence.

"Rorke, Rorke," he said, raising his eye to, in some strange fashion, bore through both of mine—and far more. Into everything I was, or had been, or would ever be, and with still greater secrets than the human mind could ever approach in questioning, let alone satisfaction. "Why do you look so frightened upon your progenitor? You who bear my blood know me even now."

I hardly knew what to say, though my mind was so clear I may as well have been fully awake. But, had I been awake, I would have struggled just the same. How could I say what I thought? I only spoke because I knew the futility of lies.

"Aside from the circumstances of our last meeting being unfavorable for me," I answered, "I suppose I did not anticipate I would find you looking so...old."

For old, he had become. Hildolfr, when I knew him as that man, had been older, yes, but strong and vigorous, his mind and body exhibiting an admirable dexterity. Now, all that had changed. As the hood fell from his raised head, new shadows cast their dramatic way down Weltyr's cheeks and the hollow of his eye, and even the impression under his lip visible at either side of his now unkempt beard. The lines in his brow were severe, and the gnarled hand that gripped his broken spear was withered by time, or so it would seem. The snake of a blue vein haunted me, disappearing up his sleeve in a pursuit my eye aborted when he suggested, "You'll look like this someday, Burningsoul. In fact, you may be even worse... but I won't be around to see it."

"What a curious thing for a god to say."

I had said this in a jesting tone, attempting to inject levity to drive away the fright I experienced when he spoke this way. He did not laugh at all, however; he barely even smiled. I let my inappropriate mirth fade as he asked, "What do you think a god is, Rorke?"

"I—"

My mind raced as I struggled to articulate a suitable answer. "A god—a god is a kind of advocate. The guardian of a certain discipline or sphere of reality."

"And is that all you reckon I am?"

Chastened, I said only, "No. You've accomplished miraculous things before my eyes. You gave life to my lineage, if indeed I am a Wotsung, and indeed that title has meaning."

"Yet, my power wanes. My influence in this world is limited. And why is it limited, boy?"

Feeling less like he used the word to diminish me and more like he was speaking to me as what I was in comparison to him, I betrayed myself with a brisk glance at his shattered spear, then met his eye again. "I have my theories."

"Theories—because of the choices you have made with the sword I gave you?"

His eye dropped to my side. Exigence was in my hand, weightless as in any dream. I raised her, looking long upon her blade and seductive hilt of glittering Deepgold.

"You've killed me, Rorke," Weltyr observed, looking back into my face.

"If I have done such a heinous thing," I replied, defensive as any small animal backed into a corner by a being far greater in power and scale, "then surely it must be because you permitted it, Lord—but I cannot imagine why."

"I am bound to those contracts I enforce, which are my sphere to rule. I cannot defy myself. Only a man with the strength of a god could do what I needed. And you did it."

"Then you did not just permit it, but you wanted it." Incapable of grasping this, I tore my attention away from the sword to find Weltyr now stood just before me. Somewhere, a raven cried a hateful seven-note laugh. "Why would you want your own death, my Lord?"

"Renewal can only follow destruction…something you've never wanted to face." Now a slight smirk quirked his lip. "If you had your way, Rorke, every day would be Winter Festival. That's why it always surprises me you would choose to leave the Valor Hall."

Frowning, I sheathed Exigence with respect to his nearness and said as I did, "Of course I chose to leave it—I had to, for my children and my wives." Hesitating at the meaning of the rest of his words as much as at the ease with which the evidently natural state of my relationship with Valeria and Elishta-bet (and, it had been prophesied, a third) emerged from my mouth, I asked, "What do you mean by 'always'?"

"I'm proud of you," he told me instead of answering, his expression the gruff one of an otherwise stoic father suddenly getting the words out before it was too late. To hear him say it twisted my heart, and I opened my mouth, but he would not give me time to speak. "Know," he went on, "that you can never disappoint me, Rorke. You can only be exactly as you were created to be, even within the movements of your will throughout this world whose order I maintained. And that, my son…"

Valeria's cool hand caressed along my cheek, and

Weltyr smiled as the dream came to an end.

"That is a mystery even greater than my death, and all that will happen after."

"Wake up, slave," my durrow mistress groaned in my ear, her caress turning into the tight clench of her tapered fingers into my cheeks. "I need you to fuck me—wake up, I say!"

Rest assured—at her blunt command, I was awake.

SUBJECT OF NEGOTIATION

VALERIA HAD TRANSFORMED during our time since leaving the Nightlands. I had watched her experience not just the loss of her privileged station and all the treasures it implied but also the exposure to realities she had never been made to face. She had never even experienced jealousy, I think, until quite recently, as when we argued before the captain of the *Flying Rhinemaid.*

But the change that had come upon her since our return from the Valor Hall had been strange. Her sexuality had become more aggressive again, as it had been in the Nightlands, but there was a new softness to the center of her soul that exuded from her every command. Why shouldn't it have been like that? Of all three of us, myself and Elishta included, she was first to realize we were dead, and that realization affected her transition back to life. When she saw I was awake enough for her liking, she lunged upon me to pour a heavy kiss into my mouth, her tongue stabbing against mine but quickly retreating to coax me into pursuit. As her hand slid down my stomach and beneath the sheets that had tangled around our waists, she raised her mouth from mine with a breathless gasp for air.

"Your sleep-murmuring kept me up," she remonstrated, lowering her head to sink her teeth into my jaw. Her teeth shocked me with pain even as her hand shocked me with pleasure by leaping down upon my tumescence, and both sensations combined in a heady, irresistible way. Beneath the sheets, Valeria took to petting me with that slow, soft hand of hers, then suggested, "Or perhaps it's the scent of you, your body. You need a bath; you smell like an animal."

I twitched in her hand, my palms enclosing the beautiful black heart of her face to draw her back into my kisses. "And that's what makes you want me to fuck you, is it, Materna?"

This was that softness, that longing hidden in the center of her words. She berated me for her greater pleasure, got rough, and guarded her heart. But I now had the sense that, as she had relied on my protection in the Nightlands, she now knew her own helplessness, and my strength, and the depths to which my love for her truly ran.

In those days, she was still newly pregnant; but I suspect that the condition was already having some effect on her temperament, which was that of a passionate woman who wanted to have it proven to her she could still be loved in the heights of that passion, that bad behavior that had the curious effect of making me love her only more.

"It is," she said through clenched teeth, an adorably fierce expression that sent another rush of pleasure bounding through me at the tighter grip of her hand. "It reminds me you belong to me...that I permit you the luxury of freedom to sweeten your nature as my willing possession."

My hand lowered from her cheek, thumb trailing along the column of her throat and over the sumptuous hillock of one perfect breast. Valeria, with child...soon, her body would be swollen with my heir and the sustenance to feed him (for I sensed with certainty that Roserpine's words were true and this one would be a boy in defiance of the ways of durrow), and I would see her endure a delicious internal conflict liable only to increase our enjoyment of every interaction. How would my durrow mistress, who fancied herself my owner even though the days of our Nightlands games were long past, interpret the experience of having her body serve as the field from which sprang rich and vibrant life?

"You're so hard," she commended, oblivious to the true nature of my thoughts as I rolled her over and planted kisses down her supple body. "One would almost think you enjoy being demeaned by me, Rorke."

"I just enjoy the sound of your voice," I told her, savoring each press of my lips along the soft elf-flesh of her still taut tummy. While, sighing with pleasure, she spread her legs in anticipation, I slid my hands along her inner thighs and let my tongue flicker along her mound, kissing the patch of white hair poised above the cleft of her tender cunt. "I enjoy everything about you, Valeria... so much so that it doesn't matter that you're cruel to me. Even that is sweet."

"Rorke," she murmured, some of a plea in the sound of my name as it emerged from her that time. Responding so she would not have to accept the influx of her emotions in this precious moment of lovemaking, I kissed along the pouting lips of her labia and let my thumbs ease her open just slightly. She gasped as the air hit her already soaking flesh, the high contrast pink of her inner folds glistening with need even before I traced my tongue along them. Crying out and gripping the bed covers beneath her, then the pillow behind her head, Valeria made no effort to stifle her pleasure from the women asleep in the *Flying Rhinemaid* cabins beside ours. The thought of her exhibitionism made me ache to be inside her, each low groan of her mouth or flood of pleasure along my tongue another pulse of desire that turned me into the animal she wanted me to be. It helped that she was so especially eager, even for her: as I pressed my mouth more completely against her gorgeous sex and let my tongue flicker just in and out of that sweetly flowing hole, she produced a sound almost akin to surprise, and I sensed she had climaxed without meaning to. Yet, as I tried to ease my mouth away to give her a moment, she caught me by the hair to keep me pressed there, arching her hips and grinding herself against my jaw.

All the same—hilariously, I should say—she complained like the spoiled brat she's always been, demanding, "Did I tell you to eat me, slave, or did I tell you to fuck me? Oh—oh—ah, by Roserpine's tits—"

"I'm sorry, Materna," I told her, slipping a finger just barely inside and inhaling sharply at the insistent clench that dragged my digit deeper. "I heard what you said, but your impudent slave can hardly resist...and you like it, don't you, Madame..."

"I'll tell you what I like, damn you—ah—"

Mouth upon hers, I shut her up with kisses, the plunge of my tongue toward the back of her throat silencing her into a pretty little moan. At her insistence, I withdrew my finger and forced her legs wider, bearing down upon her center with no further warning or preparation. As I plunged into her soaking core and groaned at the inundation of pleasure, feeling as if I had just leapt into the crisp blue waters of a perfect lake on a hot summer's day, Valeria nearly choked on her own tongue with the intensity of her scream and arched her hips to meet mine, offering herself to me absolutely, gasping, "Oh, yes, sweet fuck, yes, plow me, slave—oh, you stud, that's right, cripple me with that big, human cock, run me through—"

Valeria! There is no doubt I take immense delight in the women I most love, but Valeria has a way of plunging my soul into infinitely deeper ecstasy each and every time I take her in my arms. As my durrow mistress thrashed beneath me, I wrapped an arm around her hip to grab hold of one fleshy globe of her sumptuous ass, keeping her pinned to my body and open to the deep, merciless hammering of my cock into her womanly grotto. As her torso flexed and contorted, her nipples hard pink beads against her dusky flesh, I bruised her with kisses and sank my teeth along the sensitive ridge of her highly sweeping elvish ear, each bite of her nails into my back only furthering my pleasure. This is something else too wonderful about Valeria for me to resist—how eager she is, now away from the Nightlands and the pride of her station there, to pay the penalty for her wicked mouth, to entice me to great heights and then eagerly receive every scrap of the attention she's merited. She loves to be pulled from her pedestal and stripped of all her power until, captive to my cock, she's helpless beneath me and given no other choice but to recognize how much she needs the pleasure I give her.

How much she needs me.

"I want you to cum inside me," she whispered harshly, her eyes blazing as I released her from a kiss so we could gasp together. Even speaking this command made her grip flutter around me, and she enticed me on as, arching her hips and letting her bare feet slide along the muscles of my thighs, she shuddered. "I need it, Rorke, oh, yes, Rorke— I—"

Her face changed, and her eyes darted askance with the utterance of a single syllable: "Sh!"

My body was so calibrated for danger—after not just my training but all we had been through since our time in the Nightlands—that I stopped short mid-thrust, hyper-aware of the nearness of Exigence, my arm ready to sweep the blade out from beneath the mattress; yet when Valeria remained supine beneath me, a half-smile on her lips, I realized what had caught her attention.

A soft little moan, poorly stifled, tapered off through the wall separating our cabin from the one Elishta-bet shared with Branwen that night. My cock throbbed at the sudden knowledge that Valeria's antics were reciprocated with suitable voyeurism. Seeing I had heard, my durrow mistress moaned low, her fingers carding sensually through my hair.

"You must let me fuck that adorable girl of yours," she purred as I resumed thrusting into her, all the harder now. "That pretty human, Elishta. I've never fucked a human woman before, and besides—mm, she's so shy but so curious, it makes me want to do all manner of sordid things to her."

"She might not agree to it," I posited, for Elishta's benefit as much as for Valeria's consideration.

Valeria was quick to brush this off as a minor detail.

"She would walk over burning coals for you if you but asked...I'm sure you could persuade her to relent to some fun. Oh, mm—fuck—" Eyelids fluttering, Valeria gripped my shoulders and rocked into my slightly faster thrusts. "Besides, oh, ha—it's as we discussed before. If I'm not to keep male slaves aside from you, then I must be recompensed...give the girl to me as a pet, and I'll be mollified."

"How reasonable."

"Don't act like you don't want to help me...this cock is harder than your sword at the mere thought. Don't you want to hold her down for me while I introduce her to all manner of pleasures her innocent mind has never imagined?"

Elishta's sharp little moan, renewed, was quickly stifled as if by hand or pillow, and Valeria and I both laughed together—then Valeria's face changed, her perfect brow furrowing and her pelvis pitching up against mine. "Oh fuck," she gasped sharply, "oh fuck, that's it, that's it, Rorke—go on, slave, promise you'll give me Elishta-bet and I'll let you cum, go on—"

"I'll give you anything," I told her, overwhelming her mouth with kisses as our bodies were overwhelmed by pleasure. "Anything, anything at all—Valeria, oh, my love, my queen—"

"Rorke," she shouted, her words a blaze as her body collapsed into an Urde-rocking climax that dissolved my composure and brought about mine, "Rorke—oh, my love—"

"I love you," I growled, catching her face in my hands and enjoying her surprise as I laid out my heart so plainly amid all her rough talk. "You're the song of my heart, Valeria—my joy, my love—my soul."

"I love you." She whispered it like a defeat, an admission, but seemed so relieved as the words burst from her lips to cling to my heart the way her body clung to mine. "I love you so much, Rorke—oh, Rorke—what am I to do?"

And, looking at me in helpless fright as our climaxes eased into what normally should have been tranquility, my beloved burst into tears.

THE MORNING LIGHT

SEEING VALERIA WEEP is a startling thing, for she is a woman whose level head and steady demeanor does not easily succumb to emotional expression. Only truly immense movements of the heart could provoke such an experience from her—and it was these types of movements that her heart could hardly stand. She let me hold her, yes, and wept in my embrace as other women might have under more typical circumstances; but rather than hiding her face in my chest as Elishta might have, or wailing and gnashing her teeth between provocative kisses like a certain mad witch who had begun in a strange way to occupy the background of all my thoughts, Valeria kept her face twisted away, hidden in the pillow, sullen as she soaked the fabric with her sorrows.

Yet even with her precautions, she could not hide the truth from me. I knew what she dreaded, because it was what I dreaded, too. Eventually, I knew, we would find Roserpine's ring. Eventually, she would hold in her hand that reason we had left the Nightlands, and she would have renewed claim over the throne of her people. The time for her to reclaim her role as the priestess-queen of the durrow would be nigh, and Valeria would need to make a choice. I could only pray she would make the right one for her soul—and for mine, too. For I could have all the women in the world—even the two others for whom I most deeply longed—but they would be cold comfort if I could not clasp Valeria to myself and kiss her until her derisive little scowl melted into that contrite glow of amorous trust that overcame her when, caressing her, I drew her from her wave of tears and into another hot embrace of love. When she fell asleep, I was tempted to join her; but I could also tell by a peculiar quality to the light of even that windowless room, thanks perhaps to some cracks in the boards here or there, that it was nearly sun-up, and I wished to see what I could of the dawn before the captain sped away from it again. Therefore, silent as I could be, I slipped Valeria more completely upon the mattress, depositing her gently from my arm and drawing the covers up over the delicious curve of her bare shoulder. There, I kissed her. She sighed in the voice of a dove, then dozed deeper, inundated in a dream that, if my own since returning from the Valor Hall were any indication, was more likely to be prophetic than not.

In the dark, I dressed, drawing my tunic over my head and silently stepping from the cabin. Over the course of the past week, the deck of the *Rhinemaid* had been considerably repaired by the undead crew, but progress was slow and supplies frequently ran short. This need to stop was what delayed our disembarking, as the captain was more interested in waylaying other airships to plunder their repair supplies than in finding a suitable location to drop us off.

"What the hell are ye in such a rush fer," she had barked at me only the night prior, the little light within her empty eye socket blazing at my impatience. "All yeh's do is eat up our wares an' screw yer women! Seems to me we'd oughter be chargin' yeh fer comin' on a cruise."

Maybe she had a point. But, my moral problems with her enterprise aside, I couldn't help being restless. My duty to find Roserpine's Ring now extended beyond even that fealty I owed to Valeria. When we found it, I would have a decision to make: for it, along with Hamsunt's Lantern and the hilt of Exigence, was Deepgold that belonged by rights to the daughters engendered by Weltyr in the womb of Valeria's dark goddess. The last of the three most precious objects in the world, still eluding us, and, by extension, the Deep-children. When I contemplated it out there and turned carefully over all the implications of finding it, my heart could enjoy no peace.

Nor could the Selectrix whose red hair billowed in the pre-dawn wind, her gentle, virginal features haunted by the intense inward-looking wisdom of ancient sages and the terminally ill.

"We'll land soon," she told me without turning to look, her words in fact the only acknowledgement of my presence at her side. "There is still a long way for us to go. If you don't get your rest now, it may be some time before you find relief."

"What about you, Brynhildr? Don't Selectrices need sleep?"

A sardonic smile such as I had never imagined her wearing twisted across her pretty lips. "Sleep," she answered, "is the least of my worries. No—I won't sleep now. It's battle that fills me with vigor...so I'll have plenty of spirit in me soon enough. Rorke—"

She turned to look upon me, her blue eyes sharp as they bored into my face.

"You must promise to listen to me," she said, "no matter how frightened it makes you. Remember that following my guidance has served you well so far, and don't forget. Do you understand?"

Hesitant, I answered, "Yes—but I must admit, Brynhildr, when a man's Selectrix says a thing like that with such gravity, he can't help but find it unnerving."

"Good." Her gaze trailing away from mine now, sliding along the horizon of the world as glowing sunlight warmed its edge, Brynhildr said, "You should be unnerved. You must be ready for anything, Burningsoul. There will be things I cannot warn you about—things you do not understand—things that will horrify you about the world. About yourself. But...no matter what, you must remember—I have no choice but to do my Father's will. My existence is an expression of that will. And so, when I speak that will to you, no matter how contrary it may seem to even my own wellbeing—you must hear it, Man, not as my will, but as Weltyr's. Do you see?"

"Yes," I told the battle-angel softly, frightened to look upon her in that moment and instead transfixed by the growing light of distant dawn. "Yes, Brynhildr, I see."

Satisfied, she nodded. Her eyes fixed ahead, she who charged so boldly into the most treacherous battle seemed to hesitate. I waited in silence for her, the parting of her lips louder than the least word. When she moved, it was not to speak on, but first to turn her eyes to me.

How strange, to see a Selectrix at all—let alone one with tears in her eyes.

"I'm frightened," she whispered to me. "Rorke...you men can't understand. Love strengthens you—it props you up. Yet it kills a woman, Rorke. And how frightened I am to die to myself as I am now! How frightened I am by how much I will love him—by what I will do for him."

Her gaze lowered to the spear whose silver tip shone in the light of dawn as she shifted her hand. "Who will I be," she whispered, the urgent whisper of one prisoner to another shortly before the former approaches their date of execution, "when I am this no longer? Who will I be, what will I be, when he has taken the spear from my hand, and stripped me of my armor, and I am left helpless beneath him, as your women are reduced beneath you?"

Once, Brynhildr had said something strange to me, and in an inundation of other strangenesses it became lost like one droplet in a mist. Now, though, I recalled that same droplet striking my cheek. This Selectrix was the one prescribed to look after me, yet she was destined, it would seem, to love one of my offspring. The notion of a Selectrix being tamed by love was so foreign that I nearly protested her assessment of the feminine experience, wanting her to see that she was an extraordinary being designed for battle and service to the All-Father in the fetching of fallen warriors destined for the Valor Hall. But quickly, my thoughts on Valeria re-entered my heart, and I considered how even Branwen, in her fondness for me, became docile at certain moments beneath my touch—though the effect was not so pronounced as it was in Valeria, whose deep love for me felt more mature than the high elf's hot-and-cold crush.

Overcome by a paternal tenderness for Brynhildr, I slipped my arm around her shoulders and drew her nearer to me, where I dared to press a fond kiss atop her head. With a hitch of her breath and a gnashing of teeth, the warrior maiden—truly a maiden, I felt in that moment, again staggered by the surreal awareness of some metaphysical nature belying all artifice—pressed her face into my shoulder and hid herself there, unspeaking.

"Bugger off, Burningsoul, and save some women for the rest of us!"

As my hand stroked supportively between the suddenly laughing Selectrix's shoulders, which shook slightly as her tears of fright turned into unanticipated mirth, I glanced up from her mane of fiery hair to find Grimalkin marching over. The dwarf's chest was puffed, his shoulders thrown back and his expression so dynamic I had trouble discerning whether he was serious. That had always been the case with Grimalkin, in truth. The trouble with a man who takes everything personally is that one can never comprehend his sense of humor.

"I was only comforting my friend," I assured him, my hand raised to rest gently upon the back of Brynhildr's head, then releasing her altogether as she briskly wiped her tearful eyes and flashed a small smile up at me. "I assure you—though, if you're hoping to compete for her affections, you may have lost that race before it's started."

"Let's let her be the judge of that," Grimalkin said, leaning against the rail with his fist propped against his cheek and a leer lighting his eyes as he assessed Brynhildr.

"What d'yeh say we help ourselves to a bit of brekkie before the rest of the ladies are up, Bryn?"

"I'd say you're already too late," she said, gesturing starboard with her spear tip. "That one's been up for quite some time already."

My heart stirring, I followed the tip of her weapon and let it guide my eye across the ship. Carefully negotiating her way over and around discarded supplies of the half-repaired mast, her nose wrinkling at a whiff of drying tar, Elishta-bet looked about for something I knew not of. My attention snatched from the conversation, especially as she vanished out of sight around the edge of the forecastle, I smiled at my current companions and said with an apologetic wave of my hand, "I'll let you two get a head-start on breakfast and find out if Elishta feels up to joining us—see you in a moment."

While Grimalkin snorted and muttered, "More like thirty-five moments," I strode after my friend and wondered in what condition I would find her. It seemed to me—or had seemed to me, at any rate—that Elishta was, of all the women who had gathered around me, perhaps the least suited to the promiscuous lifestyle preferred by the durrow women with whom I traveled. Yet, well…I was also beginning to sense a certain intrigue from her, and I could hardly resist my own urge to foster it. I rounded the corner after her, calculating how best to approach her and plant seeds in this fertile ground I had noticed with Valeria's help—

And fell short, ashamed to find her silently praying.

How chastened I was by that vision! I, a paladin— once a paladin, at any rate, though now I was but a wanderer in the confused service of my weakened god, rather than one of the appointed knights in the service of his Church—was stricken by the stark reality: it had been a great many days since I had truly prayed. Even in the Valor Hall, or perhaps especially in the Valor Hall. In that place where my god had been so literally and bodily present, I had managed to disregard the foremost duty of my station, which was not battle, but piety. I had become focused on active service, (so I told myself I was focused on, at any rate), and had allowed the quest to fetch the Deepgold consume me.

Though...perhaps there was another, deeper reason my prayers had been so stymied until my witness of Elishta's deep devotion. For, intending to join her, I took a step forward—and a hateful voice, an alien voice, rose up in my soul to speak through my consciousness in a manner I had not experienced since before my departure from life and into Weltyr's house.

The fool! Wasting her time—she does not know you struck him down with that sword he gave you, Eradicator. Perhaps you ought to tell her the truth...that your god is dying, dead, and she would be better off praying to those deities that still thrive, capable of working in the world. What does it matter? They are all the same, the lot of them. Mere fleas on the hide of the Sleeper.

My head throbbed with an ache that pulsed in the same rhythm as the hivemind entity of the spirit-thieves, that mass of heinous red tissue kept beneath the saltwater of some dark place I had never seen outside vague visions. Damn Al-listux—would this accursed connection remain for all time, for so long as I was upon Urde? Ever since the spirit-thief had afflicted me, the inescapable knowledge of my connection to their network was another thorn in my side. Humiliated by my own negligence and, I will confess, frightened by my own weakness owing to my connection with this demon, my heart inclined strongly toward prayer. I stepped forward, intending to join her.

Starting as if in fright, Elishta cringed up from her place, whirling toward this interloper—then, with a new and prettier color about her cheeks, relaxed. "Oh," she said, laughing and pressing a hand to her bosom through the soft blue fabric of her boy's shirt, "Rorke! I thought you were one of the crew."

"I don't think they'll hurt you now, Elishta, even if they found you alone. They have something of a sense of honor, from what I've witnessed."

Before I could apologize for interrupting her, she shook her head. "Mm-mm, it isn't that. I'm just—well, I'm not sure how sensitive they are! What if they should behold my praying and be turned by the sight?"

Adorable Elishta! There has never been a woman as innocent and tender of heart as she. The art of 'turning' the undead, as it was called, was a foremost specialty of paladins in the service of Weltyr, for it was not killing, as they were already dead; nor was it wholesale destruction, because that was not the method, though it seemed often as such. Rather, it was the generally held opinion of scholars of these matters—such as Father Fortisto, the old mentor of mine in the citadel at Skythorn—that exposure to anything above a certain degree of holiness would make it impossible for the undead to continue their unwholesome existence, as it provided them with a knowledge of divinity and the human soul that was incompatible with the reality of their condition. While it was true that some such beings could hold on to their deluded, degenerated forms longer than others, (for instance, I would anticipate the captain and her crew far more challenging or even impossible to turn compared to, say, a simple zombie, as they were conscious, thinking beings despite their abominable status), in the long term, no undead could resist the will of God. And, while it was also true that turning was generally a deliberate act apart from prayer, prayer was a part of turning; therefore, Elishta's thoughtful initiative to pray in secret was not altogether baseless, and was another glimpse into the compassion of her heart. My soul aching, I stepped near and, finding no resistance in her body language, slid my arm around her back to draw her close to me.

As I did, my body took up aching for her, too.

"Are you sure, Elishta," I told her, slipping a knuckle of my free hand beneath her delicate jaw to raise her eyes back to mine when they fell shyly away, "it's the crew you're hiding from?"

Her blush deepened, those eyes of hers clearly longing to dart askance from my face but instead transfixed, shining with fright and excitement as my hand began a slow trail down her spine through the fabric of her shirt. "I—I don't know what you mean, Rorke—ah!"

The breeches she wore were form-fitting to such an extent that they flattered her shapely form beautifully. The Temple priests might have considered her unchaste had they seen her in such a garb during her time in their care. The elves with whom I had become close, especially Valeria, had provoked such a perversion of my morals that the brief imagining I had of Elishta suffering a few lashes for this impudence was sweet, rather than abhorrent. I confess, I enjoyed a twitch of pleasure as I let my hand glide down her rear. Although she gasped, Elishta nevertheless remained still as a doe before the wolf destined to consume her, staring with intense excitement into my eyes, her lips parting for an intake of deeper breath as my fingers molded to the flesh of her hindquarters. My grip of her lowered, that delicious peach cleft of hers inviting my caress so deeply in those trousers that my middle finger nudged against the plush outline of her sex. I fondled it through her clothes along with that beautiful backside.

"Don't be shy, Elishta," I coached, bending to graze my mouth along hers as she released, despite herself, a winsome moan. Encouraged, I took to moving my fingers, gently massaging the edges of her concealed femininity and loving how she trembled against me. "Valeria and I heard you this morning, you know...there's no shame in it."

Stammering, Elishta gazed up at me with uncertainty and more of that fright. "Oh, no, I wasn't—I couldn't—I could never, Rorke—"

"Why not? I think Valeria loved the thought of you taking pleasure from the sound of her riding me. I certainly do."

My exploring hand eased its grip on her rear, sliding up beneath the fabric of her shirt to glide along the soft flesh of her stomach. Here dwelled my third son. Here was the proof that this body I had never imagined myself worthy to receive was mine. That enticing slope tightened a little, and by the time I reached her breast, her nipple jutted against my fingers like a diamond. Panting, uncertain yet desperate to be held by me, Elishta squirmed and gazed into my eyes.

"How could I dare intrude in such a way, even as witness? I have no business, I—"

A strange thing happened. Tears appeared in her eyes, a gloss that ached my heart.

Drawing her closer to me, I murmured, "What do you mean, you have no business?" and she shook her head.

"You love Valeria. How sweetly you condescended to me in our shared dream of the Valor Hall! Oh, Rorke—you were everything I prayed you would be to me, and more. But...." As a twitch of pleasure brought her attention to the tumescence of my desire pressed against her thigh, Elishta-bet glanced down, bit her lip, and gazed back up at me. "I understand the difference between what is done in love, and what is done in desperation. I would not have the delusion to think that a man like you, Rorke, would want anything to do with a meek little mouse like me when you instead have Valeria, a woman whose body invites compare with any number of sublime fertility idols I have seen established by the heathens."

A meek little mouse! Heart breaking, I looked at her in shock. "Is that really how you suppose I think of you? Elishta—I love you."

Her entire face and neck bright crimson with longing, Elishta demurely lowered her eyes. "I beg you, Rorke, don't tease me—my heart is fragile, especially after all we endured."

"I have always loved you, Elishta," I told her in earnest, gaining from her a more wholehearted lifting of her eyes in a look of beautiful hope. Raising both my hands to frame her lovely face, my thumb trailing along the edge of her mouth, I lowered my head and vowed to her, "And I always will. You'll never be parted from me if you don't want to be."

Easing in my embrace, Elishta let her smooth brow furrow with emotion as she breathed, "Rorke…" I could see in her soul that she wanted to kiss me, and I was poised to receive it and deliver more in turn; yet, still hesitant, she bit that lower lip I longed to taste. "Won't Valeria be angry to think of you saying such a thing, making such a promise?"

Letting the natural strength of my body push Elishta to the edge of the ship so I might savor her gasp as her rear hit the wood, I tipped her head back to ensure her view of me was inescapable.

"Far from it," I assured her, letting her feel the pressure of my desire as I pinned her delicate form to the rail. "Valeria sees the love I have for you more clearly than even you do, Elishta, and she revels in the thought… particularly in the thought of loving you along with me."

Squirming now, helpless to do anything other than offer the pink lips of her open, panting mouth to the brutish depths of my kiss, Elishta moaned with pleasure and relented. Her tongue ardently greeting mine, receiving mine, Elishta suckled gently upon my exploring tongue and gave my body the fever for more of her. As her nervous hands found an unsteady rest upon my chest, then began more boldly to explore over my shoulders, I raised my mouth from our kiss enough to rasp, "Join us next time."

"But, Rorke—"

"How shy you are…so pure and virginal, even changed as you are by what happened in the Valor Hall."

Her eyes by now glazed with pleasurable memories, Elishta murmured, "Yet not so changed. For, whatever was the case in Eternity, here in Time again with you I have never known a man."

"Good," I rebutted, bending my head over hers for another plunging kiss. "That means Valeria will have a second chance to enjoy your defloration with me...you'll see how fond she is of you."

Whimpering with shameful pleasure, Elishta received my kiss a second, deeper time, her fingers tightening into fists around the fabric of my tunic. I reached down with both hands to grab her luscious backside, dragging her close against me, uncertain if I had the self-control to wait until Valeria was available—

When Providence interfered until a moment more suited to Elishta's beauty and dignity.

A voice rang out across the decks of the ship, crying words so welcome they almost seemed foreign—and so unexpected they hardly pierced the veil of my consciousness until, also hearing the voice, Elishta turned her face away from our kiss and toward the source of the sound.

"Land, ho," cried one of the crew members, unseen as she hollered from the darkness of the ship's open forecastle. "'Tis time for our illustrious guests to depart. We've reached Rhineland, and we're landing imminently. Land, ho!"

Relieved, Elishta smiled up at me, and I returned the expression. It would be so good to touch land again! Good to walk among the living, rather than be on this ship of dirges and wraiths. Now, we would have the opportunity to resume our quest: to obtain Valeria's ring and put an end to all this ceaseless wandering.

So why, then, did the thought of reaching land give me such presentiment of dread?

4

ABANDON SHIP!

AS I STOOD in the Captain's quarters, a new serenity washed over me as though to compensate for that queer dread. I cannot truly explain why it broke in the way of a wave crashing against rock, this trepidation of the soul; I think it was only a form of acceptance, the mortal response to one's insufficiency to save oneself. This is not so much a question of weakness, as even the strongest man on earth dwells in this condition. But the response to that truth is what makes one weak or strong, for those who know they are of their own self insufficient are far more likely to surrender to the divine will. So, I surrendered; for I knew that even in his weakness, my god was stronger than any terrestrial creation, myself included.

Why, then, had he permitted me to hobble him by the destruction of his spear?

"Yeh's lookin' far off, Burnin'soul," my hostess observed, drawing her many-times patched and stitched and otherwise poorly repaired robe tighter around herself. Extending a withered hand toward the carafe of wine on the table to her right, she asked wryly, "Now, don't tell me yeh's think y'er about ta be missin' us."

"With all due respect, Captain"—I chuckled and lowered my eyes as one does from the wild animal one wishes to avoid antagonizing—"there are few I have met from whom I would more happily depart."

Thankfully, she found this relatable, laughing alongside me, the rasp of her voice like the sound of bones rattling at footsteps through an ossuary. "Aye, 'tis a mutual sentiment. There ain't no love lost 'tween us, Burnin'soul, though I confess y'er not all bad. That really is y'er problem, yeh know...consider tryin' a bit a' bad sometime."

Weltyr's spear, which had only just been on my mind, once again re-shattered in my heart. "That you think me good," I responded with measurably less mirth, "only serves to reinforce what's lacking in my heart. No one is truly good, I begin to think, Captain. There are only those good at pretending to be good, and then there are those who do not see the value in the pretense."

"This is what I like about yehs, boy...ain't afraid ta speak the truth."

While she raised her dusty chalice to her lips and took a sip of the sludgy-looking contents, I politely studied the couch upon which Valeria and I had sat before the breaking of Hamsunt's portable prison and all the chaos that ensued. "My god will know if I am false."

"Fie! Gods lie all the time. What business have they, measurin' the honesty of mortals?"

"It is the prerogative of divinity to present whatever information pleases it, but the lot of men such as myself to maintain an orderly world in which to parse that information, for good or for ill."

"The 'prerogative of divinity'." She repeated this in such a tone that the jagged portion of lip which had long since decayed off now appeared to my eye to be curled in a sneer. As I averted my gaze to avoid the sight of her withered tongue running along her teeth to mop away what I suppose was once considered wine, the captain went on, "It's fascinatin' ta me how yeh's have a courageous heart, Burnin'soul, yet yeh's just lie down and let yer 'god' do as pleases—and with such confidence he exists!"

After the experience I'd had, what little doubt had ever been present in my heart had disappeared forever and would never, I was certain, re-emerge. Already, disbelief in Weltyr had been befuddling to me, but now having received ample proof that Valeria and Elishtabet both recognized—indeed, one of them not even herself a servant of Weltyr—and knowing the nature of the Selectrix in our company far better than the undead captain, it seemed to me the issue was not of his existence, but of his godhood. I asked, "You, who sit here drinking wine after you are already long dead, the captain of a phantom ship full of women like you, don't believe in the gods? In Weltyr?"

Given the context, the chuckle I would have found patronizing now moved me to pity. "Burnin'soul," she said with a shake of her head, "I've walked this world—

flown above it, any rate—for centuries now, and I've seen some strange and terrific things in all that time. Men and women of every race; strange magics that I do admit seem to be of some tier beyond our understanding. Yet in all the time I an' the *Rhinemaid* have cruised above Urde, yeh's know what I've never once seen, not once, anywhere? Not yer god, nor any other."

"There is no god but Weltyr," I informed her. "Only those idols permitted power enough to satisfy the primitive needs of men."

"It's all semantics if they don't exist; and, if they do, why's yer god better than the others?"

"God reveals himself to those for whom he has some special love or purpose," I explained to her as gently as I could, quick to add, "and that is not to say he does not have some great fondness for you, for otherwise those thoughts of the divine mind that sustain your existence would be farther from Him than the nature of a microbe is from human nature. Yet—he desires that we should have free will, too." Realizing I had not said his name in all that, I clarified, "Weltyr desires that we should have free will," and felt odd.

The splinters of the world tree wood, exploding as Exigence struck the spear in twain.

"Even," I told her, unable to disguise the distant, solemn expression of pain I am sure made its way into my face as it overflowed out of my heart, "when that free will's exercise means we alienate ourselves from him by our own choice—still, he has for us a deep enough love to let us fall into ourselves, knowing that we may also make the choice to return to him again someday."

Those such as myself for whom belief is a natural

way of life or in relation to an established fact are always so naive! We think so often that when we speak from the heart, those hardened into disbelief around us will grow soft at our words and will see reason enough to change. My pride was wounded by her laugh, therefore, and I reminded myself that pride did not serve my master half so well as humility while the captain shook her head.

"And they call him the All-Father! What sort of father lets their children toddle off? Will yeh's do so, Burnin'soul, when yer children are brought forth by the dark elf and that mousy little mage with a new flutter in her tummy?"

The question struck me, succeeded in drawing me out of my religious ruminations and into new questions: ones so deep and important that I could not spare much conscious thought of them in that moment and instead had to permit them to pile up within me until they had a chance for later review. "You can perceive that, can you?"

"Aye—though I admit I'm impressed, since she seems ta be the only one neither I nor my crew ever seen yeh's lay hands on."

"The ways of life are mysterious," I agreed, trying to think how I might explain Elishta's pregnancy to someone who did not believe in Weltyr and therefore would probably not have been capable of accepting the existence of the Valor Hall. "I would imagine after all your time in the present condition you must have lost a certain sense for what it is to be alive."

Slightly shrugging, the captain said, "Felt more or less like this, 's I recall," though I could spare little time for contemplation of her answer.

Indeed, barely had the sentence left her mouth

before the ship gave a buck, jolting like a stallion leaping against the bridle.

Lurching, I caught myself against the nearby door jamb, astonished by the practiced way the captain leapt up from her seat and hurried toward her desk. There, an apparatus I recognized as a periscope extended down from the ceiling with the flick of a small lever built into the wall behind. It lowered as another rattle rushed through the ship, leaving the captain gritting her teeth while she peered into the glass.

"Seems ta be an enemy vessel," she groused, raising her face away from the periscope and studying me with an expression of dark frustration. "And us, just havin' fixed the ship. Well...if it were my problem, I'd be havin' an episode."

"You mean you intend to leave the ship undefended?"

"I mean," she said sharply, striding up to me to poke me in the chest with one sharp finger bone, "that if left ta our own devices, this is a fight we'd cruise away from. Ain't no reason ta suffer an assault when there ain't no reason for us ta be here. Besides, it's daylight. The expedient thing ta do is fly the ship away, and it's what I'm doin'."

My blood beginning to rise within me as I interpreted the urgency of her words, I asked, "Are you not going to let us off here?"

"Oh, aye, I'll let yeh's off, Burnin'soul. But—" The atrophied muscles of her dead arms strained as she bent to pull up a trap door beneath her desk—one of the ones which, I assumed, were built throughout the ship to prevent sunlight exposure to the captain or her crew. "If'n yeh's don't want ta wait until the next, more accommodatin' stop, it's y'er jobs ta lay the defense and make it ta ground without getting' yerselves killed...we're departin' in 10 minutes, regardless of whether y'er still aboard."

Puzzling all this together along with the consideration that we were still high in the air, I asked, "Where are the lifeboats," which only yielded a cackle from the descending captain.

"Lifeboats! Lifeboats, he says...I think I'm almost gonna miss yeh's."

The trap door banged shut as she pulled it closed, and by the time of the next direct hit, I was standing in sunlight and looking for my friends.

One can hardly blame the dwarvish armada for taking an interest in the *Rhinemaid* idling within ten miles of Ironforge's city walls. Were I them, perhaps controlling Skythorn's ships or otherwise responsible for the wellbeing of an entire city, I am quite certain I would have reacted similarly. It was a little annoying that in all our time aboard, it was only now, when we had our chance to depart, that our mortal fellows were taking too much interest.

"Rorke!" Branwen's urgent tone drew my attention to my right, where, already with her leather armor hugging her soft curves, the elf dashed to me, stumbled with the latest impact from the dwarvish cannon fire, and had to be caught in my arms or else meet the deck far too intimately.

"These damn dwarves," she cursed, pushing herself back up and turning a blazing eye off in the direction of the enemy ship in the distance. "I'm never going to let Grimalkin hear the end of this."

"They're doing what anyone would do in this situation—it inconveniences us."

Another projectile arced toward us, slightly mis-aimed. With its trajectory just a bit too high, it arced over us, shattered only the edge of a rail, then continued its course back down to the planet from which its metals had been mined. Branwen, who had crouched with me upon witnessing this latest cannonball, cringed a little as I took her shoulders in my hands.

"We must find a way to get to ground, and we must do it immediately. Gather the others—Brynhildr can bring at least two plus what of our possessions we can't bear on our persons, and Elishta's powers will allow her to reach ground safely on her own."

"That's Indra and Odile accounted for, then," Branwen said with displeasure that nonetheless indicated a depth of secret affection that made me fond of her no matter how haughty her manners. "And Elishta. Wind spirits will help me, if I ask, but I can't gather enough of them to bear many more than me alone."

"Grimalkin?"

Hesitating only briefly, she nodded. "Yes, they can take Grimalkin, but—" Her emerald eyes pierced deeply into mine. "What about you, Rorke? And Valeria, too?"

I didn't know the answer to that, and there wasn't much time to ponder as another blast rocked the ship—especially not as a shift in air pressure indicated we had begun to cruise. Gritting my teeth, I admitted, "I'm not sure yet," even as a memory of tangled voices sprang up once more in my heart.

Deepgold! Deepgold! Deepgold!

"But I'll figure something out," I told her, reluctant

to reveal—indeed, to any who were not there in the Valor Hall with us—the nature and extent of the artifacts I had temporarily kept in the name of seeking Valeria's ring. Releasing Branwen with a squeeze of her shoulder, I stood. "Gather the others—I'll find Valeria."

A funny sort of expression crossed Branwen's face, a slight knit of her brow paired with an exaggerated moue of displeasure. There was no time to ruminate over its meaning, however; my mind was driven toward the urgency I felt to find Valeria, more intense than what I felt for any of the women present except, perhaps, Elishta-bet. Yet with Elishta, I had some confidence. She had been raised in the Temple of Weltyr in Skythorn, a massive city she was used to navigating on her own or with others. Elishta had real-world experience. Valeria, on the other hand—a pampered priestess-queen who, so far as I had been able to divine, hardly left her luxurious home—could not even see well in full daylight owing to the nature of her people's subterranean lifestyle. I couldn't assume her self-sufficiency in matters of escape; not in conditions like this. Hurrying onward, I burst below deck and practically overleapt the stairs, landing with a thud upon the bottom one and launching off to round the corner to our cabins.

Yet as I did that, everything changed.

I do not mean this in an internal sense, as referring to some mental or emotional cliche. What I mean, rather, is that as I rounded the corner, I was transported elsewhere. The transition was so abrupt that my brain managed not to think too much of the fact that I was now striding through a field of pink and violet flowers, their effervescent petals blowing lazily in a breeze

I barely felt. In the same sense one has when one awakes from deep slumber and has to puzzle together a change in circumstance or difference in location that occurred while waking, I had to stop and assess myself and my surroundings, striving to regain the lost thread of spacetime continuity that had been snapped by this change in environment.

Yet how much more of that was lost when I set eyes upon her!

"Burningsoul," Gundrygia called to me, raising one pale arm and coaxing me near. When I did not respond—indeed, could not move—she slipped away one pale shoulder of her gown. Even in that uncanny moment, and even with so little of her beheld, I was captivated by her beauty; perhaps even more than I normally would have been, since my glimpses of her had been so fleeting after that first handful of times, culminating in our encounter with her in the tunnels beneath Skythorn. Indeed, with all the urgency of a dream, my mind knew that danger was pressing elsewhere and comingled that information with the vision before me to elicit in my heart the powerful need to rescue Gundrygia, too. And all the rest of me, in an even deeper and more primeval way, bucked this idea as the horse its rider. Whatever she was, Gundrygia was not in need of rescue.

"Like an arrow through my heart, Rorke," Gundrygia teased, her eyes glittering as they fixed upon me. One pale hand framing along her own curves to entice me nearer, she cocked her head in an owlish way, asking, "Am I not a woman as much as the others?"

My instinct was to answer yes, but for some reason, I hesitated. "A woman, certainly—but not like the others."

"And what is the difference?"

Her voice was a whisper in my ear even though she stood before me, and I whirled to face this other her, the muscles of my legs and back locking with the intention to step away. The first vision forgotten, this new Gundrygia wore animal skins and tattered garments and was the one I'd awoken with a strangely compelled kiss. Looking once over my shoulder to see the first Gundrygia had gone, I caught hold of this one's bicep, forcing a lewd gasp from her hot little mouth and inspiring a heavier bedroom droop of her kohl-shaded eyelids, dark as the arrowhead tattooed upon her chin.

"The difference," I told her as she swooned against me, responding to my touch with a mere pantomime of submission, "is that you are female, but I would hesitate to call you a woman any more than I would call an ancient tiger the same as a housecat. You're a wild thing—not to be trusted."

The image was perhaps because the edges of her plump lips were tweaked by a feline curl of satisfaction. As her hands rested upon my chest to explore my musculature through my tunic, Gundrygia tried her best to pout and only looked all the more haughty. "What is trust, Rorke?"

"The capacity to rely on another's promises."

"And you suppose you can't rely on me?"

"There's a difference between being dependable and being dependably mad."

Her head tipped back with her gay spate of laughter, a high cackle that brightened those eyes still smilingly fixed on me. The tips of her fingers glided down my arms, following the path of my muscles to grasp my hands.

"If I'm mad," she insisted, raising onto her toes to let her nose and lips brush mine as she spoke, "then you are just as mad as I. What will we make of our little Wotsung then? The child you gave me? He'll be twice as mad as both of us."

He'll be. An inopportune surge of excitement rolled through me, a joy to confirm that a third son was to be delivered to me even if through her. Yet as I had that sense, her head tilted and her smile grew. "You trust me well enough to take excitement at my presentiment," Gundrygia rightly pointed out, "yet you still think you cannot trust me otherwise. What makes the difference to you?"

"What makes the difference," I told her sternly, catching the thick mane of her hair at the roots of her scalp, "is that those deceptive words which spring from a greater truth are recognizable in the soul for those who are true children of Weltyr."

But before I had even finished speaking, the cruelest of smiles curled the corners of Gundrygia's mocking lips. "Then," she observed, staring sharply into my eyes, her own glittering with a kind of poison that made some deep, secretly knowing corner of my soul cringe with dread for what was still to come, "when spoken by a Wotsung, the truth must be twice as recognizable, Wanderer."

I could not understand what she meant to imply by this: could not, would not. Yet before I could even begin to puzzle it out, Valeria's voice gripped my attention and drew me back to the *Flying Rhinemaid*, where Gundrygia's wild mass of hair regressed, in my grip, to what it perhaps had always been while I was in that dream-state.

The glittering chain links of the Helm of Dunnun.

BEAST OF BURDEN

THOUGH A MAN may grow used to nearly anything in life, there is no way for the human mind to assimilate habitual visionary experiences into one's normal routine. Perhaps it is different with elvish minds, for their souls, I have heard it said, are more elemental in nature, more in tune with the ebbs and flows of seasons, chemicals, and even divine effects upon the psyche. Yet the minds of human men, grounded and sharp, adept at knowing and arrogant in the capacity to know and apprehend, are not so well-equipped to endure changes of state. Upon the retreat of such a vision, one's mind—at least, my mind—rather feels as the steel must when, drawn from the heat of the forge, the metal glows with molten otherworldliness and in those precious seconds is vulnerable to a more permanent change of state beneath the clanging blows of the hammer. Dizzily, I reoriented myself as best I could to the situation unfolding around me—and nursed a perhaps inappropriate sting of disappointment to find that alluring witch had once more escaped me before I could mete out proper chastisement. The loss was mitigated, however: Valeria hurried to me and flung herself into my arms, having come upon me in what I dimly perceived to be our cramped quarters aboard the ship.

"There you are," she cried breathlessly, drawing back to glance into my face before turning to note with relief, "and by Weltyr, already packed."

I remained so delirious after the shift of reality around me that I could not in those seconds even comprehend the thought that Valeria had just sworn an oath by the name of Weltyr, rather than by her idol, that dark creature of prophecy. Yet, though my consciousness could not absorb this information, the words fell strangely upon my ears. More strangely still to find that I was evidently in the middle of packing when she found me, or perhaps unpacking, since the cool chains of the Helm glittered in my hand. Had Gundrygia influenced me to this? Why would she afford me help, even if only by driving my body through mesmerism while she taunted me in that other place of hers?

Frowning, Valeria caught my face in her hands. "Are you fine, Man?"

"Fine," I managed to stammer, shaking my head and then, as another blow rocked the ship, catching her around the waist to steady her against the violence. "But we need to move fast"—surely I said this to myself as much as to her—"especially since the others are evacuating. If our opponents see them disembarking from the ship, they may coordinate troops to pursue them. We can't risk separation, especially as the *Rhinemaid* prepares to take evasive action."

"How will we escape," Valeria asked with alarm. "If the Selectrix and her horse are inaccessible to us, and the magicians are already free from the ship—"

"Trust me," I told her, words that were firm yet tender; a command, yet a lover's plea. Valeria's bosom swelled with a great inhalation as I went on. "There are things I learned during our time apart in the Valor Hall. Methods and strategies that have unnatural effects and are, I think, to be kept as a last resort for any man—even the lesser idols, these demi-immortal beings making up Weltyr's family and court, could succumb to them."

"The Deepgold," Valeria surmised, glancing at the Helm in my hand and then back into my face as I nodded. "Are you sure it's wise for you to put it to use? Exigence was a gift from your god, yet this thing—what is this thing?"

"The Helm of Dunnun." As I turned toward the entrance of the cabin, Valeria plucked up the bag with only the briefest grimace for its weight. I caught her other arm and drew her along briskly after me, explaining, "I watched the figurehead of the dwarvish people use this to assume a different, altogether more terrifying form—one of beast and not of man. I am not certain of the extent of its utility; but if he, so much a lesser being than Weltyr, can transfigure himself so completely with its help, then surely a son of Weltyr may accomplish the same."

A noise like a hiss of frustration expelled from Valeria's lips. Before I could hurry her up the stairs behind me, she jerked to a stop and caused me to look into her face. "You impudent man! You may be a Wotsung, but you're mortal, too. Do you really think that, from the heart of a beast, you'll remember yourself well enough to accomplish the change back to a human?"

I understood her point well, of course, but the nature of the situation was such that I could not help but gamble. "In a ship with no lifeboats," I told her, my tone conciliatory in exchange for her concern, "I would gladly give my human life to be the vessel of your rescue."

Seeing how her eyes shone—then blazed with a new anger, as if the stirring to emotion stoked the flames of her rage twice over—I bent over Valeria and caught her lips in mine. She yielded with a soft murmur of mingled displeasure and intense love, pressing back into me, pouring her whole self into my mouth until I drew back with a grin for her still obvious indignation.

"Besides, my love," I teased her, turning back to resume pulling her up the stairs to the deck, "between your wisdom and that of the other women, I'm sure you'll figure something out to change me back...assuming Grimalkin doesn't see fit to slay me to try and woo all of you."

My beloved did not look particularly amused by that bit of gallows humor, but it was all I had to get by on, for Valeria was quite correct. I had no idea what I was doing, in truth; it was not as though the Helm had entered into my possession in the company of a helpful instructional parchment, or perhaps some chaplet by which one might have a clearer idea of its utility. There had been no incantation required for its use—none that

I had heard, anyway—but that just begged the question as to how the transformative powers of this relic could be unlocked. Would it happen by some automatic cause-and-effect, a matter of physics as simple as hitting a ball with a bat and watching it arc into the sky? Or would there be some special activation necessary on my part? Would this work at all, I wondered, or would I be forced to scramble for an alternative solution?

There was no chance to find out. When this next cannon blow arced over the ship—a glittering fireball of black and greenish red glowing with the hallmark phosphorus of the dwarvish people of Rhineland—I realized that the Captain had made good on her promise to spare no time. Like many solutions I had cobbled together since my initial time in the Nightlands, I would have to go along with everything and figure it out in the moment.

Yet, in this particular instance, that method had some interesting consequences.

Releasing Valeria, I threw the Helm over my head, and a strange sensation swept through my entire nervous system. It was as though fingers crept down along my brain, trailing the outline of pathways that made me Rorke and immediately commencing the process of shifting these into something else.

A kind of instinctive panic surged through me: would I become? Was there no way to steer this process? I opened my mouth to warn Valeria that I may well have suddenly taken on the appearance of that same erratic dragon Dunnun had assumed as his new shape, but all that emitted from my throat was a kind of staggered croak—the noise of a man whose wind had been struck from his diaphragm.

Valeria said my name, but her voice was distant already. My shifting mind was losing the capacity for meaningful language, and a new urgency caused my thoughts to fly from one imagining to another. A dragon seemed not only unsafe for Valeria, but unsuitably antagonistic should the dwarvish militia set eyes on me and take me for a threat. Was there no way to assume the form of a fairy tale bird, perhaps? Some giant creature with the wingspan of the ship we sought to flee? Or perhaps I might take on a shape not unlike the flying horse of the Selectrix—Grane, who had already made good his escape from the ship, Indra and Odile along with his mistress upon his sturdy back. All these images flew through me without words, with such a rapid pace that I did not realize until my talons hit the deck that the change had been accomplished.

I was not one of those things that had caught my consciousness, but in some measure or another a being encapsulating all three: the haunches of a horse, the beak and wings of a bird, the claws of a dragon whose reptilian scales shimmered within the wild panoply of feathers and short fur making up my new hide.

Valeria's breathless gasp drew my eye's attention toward her, and how strange it is when I reflect on my regard for her in that moment! She was both my beloved and something more. Something holy: a sweet-smelling, familiar being of softness and mysterious power. A being that, while I was in the form of some animal, was so far beyond my purview in terms of ability and wisdom I could not help but succumb to the folding of my legs beneath me. Holding her breath, this otherworldly creature whose presence made my heart pulse with new vigor extended a hand toward me, her delicate feet slowly lifting and softly landing, each step silent. That dainty, warm palm of hers pressed against the crown of my skull, her fingers tunneling through the pelt of feathers and fur that had sprung up from the Helm. As she caressed me, I forgot, for just a few seconds, the chaos unfolding around us: it was only as, finding me docile, she snatched up our bag and spared no time in mounting my back that I awoke to the urge to flight.

And fly, I did. As cannons fired around us and the *Rhinemaid* gained momentum enough that the wind whipped through the feathers of the wings unfurling from their place against my back, I galloped forward, following some instinct as if I had obeyed it all my life. Not even Valeria's small fists, gripping my feathers at the root and then releasing only so she could drape her body over my back and weave her slender arms around my neck, could divert my attention from what seemed as simple as walking—or, perhaps, it would be more apt to compare it to swimming, for when one has wings, to fly through the sky feels as ecstatically free as a man does while swimming in the sea.

As I launched myself from the edge of the deck, Valeria gasped, and the lurching of a sudden drop jolted us both: then the wind caught the great wings that extended on either side, and I was weightless, borne aloft by the whistling breeze so that our fall became a smooth glide. Second by second, we broadened permanently the gap between us and the ship that had held us captive for what had seemed like ages. We were free; I would never in my life see the *Rhinemaid* again.

Yet there was no chance to celebrate! There were new dangers—always, new dangers. For the experience of flight was so exhilarating, and that falling-buoyant forward thrust propelling me and my beloved liltingly along the air was so simple, so easy to engage to my newly reformed mind, that I got caught up briefly in the thrill of the moment. The extraordinary and sublime being upon my back called out in short rotation a rolling thunderclap of sound that was known to me (my name, my wife assures me), and others called out similarly below. As I looked down I caught a glimpse of something heavy and black in my periphery, and it is now that I understand that by the grace of the Maker of us all I was spared a direct hit from the dangerous armament thanks to the raising of a magical shield by Elishta-bet, who was having her own problems as she drew closer to the ground. As I hear it transpired (which I have requested to re-hear, in a particular mood, more than a few times over the years...perhaps some readers will sympathize with my appreciation, a little gift to apologize for the fact that the psychic depths and actual lengths of my journey will here on out leave little time and space for leisure, for in truth we ourselves had little to none, and what was enjoyed was stolen between heartbeats amidst violence and strife, or will be recounted to aid in your understanding of why things happened the way they happened), Odile and Indra cried out for surrender and mercy even as a militia below drew their bows and took aim, not hearing their feminine voices over the sounds of the canon blasts above.

"They think we're pirates," Odile hissed as, above us, the durrow looked urgently at one another around the

Selectrix's shoulder. "What do we do? If the flying horse isn't going to stop them—"

"The flying horse is egging them on," Brynhildr said, not tearing her eyes off the threats in the environment for even a second, aware of all angles and opponents. "Do either of you have a handkerchief available? Anything white."

Patting herself, dismayed Indra cried, "No!" while Odile looked around with gritted teeth. It was then that, seeing what Valeria saw, Elishta-bet also cried out—first to see Valeria astride a strange beast, and then to see that same beast subject to a cannon blast. Throwing high her arms, she raised her shield: and so, at the moment that the force of the cannonball impacting the shield knocked me heavily off-course—doing no physical damage aside from a slight misalignment of body that came with the unexpected momentum in a new direction—Elishta was helpless to preserve her modesty from the winds that dramatically bustled her clothes about and revealed the chemise beneath her leather tunic was of simple white cloth.

With a cry of victory, Odile pointed, enthusing to the Selectrix, "Take us higher!"

As Brynhildr obliged, Odile extended her hands and unceremoniously grasped Elishta's ankle, the sorceress being, as they all were, mid-air. Yanking her down and provoking a cry, the durrow called to her compatriot, "Hold her down," and to Elishta, "We need your underthings!"

"Why, what? O-oh!"

With the durrow half-hanging from the massive horse and Elishta entangled with them in the sky, Odile and Indra tugged at the laces of Elishta's bodice. My innocent friend struggled, shrieking outrage. "What are you doing, in Weltyr's name!"

"Hush, girl! This is a matter of life or death—stop fighting! Indra, catch her arms—"

While Indra obeyed, Odile removed her dagger and made swifter work of the laces than could fingers. Crying out, Elishta thrashed some more, her stomach flexing bare beneath the white chemise that whipped up in the wind and around her delicate breasts without the leather bodice holding it in place. As Elishta emitted another cry of shocked protest, Odile tore the white fabric away from Elishta's body, leaving her bosom exposed and even her short-hacked boy's hair in disarray. After brisk examination of this shredded cloth to determine it would be seen from the ground, Odile sighed in relief, then released her hold of Elishta with a grin.

"We owe you. Hey! Mercy!"

While Odile raised her new white flag high, waving it back and forth, Elishta regained her magical footing in the air and, blushing furiously, folded her arms over her breasts. "You could have just asked!"

"There was no time to convince you if you said no," Odile assured her, gasping with relief as the sight of the white flag brought new hesitation to the archers below. "They see it! They see it, oh, Roserpine—"

"We're not out of the woods yet," Brynhildr assured them, glancing up at me as I righted myself in the air and managed to keep Valeria on my back. "Let's just get everybody safely on the ground. Then we can figure out what to say."

For some of us, that was easier said than done.

Yes, while it was true that the ladies drew a fair bit of attention—especially now that poor Elishta, clutching her bodice closed with her arms, was drifting nearer to the ground and looking as if for a place to hide even with enemies on all sides—something about a durrow riding an unknown beast managed to draw most of the fire.

By Weltyr's grace and a great deal of frantic flapping of my new wings, I found myself upright and identified new threats, finding there were more canons to duck beneath, and now even rifle fire that only seemed to strike me as deadly when the crack sounded and something whizzed near enough for my sensitive ear to ache with the lucky miss. A cry of surprise exploded from my maw, which clacked open and then snapped shut again in a soundwave that bombarded the nearest ship to send it rocking back. As Valeria emitted a victorious whoop, I swept down, pursuing the only flying objects that were not the ships: these great, looming structures of danger. I followed what appealed to me. The women.

The fragrant and gentle being on my back was like these, and I felt some degree of sympathy with them, for we were all subject to our assailants. More than sympathy—I experienced responsibility, though in that moment I could not discern why. There was only the heightened awareness of an animal in danger, and of that animal's need to protect that which was good in its life. As the women landed one at a time—first Branwen in a fantastical cyclone that kicked up dust enough to blind nearby dwarvish warriors who grimaced and covered their eyes and mouths, then Brynhildr and the durrow women upon her steed, and finally poor Elishta, who had been in no hurry to get down to eye level once she had drawn close enough to the ground to determine there was nowhere to actually hide. Grimalkin, on the other hand, having been clinging to Branwen's waist with far less lascivious pleasure than I had ever seen him taking in the touch of a woman, literally leapt down upon the ground to kiss it. The poor fellow's gasps of relief were so deep they renewed the color of his unnaturally pale face. "Oh, sweet mother Urde! Never let me leave again, merciful Dunnun— No more airships—"

"Put down your weapons and release your captive," shouted one of the helmeted warriors standing against us while the dust was clearing. "We won't hesitate to use force."

"You've made that much perfectly clear," Valeria responded coolly. My feet scrambled unsteadily across the ground, finding purchase and then stabilizing into a gallop around the perimeter. I ran off my momentum and snapped at the dwarves, causing them to flinch away and ready their arms. Seeing this, Valeria produced some word of power from her lovely lips, leaving the men to cry out as spiders from beneath the rocks strewn about that gloomy heath rushed up into the armor of the men on the front lines. As Grane reared, the durrow women on his mighty back cried out, and my wings fluttered in stern warning that our assailants come no closer. Certain of the men murmured among themselves, eying the armored woman who dismounted her steed and strode toward me with confidence.

For a heartbeat, I cringed away, flinching from her approach until our eyes met. No predatory hardness or intent to harm lay there: indeed, the deepest peace and safety, even in that treacherous moment, seemed to exude from her being. I laid down upon the earth beneath us, and as Valeria sprang from me to scramble upright upon her dizzy feet, the towering woman with her billowing hair the color of flame stooped to grasp me by the scruff. As the feathers she pulled from the back of my neck took on the quality of gold chainmail, the ambiguities of animal existence were keened and hardened once again into the awareness of a human man.

Not just any human man: Rorke Burningsoul, who, with Exigence and the Lantern strapped to his hip, looked around as if awakening from a dream—or plunging back into one. The fellows around us were startled by my appearance, but only for half a second or so. Apparently more hardened than to be taken aback by the transformation of a beast into a man, they shored up their ranks, arranged around us three men deep to keep us from fleeing while their ships made futile pursuit of the *Rhinemaid*. The ghost ship was already screaming off into the distance, vanishing westward, into what of the world was still the darkness.

"You have one minute to release your captive," shouted the unruffled leader of the men. "We will not give you another warning."

"Captive," I repeated dumbly, looking amid our number as I fought through a strange combination of adrenaline and disorientation. My uneasy eye fell on Grimalkin. I laughed.

"As captives go, he's not worth much. What do you say, Grimalkin?" Waving a hand toward the line, I asked our still slightly queasy-looking friend, "Care to put in a good word for us?"

"I've half a mind to throw you lot under the ship for all the troubles you've caused me..." Shaking his head, then glancing up at Branwen, Grimalkin stomped forward toward his kinfolk, waving his arms over his head as he did.

"They're fine," he called as a few of their number rushed forward to detain us, men from the second row producing manacles and hurrying to participate in the binding of the women.

The leader of their number removed his helmet and strode forward to meet Grimalkin, and, having sheathed his sword, even extended his hand in greeting. Though I could see them speaking, I was distracted by Elishta-bet, who, afraid to so much as breathe too deeply lest her open bodice reveal too much of her flesh, fell against me, concealing her front against my chest while squirming in the cuffs with which her wrists had been bound in the small of her back.

"Elishta," I tutted, concerned and frustrated there was nothing I could do for her while I was similarly bound at sword point, "what happened?"

"Necessity is the mother of invention," Odile said while Branwen, still in cuffs, jerked her chin toward Elishta and said some ancient words. The grass of the heath at our feet sprang up, six lucky fronds of it twisting themselves together in a fine braid that wiggled up between Elishta and I and made short work of weaving shut her bodice again. Yet this demonstration was more than handy necessity: it also caused the dwarvish men around us to recoil, all of them scrambling back a few steps to realize that at least one of our number had the power to leverage nature itself as a weapon, in addition to Valeria's command of the many spiders men were still plucking from their beards and shaking out of their grieves. As a few of them began making eye contact as if in consideration of how to act should we buck against the goad, the one with whom Grimalkin discoursed raised his voice.

"He claims these are all victims of the pirates," barked the man, his gruff voice no more lighthearted for finding we were not true enemy combatants. "But there's too many women among 'em for me to trust that without investigation. That's a female crew aboard the *Rhinemaid*, I hear. You there—Burningsoul, he says?"

I nodded, exchanging a grateful glance at Grimalkin before affirming verbally, "I'm he."

"Do you agree to come with us peaceably, unarmed, to submit to questioning in the Rhineland town of Ironforge?"

"Peaceably," I agreed with a small smile, "of course. But unarmed, well...that might pose something of a complication."

Grimalkin, irritated, scrubbed his palm vigorously over his brow and eyes. "Just leave the blasted thing here and come back for it when we've sorted this all out! Who's going to manage to take it?"

"What are you on about, exactly?"

When Grimalkin and I exchanged a glance on the commander's question, I cleared my throat and began, "You see, it's a small detail about this sword of mine…"

6

NORHALM OF IRONFORGE

OUR TRANSIT BACK to the dwarven city of Ironforge was slow and terribly hot, which I have learned since is out of season for the area where we finally had to leave the so-called 'free' transportation of the *Rhinemaid*—by far the most expensive thing I've never paid for. Although I had my share of hot, humid days in Skythorn, this proved taxing for us all save Valeria, who was never as substantially dressed as I might have preferred while other men could set their eyes on her glory. The dwarves transporting us took no shame in staring as they strode up to confiscate Exigence from me; yet I let them make the attempt and laughed along with Grimalkin and the women when each who tried wound up pinned to the ground beneath the impossible weight it seemed to be for any but a Wotsung or a god. Thereafter, seeing they had to trust I was honorable enough not to use the sword—which seemed of far too great a value to force me to leave behind, especially given we were vouched innocents—they dropped their gazes, surely not wishing to test me on that matter.

In truth, I trust all my women—most especially Valeria—to take care of themselves. Indeed, there is more than one I know could best me in combat, or so I humor them in believing for my own admitted enjoyment.

However, there is one among their number toward whom I have always felt especially protective, and I found myself even more so knowing she carried one of my heirs. It was therefore exceedingly painful for me when, shortly after our jailers finally shut the doors of our holding cell while they went off to collect a clear, formal report from Grimalkin which they would then corroborate with at least a few of our number, the frantic hitching of Elishta's soft breath reached my ears. With a tut, I looked, and was amazed to find her crying—then considered that perhaps I ought not to have been so amazed after all.

"Elishta-bet," I murmured, sliding my hand into the small of her back and sitting down beside her upon the splintered bench where she'd sunk. "Don't be afraid. It's all right."

"Oh, Rorke, but it's not." Wringing her cloak with a tragic sob, Elishta sank into my chest, her shoulders trembling. "I never should have left Skythorn! Oh, I'm so afraid—what's going to become of us?"

"Now, Elishta-bet—these seem like reasonable men. Surely they'll get this straightened out and let us go along our merry way."

"Not the dwarves," my sweetheart sniffled, dabbing her eyes with the corner of that garment, then sighing as I took her face in my hand to wipe her tear back with my thumb. "I mean," she resumed when she was steady enough to manage it, "I mean—all of this, this business! What are we moving toward, Rorke?"

"Why, toward finding Valeria's ring, and deciding what to do with it."

Deepgold! Deepgold!

"And then?" pressed Elishta, trembling, oblivious to the phantom voices that sang in my ears. "What next? Where will I go when all this is over?"

"Why, Elishta..." Craning her chin up to look more clearly into her pretty face, I assured her, "You'll stay with me, won't you? We just discussed it."

"Y-yes, Rorke, of course I will—" With a brisk glance at Valeria and my soft assurance to her that we would discuss it more later, Elishta looked then again at me and continued, glowing even through her tears, "But—but what will we *do*?"

"What's to be done? Why, we'll live, of course, whatever that means for us."

"But how? Will we be farmers? You were meant to be a paladin—and me, some other paladin's unhappy wife."

"And now you'll be a wanderer's happy one."

"But that's just what I mean," she pleaded, looking into the heart of me as she gripped my tunic. "No more of this—oh, Rorke, no more wandering, for you or for me, or for your Valeria."

Now hearing her name—having no doubt already noted the glance, as astute and alert as she was to all things unfurling around her—Valeria had her attention diverted from her conversation with Odile and Indra enough to come slinking over while the two resumed murmuring. "Now, Rorke," she tutted, seeing Elishta's face coated in shining tears (the girl suddenly blushing), "what have you done to make our little pet cry? What's the matter, Elishta-bet...has he said something foolish?"

"N-no," said Elishta with something close to a laugh, sniffling and then looking startled as Valeria cupped her jaw and wiped her tears as I had done, albeit in a manner more forceful and possessive than tender and comforting. Apparently taking it for play rather than the genuine possessiveness I knew it was, she explained, "No, I've just—I'm having a difficult time with all of this, suddenly, I think."

"Oh, tosh..." Her thumb coming to rest at the corner of Elishta's mouth as a natural consequence of following the tear track, Valeria looked like she was thinking about doing something more aggressive, but then thought better of it and let her thumb continue gliding back down to Elishta's chin. "There's no shame in being weary, of course—we all are by now—but come, girl, you must try to find some cheer. Our beloved conquered death for us. Surely that's a reason to rejoice."

"He only delayed it, really," Elishta countered, adding with true woe what I had already pondered: "And who knows what will happen now that Weltyr's spear is broken? Oh, horror—ouch!"

With fingers as quick and strong as the pincers of a Nightlands gem beetle, Valeria pinched Elishta's cheek and commanded her, "Snap out of it, or I shall begin to think I'm sharing Rorke with a child. Be reasonable! Don't you know I'm the Materna of Roserpine, the priestess-queen of the Nightlands and all the durrow within it? Do you think I've done much traveling, hm? Much 'roughing it', as they say? No, you silly thing! I've lived quadruple your life and my hands have fewer callouses than yours. I'm tired, you're tired, Rorke's tired—everybody's tired, Elishta, darling, but we've come this far now. Haven't we come this far?"

"This far toward what," moaned Elishta, looking inclined to expire from grief.

"Toward the moment when the dust settles," I promised her gently, drawing her into my arms and letting her rest, weak, against my chest. "My wives and I will retire someplace in peace, living by whatever means necessary, in a manner that will never leave you so burdened again, Elishta-bet, my darling, my love."

"Please don't spend our lives as an adventurer," murmured Elishta with a soft hiccup.

"There are other ways to make a living sweetheart. Don't worry about it—that's my affair."

Deepgold! Deepgold!

If only the ears of the soul could be stuffed up! I stilled my thoughts, thinking of nothing but the present, and this seemed to aid me. Still, my conscience waged war with an idea, and the maiden spirits who pursued me as did the heinous hivemind of the Spirit-Thieves rebuked me for the first hints of that notion which struck me then, but which I assured myself I would studiously reject.

"All right," Elishta whispered, exhaling shakily against me, and nodding. "All right, Rorke. I trust in you. Please be patient with me...I've never been so far from home before."

"Us, neither," I assured her, squeezing her delicate shoulder with a smile, gratified by the way she shyly hid her own smiling face against my chest. There, she half-silently prayed to Weltyr in a prayer whose rhythm I knew too well to avoid recognizing, even at such a soft volume. I thought of joining her, and was indeed about to, when the door to our holding area opened and a pair of guards stepped up to the bars.

"Let's hear from the man first. Everybody step apart, six feet from each other. You—Rorke Burningsoul—come over here, put your hands through the slot."

"Just relax and do as they tell you," I advised Elishta, who had tensed at the dwarves' arrival, but who bravely nodded and watched me set a good example of how to obey when justice demanded.

While it's true that the rituals of the courts are designed to be humiliating in their nature—criminals being a prideful sort, and would-be criminals yet uncertain enough in their character that they may be shocked from such awful fates—I had suffered worse humiliations by far in the Nightlands, where I had been not a justly captive prisoner but an unjustly captive slave. Between this reality and the openness the dwarves were showing to the possibility that what we had all claimed was in fact truth, I was unbothered enough that my mind wandered as I was escorted away from the rest of our party to the upper halls of the magistrate's complex. It was one of several broad, perhaps aptly squat station buildings located some ways out from the edge of a city we had hardly glimpsed above its fortifications. While their architecture was distinct and beautiful, their buildings adorned with half-timber grids that leant a peculiar character to the beige, green, or sometimes rose plastering beneath, I had seen such wonders of construction and botany in the Valor Hall that what little I had already seen hardly struck me as noteworthy. More noteworthy, more beautiful than any work of man, were the tears of Elishta-bet.

It occurred to me now that I had taken some things for granted in our journeys. After growing used to women for whom adventure was natural—brash Branwen, daring Indra and Odile, certainly the Selectrix and her vibrant willingness to go wherever her father sent her—I had not critically considered the fact that Elishta had been swept up into our journey as a matter of circumstance. Indeed, among all of us, Elishta had undergone perhaps the greatest sufferings; for she had, in a literal sense, no home or property or anywhere to go. Had Zweiding taken her in marriage, she would have lost great portions of what made her herself, but in body she would have been accounted secure—even the recipient of good fortune. Now, she was bereft: the Temple of Weltyr had withdrawn its support; the Order no doubt considered her an enemy, much as it considered me; the city where she had spent her life until that point would no longer have welcomed her, and if it had, under some assumed disguise, permitted her to slip past its borders, it would have offered her no charity and would instead present her with job options such as the withering chemicals of the laundresses or the soul-rotting excesses of the Nixie. That, or maybe she might have found some quiet life as a flower girl, living in a boarding house alone for a year or two before a kind and gallant man came to take her away, for surely even the impetuous gods could never have long been cruel to a cherished little flower like Elishta-bet.

At the same time, I have oft heard it said that great holiness is to be found in suffering, and now I see the wisdom in this more than at that time, when my heart was bruised by her sorrow. It made me long to replenish the vigor and joy and peace of that girl I knew in my youth, who had so carefully, reverently lit candles at altars and swept up the church, and who had the carefree trust of a daughter who knew with certainty her Father had all things comfortably arranged for in her life. A girl who had faith.

Yet who could have faith as once we knew it, having seen what we had seen?

It was reality-altering. To be among the bureaucratic, legalistic frameworks of Urde and her people was bewildering, I will say, after having spent what seemed like an endlessly long span of time subject only to a higher order of logic which, at times, took on a hue of nursery tale foolishness. In our case in particular, all this seemed petty. I felt as though I were playing some sort of game, some make-believe thing that struck me with greater acuity still as I was pushed into a lift that, like the one embedded in Valeria's spire, ran smoothly. Every mechanical thing the dwarves touched, even the berich dwarves of the Nightlands, proved a magnificent testament to the ingenuity of mankinds. This was, even though it belonged to a legal complex, particularly stunning. The ceiling had been installed with glass so one could study the pulleys, with safety catches above (and presumably below, one would hope, though the opaque floor was polished) clicking as they rotated their teeth away like curious waves of metal for each length the box drew higher.

"Remarkable craftsmanship," I commended. Met with no response, I lowered my head to find my dwarvish captors exchanging a wry look. For whatever reason, I had the instant impression they knew full well I and the others were innocent of any crimes (well... in *their* particular legal system, at any rate...) and so, emboldened, I took it upon myself to inquire, "What are your names?"

"Phildrin," said the fellow to my right, an older fellow, streaked with grey in the texture of his once solidly black beard. "That's Shemrin."

"You're a paladin, aintche," Shemrin inquired, his bald head—save for the russet pelt that sprang from his cheeks and jaw—jerking toward the tattoo of the black sun emblazoned upon the side of my neck. An odd feeling passed over me, this deep knowledge that here in this unmistakable feature I would, for all time, bear the visible hallmark of that god I had embarrassed, yet whose work I needed, more urgently than ever, to finish.

"I was brought up by the Order, but I'm a wanderer now." When they looked at me with curiosity, the doors opened. I adopted a lower tone to ease their sudden spate of obvious (and valid) questions, bending down to half-truthfully explain, "They prefer us to have only one woman at a time, you see."

The tension broke, and the men let out a merry pair of laughs, their heads tipping back and Phildrin's shaking even as he reached up to catch my elbow and push me along. "Maybe I oughter take up adventurin'," mused Shemrin, suddenly sobering and looking quite serious. When I raised my head upon ducking under the elevator doorway, I noted the sight that had silenced him—we were awaited, at the hallway's end, by that same fellow who had taken the lead in our detainment.

"Anything's better than sitting around in this hellhole, eh, Shemrin," said the man in a tone that didn't even pretend to be amused, his dark eyes flashing sternly. "Go on then, uncuff him. You might as well, leaving him manacled in the front like that, laughing with him like he's a friend from academy. Can't believe we let him keep that blasted sword."

Having the sudden impression that the issue here was the concession that had to be made to permit me to come along armed, along with all the many unaccounted-for powers of the women, I cast a sympathetic look at my guards—or tried to. In reality, they so hastily freed me and hurried away that I could not catch their eyes. As they strode off, I offered my hand to the man in charge, who looked at me and my offer with a barely repressed sigh. As his visible reluctance ultimately turned into a sporting shake, he introduced himself as "Norhalm Thunderson, Commissioner of Ironforge."

"Rorke Burningsoul, Wanderer of Skythorn."

"Come in then," he gestured, waiting for me to move before briskly following me and shutting the door to an office that already contained Grimalkin. My so-called friend sat there looking pleased, stroking his beard with enjoyment and, of all things, puffing on a cigar as he savored a finely stuffed scarlet chair. I occupied its twin, but of course, as one may imagine, I was ill-suited to its scale and could not seem to take comfort in it, my knees pushed comedically toward my chest—while at the same time not giving me any particularly adequate place to set my elbows, for the dwarves were fairly broad-bodied people along with their short statures. As a result, I sat with my hands folded awkwardly upon my knees, no doubt affecting the impression of a school-boy on the timeout step, sulking as the other lads laugh at recess. Grimalkin certainly laughed at me, merrily savoring the sight while waggling his cigar between his thumb and finger.

"Turnabout's fair play, Paladin." Tapping a bit of ash away on the ashtray, then rotating it in the hook of his thumb, he wiggled his eyebrows while Norhalm stalked around us to sit behind his desk. "How're the accommodations?"

"Compared to the last cell I was in," I ruminated, recalling my brief time in the brig of the *Rhinemaid*, "not so terrible. The engineering of this building is certainly a feat."

"We've been making some progress here in Ironforge—a necessity of modernization—but not near so much as I would like." Folding his hands upon the desk, the commissioner looked me straight in the eye. "Care to explain to me how you wound up sitting here today?"

"Let me think where to start," I bade him, glancing off toward my left shoulder as I sought to answer my own question. So much had happened! Ultimately, though—

"My friends and I were aboard the *Battle Swan*, actually coming out this way to Rhineland, or hereabouts—"

"What for?"

"To track a thief who stole something from my beloved. A ring."

Tilting his head, his eyes consulting plainly with mine, Norhalm observed, "Long way to go for a ring. Skythorn's on the other side of your continent."

He had the cool, cultivated tone of a man educated for his field—maybe overly so. I decided not to play it too stupid with him, but remained devoted to revealing as little as possible, lest he become too interested in matters such as Valeria's pedigree...or, Weltyr forbid, the pedigree of the Deepgold.

"One of the ladies of our entourage is a holy woman among her people, as well as the heart of my heart. I would do—have done—foolishly much for her, I am afraid to say."

"Mm." Leaning back now, less intense, Norhalm folded his fingers over his gut and nodded. "Continue."

I spread my hands slightly, then replaced them upon my knees. "As I was saying, we were aboard the *Swan*, and while we attempted to fend off the pirates, they took notice of the same peculiar qualities you and your men noticed of this blade, and some of our other precious objects. We were obligated to join them on their ghost ship, the *Flying Rhinemaid*."

"And how is it," asked this shrewd fellow, having carefully listened to every word and weighed each against whatever variation Grimalkin had used in his telling, "that rather than slitting your throats and tossing you overboard to find a solution to the sword in the eternity of time had by dead women, these pirates instead gave you a free ride to your destination and permitted you to leave with your lives and your goods?"

"Norhalm, my friend: you wouldn't believe me if you had time for all the telling."

A muscle at the edges of his left eye visibly spasmed, a reflexive twitch in his brow and eyelid that was no doubt a sign of long internalized anger. "How about you give it a try."

"Well—ultimately, I think the relevant piece here is that there was a magical fire aboard their ship, and my companions rescued the captain while I dealt with the fire rather than let them all immolate."

Nostrils flaring, the commissioner leaned forward again, as close to incredulous as I'm sure he ever got. "Aiding and abetting a bunch of terrorist banshees rather than letting them burn to a second death—and you're a paladin?"

Now confronted with the question for a second time in such a short span, I attempted not to grit my teeth as I maintained my polite smile. "I was raised by the Order," I repeated.

"But not a proper paladin. You're a dropout, in other words—or you did something. What was it? Murder? That's how a lot of drifters wind up getting their start."

"I found true love on the mission I was given as part of my initiation, and I discerned that the Order was not the manner in which God was calling me to serve."

That piercing gaze keeping mine held in place so firmly I felt uncomfortable, the commissioner pressed, "But you're still a follower of Weltyr?"

"Well—" Was I? "—yes."

"You still know the prayers?"

"Of course." Though for half a second I was affronted, I recognized how understandable the question was of someone in my position, and a great sadness swept over my heart—to be quickly dispelled as I conjoined this conversation to my last, brief interaction with the two guards. "Why do you ask?"

His posture far more businesslike than interrogatory, Norhalm gave me one more brisk look-over and, deciding I was telling the truth, tightened his folded hands one upon the other where they'd come to rest on the desk.

"How are you at turning the undead?"

THE TASK AT-HAND

FEW THINGS CAN be considered a universal truth, I have found. Particularly among the mankinds, any form of universal moral positioning is, I should say, evidence enough of the existence of a perceptible God of *some* kind or another. One could even look at the excluded races and beings, as it were, and see precisely why they were outliers from the brotherhood of men: the durrow and the berich dwarves had both incorporated a cultural acceptance of vice to so great an extent that their eyes had literally adapted to serve those vices, which must, like all vices, be performed in the dark, consigning them forever to the Nightlands; the wajita, too, lived this way, and neither could a skin-crawling demon like Al-listux or any other spirit-thief remain in the world for a prolonged time without some tangible connection to its bloated hivemind. So are other races generally stereotyped to lesser or greater accuracy upon Urde. Yet I have never been able to agree that a person's essence can be measured against such a dubious counterweight, for I have discovered, in for example Valeria, superlative examples of character where I personally have been found wanting; and in other discharges of those races which are generally commended for the production of great virtue, I have found men and women of the most truly disgraceful, evil hearts—Elishta's hateful former betrothed, Zweiding, being only the most prominent recent example. It therefore cannot but be assumed that, with character coming on an individual basis, so too would tastes and opinions, passions and compassions. We all have things we support, things we tolerate, and things we instinctively shun.

But the one universal truth that is clear and strong and, to me, the ultimate evidence that holiness is some inborn trait or measure of something not fully understood by any but the divine, is this:

The undead are repulsive.

Because I had grown so used to witnessing the *Rhinemaid's* banshee women, and then had been quite numb to most everything else aboard the ship but the comfort and company of my beloved Valeria due to the powerful malaise that had come over me in the wake of our time with the gods, I had released my personal sense of offense, at least insofar as the conscious undead went. I tried to view the crew as the unpleasant articles by which Providence had chosen to steer me along in the manner my journey needed to go, rather than the way I envisioned it going. However, they were still frightful to look upon: missing teeth, some of them sections of scalp or skull; gnarled lips; once I even saw a rat moving around in one, which makes me cringe on the retelling. And then, there was the general aroma of the ship, a mummified odor of beige death, long-present, infused in the environment like the cadaver of a rich man united with the chair where they find him in his winter home some seven months later. And, I remind you, these were creatures who seemed perfectly autonomous, still retaining sapience, individual characteristics, cognizant memories. They did not seem prone to some of the more typical properties of the undead, though sunlight—in particular, sunlight while sleeping—was a surefire bringer of their permanent death. In a sense, they were more like lepers, or so I told myself to get through our voyage.

Less conscious undead—less open to reason, less or even not at all aware of what virtue even was as a concept, with no memories of life instilled in them—well…

"All paladins have a particular relish for turning the undead," I assured Norhalm on the other side of his desk, using the technical term for the eradication of these taboo un-beings. "Are you having a problem, Norhalm?"

"Oh, yes," agreed Norhalm, his mouth so sternly arranged that Grimalkin lowered the cigar which was his consolation prize for the undignified greeting of the envoys sent to welcome us upon our landing. "Yes, we are having a problem, Burningsoul."

Taking that to mean there were substantial numbers, some sort of colony we would be dealing with, I arched a brow. "Why has it gotten this bad? Surely there are paladins in the area. Many dwarves serve Weltyr, though even Dunnun's adepts have, I believe, some talent against the undead."

"That's a question with a complicated answer."

"You're more likely to have an appointment booked than I am."

With a slight snort, Norhalm lowered his eyes from me, flipped open the leatherbound appointment book beside him, and looked at the time on the deviously beautiful—also glass-enclosed—desk clock, whose swinging pendulum counted the seconds toward a proper quarter to ten. Then he shut the book again and pushed it off to the side.

"Do the women typically fight with you? I suppose I ought to have them up here to join in our discussion. Can I trust you, and them?"

"Aside from the holy woman, there are two aside from myself who are of deep devotion to Weltyr, and—"

"Bring the rest of the group from this morning up here," said Norhalm into some small mesh device, an intercommunications line so stylishly built into the desk's surface I had hardly noticed it. "And bring more chairs."

As the line cut off, the commissioner leaned back in his chair, looking chagrined. I was sympathetic, and found myself saying, perhaps oddly, "We really are sorry for our arrival causing so much trouble for you, my friend. I can assure you, it was our every intention—"

"The *Swan* was big news, as big of an airship as it was. We already checked the passenger manifest; all but two of you are listed on it, for reasons I don't feel like interrogating you about...although I should." His eyes dashed from my face to my sword and the lantern which still hung from my waist, an additional concession he regarded with a nostril flare so wide I caught unfortunate sight of the hairy undergrowth springing from there down into his moustache. This became an unfortunate point of focus for me thereafter whenever I looked at the man, so I focused intently on his eyes and suffered the sternness there as he lectured on, "For all I know, you're some kind of terrorist organization."

"I can assure you, we mean you no harm."

The fellow lapsed into silence, brooding over my words for a hefty handful of seconds before he rose from his seat to make his way to the bar. This relieved me of his unfortunate nose and gave me a chance to recognize the signs of a true soldier: a slight limp, the proud carriage. He had the look and bearing of a man who was not just a veteran but who was *actively* fighting. And then, it occurred to me: the newness of the building in which we had been detained, its unusual location as an outpost rather than closer to the centrally based, city hall-adjacent locations where one usually found a commissioner's office in a town this size.

"Are you at war with something, Norhalm?"

His hand, which had already come to rest on an overturned glass, paused there as he offered me a look between reproachful and relieved. "That's exactly what we're doing," he replied coolly, turning away from me now and twisting open the cap of a bottle. "Drink?"

"Thank you," Grimalkin and I said in unison, exchanging a smirk of kinship before returning our attention to Norhalm. "Skeletons, innit, Norhalm," asked Grimalkin with a tap of his folded fingers along his stomach, where he had settled his hands while leaning back in his seat. "I been hearing some reports about you folks having a problem, but Rorke's right. Any paladin should be able to take care of a few skeletons!"

"If that was the only problem, we wouldn't be so desperate. It's why we were so concerned about the *Rhinemaid*—we don't know what the necromancer in charge of this operation is capable of. To be frank, we're not even sure he's really in charge. I don't think that he is. But—"

More interested all the time, I leaned forward in my seat to receive the glass of whiskey I was handed. "What do you mean by that?"

"What I mean is—when I tell you the problem isn't just skeletons, I mean the problem isn't just undead, either. And even if it were, we're not discussing a typical inconvenient wave or raiding party of skeletons from some megalomaniac who wants to negotiate something out of us, like money or provisions. We're talking about a steadily growing infestation of the undead that's been endemic in this region going on for decades now, and that's lately gotten out of control. Within the past five years, I mean to say."

After handing Grimalkin his drink, Norhalm returned to his seat with his glass already half-drained. "They're disrupting trade routes and mail carriers, now. Our economy is drying up, and we can hardly farm anymore. They say there's a hermit who lives in the bogs to the northeast of here, and how he survives, nobody can tell; they say he's immortal. Sounds to me like a wives' tale, but, if he's real, he's the only living thing that's between us and civilization, aside from the animals that haven't been so repulsed by the undead they've migrated away."

"Are the skeletons trying to drive you out?" I asked, studying him without yet imbibing. "And to what end?"

"At first we reckoned it a curse on the land. You know skeletons—they're like termites. Not everybody has to deal with them, but they're common enough in certain areas. But—"

At the end of the hall, the elevator chimed, and the doors slid open to emit the excitable flurry of voices that signaled the arrival of the women. I straightened up, then decided it was better if I stood, which wound up ideal when Norhalm also stood—not out of respect for the latecomers to our meeting but rather out of necessity, for he drew my attention to a map hanging from the wall adjacent the fireplace.

"Rorke," Valeria sighed gladly, hurrying over to slide into my arm without delay. I smiled despite myself, as glad to see her as she was to see me; but her relief soon faded when she saw Norhalm looking seriously upon them all, his black eyes sliding from face to face as each filled the room and made the dwarvish architecture seem all the more close-quartered.

"Something tells me," Valeria observed, "that walking out of here isn't going to be as simple as some paperwork."

"Norhalm here has a favor to ask of us, ladies," I explained, gesturing to the map around which the group assembled. "It would seem that Ironforge is in the midst of a pestilence. We're perhaps better equipped to take it in hand than most of the natives in these parts."

"More like we're a captive audience," muttered Odile, folding her arms and studying the map. "Is he going to keep us here if we don't do him this 'favor?'"

"There's nothing that legally permits me to hold you if you've committed no provable crime," Norhalm told them in that permanently gruff tone of his, his expression grim. "But I can't imagine even a durrow could sleep at night having left us to our devices while knowing all that I'm about to share."

As he gestured to the map, I leaned in to make sense of the pins scattered across what I could only assume to be an image of Ironforge. I wasn't entirely certain what they represented—skeleton attacks, I assumed, since they were dense at the perimeter of the city and became increasingly scarce as one drew toward the center—but was chilled as Norhalm explained, "These pins represent abductions: instances where men, women, and children were spirited away in the night, about half of them never to be seen again."

Appalled, I asked, "The necromancer is doing this? Why?"

Norhalm shook his head. "The 'why' isn't clear to us—the 'why' is what's sinking us, because there is no real, sensible 'why' that the human brain is capable of comprehending when it comes to the motivations of spirit-thieves."

The room was so silent a board creaking down the hall would have been loud enough to draw my attention had my thoughts not been so preoccupied by the act of parsing his words.

"Spirit-thieves, you say?"

With a nod and a look in my eye, Norhalm emphasized, "More than one, we know, but we're not sure how many in total since they all look the same. All we can be sure of is that over the past seventeen years we've been keeping records of it, more than 900 citizens have had some contact or confirmed sightings of the creatures, and at least 150 have been permanently spirited away, assumed dead in our city registry."

"That's a large proportion of a city this size," Branwen observed, frowning. "Have you found any bodies?"

"We suspect that some of the missing now make up a negligible percentage of the skeleton waves we're being forced to deal with on the roads leading from here, but mankinds have inhabited these lands for millennia, so the necromancer has no shortage of raw material for his work."

Rubbing my jaw, I studied the map. The visitations were densest on the northern edge of the city. "And you're certain the two are interlinked?"

"The spirit-thieves have been said to have skeletons for attendants, or for the heavy lifting. In fact, in cases where there were eyewitnesses able to describe what happened when they were taken away, most explained they were taken by the skeletons to the location where the spirit-thieves operate. And our police force have consistently reported black objects departing from and returning to the flying citadel controlled by the necromancer, which is reported infrequently but which, we are certain, is tied to both abduction cases and high prevalence of skeletons in a given area."

"A flying citadel!"

He nodded. "The people here call *it Shooting Star*."

I had heard of such things—that they were common long ago, and were even utilized by the proto-mankinds as a form of transportation between planets and dimensions—but the idea that one was still around seemed surreal. "With a device like that, approach can be hard." Musing on this for a few seconds, I folded my arms and studied Norhalm with a grim expression of my own. "I think I'm starting to see your dilemma...and why nobody wishes to help you. Have you attempted to communicate with the necromancer? To understand his motivations?"

"Every messenger we sent has disappeared," said Norhalm with a shake of his head. "There's been no line of communication between us and him, whatever the case. But this, we know—he's never left the blasted place a single time. Not once that we've ever seen, anyway. This fellow doesn't need sunlight, doesn't even seem to need food—they leave all the provisions to rot when they raid our merchants and cut off traffic moving in and out of the region around the city. Unless he's found some means of providing his own agricultural infrastructure in the building itself, he's something inhuman—we think he's a dirge."

A certain raw feeling, as one gets when smelling rotting flesh, settled over my stomach. Of all the unnatural undead there were, there was nothing more repugnant and despised than a dirge. Unkillable, unspeakably intelligent, dirges tended to harness black magic to ensure their permanent survival. You could destroy a dirge's body, it was said, but never a dirge's mind— and that was why it was not impossible to find one in in this state of symbiosis with the spirit-thieves, who did not just leverage and corrupt information but who were said to literally consume it in some metaphysical manner that was beyond the grasp of my reason. The qualia of information making up an individual's sense of self and awareness has some ethereal shape: this and all information contained within it apparently provides some conceptual substance that contributes in a queer way to the metabolism of the spirit-thieves' satellite members, who by their connection to the hiveminds sustain themselves and the capacity of their species to remain in a particular area. It was almost as though, in absorbing the details of the realities of others, spirit-thieves could solidify themselves within that reality, our reality, much more clearly and aggressively, concretizing their powers and deepening the roots of their hivemind into the earthly place they had come to despoil.

"And nobody has seen him, really?"

Norhalm shook his head more emphatically this time. "Not once. But there must be someone behind these skeletons. Spirit-thieves have their little experiments, but they have no power to raise the truly dead. Their servants are still living, breathing men, even if they've been robbed of their mental faculties. Beyond that—if the spirit-thieves were the ones in exclusive control of these skeletons, we'd surely only see them during abductions. Instead, we see them all the time. Walk no more than five miles north of here and you're likely to take note of more of them than could be counted...it's a real war zone, Rorke."

Feeling that some degree of progress had been made if he was using my first name, I nodded, my brow lightly furrowed but my eyes lowering so as not to steep him in my pity. "So I can see. You and your people must be exhausted."

"We've considered evacuating the city, but there aren't many equipped for so many refugees, and at any rate, it seems too late for that. The kind of exodus required would make us sitting ducks. If it's the dirge's intention to eliminate our population for whatever reason he's decided, we'd be handing ourselves over without the least fight. We'd be knee-deep in a bloodbath, and I have little doubt they'd wait a good while to descend upon us so as to cut us off from the city."

His certainty was so pointed, yet still I could not understand—*why?* The women looked dubious, Odile and Branwen in particular. These skeptics exchanged a glance while Valeria, who was no stranger to military strategy thanks to her upbringing and her need for occasional contribution in times of economic or social upheaval in El'ryh, studied the map and stepped up to it, her eyelids shifting slightly as the pale surfaces of her sensitive durrow eyes skimmed back and forth along the sea of pins.

"Why salt the earth in this way, though?" Bracing her arm above the map, which had been set for the height of a dwarf, Valeria leaned against the wall while turning her body to regard Norhalm. Her scrutiny was as deep or deeper than what he had given us all upon our landing. "Come now—doesn't that sound a little absurd? What would be the point in doing a thing like that? If this fellow is benefitting from the trade he's interrupting and he's not taking the food, then it must mean he's taking *something.*"

"Precious goods and luxury items, for the most part. The food is left to rot universally."

"So why disrupt that flow of goods with the skeletons, since I presume he's taking these items as income for himself to fund his magical workings?"

Valeria's beauty struck me as so extreme in that instant, a cord of white hair falling down along her temple to plunge like a stream along the hillock of her abundant breast. Norhalm, though, looked at her as though he were made of stone, his pinpoint attention dominated by the blight destroying the lives of his people. "If I knew that," he gruffly rejoined, "I would be able to barter with him."

"Perhaps...perhaps not." Straightening up from where she'd bent down, Valeria asked, "These blue pins are those that returned?"

"And the red the unaccounted for, aye."

Her hands resting upon the flares of her hips, the Materna of Roserpine asked in a tone of open-minded interest crafted to disguise some form of calculation I could recognize but not yet guess at, "What do the survivors all have in common? There must be some reason they made it back. Or were they returned?"

"A little of both. Some are returned to their beds, if the span of time they've been absent is short enough. Most of them miss some time and wander back into the city in a daze."

"And they have nothing to report?"

"Nothing helpful. Lights, figures. Slender undead, tentacle-faced spirit-thieves, a man in black."

A queer feeling came over me. I looked away, dizzy, as though I had peered too long over the edge of some cliff and needed to regroup.

When I did, my eyes locked with those piercing ones of Brynhildr, who waited with my gaze in hers to ensure I knew her stare was deliberate. Then she resumed her study of the map.

"What about things like enchantment detection, bloodwork? You dwarves are men of great engineering. Did you truly find nothing of value in your rigorous investigations?"

Though her questions were reasonable, Norhalm wrestled with the need to show some humility and said through his teeth, "If I had, I wouldn't be standing here talking about all this to a bunch of strangers."

"There must be a pattern," she reflected. "Don't you all think so?"

"For some of them to come back and others to not, yes ma'am," Indra agreed with a nod. "There must be a reason...and they're not enslaved by the spirit-thieves?"

"We've had our experts look at them. There's no sign of mesmerism or conventional mind control."

"Are there a few we could talk to?" Valeria's interest was unfeigned, though I was sure it was rooted purely in the hope that her ring was close at hand. "My people regularly deal with spirit-thieves; I only recently experienced infiltration of them, disguised among my staff."

"We may be able to arrange that, but I can't make any promises. Either way—you're willing to help us?" Though he spared a look for the others, it was to me Norhalm asked this question, evidently holding me to a high value owing to the clerical specialty in destroying the undead. "There isn't much we can offer you in the way of reward, but—"

"Letting us leave your town untroubled is reward enough," I assured him. "Especially after the time we had aboard the *Rhinemaid*, the last thing we want is any kind of trouble with or for you."

Visibly relieved to hear this, Norhalm nodded. "May your god bless you all your days if you do this for us, Burningsoul."

Something about this blessing pained me, but all the same, I smiled in a courteous manner. "And you, friend."

"There actually is something we can do to repay you somewhat. Our hotel doesn't have many visitors anymore, as you can imagine. I'm sure they'd gladly put you folks up for the night. Why don't you lot rest—I'll arrange a few meetings for tomorrow. Maybe after you've had a chat with a few witnesses we'll be able to determine next steps…if here's anybody willing to be forthcoming, anyway."

8

A MOMENT OF PEACE

WHILE THEY ARE a frequently stubborn people, let it be known that the mankind from which my complicated friend Grimalkin hailed had within them a great spirit of generosity and compassion. They were good-hearted, with a sense of not just their own dignity, but the dignity of others. In addition to the dangers we were about to undertake and what the success of our venture would mean to these people, I believe they felt that they had offended our natural dignities by mistaking us as enemy combatants when we were in fact the victims of a great injustice. In response, that same commissioner who had been so instrumental in detaining and questioning us now put us up in an excellent series of suites in what remains the only "fine hotel" in which I have set foot, let alone stayed. I confess, I see the appeal of the luxuries that delighted the women, (for whatever reason, everyone—in particular Valeria—was thrilled by the curtains enclosing the bed, and most especially the fringes on these curtains, which for some reason even now amuses and charms me, because I would never have noticed such a detail), but after all this time in the air, I was ready for a bed in a building rooted firmly to the ground, and anything fitting that description was more than good enough for me. They fed us, too; and the baths were most inviting, a moment to sink into water and dissolve into steam. As the women chatted on the other side of the wall, giggling and splashing and making merry, I found myself in a state of solemn reflection on the otherwise empty men's side.

What were we going to do, really? Given the unknown number of spirit-thieves and the tactical advantages provided to our foe by the flying citadel, there was an excellent risk we would lose our lives making this effort. And what would happen then? Would the Valor Hall be closed to me? Would it even be there?

Indeed, had it ever been there?

Oh, cruel mind—cruel and petty heart, changeable and faithless! In that moment when the majesty of God is laid bare before us in even some small part, Man can do nothing *but* believe, for God is truth and in all His degrees is naturally ascertained as Himself by the human soul. But after—especially when that moment was linked to death, or to death's nearness—the mind begins again to doubt, and to trick itself with excuses to avail itself of the things of this world. What if that was only a dream? Some fancy concocted by my brain, by all our brains; a shared hallucination, a delusion, or worse?

Then I would look at the Lantern, which I kept near to me along with Exigence and the Helm. Even here at the baths, they sat alongside the water, within my reach should anyone enter with malicious intent.

But the one who entered instead could not have had that intent further from her mind.

"Rorke," breathed Elishta from the open doorway, her voice echoing softly, dreamily, from the entrance to the dressing room. There she stood in a wrap that revealed her comely legs, her soft décolletage, the pink-kissed curves of her shoulders, all her skin given a rosy flush by the heat of the baths. "Aren't you going to join us?"

"Well," I chuckled, trying to avoid objectifying lewdly this woman I loved—had always loved—as a dear childhood friend and now so much more, while still appreciating her beauty and sweetness, "I confess, I was tempted...but I don't relate to the Selectrix the way I relate to the rest of you, if you see what I mean. Besides...I suppose I'm feeling pensive. All the less reason to remain alone, though, you're right...come, Elishta-bet, sit with me, and I won't feel so preoccupied."

"I think we're the only ones in this place," she observed, stepping into my side of the baths and flicking a glance down at the waterline. Her face turned an even darker hue. "Oh," she said, sucking in a breath while I realized with a twinge that I hadn't considered modesty, having seen the empty pool and thought of nothing but the peace of submergence.

"I promise to keep myself under control," I told her playfully, thinking her reticence was related to my nude state. Yet her hand pressed to her heart as she continued stepping down into the water, her towel still wrapped around her.

"No, Rorke, I don't mean that—if anything, I'm the one who needs greater control when you're in a state like this."

Another, far sweeter twinge of pleasure caught me, increased by the way Elishta's eyes flickered down again to witness it. "You don't ever need to be in control of yourself with me," I told her, my voice low as I extended an arm. My soul gasped with joy as—adorable, sweet, tender Elishta-bet Highwind, my darling friend, my first love, the woman who, of all three of my wives, makes me feel most fully safe, almost as if I am experiencing some glimpse of what it is like to have a mother, but so much more—she sank into my embrace, her delicate body and soft bosom plush against my chest. How she gazed at me! Her pupils were like saucers, and even though we were both finely misted in sweat from the humidity of those hot baths, she trembled.

"I want you to be in charge of me, Rorke," she whispered, her hair in wet tendrils plastered to her brow. I pushed a few of them away as a pretext to touch her mouth, which I then bent down to deeply kiss. Elishta's breath released into my mouth with her soft little gasp, and she yielded, making good on what she had just said by letting my tongue probe as far as the entrance of her throat.

How sweet and responsive Elishta-bet was. Valeria was no stranger to sensitivity, but Elishta had never known a man aside from that encounter in the Valor Hall. Within her grew my child, sibling to the one being nurtured by Valeria's womb. This knowledge, along with our wholehearted friendship, made me wish to be extra gentle with her, and to take extra care of her.

Yet...I sympathized with Valeria's desire to dominate pretty Elishta-bet, too. What I wanted was not so much to control her as to shepherd her—steer her gently into deeper levels of intimacy, pleasure, total trust. I wanted her to forget all her fears and worries and trust that I would always take care of her: that she could surrender to me, and obey me with her whole heart, and know in the fullness of confidence that I would always protect and care for her, and love her unconditionally.

Hearing her invitation, I took it gently, untucking the towel from around her waist and drawing back from our kiss to gaze into her eyes. Her breath hitched, but she allowed it, suffering herself to be wholly exposed to me: from the sweet dark red curls around her mons pubis to the kissable divot of her slight but soft tummy and those sweet, soft breasts tipped with adorable pink nipples already beaded with desire.

"You're so beautiful, Elishta," I murmured to her, my hand gliding along her outer thigh and up her waist, where I used firm but gentle pressure to draw her into my lap rather than leave her by my side. As she gasped to feel me, her back arching, I caressed back down, this time following the entire line of her leg to catch hold of one delicate foot and lift it from the bath. "Even your feet are beautiful," I told her, taking advantage of the water and the way she was half-curled against me to raise her foot to my mouth. Amid this experiment in Elishta's flexibility, as I stooped to kiss her pretty instep while she whispered my name in surprise at the pleasure this gave her, I followed the curve of her calf and thigh with my palm, coasting to her slight but pretty rear...and to the velvet lips of her sex, already warm against my hand, and slick with something more than mere water. As my fair lover squirmed, pronouncing my name in a surprised voice amid this pleasure, I gently explored all of her, following the inspiration of my fingers to trail along the soft skin of her perineum and into the crevice between the cheeks of her rump. "You seem excited already...I never knew you were eager as this, Elishta-bet."

"Oh, Rorke..." Moaning in shock but not in protest as my finger trailed an exploratory circle around the rumpled flesh of her tight sphincter, Elishta's trembling doubled, but she made no move to discourage me. My passion for her firmed to know for certain that she would deny me nothing. "I never knew myself to be like this, either, but you—I love you so—"

"I love you, Elishta," I told her breathlessly, lowering my head to crush her mouth in more kisses. When I raised my head, I murmured on, my fingers dancing through the water and back up to the flower of her pussy. "But you must tell me...after all we've been through today, how is it I find you already so eager for my attention?"

"Well," stammered my shy beauty, rocking in my lap just enough to exacerbate my pointed yearning, "it's from thinking about you, I suppose, and—well—"

As my fingers sank between the plush, soft labia enclosing the petals of that gorgeous flower of hers, Elishta lost her train of thought, or became too embarrassed, or both, and moaned without going on. I punished her for this impudence with more pleasure, my finger sliding up around the noticeably swollen button of her clit while she panted in need.

"Well, what, Elishta," I asked, assailing the nub directly with one finger while the others kept her lips spread to make the attack easier. "Tell me...we must never be so embarrassed to share pleasure that we deny our loved ones pleasure through our embarrassment...I have the feeling that whatever you're about to say will bring me great pleasure, indeed."

"It was the way Valeria was looking at me," Elishta moaned, her legs parting slightly to accommodate my touch, her mouth open as she panted for air, "and Valeria, herself, touching me so brazenly—every time I set eyes on her, I imagine—oh—Rorke—"

Though she groaned in a way that seemed as much of agony as pleasure, Elishta made herself go on, whispering out the words. "I remember the sounds of your bodies— of your—you being inside of her, and how much pleasure it brings her..."

With a shudder of my own pleasure, I teased my finger along the slit between her legs, nudging between her labia and brushing that alluringly slick channel whose attention made her weak. "You certainly do have a habit of witnessing, don't you, Elishta? First me and Branwen, now me and Valeria..."

"N-no," she stammered, her legs trembling, her eyes fixed helplessly upon mine. "No, Rorke, I don't mean to, I don't. And in fact, I hate it—oh, I'm so jealous—"

"Tsk! Jealous, you? My oldest and most treasured friend?"

"Yes," Elishta moaned in response, a moan of protest and ecstasy uttered as my finger pushed just slightly into her sweet cunt. "Oh, yes, Rorke, I hate it—I hate knowing you've been inside all of them, yet oh, I love you so much, I want that for you, and it excites me, too—and this excitement makes me hate it all the more. I'm in such confusion."

Unable to help myself upon hearing her confess all this, I used my free hand to steer her mouth to mine for a kiss. As our mouths met, Elishta-bet's tongue leapt fiercely, needily against mine, flickering into my mouth in an amateurish but desperate way that expressed how deep her desire ran. As we kissed, my finger sank more deeply into her, and she made a little choking noise, breathless with pleasure.

"That's the same type of holy jealousy I think of when Valeria talks about having her way with you, Elishta," I told her, working my digit in and out of her in a few slow, steady strokes, not intended to overwhelm her but only to give her pleasure, and to help her get used to the sensation of being filled by me in even this small way. "But it's a sweet jealousy, a jealousy of love... and I sympathize, for I could never deny either you or Valeria the pleasure of playing together, as sweet as I find you both. In fact, Valeria is jealous, herself...she's used to a life more luxurious than even someplace like this hotel can afford to can afford to provide, of lovers and slaves provided her in droves from both sexes...and I have asked that she refrain from opening her heart or her body to other men, if she and I are to give one to another in the fullness of love. But, because I know her needs are great and her passions are hot, I've made it clear to her that I don't mind her pursuit of women, within reason... why don't you sleep in our quarters tonight," I suggested, drawing my finger from Elishta in an act that took as much will as I was already expending to keep myself from taking her. "We could make you jealous in-person, and show you our jealousy...no need to hide, Elishta, my dove, my love." As she made a soft exclamation of joy upon hearing my words, I took her face in my hands and kissed her once more, deeply, then set her free. "Let's share in one another's joys...let's work together to decide how things will be when we're finally through, and we've dealt with Valeria's ring, and all the rest."

"Rorke..." An admixture of joy and relief easing over her features—as if she hadn't been certain I would really want to keep her when our journey ended, despite all I had said before—Elishta-bet took up her soaked towel and wrapped it around herself again while emerging from the bath. "All right...I'll move my things, if you mean it. If you really don't think Valeria will mind."

"Rest assured, Elishta..." As she turned to go, the wet towel had ridden up along her backside to give me a painfully gorgeous view of her nates, along with the barest hint of her labia each time she took a step. "I think she'll be even happier to see you than I."

9

FAMILY

ANTICIPATION SWEETENED THE air as I waited, giving myself time to collect my thoughts and spend time in prayer for the gratitude in my heart. Lord, what a gift these women were to me—are to me! I felt it acutely now that they were more than an assorted harem of vigorous lovers. Knowing two of them (and that beautiful, insatiable, deadly witch) were with child by me was a contributing factor, I am sure; but more than that, it was the intimacy and sweetness of the spiritual companionship that had intertwined us as a consequence of what had happened in and around the Valor Hall. Yes—they, like the Helm and the Lantern, were great reassurances of the reality of what we had undergone. It had been real: every bit of it.

That notion was more frightening than the possibility of it being a hallucination, and I shuddered, rising from the baths to pursue the lovers who were tied to my soul as much as to my body. One was already accounted for.

And the other, to my pleasure, was coming already to find me just as Elishta had. Valeria's inviting curves were left half-exposed and gorgeously accented by the gossamer pale fabric of the gown she wore, which, having been donned while her luscious black flesh was still wet, had gained a transparent quality that once again exacerbated that quality I had spent the past minutes ignoring into a state of relative calm. Seeing this, Valeria tsked, her eyes glittering with pleasure.

"There you are, slave...here I was, thinking I would find you hard at work on that pretty human girl of yours. Didn't she come find you?"

"She did, Madame," I told her, leaning playfully into Valeria's feelings of possession toward me—but also reminding her that it was only out of love I submitted to such banter by lowering my head to fiercely kiss her mouth, my free arm wrapping around her waist to grasp firmly one globe of her ass and pull her against my body. While we kissed, I rocked my tumescence against her stomach as I knew poor, helpless Elishta wasn't yet ready to endure on the basis of teasing. Moaning with pleasure, Valeria let her tongue work hotly along mine, a low purr in her throat even as I pulled away for air. "I was thinking about what you said up on the *Rhinemaid*," I told her in a murmur, my fingers massaging that tender rump, "and also about what our future should look like...and, well...I just thought it might be nice to take an opportunity to let you and Elishta-bet get to know each other. Would you feel cross to know I invited her to bed in our quarters tonight?"

"And she agreed? Oh, this I need to see for myself... what are you doing, leave that off!"

"Not every place is as liberal as the Nightlands," I told her, setting down the Deepgold implements long enough to replace my breeches. While Valeria eyed the hand with which I tucked myself away, she crossed over to tie them for me, her knuckles brushing the straining bulge every chance she had, her eyes fixed on mine.

"I thank your one-eyed god for that," Valeria crooned, giving me a quick squeeze to elicit a grunt before she turned and swept down the hall, the trailing white cloth of her dress clinging obscenely to her backside thanks to the slit running down the leg of the wet fabric. "If not for Weltyr and his ways, there'd be no taboos for us to break."

"The taboos the gods give us are gifts to preserve our souls, Valeria..."

"And gifts to sweeten the pleasure of those who break them. Now, come on...I want to see my new pet."

Before I could even pretend to tut, my beloved dashed up the stairs with the unfeigned sincerity of a spoiled child rushing to find a gift from some new adorer. I chuckled to myself, marveling over the utterly spoiled brat of a girl my mistress must have been when, anointed as the next high priestess of the spider goddess from birth, she was surely raised to enjoy whatever she pleased whenever it pleased her.

Then, for the first time—then, of all times!—it struck me that I had never heard Valeria describe her family. With men counted as slaves in the Nightlands and male durrow unheard of, I couldn't imagine she'd had much in the way of a father. And a mother? The prior Materna, I supposed. What, then, of our child's future?

What, then, of our future at all?

It seems perhaps an odd time to think of it, but suddenly, as Valeria threw open the door to our suite without waiting for me and hurried in to gasp with delight at whatever she found there, I could think of nothing *but* the future. Suddenly, realizing the divine will might permit this and moments like this to make up our every day, far more than my loins were set on fire. It felt as though my soul combusted (aptly!) and I shut the door behind us, knowing in my heart this would be our last night of peace before a long storm—but also knowing that this would not be our last night of peace for all time.

"Rorke," purred Valeria as I came around the corner of the suite's small sitting room and into the opened bedroom, where Elishta, though covered by the sheet, lay already naked and sweetly flushed in the embrace of the bed. "You certainly do keep your promises, don't you..."

"I take vows as seriously as Weltyr does," I told her, setting down my implements and turning to fit my hand upon Elishta's cheek. "I vowed to you, Valeria, that as long as you love me, I don't mind the thought of your having Elishta for a pretty pet...and I vow to you, Elishta—" I looked sincerely into her eyes, knowing that she wouldn't be frightened to hear me say, "If you swear to be my wife, and to love me as I have always loved you, I will cherish and honor and protect you all the days of your life, and the lives of our children, and I will guide you in the experience of pleasures few would dare to taste."

"Oh, Rorke," whispered Elishta-bet, gazing in awe up at me. "Do you mean it?"

"I want you both," I told her, and Valeria, looking back at her with relief to see she looked as if this were lighting a new kind of exuberance in her. It was this passion (and my own growing joy in the matter, and the need for them to stay safe) that made me say, with great emphasis, "I want—I must have—the three mothers of my children with me, always."

A curious shift occurred in the room. Elishta herself did not understand at first; and whatever Valeria in particular had been expecting me to say, it was not that. Hearing it made her look at me sharply, then strangely. Then she looked at Elishta-bet, her features arranged in intense concentration until she released an astonished breath she'd held amid some careful study by her elf-senses, magical or otherwise.

"You're right! She *is* with child...Rorke, you—" Looking at me with new urgency, Valeria demanded, "How did you know?"

"Anroa revealed that an additional life had been added to our number while in the Valor Hall." Looking at Elishta-bet, whose eyes were wide with growing understanding, her mouth open in astonishment, I explained, "That was yours, Elishta—your baby. For Valeria's had already come with us. I suspect, based on what I know now, that she has been pregnant since the Nightlands, when we were first making love."

Her hands first clasped to her heart, then in prayer of praise to Weltyr, Elishta-bet forgot her state of undress and threw herself up from the sheets to fling her arms around my neck. "Oh, Rorke," she cried, kissing me passionately, joyful tears in her eyes. "I've never been happier! Is this true? Oh, please—yes, please, keep me with you."

"Of course," I murmured, gratified by the way Valeria slithered up to lean into the embrace of my other arm. Though her joy was reserved, as were so many of her greatest emotions, I could see by the light in Valeria's face that she was as moved as Elishta—perhaps even more. As I tipped my head from kisses with Elishta-bet down to Valeria's plush, wet mouth, the dark elf emitted a murmur of pleasure, sliding her hand along the muscles of my stomach and down the front of my breeches.

"What a virile stud you would have been if I'd have gotten a chance to put you to the task of breeding bitches in the Nightlands… But, that third—" asked Valeria, before pausing and, with a sort of start, withdrawing her hand from me to look at me seriously. "Surely you're not intending that the witch— On a *permanent* basis?"

With my expression grimly arranged and my gaze fixed on hers, I told her, "I'm not sure how such a thing will come to pass—but, yes. She will be as a wife to me. In my soul, I know it as naturally as I know that right now, I hold the other two."

As I spoke these words, I swore I felt a cool breeze, like fingertips dancing along my neck. Just as quickly, it was gone. While Elishta, who had not been present for Gundrygia's grandest appearances, looked at us quizzically, skeptical Valeria paired her arch look with a tolerant shake of her head.

"You men are so emotional, though you claim you're not...Rorke Burningsoul, you give your heart away to the wickedest women."

Now it was Valeria who leaned up, her tongue sliding into my mouth in a stroke that sent pleasure coursing all the way to the bottoms of my feet. After a few seconds, she moaned, her mouth opening wider, encouraging me to deepen the kiss; I did, unapologetically devouring her, and pleased when we parted for air to find that Elishta-bet watched with a peculiar alchemy of pleasure and jealous pains commingling in her face.

"How shyly our new slave watches her master and mistress kiss," Valeria said with a cruel smirk, catching up a fistful of Elishta's hair and craning her gaze over to be fixed on Valeria's. "Like a girl, spying on her sister and the stable boy...you like seeing it, don't you, though, darling?"

The blush of her desire deepening, Elishta nodded her head and looked timidly between us. "Y-yes," she whispered, her throat tensing as she swallowed.

Amused by this sweet shyness so foreign to her and her people, Valeria leaned in to apply a kiss in which Elishta was slow to respond—but, after the delay of a second, eager in a pure, innocent, wholeheartedly pleasing way. There was nothing ribald about the eroticism of Elishta's love: for love, indeed, it was, and she poured it into Valeria, remaining there with a bitten lip as the durrow drew back.

"Don't worry," purred Valeria, "it's our little secret... no one ever needs to know what you and I and Rorke enjoy together as a family. That is the word, isn't it?"

"It certainly is," I murmured with pleasure, eyeing Valeria as she stepped back.

"Well, my little pet," crooned Valeria with a crook of her finger, "come, undress your mistress...and then, I'll permit you to do what I know you like to do so very much..."

Her eyes raising up to me, then falling with excitement upon Valeria's wet garments, nude Elishta scrambled upright, hesitated only a moment, then threw herself into aiding her 'mistress' in disrobing. As, with a deft hand, she untied the halter of the priestess's gown, the damp fabric fell away and Valeria's sumptuous breasts bounced forth, having been poorly restrained by the fabric anyway. Seeing this, Elishta held her breath as I did, and knelt to draw the remainder of the fabric down Valeria's long legs to reveal the full glory of her body beneath. Then, as Valeria stepped out of the pool of fabric and reclined upon the bed, she waved a regal hand. "Now your master," commanded the imperious priestess. "Go on...look at how big that cock of his is, he's bursting out of those trousers..."

For some reason, Elishta looked even shyer now, and met my eyes furtively; a little smile cracked across her features then, as it did across mine. I stooped into a few kisses to make it easier as her trembling hands untied the bow Valeria had used to bind me up. My length sprang forth before she'd pushed the breeches down more than a few inches, and with a soft cry of my name, Elishta looked at me with a kind of fright that gave me supreme pleasure.

"How hard your presence makes him," Valeria commended, crooking a finger for Elishta. "Come here, girl. Lean back in my arms—I want him to look at your body."

My cock ached to see her shedding her inhibitions. Sweet Elishta obeyed, reclining back in Valeria's arms and gasping to feel the nude woman's flesh pressed against hers. Unhesitating, Valeria tilted Elishta's head over and drank up her kisses, her tongue lashing into the tender girl's mouth as her hands roved along her breasts, paying special attention to her nipples. Shocked by the pleasure of this, Elishta writhed. I sighed at the vision and couldn't help but stroke myself in anticipation of what was to come.

"See how he can't resist the sight of us both here," Valeria crooned, hooking her legs over Elishta's thighs and using an incredible gymnastic strength to 'force' the slender human woman's thighs wide apart. "Oh, Elishta, I'm so pleased you're here. Now that Rorke has proven to me he's willing to give you as a gift, perhaps I really will let him think he's tamed me...and what better way to do that than to help him break you in? Come, Rorke... Husband..." Her intense gaze raised toward mine at this word that, especially from Valeria's lips, made my heart an oasis of peace. She lowered her hand along Elishta's stomach and, plunging lower, delicately spread the outer lips of her vulva so that Elishta could hide nothing from me if she had even wanted to. "Lay first claim to this gift you've given me. Let's give Elishta a proper welcome to our bedroom."

"I'll be gentle," I promised Elishta as I knelt between her legs, still forced wide open by Valeria. Yet, to my delight—as Valeria reached forward to grasp me from the base and, stroking me, guide the tip of my scepter to the delta streaming forth with Elishta's nectar—my beloved lifelong friend shook her head.

"No, Rorke, oh, no. Don't be gentle, please. Don't be gentle. I want the real you. I want whatever you want!"

"She's a big girl, Rorke," encouraged Valeria, tugging on my shaft to push me down and into Elishta's velvety vise. I obeyed, unable to help myself, making all three of us gasp. "I know she can take it...oh, yes, I know she loves it, too...just look at her..."

From the second of penetration, Elishta's face had changed, the wideness of shock narrowing into a sultry, almost glamorous look of absolute submission and trust. Cared for and held by both me and Valeria, with my child inside her womb and the womb of the woman who held her vulnerable to me, Elishta could do nothing but moan and cry out in soft pleasure—pleasure that grew a little less soft as Valeria, satisfied with the depth of my penetration, rubbed her middle and index fingers along my girth, then down over Elishta's clitoris. I found a rhythm that satisfied my needs and Elishta's without overwhelming her, so close to a virgin as she still was. Yet, even as I held back, I could tell she wanted more: her hips bucked as much as was possible with Valeria restraining her, and the slippery channel of her sex gushed with a special type of pleasure while the priestess encouraged us both on. That moment of looking down at them both instilled in me such a feeling of rightness, of goodness, that I could have given up right there: but, the opportunity was too sweet, for just beneath Elishta's welcoming flower, Valeria's also was invitingly poised due to the way she cradled her human counterpart. Therefore, after a few more thrusts, I drew out, keeping my eyes fixed on Elishta's as instead I slammed myself to the hilt in the unexpecting durrow. Valeria responded with an expression that resolved from shock to overwhelming, unbridled pleasure...especially as I began to hammer into the depths of her, stabbing her with myself again and again to make her scream in pleasure to be invaded by me while still coated in Elishta's juices.

"Oh, Rorke," moaned Valeria, her eyelids fluttering as she received this ecstasy, "you wicked slave, I'll whip you for that—you should beg for your mistress's pussy, oh, yes, but now that you're here, mm, keep going, oh, sweet Roserpine, oh, yes, stretch me open—"

As Valeria responded deliciously to my thrusts, I looked Elishta in the eyes and continued my pace. Each time I thrust heavily into Valeria, bottoming out against the soaking, spongy spot in the depths of her needy grotto, my pubic bone would strike heavily against Elishta's sex. Each time, she would moan, and that moaning mouth incited me so that as I rode Valeria savagely, I bent down to kiss Elishta with great adoration, my tongue asserting ownership over hers with every lap and thrust.

Yes—we could play whatever games they wanted, but now that I had procreated with them, they were mine in a deep, instinctual way that I had not been expecting. The mere notion made my pleasure intensify, my balls tightening, my speed increasing. As Valeria's voice raised in a desperate shout, I angled myself up, more specifically striking that spot; but it was only as I turned my mouth from Elishta's to kiss Valeria and enjoy the sensation of her sucking on my tongue that my loins erupted, inspiring a like response in hers. As, overcome with pleasure, I tensed, pulsed, burst inside of her, Valeria groaned, kissing me passionately, gasping with delight as I slid my twitching cock out of her and, with a few false thrusts and at least one jet expended across their thighs, remounted Elishta, who received my last few brutal strokes and thick, pearlescent emissions with a moan and a shocked orgasm of her own. Pleasure raced through all three of us in waves, overwhelming our minds and uplifting our hearts.

And when the ecstasy passed us by in a sublime afterglow, and I looked upon both the tranquil faces arranged before me, all the many other pleasures I wanted with them rose up in my heart in the wake of that sexual fulfillment: profound words, simple gestures, hands held, fevers tended, peace, peace, nothing but peace and companionship.

And I knew I would fight any battle to get to it.

10

THE OLD MAN

THAT NIGHT, I dreamt of myself.

This was not the first time I had dreamed of the old man in the tower somewhere far away; only now, within the dream, my soul was moved by some powerful instinct to know that he was close. In a reflection of that, or in some law of nature, or for some other reason known only to my Master, I sat face to face with this fellow at table. Even in that dream space, I remembered the tales of old and would never dream of touching the food, for the man looked exactly like I would have were I perhaps forty years in advance of my own age: then, the far-roving youth of my twenties. I could chart the continents in the crags of his face, yet I looked into it and, as if recognizing the face of an old friend, knew intimately therein myself, and marveled, afraid of him.

"Still stuck on these women." The old man spoke as if amused yet curious, like a researcher whose interest in some primitive tribal member had been piqued with a new note to be added to his journal. "And still hung up on old Weltyr, huh? Well, what can I tell you... I suppose, if I were you, I wouldn't be able to resist them, either."

"Aren't you me?"

"On a genetic level." He paused, hearing his own words, and after a second opened his gnarled hands on the table where they rested. "Do you know what 'genetic' means, son?"

I nodded, understanding precisely, my heart full with thoughts of the small durrow son likely to be the eldest before his fairer brothers joined him. "The traits the boys will take from their mothers."

"Rightly so," said the old man with a wave of one hand, adding, "Congratulations." Again, I nodded, and he went on without further delay. "You could consider me a disciple of the beings you call spirit-thieves. They have ways of producing a child without the need of conventional conception. That's the way I prefer it, as my concerns are deep, and require deep focus to plumb their depths. This is all I can say for now without going over your head."

While I sought to contort this knowledge into something congruent with what I already understood—that I was a Wotsung, with the blood of Weltyr—the old man showed he was either privy to my thoughts or knew my nature from some cryptic form of observation. I decided that, likely, he was linked with the same den of spirit-thieves who had obtained connection to me through Al-listux, thereby opening the doorway for the entirety of their species to have unfiltered access into my mind…which I had not fully grasped until that moment.

"Do you not love women?" I asked him, sincerely confused and needing someplace to start amid all my questions. I had then in my heart still no comprehension of a life better than doing Weltyr's will while as often as possible buried under and within the bodies of my brides, save perhaps for the tender notions of domesticity with them and the sons they would bear me—and perhaps even daughters and more sons someday, if divine generosity did not stick to the letter of prophecy. My question made this fellow laugh, and he gestured as he spoke in a more animated way now.

"Oh, of course! I love women. But I don't have the time for a woman…let alone three. You've got your work cut out for you, kid, I'll tell you that."

Leaning back in his seat, he studied me in a shrewd, piercing way that made me wonder if he had some form of extraordinary vision—a gift from the gods that made him super-perceptive in a manner requiring an action of the will, rather than some passive knowingness as enchanters or sorcerers were said to conjure up.

"Listen to me carefully, now, Rorke," he said when his scrutiny was complete. He leaned forward in his seat, looking me hard in the eyes. "Or should I say, Nothing… for that's what you are, yes? Nothing. Nothing at all. An identity, a dream, suspended on a mote of fairy dust floating in a galaxy that will explode someday when the sun consumes it—even if what's going to happen doesn't happen. But I wouldn't hold my breath. It seems to happen every time. Stop me if I'm going too fast for you."

There was no hiding the bewildered expression from

my features. "What do you mean?" I asked him. "What thing?" Although, in a strange way, I knew—and I had the distinct impression that this was one of the many truths Gundrygia whispered in her garden that day of our child's conception amid the flowers, when she pressed her lips to my ear and filled me up with knowledge my mind was too overwhelmed to contain.

A sympathetic furrow excavated further that spotted brow, but there was less sympathy in his eyes, and less so by far in the dismissive bent of his mouth.

"I don't think it's a good idea to overwhelm you with information. I came here tonight to tell you this one thing, Rorke—that Nothing is more powerful than Weltyr."

The snap of his spear beneath shining Exigence, that sharpened blade enhanced by its crossbar and grip of Deepgold.

"Yes," I agreed with a nod, though on multiple levels. Indeed, I thought he punned in the way I wanted him to, acknowledging the power of Weltyr and his might over the lesser idols of the other gods whom Weltyr made.

Yet my aged reflection had in mind arithmetic rather than wordplay.

"If Nothing is more powerful than Weltyr, then Weltyr, too, must be Nothing. Maybe even less than nothing. You see?"

A cold chill passed me by, as if I became aware that I had been doing something wrong. What was it, though?

"I have seen Weltyr's power close at hand," I assured him. "Surely you know that, Sir, for it would seem you know a great deal about me and my mannerisms, and my mind. Add also the thought that the sword which defeated Weltyr was the creation of Weltyr, and—"

"And who created Weltyr?"

"W— I—"

Not having anticipated this question, I took a few heartbeats to respond. "He was self-created, and the byproduct of his creation was this universe."

"So he isn't pre-existent, or truly eternal in any meaningful sense. Then how can he be king of the gods?"

Again, I hesitated, lingering on this question, not understanding it. "By his might, of course," I said in a tone that was more like a question. "And by his Will, within which even he is bound."

"Then, again, I have to ask—is he king of the gods? How can he be? Wouldn't the king of the gods, the singular monolithic God, be beyond all truly fathomable definition when compared against the containable beings who have names and sexes and particular aspects that don't encompass in any valid way the fullness of reality?"

How pleased Weltyr had seemed to let me escape, him defeated and humbled in his own court. How disenchanted I had become with his church and its barbaric ways, embodied in the fate from which we narrowly freed Elishta-bet. How difficult it was becoming to pray in the old ways, not knowing what consequences my actions in the Valor Hall would have on my ability to return to it.

Yet, I could not make myself nod or shake my head. All the thoughts and emotions that had been roiling in me since our journey through death rose up newly even then in the dream, and I found myself awed to the point of fright by how much I had changed since I first left Skythorn for my goal, which had once been Weltyr's Scepter.

O simple dream! What vainglory, what arrogance had filled my heart when first I set out. Other men had gone out of the Temple and returned within as little as two weeks, or maybe the span of a month. Only rarely did a man's first completed mission and induction into the Order require more time than that, and more rarely still did it result in a death, though they had happened on occasion with those who had not taken sufficiently the seriousness of their studies. Surely, I thought, I would not be among these, the dead, nor even among the late-goers. I was quite sure that, especially with assistance from the adventurers I happened to meet and collaborate with along the way, (Hildolfr! What far away days, what naivete filled my heart), my time away from home would not amount to more than three weeks. Then I would be seen for a genius adventurer, an excellent paladin, and I would have a comfortable career serving the Citadel until it was time for me to retire or die gloriously in military service, lest the unthinkable happen and there be widespread war. More likely any combat-related death would have been in the service of missionary work.

But now, I was months unmoored from that timeline, (even the period of adventure with Grimalkin, Branwen, and Hildolfr unrecorded here had exceeded in length my ambitions), and had managed in that time to be expelled from the Order entirely. Now, I was a free agent who had been working in the service of my god.

My god, who was a created thing, a being who did not exceed in age the universe, even if indeed he was self-created. That one whom I who am Nothing defeated in his court, the impregnable Valor Hall which he won through the seduction of Roserpine, the theft of her gold, the deceit and betrayal and unvirtuous doings that had tarnished my estimation of him even before the strength of my arms met no further resistance beneath the shattered spear.

"No need to answer now," said the old man, raising his cup to his narrow lips. "I can tell that you don't want to talk about it. Just a little something for you to keep in mind."

There was someone else who was invoked by the features of this old man. I studied and studied, fixated on his stare, until the raising of his eyes from the lowered cup triggered a steep recognition, furthered when I considered with whom I had seen him. A wild voice, referring merrily to her father.

"Gundrygia," I placed, pleased with myself and hitting the edge of the table in a jovial manner.

The old man rolled his eyes and commenced sawing apart his steak.

"Well, now you've done it. Nice talking to you, kid."

Her lips on my ear and the weight of her sweet-smelling arms around my shoulders were the change in scenery that my brain could no longer accommodate. With a start, I awoke—

And as the women slept on, Valeria's arms folded comfortingly around Elishta-bet while the dark berry of her rump stayed pressed to my hip, Gundrygia, already straddling my thighs, bent down low to let her hair brush along my face.

"Sh," she whispered, touching my lips with one slender finger, her mouth poised in a bow of wicked amusement. "It was only a dream, my love…a dream, and nothing more."

Again, I startled; and now the scene was the same, without the succubus.

Something about these dreams—these dreams that were not dreams, though they utilized the same faculty as were occupied by those nocturnal visions—disturbed me immensely more than any nightmare. I lay awake in the early hours of the morning, puzzling over this, wondering what my mind wished to indicate from this strange construction. Wondering if it were really possible that another person could have sent it. As it occurred, the certainty was unshakeable; but now, as with the Valor Hall, removed from the stimulus I could not help but doubt. While my mind rushed, I could not return to sleep, and I didn't wish to disturb the women since they were most in need of rest, these two gifts to my soul. Therefore, sliding gently out of bed, I dressed in the thick bluish dark of early morning and crept out of the room in pursuit of a maid to furnish breakfast.

Perhaps it was the time in the Valor Hall, but I already had a steep internal sense that something about these next days would be different from all the rest we had spent together. That these days would be different from the days before Valeria, and the days, even, before my adventuring began. As I made my way down the hall toward a (highly inaccurate) bearded carving of Dunnun, the awful thought occurred to me that I myself was actively living the kind of life one normally found encapsulated in fiction for the inspiration of others. I thought of the heroes of the Ancient Days, before the genesis of all the mankinds at the climax of the wars inaugurated by the engineer Oppenhir, Death himself, who sold his soul to be counted among the ranks of those such as Weltyr and Anroa; and whose fearsome weapons of war, I have heard it sung in poetry, attracted the attention of the spirit-thieves in the first place, seeing in these tools the hallmarks of a species advanced enough to sustain their own.

In those days, there were only the proto-mankinds. The origin of the separate mankinds was a source of great disagreement among scholars and Theologians of all sects. In some legends, the human race was once an even more formidable one than it is now; and the gods, disturbed by their power, shattered them into the mankinds to disrupt their unity, for otherwise they might well have conquered the spirit-thieves and, obtaining their technologies, would have destroyed the galaxy and even the gods. Yet, other learned men pointed to the stories of great heroes, such as Odizeus and Gil-gamesh, whose tales teemed with curious beasts and demons that some said were only late created from within the human race, or by some magical means after the distinction of the plurality. I was living the life of one such as these, on the precipice of reason and realism, pushed along into something that yet still more tenuous. Something that I felt only I could do, however arrogant and confusing that intuition seemed at the time.

But it did not remain so absurd when my foot hit the landing and, having rekindled the fire in the great hearth while the morning was cold, the Selectrix sitting in the lobby's most appealing armchair raised her eye to mine. For how many could say they kept such company? How could I deny the compilation of evidence before me, these indications that despite the chaos and the pain and even the moments of hopelessness, my existence held a special relevance to the divine forces that sent me from the Valor Hall in pursuit of the last of the Deepgold?

"We must speak, you and I." Gesturing to the chair across from hers without rising, her helmet upon her knee and her hair falling in wild rivers down her cheek brightened by the hearth's flames, Brynhildr insisted, "Sit, cousin. There is little time, and once we are on our way, we shall have no more to talk between us."

An odd lump in my throat, I did as the harbinger commanded. "No time to talk until when, Brynhildr?"

How beautiful, Brynhildr's eyes! There's a not uncommon joke between crass men who, when speaking of a woman's assets, comment ironically upon her eyes to draw their peers' attention to certain other features of interest; but with Brynhildr, there is no question that there are truly no eyes like hers upon all Urde. Innocent and infinitely wise; open-hearted and shrewd; merry and profoundly solemn. These great pools of glittering sapphire, framed by plush lashes that only seemed to enlarge them, shimmered slightly as if in the containment of a tear.

"Long have I waited to know you, Rorke Burningsoul," she said, reaching out to take my hand. "Yet longer still must I wait for him who my heart loves. I must surrender everything I am to be with him."

Her grip tightened so I almost felt fright. I looked at her sharply, uncertain if she knew her own strength. Seeing she had my full attention, her hand relaxed again, and she said with great sincerity, "You must not interfere, Burningsoul."

Taken aback, I could only think to ask, "Why would you think I would ever interfere in your love? Particularly if your betrothed is indeed to be one of my sons, you have my full blessing, and I'll be overjoyed to say so again on the day of your marriage, whenever that will be."

How stricken Brynhildr looked! With tenderness, and once again with that sorrow. Touching the palm of one hand to her breast, her head tilting with the tension of a smile that seemed liable at any second to tip wider and expand into a grimace, Brynhildr whispered, "How sweet a day," in the adoring, hopeless tone of a parent whose dying child makes some vow or dream for their adulthood. "Aye, Rorke. When your son is by my side, I know I will have your blessing, and my heart will have a moment of holy peace."

"You say that as if I will not be there," I observed, a cold sensation rushing from my cheeks and through my body.

Making no response to this—in itself, the most alarming response she could have provided—Brynhildr leaned forward to gently take both my hands in hers and look me in the eyes.

"I beg you a second time, Rorke. Not for my sake, but the sake of your son and your grandson, too: Do not interfere. It is not your business. Not everyone is for you to save; and for even those you save, you are but the implement leveraged by a higher savior. Even my Father—well."

With a slight smile, dark and fleeting, she released me and stood from her seat. "You have already won your battle with him; you need prove nothing more. So let what is between him and me stay between him and me."

The mystery of her words was alarming, certainly, but I could do nothing to extricate from her greater knowledge than she had already revealed. Whatever awareness Brynhildr had of her fate in repayment for what she had done to aid my flight from the Valor Hall was hers alone, and there was no doubt that its premature release would in some manner interfere with the order of events preordained, or would at least increase my suffering by my remembrance of them. Yet the uncertainty was its own pain. It ground my teeth to think that Brynhildr had weighed the options and found this to be the least disagreeable, this knowing-but-not-knowing. Yet, looking back now, I can see if she had not had such a firm word for me, I would indeed have made some choice mistakes in the coming days.

At least for now there was much to distract me from the pondering, I was wont to do over matters far beyond the realm of my concern. By the time I managed to find any of the staff who could be pressed into service, the second floor bubbled with the vigor and energy of the rousing women beginning to cross the boundaries of their quarters to review the quality of their sleep the night before, the softness of the beds, the dignity afforded our travel-weary bodies by a nice thick curtain and a pillow of goose down. There was much chatter and speculation, and exclamations of relief seemed to be a great chorus. No matter what we were doing, where we were going, or what kind of trouble we were in: we were all on the ground now, all of us alive, and all of us together.

Even if only for today.

11

COLD CASE

AFTER MUCH DISCUSSION, we determined that the best course of action was to assume we would need to set out immediately from our interviews to whatever destination our intelligence called us toward. There was no clear indication of precisely where the flying citadel of the necromancer was, for its unreliable appearances meant it was either highly mobile, or capable of invisibility. We did not, therefore, have any definitive plan as to how we would find the thing's current location aside from the idea that we may have luck locating it at recent abduction sites. There was also no clear indicator on whether there would be greater, more dangerous undead threats between us and our nebulous goal.

Ultimately, it didn't matter. If there were spirit-thieves involved, that was enough for us to know we had to take things with deadly seriousness—and I could see that, among all of us, Valeria was the most quieted by the possibility that we were about to have a renewed focus of our original task, which sent her out of the Nightlands to begin with. While the other women chatted on, Valeria remained pensive, her gaze distant, her features brooding. I squeezed her hand as we convened in the hotel lobby, where not just Norhalm but Grimalkin arrived to greet us—this latter lacking the leather armor of a journey or even the helmet to which I had grown accustomed to seeing him wear. He was balding. Something strange and melancholy struck me about that knowledge as he extended his hand to me.

"Are you separating from us for now, friend?"

"With all due respect, Burningsoul, I pray by Dunnun's beard that it'll be not just for now, but forever. There's only so much a man can take before he recognizes it's time to stop testing the gods...a fire aboard a ghost ship is that limit for most of us, and most especially for me."

"I understand. I won't say I'm entirely sad about it, myself"—I smiled at him in a way that showed him I meant no harm by an observation we both knew to be true, and he laughed in a surprised ejaculation of agreement—"but aside from a few bumps in the road, you're a man to whom I think I can relate."

"I'm sorry to see you go, Grimalkin," Branwen lamented, bringing to mind in a bitter flash how she and he and Hildolfr, too, had been against me that time in the Nightlands.

Yes—even my god, disguised, had been against me in the Nightlands, or had appeared to be. And now here I was, doing his will even after bending it, testing it, breaking it.

"Are you lot really going to look into this business with the skeletons?" he asked, dropping his voice a little as he passed me.

Faintly, I smiled.

"If I am not to serve Weltyr's will by the assignments of the Order, then I do not see the harm in doing Weltyr's will by assignments from wearied men to whom he leads me. Besides…" With a sidelong glance at Valeria, who, like a child anxiously awaiting a journey, stood by the window with her hand upon her heart, I assured him, "There is more at stake here than even the soul and livelihood of this town."

"We've a list here of witnesses who returned from the clutches of the spirit-thieves," Norhalm announced impatiently, slapping the document he held with one hand and nodding toward the door. "There's some fellows here from the city guard who are willing to accompany you. These are sensitive people, so we ask you not upset them. They've been through a lot, some of them fairly recently, but these of all the list seem like the best candidates for closer discussion…if there's anything to discuss."

"I'm sure there will be something to glean," I told him mildly. "How many are on the list? Perhaps we could split the group among our number and each of us attend to a portion."

"That'd be best, especially since most folk don't care to answer the door after dark round here."

"I can imagine." Looking between our number, I gestured. "Indra and Odile, perhaps you two could form a group and Brynhildr could come along. I think Branwen and Elishta-bet can take care of one another perfectly well."

Scoffing, Odile protested, "We can take care of ourselves, too! What are you worried about, anyway? A bunch of traumatized peasants in broad daylight aren't likely to give us any trouble."

"We're durrow, though," Indra observed, frowning a little as she pushed an icicle shock of white hair back from her face. "They're not used to us in these parts, especially not in dwarven regions. They might not even open the door during the *day* if we don't have someone who looks at least human...and even then…"

"Fine," Odile muttered, flicking an annoyed glance at Valeria. "I guess that leaves you with your bodyguard, Materna."

"There's four of my men outside for you to split amongst yourselves," Norhalm said with a gesture. "We expect you to share information you glean with them and to follow their lead if suspects get too emotional. I appreciate your desire to obtain all the information you can...surely you can respect my desire to protect the fragile minds and hearts of the people I've been assigned to protect."

"I promise"—I raised my hand—"we will handle these good neighbors of yours with the utmost sensitivity for all the troubles they've endured."

Outside, I was none too surprised to discover Phildrin and Shemrin were among the four who had come to act as our escorts through the interrogations. Now having the perspective to understand their interest in my place in the Order, I saw that they were savvy fellows. Though they had no imminent awareness of a threat, after the kind of life they and the rest of the Ironforge citizens had lived, I was not at all surprised to think that anyone with the least awareness of the Order would have hastened to stick with one who was versed in its practices. I had the sense they wished to talk more, but they could see clearly that my attention was fixed on Valeria. While I allowed them to lead the way through the gloomy streets toward a witness from the list, I caressed my lover's bicep and drew her gaze up to me.

"What's wrong?"

"My mind is full of strange things," said Valeria with a solemn shake of her head. "Is it not frightfully queer to wind up here, in proximity to those beings whom we seek? Has not this entire journey been troublesome? You yourself, Rorke—we—"

As she had been before the chamber of Roserpine, Valeria fell speechless. We walked side by side, together behind our guides, for the pace of perhaps half a block. Then, she looked up at me and spoke again.

"What do you experience, Rorke, when you pray to your god?"

Taken aback by the question, I hemmed over my answer while I laughed out my surprise. "Well—what I experienced before was strength, and the security of his guidance. The knowledge that he was a just god, a god who always keeps his agreements and who would honor me as long as I myself was honorable in serving him."

Nodding, she asked, "And now?"

"And now—" My tongue darted across my dry lips. I glanced askance, almost frightened that I might find Hildolfr or another manifestation of Weltyr standing off to my side. "Now," I murmured, "I'm not sure what to think about how I feel. Now it seems like there never were any gods at all—although I saw them with my own eyes."

"Almost as if in seeing them," Valeria agreed with a forlorn expression, "they became less gods, and more men."

That was just what had happened. It occurred to me at Valeria's observation that there was something to this notion, the idea that perhaps I had draped something profoundly incomprehensible with the trappings of metaphor because it was all I could perceive. Weltyr, Anroa, Dunnun—if they were gods, why could they be tricked? If they were worthy objects of my worship, whatever powers they generously provided at this moment or that, then how was it I had defeated in battle that one among them whom I held in esteem?

Perhaps that same power that had allowed my hand to defeat him had been delivered unto me by his own will and, at times, his direct intercession. But there was a far more fundamental problem—the plurality of it. Having by now become accustomed to the mental and heartful experience of being interlinked romantically with a handful of women at once, I could not rightly say, even if pressed, that one of them was preferred to all others, truly. Valeria's eroticism and Elishta-bet's innocence both delighted me in different ways at different times. Gundrygia's wildness versus Valeria's structural knack for leadership. Their complication; Elishta's simplicity. No one of them was 'perfect', for perfection was not a relevant component of my thinking toward them. This was the way it was, like with the gods. Different characters and temperaments and specializations had been applied among them, and they had taken to some sense of living in a manner that seemed at times beneath them: for, just like many wives, many gods have a tendency to quarrel among themselves, and this, again, was a component of imperfection.

What then even *was* a god, if not perfect? Well— not a god, in truth.

And what was *a* god? For, in my heart, I had only ever cherished Weltyr, and had dismissed the other gods as mere emanations of his glorious Will for all things. Now, having seen him standing face-to-face with his wife, or take into his arms in paternal embrace that Selectrix with whom I broke bread, (or so she deigned to appear as doing while we dined in her presence), things did not seem to be that way at all. It seemed to me that Weltyr was of the same stuff as the other gods. The king of those who dwelled in and around the Valor Hall, yes. But a king among the mankinds is still one of those same mankinds he rules. Therefore, whatever Weltyr was, the other gods were, also. This implied there was nothing to differentiate him from the others aside from the value I had been taught to place on him.

It troubled me. As we walked through the gloomy streets of Ironforge, I wondered, heart heavy, what all this implied. Had I been wasting my time? Entrapped by tales of beings which, though exceedingly powerful, were not what I thought they once were? Was there not evidence in their plurality of their imperfection and inferiority?

Would not the only God worth worshipping— worthy of the title—be so far beyond them in comprehensibility, glory, and perfection that the experience of His presence in naked fullness would be so infinite, so much the source and substance of life itself, that physical existence could hardly be compatible with even the least awareness of His immediate presence save by some tremendous grace bestowed by His sovereignty?

I ruminate on all of this now because the unfortunate reality of that dusty gray morning is that it was a ponderously long series of failed attempts to make a connection with anyone. Norhalm had rightly warned us, and the experience showed me one of many reasons why the town authorities were reluctant to push.

No one would talk with us. The pattern became evident sometime in the first hour. The first door we knocked upon yielded no response, which was easy enough to chalk up to a trip to the market or a moment of indisposal. The second house was where things became strange, however. A stocky maiden, dumping a bucket of soapy water out into the gutter outside her house, looked up at us, then froze in place as she realized we were coming off the road to take *her* path.

"I paid my taxes this year," she said, leading to Phildrin flashing a smile and tipping his helm.

"Nothing like that, ma'am; no trouble at all, we assure you. Could we just have a few minutes of your time to follow up about that incident from the other month?"

A wave of corpse green despoiled her complexion. The woman turned, empty bucket hanging from her hand, to march directly whence she came.

"Told you," Phildrin said with a shrug of his shoulders as the door, closed harshly, vibrated in its frame with the energy of the rejection. "These lot'll want nothing to do with us. Sometimes I think they'd rather return to wherever the spirit-thieves took 'em than even open their mouths to describe what happened."

I frowned, studying the little cottage as we retreated, my mind spinning with questions. "What could it be? She looked terrified."

Shrugging his shoulders in time with Phildrin, Shemrin pointed out, "It's like Norhalm says—if we knew that, we wouldn't need you, Burningsoul. Don't worry...it'll get worse, you'll see."

I had no idea what was intended by that remark, but to my great befuddlement, I soon discovered he was right. That first encounter was to be our most successful. At our second stop, some ten blocks north in a district that seemed in desperate need of street cleaning, we merited a double-glance from the young lad playing with his friends at the mouth of an alley. Without even a second's hesitation, he leapt from their game of astragal and darted into his mother's house, whence came no answer when we knocked.

How can I describe this day without causing you, friend, to grow as agitated as Valeria was by the third such repetition? Yet perhaps from that perspective, the fact that there was no fourth was a better respite than I considered at the time—for from our third rejection on, there was no one about to reject us. Coming upon a procession of three small homes where, Phildrin informed us, each had been the subject of one of these abductions, no one worked or played in easy sight, and the houses themselves might as well have been abandoned. Their doors were locked and their curtains forbiddingly drawn across their windows. At a certain point, we ceased even knocking. I had the impression that our presence harassed them, and I did not want to agitate them further by insisting they answer our inquiries and detail the horrors they had witnessed.

But that all begged the question—

"Why is it that they appear to know we're going to come round for them?" Valeria's question came as noon approached and the heat of the day climbed unpleasantly, the unseasonable beat of the sun a discouragement worse than any shut door.

"We've noticed that, too," Shemrin agreed. "The survivors seem to have some network of information, because as soon as you talk to two or three, the whole lot disappears. The trick is, we never see them sending messages."

"That's just a small town fer ya," Phildrin responded with the bored shrug of a man who had seen it all and didn't really care anymore. "We all know one another's business."

"That Norhalm fellow seems like a strong ruler, though," suggested my beloved, thinking always in autocratic terms. "Pray tell me, good sirs—just what is it that has made him fail to glean *any* information about these sordid demons and whatever it is they are doing to those whom they spirit away?"

Shemrin, who had come without helmet or any sign of a weapon other than a miniature blunderbuss hanging from a holster at his hip, looked at her sympathetically, understanding her veiled frustration. "Some of them just don't remember. I talked to a farmhand who was so changed he moved to town and got hooked up as a bookbinder's apprentice, like. Real decent feller. Strangest thing though is he doesn't even know what happened to him. Says there was a light that woke him up while he was asleep in the loft of the place where he was workin', where they put him up to sleep and the like. About two days later we found him walking along the roadside looking dazed."

"You get to know that look after a while," Phildrin ruminated, stroking his beard and then digging for a pipe from the pouch at his waist, beside a slightly larger musketoon. "It's a pretty troubling sight the first few times, whatever it signifies, but after a while it just sort of takes on a different character."

Interested in this, I asked, "How so?"

Thoughtful as he sprinkled some tobacco into the bowl and fished for a match, Phildrin suggested, "Just sort of seems like drunkenness, after a jot." With a frown, then, he glanced over at Shemrin, elbowing him. "Got a match?"

With a flick of Valeria's finger, a blue wisp of flame bounced up over the tobacco, then was gone.

As Phildrin removed the pipe from his lips for a few impressed seconds, I asked Shemrin, "Where is that bookbinder you mentioned? Does this man still work there?"

"I think he does," agreed Shemrin. "It's at the edge of the commercial district over this way, half a mile or so."

"Is he on the list?"

"Hm…" Checking it over for a few seconds, Shemrin eventually confirmed, "No, he isn't."

"All right…then let's do a little experiment."

At least finding the bookbinders closed told us one thing: if there was a conspiracy afoot, this list of names had nothing to do with it. These were not previously warned townsfolk who had been tipped off by someone in the police and prepared to spend the day making themselves scarce.

And, of course, that just left me with many more unanswered questions.

12

SUBTERFUGE

BY THE END of our unproductive day, we were hot, tired, and ready for rest and a meal. To no one's surprise, the other groups fared the same, and we were all wearied by the pointlessness of it all.

"I say we forget about any investigation and just move on," Odile said with annoyance, her arms folded beneath her breasts and her boot rocking against the edge of the table in the hotel lobby. "We know the flying citadel and these abductions are related to these skeletons, right? So, we just follow them. Look for the greatest point of infestation and go there. There's your source."

"Except, as you yourself said, it's a flying citadel," Branwen reminded her, a bit of a snip to her voice. "There could be several points of infestation, and by favoring only one, we might get into the thick of it and discover it's an area the citadel recently left."

"If the point is to find current location, then why are we interviewing witnesses at all?" Letting her chair drop forward to all four legs again, Odile kicked the list of witnesses on the table. "Half these people were abducted a year ago or more. There's no way they'd have useful information, even if they weren't shutting doors in our faces."

"You seem awfully tense, Odile," Valeria observed, her eyes narrowing. "Are you nervous?"

"You know what? Yeah, maybe a little." As if her agitation had been tempered by the question, the rogue seemed to remember in real time that she was speaking to her temporarily dethroned queen. "This place gives me the creeps," Odile insisted, a bit chastened. "I want to get out of here."

"Thank you for saying something." With a sigh of relief, Elishta turned her eyes toward me, begging me to understand. "I've felt it, too. The people are nice, but—it's uncomfortable here."

"They are a people on the verge of ruin, it would seem. All that they've been through alters the mind."

"Of course it does," Elishta agreed, then added after a brief second of reflection that visibly changed her face, her expression inward-looking and deeply serious, "of course. But—"

"But I see your point," I told her as well as Odile, raising my hand palm-out. "Yet Branwen is right. We can't rely on infestation density for our only indicator.

Regardless of whatever means we use to actually find the citadel, it's important that we have information about what we may be about to experience, if nothing else in terms of scale. When they say there are multiple spirit-thieves, do they mean there are four, or forty? This makes a great difference as to our method of approach. We must have some sense of scale before we can proceed, unless we want to end in ruin before we've even begun."

Though Odile grumbled at this, it was clear she couldn't make an argument against it. There was no sense in rushing, so far as I was concerned. The Ring of Roserpine had been missing over a month and the world had not ended. Therefore, whatever purpose it was being put to, I was not convinced that sacrificing knowledge for speed was the correct approach.

"Let's get some rest tonight," I suggested, "and in the morning, we can discuss the matter with Norhalm again. Perhaps he could give us the name of a specific witness or two who he recalled having more information than the others."

"And if he can't do that?"

Hesitating, I spread my hands over this matter. "Perhaps scrying by some means or another will be of aid to us here."

"Spirit-thieves are often resistant to such measures," Valeria reflected, her mouth in a small frown, her eyes drifting away from the hearth fire that stung them and off, off, into some distant region beyond spacetime by way of the ceiling. "Their nature is irregular. I have heard it said they hail from some other dimension."

Her casual explanation possessed a strained quality, and understood its meaning without the slightest ambiguity: of this, she was no longer certain, no more than she was of our own natures. Were we even the same bodies which had been spirited away by the Deep-Children? Had that only been some vision of death? Were we dead now, still? I supposed we—

Pay attention, now, Rorke...

Gundrygia's chastisement slipped into my ear like the whisper of a ghost which, in some mysterious way, did not pass the eardrum but still seemed like a cool lover's kiss upon my right ridge. Straightening up, I struggled to tune back in—an issue I had never had before! (How I struggled to adjust in those days.)

"We'll find a way," I told them. "Every puzzle can be solved, and I'm sure this citadel is traceable."

"If it even exists," added Odile, while even Indra, the simpler of the two, nodded along.

"That's a really good point," Indra agreed. "It could be hallucination, or some enchantment. How do we even know for sure these are spirit-thieves if they're not coming back like zombies?"

"If we're going that far," Branwen interjected, her arms folded and her expression serious, "then we need to ask ourselves if we trust the intel about the dirge they think is controlling them. Is that also a fabrication? Why would dirges and spirit-thieves sync up? Neither one is known for being especially symbiotic, to put it lightly."

"It must mean they have a common interest," I suggested. "Or perhaps they're covering one another's blind spots. Valeria—if magical techniques like scrying don't generally work on spirit-thieves, are they able to perform magical feats themselves?"

"Not generally, no. Magic is a gift to the mankinds

from—our intercessors." She gestured with her right hand downwards as she spoke, though her eyes lifted above and her hand began up there, too, against her heart. It struck me that I had been so maddeningly attracted to Valeria I had not fully seen what she really was: a holy woman, truly holy. Too holy to call them 'gods' anymore, these lesser idols—yes, intercessors—whom we served in exchange for inconstant favor. "The spirit-thieves have no intercessor in this way. Not as such. Except— Well—"

While she paused to gather her thoughts, meek Elishta spoke up, her attention divided equally between Valeria and me with only occasional remembrances to look upon the rest of the party sprinkled in. "They have some creature they worship. Some great thing far off, called the Sleeper."

"Death itself is their idol," Valeria corrected. "Their belief structure is complex. The purpose of a spirit-thief hivemind is, so far as I have heard and read, to gather as much information as possible in the course of a lifetime, and to colonize its planet with other hiveminds. When the colonization is complete—when all information has been assimilated from the planet and there is no possibility for further information, when all life on it is extinct and the planet is rendered nonviable for habitation—it is said that the planet and all its information-rich hiveminds are offered as a sacrifice to the Sleeper. Not even death in the sense of a man-god of death as Oppenhir is said to have been, but a primordial annihilation of all things into a mystery that is fully unknowable. The ultimate motivation of the spirit-thieves is self-annihilation, essentially...but self-annihilation after an exasperatingly long period of curation."

"So why would a dirge, which lives forever, collaborate with a species like that?" Wrinkling her nose, Odile shook her head. "Something still feels fishy here... and that's not a joke about those squid-headed creeps, either."

"Perhaps he's not a dirge," I felt compelled to suggest, earning an interested look from a few group members, including those foremost skeptics, Branwen and Odile. "At least, not in the conventional sense."

"Okay," Branwen allowed, mulling that over. "What is he, then? And why is he working with the spirit-thieves?"

Here, I spread my hands, demonstrating that they grasped no more information than did anyone else in our lodgings that night. "Who's to say? But the old man..." His hard eyes pierced into my soul with the look of a man who saw more of me than I was comfortable accepting—not in the pitying way Weltyr saw me, but in a different way entirely. "I think we should stay open to the possibility that the information has some grain of truth, and we need to strategize in a way that factors in two separate but interconnected threats."

More, in truth...but how could I bear to point that out to them when the immediate, most pressing issues relating to the citadel and its skeletons were weighing down upon us?

That night, as the women retired, I remained awake, wholly preoccupied. I brooded before the fire from that chair where the Selectrix had greeted me with all manner of mysterious entreaties. Odile was quite right. There was missing information at the heart of this—-but to say it was 'missing' cast the wrong character over the whole matter. Rather, I had the forceful intuition that the information was being *hidden* from me. From us.

Yet the trouble with conspiracies is that the presence of a conspiracy engenders suspicion of malice. Was that the case here? Surely the townsfolk who were abducted by these interlopers and traumatized half out of their wits would have gladly furnished any information they could to ensure it wouldn't happen to anyone else. Why didn't they? Was it truly so unspeakable?

Or was there something they were trying to hide about their experience; perhaps even themselves?

One thing was for sure: I wasn't going to find the answer sitting around, sulking before the fire. I rose and made my way softly up the stairs, for it was by then already a late hour, and one day was poised to turn into another at the passage of a moment. In our quarters, Valeria slept with the sheets tangled around her waist, her exposed breasts rising and ebbing to the tides of her breath. For a half second, I considered sneaking past her to collect what I wished, but I now had too close a grasp of my own mortality to part from a woman I loved without telling her that. I sank down at her hip, bending over her to caress her cheek and kiss her mouth—and she was so instantly responsive, her tongue eager to slip along mine, that I had the impression she'd only been feigning sleep, perhaps to see if I would do the thing I had resisted. Unable to help myself, I slipped my hand along her thigh, then back around to the flesh of her perfect, high rump.

"Where are you going," she asked me, divining my intentions, perhaps because I had come to bed still dressed.

"Just planning to do a little reconnaissance outside the city," I advised her, my fingers kneading that incredibly soft sphere of flesh while her eyelids fluttered and my heart sighed with love of her. "I'd like to get a sense for the landscape, and a few other details."

"You just want to go turn a bunch of skeletons tonight," she accused playfully, her tone already the wry one of a wife who knew full well her husband only wanted to go out brawling with his friends. "You're so energetic, Rorke...are you sure I can't persuade you to put that energy to greater use?"

"Oh...I'm sure you could." My head sank over hers, mouth thirstily drinking up her kisses while her fingers tunneled through my hair and tickled along my scalp. "But, my love," I protested, drawing back from her kiss to look her in those splendid eyes, "doesn't this seem to you a likely candidate for us to uncover information about your missing ring? Even, perhaps, the ring itself?"

Nodding, a shock of white hair sliding along her cheek and dropping into her greater mane as she did, Valeria peered up at me through the fans of her white eyelashes. I kissed them along with her eyelids as she told me, "Aye, Rorke—I feel the ring's closeness in my soul, in a manner I can't explain. From even before we learned there are spirit-thieves working in the area...it was only that I could not place the feeling until that moment."

Something stirred in my heart. The way she spoke of this object—it made me realize the strange kind of intimacy she felt toward it, as if the years it had spent wrapped around her finger had been some sort of longstanding conjugal union. A queer twist came to my heart to realize I was jealous. Jealous of a ring! Yet it was a ring that had adorned her sweet finger since she was fresh from girlhood, and which had been with her through all her highs and lows. All her greatest mysteries and most profound experiences of growth. Her ring had adorned her for decades before I even entered the world, let alone her mind. The Ring of Roserpine knew Valeria, I felt, at least inasmuch as Exigence knew me.

But was it the ring that inspired my jealousy? Or was it Valeria, who was powerful beyond measure with it in her grasp, at least among her people?

"How troubled you look now, Rorke!" As she drew me back from my thoughts, Valeria caressed my cheek and brow. "How you've changed since the Nightlands. Oh! What a curious sentence to say. They seem so long ago, don't they?"

"They do."

Something crossed Valeria's face—a tenderness I had not seen before. It was a funny sort of expression she wore; one that even I, who had never had the slightest conception of his own parents, could interpret as almost maternal sympathy. If I had doubts about her ability to be mother of our child before that moment, this gaze of hers alleviated them. Then, the slant of her smile reconfigured itself to that of my prideful queen. "Come now, my beloved...are you afraid to give me back my source of power? Afraid I will have the ring in my hand and forget everything you did for me?"

"Yes." Though she did not withdraw her caress at my flat response, her hand did pause, the tips of her fingers poised beneath my eye and along my temple. "And I fear the same of myself—or worse."

Valeria's playful smile faded. While I wished I had not spoken so, a part of me was glad I'd had the foolishness. It was something she needed to hear. The honest reality. I had possession of Exigence, of the Helm, and of the Lantern. With Valeria's ring, I would have the only four Deepgold objects remaining in existence. I had witnessed my sword destroy the weapon of a being who was near universally regarded as a god. The lantern could repel any beast lesser than a man, and with the helm, I could unlock the powers of the beasts themselves—even several beasts at once, it seemed! Whether I could take on the guise of another man, I dared not try. As difficult as it was to extricate oneself from the mind of an animal, I feared it would require a lifetime to extricate oneself from the mind of a fellow man!

But you see my point—the limits of the Deepgold's powers were not known to me, for I lacked the courage or immorality to test them. Yet would that morality of mine hold with these weapons of mass destruction in my sole possession? Would I forget my human heart, and succumb to something evil that was hidden inside me?

"It is wise of you to account for your weaknesses, my heart," Valeria agreed in a cautious voice, seeing me newly now. "But the ring knows who its mistress is. Its powers are limited in application by anyone else—little more than the interpretation of tongues and translation of written words. Only my permanent death allows the ring to change hands. That, or my sincere rejection of it, which would mean my abdication from my duties to El'ryh and the durrow. And Roserpine."

"Now it's you who looks troubled, Love," I told her, my fingers pushing the strands of her hair from her brow. "What ails you, Valeria, my darling one?"

"The same that ails you, at least in part, my hero... the question of what we shall do."

"I love you, Valeria."

"I love you, Rorke," she responded, the words coming from a great depth in her heart in a way I seemed to experience within mine. "Help me to choose you, please."

"You already help me to choose you," I told her in response, kissing her brow to seal the silent promise I would do as she asked, even if it meant wrestling into submission some sudden contrary indicator of her will liable to crop up at some undetermined time. "Each and every bloom."

While she smirked a little at the wink I added, I kissed her once more, promised, "I'll be back by dawn," and fetched my cloak along with the Deepgold artifacts I had set down from my person before sitting on the edge of her bed. "Let's see what I can glean from a study of the wilderness around these parts."

"Please, Rorke, be careful. Don't get arrogant...I don't care for you going out in the dark with your pitiful eyesight."

Unable to help my laugh, I shook my head at her. "I could say the same of you during the day...you would look quite fetching in a pair of dark glasses. Perhaps we can find someone to fashion you a pair while we're in civilization. More practical than the welder's goggles you girls have been trading amongst yourselves."

"Bring someone with you," she commanded, then added in the same breath, "but not me. I'm exhausted... this baby of yours is already wearing me out."

"He's a good son, keeping his mother in bed and away from trouble. I'll see if Indra or Odile might come along, to satisfy your worried heart."

"I'm not worried," she lied, drawing the covers more completely over herself and curling up beneath them. "I just know a little something about you by now."

That, she did. I had been fully prepared to go into the darkness of night by myself, confident the Lantern and Exigence would protect me from any threat I could expect to encounter...and, given all the ways my companions had saved me in times of trial, how could I have thought that for even a second?

Valeria was not the only one who knew me to this degree, I had already found: and it was mere confirmation I experienced when, in the hall, I found Brynhildr already there, her helm under her arm, her brilliant flame of red hair tamed back from her face with a small leather thong ornamented by a bead of bone—animal or human, I knew not.

"Where you go, friend, I go. Let's scout together and let Grane give us some distance!"

I was so grateful for the Selectrix's presence that I did not question it. "A man could do worse for a scouting partner than a battle angel such as yourself. Lead the way to your steed, Brynhildr—with you at our head, no doubt, we'll be assured the victory."

Grane's hooves beat silently across the wilderness, an astonishing experience when compared with the animal's size. As its mane whipped wildly behind, thrashing like the bounty of Brynhildr's hair pouring out from the back of her helmet, gratitude flooded my heart. How few were blessed with seeing such a creature, let alone riding it? Let alone having acted in the stead of its master for a time, as I did on the isle of Dunnun! The beast, wise as its mistress, had known I was borrowing it with the unspoken permission of its usual keeper.

How could a ring like Valeria's know the identity of its keeper? For animals, with sentient mind-experiences allowing them to sensorily grasp sight, sound, touch, taste, smell, and a certain degree of memory, (even psychic presentiment, if you believe certain stories, which seem plausible enough to me in this world of faerie fire and mighty beasts), to know one's keeper was as natural as to know one's family or tribe.

But, for a ring? A sword? Where there was knowledge, there was generally some knower. Some understanding of life. Even mushrooms, I have heard it said, pass information back and forth. Was there a quality of the Deepgold that gave it this unique connection, this imprint of its owner? Gold is a soft metal, relatively speaking. Was the Deepgold spiritually soft? Did it carry with it a sort of memory?

"All objects store memory, Rorke, even if only of themselves. The question is one of external access."

Byrnhildr's voice was strong even while low, and I did not concern myself with whether she who so transparently knew my thoughts would hear the voice I pitched low to avoid attracting attention to the swift, dark beast which bore us through the night.

"I noticed you had nothing to add when we were in the meeting with the others."

"About what?"

"No speculations, I mean."

"You may consider me incapable of speculation," she said in a way that was merry but that had a most curious pang of desolation about it, as if she had been struck in the heart by some invisible arrow. "To the brow of that hill, Grane! Make haste, my friend."

This rider needed not dig in her boots to gain her horse's clear understanding. I doubted she needed any speech, either, and in fact had the impression that she spoke only for my benefit, to give me some idea of her intentions and the sudden movements of her horse. The same way she had given me that strange warning before.

"Perhaps you know a great deal of the manner in which things are likely to unfold," I suggested as the horse fled up the high hillside around Ironforge. "But surely you cannot know all, Brynhildr. If I have free will enough to dethrone your famous father, you—"

"My will is conformed to his," she told me quickly, firmly, in a manner that made me think I had perhaps said something beyond my purview. "What serves my Father is what I must do, for he has authority over me and over Urde, and over his Valor Hall."

She did not seem herself that night. I didn't understand her ways and thought she was having some spell of temper or impatience with me, but now I see the truth.

Brynhildr was frightened for what lay along her path, and it was something she didn't want me to dwell on.

We reached the ridge that permitted us a look over the terrain, some three miles from the city. Brynhildr pushed back the visor of her helmet and studied the dark.

"Look there, Rorke—can you see them?"

Where normally I would have prayed for Weltyr's light, I paused. My mind turned toward the questions of the future that had me in a state of strange mental paralysis—what would happen in the next days? weeks? after?—and just as I was becoming overwhelmed by all the many years I had the potential to live without Weltyr's special protections, my eye caught a light of a more ethereal blue than the shining gold of Hamsunt's lantern.

How finely Exigence's hilt glowed! Indeed, all the Deepgold upon my person had taken on a sort of radiance, but with these other objects—the Helm and the Lantern—the aura was faint. Exigence, gaining so gradually as Grane took the hill that I hadn't noticed it, (or had taken it for a reflection of moonlight I now realized was absent due to cloud coverage), emanated a steady light. Astonished, I grasped the hilt and raised my gaze again, intending to ask Brynhildr the meaning of this response on the part of the sword. Midway to focusing on her, my attention was diverted across the valley beneath, and my breath grew stifled in my throat to see the answer for myself.

Though the effect was fainter in the distance, it seemed that Exigence shared the paladin charism for the destruction of the unconscious undead, or at least for their targeting: skeletons, masses of them, swayed in aimless packs that were now illuminated for me with the same light as the sword I held.

Truly, the pirate crew of the *Rhinemaid* were a different order of being, whatever they seemed. The sickly light provoked by the Deepgold in the presence of these skeletons seemed to speak of death even apart from the physical character of their bodies, which were naught but bones tangled occasionally with wiry strips of sinew. Moreover, I was shocked by the number. As bugs inhabited the house that was left unclean and made it only worse, so too did I have the immediate impression that this land was unclean in some grave spiritual way, and that the presence of this hideous brood—so many that the groups, which occasionally passed one another like semi-organized militia, bumped into one another and seemed confused as to how to proceed without guidance. As we peered down from our vantage, I could see what was surely a rolling meadow in the day, and could even admire the way it spilled out into the distance with a creek bed along the east and a brooding moor, dotted with occasional trees, yawning far off to the west and up to the base of a mountain range Grane could have reached by sun-up, or even faster if he had flown.

And all the way to the base of these mountains, growing thicker as they went, were these pallid fireflies of death, the only light on a night thick enough with clouds to blot the moon.

"I had no idea Exigence was capable of such a thing."

"Does not the Lantern of Hamsunt grow more bright in the presence of those monsters it repels? The same is true of Exigence...but now we can see the seriousness of their problem, eh, Rorke? No wonder they feel helpless in Ironforge."

"How have things been permitted to grow so out of hand? I understand this problem has been endemic to the region for a long time, but—"

"Do not underestimate the impact of despair and discouragement. You must always take heart, Rorke. Though there are trials which test us to and sometimes beyond the limits of our strength, we must persevere. A bit of laxity, and..."

Brynhildr gestured with her spear. I followed its tip, my eyes sweeping again through the heinous infestation of the undead. A shudder rolled through me. How lucky we were that the Rhinemaid had been flying at the edge of the dawn and preserved us from landing amid these hideous creatures crawling out in the night! Beneath their bony feet, the earth had been churned and torn. Now I understood the danger they posed to the farms. Any broad swath of land was liable to be destroyed by this mob, this pestilence more dangerous than any wave of locusts, for skeletons and other undead required shelter from the light of the sun; particularly while sleeping. Having no capacity to make shelter and no readily apparent caves within which to shield themselves, they burrowed with the coming of the light, throwing dirt upon themselves and resuming a corpselike state for the hours that the sun shone.

And that led to an even more horrible thought. How tempted these people must have been to make good an escape during the daylight hours, yet how suicidal it would have proved! With women and children, loaded down with the goods of their homes in caravans design for long distance transportation, they would make reasonable enough time should they start in the early hours of the morn and drive hard all through the sunlit hours in, say, one of the longest days of the summer; yet night would inexorably fall on them, and, miles away from the shelters of their homes and the walls of Ironforge, they people would have found themselves encompassed on all sides by these, the bones of their ancestors and perhaps the ancestors of all mankinds, stumbling up from the earth and seeking nothing but to add to their numbers.

What was the meaning of this? Why had these vermin been sent upon the land, and what was the endgame? For, indeed, it seemed to me that, should this pestilence spread, all of Urde would be crushed beneath it, continent by continent. Skeleton outbreaks were dangerous, a known problem to be certain—but they were never like this.

There has never been a time like this, Rorke. Not in all the ages of mankind.

Gundrygia's voice shimmered through me, and as I shuddered, Brynhildr turned away and mounted her horse with the careful posture of one pretending not to overhear a conversation.

Still staring across the skeletons, I asked in my soul, *What makes this time so distinct that we would be compelled to face these horrors?*

You would not accept my answer among the flowers, she chuckled ominously, each note of her voice like another dart of cold horror in my flesh, *so why would you accept it now? Indeed, Rorke, all you need is within you, yet you ignore it so blithely—reject it!—that it can do you no good until it is much too late.*

Puzzling over this, I accepted Brynhildr's offered hand and followed her upon the horse's back. "We must speak with Norhalm again," I told her as she wheeled the beast in the opposing direction, pointing him down the ridge. "There is more here than we have been told—I was not adequately prepared for this. Now, realizing the scope of their problems, I think if we are to effectively handle it, we must be equipped with resources."

"The question, Rorke, is whether Norhalm will speak with *us!*"

That, I could not be sure of, but all the same I sensed I had to try. Norhalm and his men had been more than adequately prepared to meet the *Rhinemaid* as it flew over his city, and he had seemed weary both on that occasion and the next day, when he came to give us guidance on the handling of our interviews. It seemed plausible, therefore, that he lived and worked in the complex where we had been detained, or that he was living his life predominantly at night—and I understood all too well why he would keep such vigil, given what I had just witnessed. We rode first to that same outpost, where lanterns burned in a great many of the windows as well as at the checkpoint roughly a mile away. We had been allowed to exit the area without attention but were now momentarily stopped to ensure we were who we appeared to be.

"Can't never be too careful," said one of the dwarves, while two others waved a pair of scrying wands along both us and the horse, presumably to discern any sign of doppelgängers or disguised spirit-thieves. "It's been some time since a spirit-thief tried to get in that way; before my time, I'd wager. But, it *has* happened."

"It's wise to be thorough," I agreed, maintaining the same friendly demeanor I had found worked well with dwarvish people, ignoring for now shaken feeling of discovering the scale of the problem. "Norhalm's idea, I'd imagine?"

"Aye."

"Do you think he's in?" I gestured at the outpost's main station, the building that had most captivated my attention, and the fellow in charge of the search shrugged.

"Might could be. Don't have much else to do, I reckon, outside of waiting for the day it all goes bad and trying to help us survive as a community until then."

"I'd have thought a man of his station would live in town, in a finer house than a barracks."

"He keeps humble and serious-like. And, well—" Hesitating, the checkpoint guard decided, "Maybe I shouldn't say."

I tried not to sound overly interested, but at the same time took the chance to remind him, "We are strangers to this town, my friend, and I believe Norhalm made it clear to his men—or said he would make it clear to his men—that he was tasking us with eradicating the blight. Whatever information you have about anyone or anything here would be welcome, as we are walking into all this with no prior understanding, and we need help putting things into context."

"Norhalm was abducted along with his wife and child," the man told me while Brynhildr mounted Grane once more. "And only he came back. I think it's just that he doesn't want to live in his house anymore…he'd rather work."

Now that was a piece of information worth knowing! My Selectrix and I looked at one another, a glance exchanged while the dwarves returned to their posts and waved us good-night. As the horse trod the road beneath us in such a way that it clearly intended to evade suspicion yet also ached to run—for its muscles rippled beneath us, and every fifth clop or so felt like a child's impatient skip—we discussed in that same murmured tone as before just how we would handle this matter.

"That's a key detail to have left out of his story," I said, merely thinking aloud and not expecting the immortal being to concern herself with these matters, as she herself had indicated earlier. "I'm sure he doesn't exactly relish the opportunity to talk about it, but—"

"But he's like all the others who have been touched by this crime," Brynhildr observed solemnly, her eyes fixed on the fullness of the central building as we approached the compound. "He won't speak of it. Or, perhaps, he can't. These poor people! They dwell in a city built during peacetime, by a folk that had never known military conflict. A valley! Piteous wretches."

"Their defenses are clearly not a match for whatever this is, I'll agree with you there. But whatever the case— if Norhalm wants our help, he needs to tell us the truth."

Sensing my rising irritation, Brynhildr turned at the waist to more naturally touch my hand. As a strange sense of peace came over me, bringing with it a dizziness, Brynhildr suggested, "Perhaps you ought to let me speak with him. All you men enjoy looking at a pretty lady while you discuss your heroic victories and future ambitions. Perhaps I can find a way to give you a few minutes alone in his office—no doubt he has some trophy or painting which can be elaborated upon while you, a mere mortal and tired, enter his office to rest."

There was merit in that suggestion. Not even Brynhildr could have persuaded these people to speak on their experiences. We were going to need to resort to more underhanded tactics if we really wanted to get information here, even from the man who commissioned us for this task.

"I shouldn't be in there too long, or he may be suspicious."

"Then I'll only keep him for a minute before we walk the rest of the way to the office, so make haste— scour every nook and cranny of his desk, and see what you find."

Rotating these words through my mind, I asked, "Are you giving me hints, Brynhildr?"

"I cannot stand to be entirely aloof, Rorke! Why— what kind of daughter-in-law would I be?"

Norhalm did indeed seem to be in better spirits than the last two times we laid eyes on him, which was discordant given the late hour yet proved me right about his lifestyle and schedule. The outpost as a whole seemed to mostly keep it; at least, men moved to and fro all through the compound, engaging in conversation or pacing around the wall, and those that greeted us at the door showed no trace of exhaustion aside from the general veil of demi-permanent fatigue that settles into one's bones after an extended period of nocturnal living. When they called Norhalm, I think we were expecting to be sent up to him; instead, we heard him say into his intercom, "I'll be right down," which led to the second (albeit brisker) silent glance of the night. Feeling that I was responsible for getting us into his office—or getting myself into his office, at any rate—I made a few swift mental calculations and decided to let him see he had the better of me when he stepped out of the elevator for a heartier handshake than I'd expected from him.

"Burningsoul," he said approvingly, "or burning the midnight oil, anyway. What brings you here at this hour?"

"We went scouting," Brynhildr said, her red hair, now free of that helmet, pluming over her shoulders and framing her face in a manner emphasizing that same strain of girlish innocence that made her so obviously a tender maiden, unsullied by the worries of existence which enter one's life as the high cost of romantic love. "What a sight you have around you at night, friend! I've never seen so great a many skeletons before—and I've seen a great many things, let me make you sure of that."

"It's horrific, isn't it? You can see why we need your help now, I'm sure."

I affected a tired little smile. "We're certainly starting to get that sense, but more information would be a nice start." With a glance toward some of the listening officers now milling about near the station's front desk, I nodded to the elevator, then turned a pointed gaze on Norhalm. He appeared to be listening, the stern energy of his focus somehow visible. "Would it be an imposition to get a second look at that map in your office, Norhalm? I'd like a visual sense for the abductions again...there surely has to be some pattern. Something in common amid the victims, even before we account for their conspiracy of silence."

Norhalm maintained his stare, unflinching, matter-of-fact.

"You'll have to let me know if you crack that particular part of this case, Burningsoul...but, certainly. If it'll help you, why don't you and Miss—"

"Brynhildr."

With a grandfatherly smile at her pronunciation of her own name, Norhalm said, "Why don't you and Miss Brynhildr come with me?"

Together we piled back into the elevator, and I saw why Brynhildr had volunteered her services. Without her buoyant presence, Norhalm would have been a stone wall to me had he the slightest thought that I was demanding more of his personal knowledge than he had already provided. Instead, with Brynhildr there, she was able to smile and jostle him upon the shoulder as harmlessly as one who had graduated military school with him a great many years before.

"What ho, man! A warrior, thou—and strategian, to carry your people so long among the heinous sea Burningsoul and I discovered tonight. How long have you manned this station?"

Unable to help but look a little pleased, Norhalm stroked his beard and confessed, "Near ten years, Madame. A decade, yes—nearly a decade now, though it's hard to believe it's been that long since it was built."

"And before it was built?"

"Mm, nigh on seventeen years I spent running our military police and doing what we could to keep the infestation at least at bay while it grew worse."

"Blast, man! Twenty-seven total years—that's quite some time overseeing this town's welfare, even in a longer-lived example of mankind such as are the dwarves. And I'd imagine you've spent most your adult life either training or serving the city in some capacity, even if with less grandeur than you could be said to possess at this time."

With a soft laugh, Norhalm stepped off the elevator with us and glanced at his feet as he did. "You would imagine true, Madame; my whole life, in fact, and not only in part."

"Forgive me for not appropriately honoring your self-sacrifice," she told him with great sincerity. Then, pausing beside a small daguerreotype framed and hung upon the wall, she exclaimed with unfeigned pleasure, "Ah! Is this the grand opening?"

"It was, indeed." Pausing there with us and smiling, or at least arranging his manner and bearing to a wistful degree, our host gestured toward this frozen moment of optimism for the town: Norhalm cutting a charming ribbon that had been wrapped across the gate of the outpost, the hands of men and women around raised in the blurred motion of applause. "Yes, that was a fine day. Since then, I think we've all been glad we invested the time and materials. Not to mention the manpower—blood, sweat, and tears, as they say."

"So they do, indeed," agreed Brynhildr. Then, she in with a smile that was guileless to all but me, who saw the artistry crafting her innocence. "But, sir! What hours you keep—I see here this girl, who bears every trace of your features in a double share! Leavest thou thy wife and child to battle back this menace? Poor soul."

"Ah—"

The vocalization did not sound so pleasant on his lips as it had on hers, and it came with the sense of a man surprised by the forceful impact of a bullet in the chest. "They're no longer with us," he said in a manner not stony so much as crystalline: a glassy, twinkling thing, transparent yet textured with a mysterious and glittering opacity, cold and sharp and desperately brittle despite all appearances, and emptied of any color or meaningful vision.

"I just remembered"—he tapped *me* on the bicep now, as if Brynhildr had infected him with some small contagion of camaraderie he now unconsciously played up in his desperate scramble to hide his grief—"I'm out of whiskey in there. Surely you'd like some, Rorke, after the day I know you had trying to get these witnesses to talk."

"That would be much appreciated," I told him, repressing a surge of optimism as he nodded to that same office where I'd met him the morning before, after our period of detention.

"Go have a look at that map, help yourself to a cigar from the box on my desk. I'll be back."

Not tarrying long enough to hear my sound of affirmation, Norhalm hustled down the hall—not back into the lift as I had hoped, but far enough away to buy time. Her part finished, Brynhildr strode to the map, hands folded in the small of her back, her eyes absorbing every smallest bit of the lay of the village and the clusters of datapoints representing abductions therein. Mid-stride toward the desk where I had been directed, I took notice of her behavior in a half-confused manner that did not distract me so much as slide beneath my focus. Brynhildr glanced over her shoulder at me with a slight smile.

"His heart needed to hear those things from me, and they were all true; yet, it would be a great sin for me or for you to act as you intend. Only mankinds are known to sin. I am not of such station. I cannot—shall not. Not any further."

Sadness filled me for her, along with shame to think that in some way her original sin—instructing me so slyly, even if in aid of her father's True Will. But had sin, then, not been Weltyr's will? So Weltyr was once more proven not to be God in a full and meaningful sense. Not if his True Will involved sins like the one I committed as I slid open all six drawers of Norhalm's desk. No— the True Will of the True God would be antithetical to all sin, I intuited suddenly, feeling strangely indicted by Brynhildr's abstinence from further involvement. My movements smooth and steady, I searched through every square inch of that desk. Its contents were as fastidiously kept as its owner; and I found that, right down to the larger drawer made up of a set of hanging files I supposed had urgency and which took at least twelve seconds to thumb through, these were more typical cases of murder or robbery, perhaps ones that had gone cold. What I did notice: no Norhalm file.

I checked for false bottoms. I quietly, gently pushed aside neat containers of pen nibs and boxed wells of ink. I did not try to open the middle drawer on the left, which was locked—never a specialty of mine, lockpicking—but I did study the contents of the other two to find in them more office supplies, a box of gunpowder, and a few replacement parts: lightbulbs for his desk lamp, boxes of screws and a driver for them, a hammer. Absolutely nothing useful or incriminating, which became doubly annoying, doubly baffling, as I shut the center drawer in response to the sound of footsteps coming down the hall.

"Did you lead me astray, Selectrix?"

It was like I had struck her, and I felt instantly sorry. My heart ached at the expression she wore while I raised the lid of the cigar box to snatch from its contents the first tube I touched.

"How your mistrust wounds me! You, who are my charge, a sacred duty sworn to me by my father—I would never act but for your good, Rorke."

Though I longed to provide her then with an apology, and indeed formed one with my lips, a floorboard betrayed the final footfall of Norhalm, who hesitated to see me standing behind his desk rather than before it. His posture relaxed as I told him, "There you are, Norhalm—I never got to see which of these objects was your lighter, old boy. You dwarves love your technology, so I'm sure it's one of these somewhere."

"It's the globe," he said with avuncular amusement, gesturing with the bottle of amber fluid he took straightaway to the sideboard. "That Urde there—that's right—"

I let out a genuine chuckle and lit the tip of the cigar I had selected, but my mind whirled with frustration— still at Brynhildr, but now mostly at myself.

I had missed something. The arts of thieves were those practiced by Indra and Odile; I was ill-versed in any of them but bluffing. I stewed on this, crossing to the same seat I had inhabited during that first meeting in this room. From this more distant vantage, I could see the map as a whole and get a good sense for larger-scale patterns. Yet, as I had discovered my first time in it, the chair was not made to my scale, and sitting in it normally with my knees pushed toward my chest also caused me to hunch forward. This position being terribly uncomfortable and the opposite of what I needed to look at the map, I reclined the chair on its back legs, having turned it more completely toward the corner where Brynhildr stood in study. In aid of this, which allowed me to extend my legs anyway, I hooked my left foot beneath the desk and allowed my right to sprawl a bit beside. Prevented from rocking back so far as to fall, I leaned the chair enough that my back was less burdened, then considered the dotted landscape.

"It resembles a swarm of bees," I commented, then added with consideration, "though, I suppose the image is appropriate, given their hiveminds."

"Don't insult bees so." Norhalm unscrewed the top of the bottle and tipped some of its contents into the glasses he had arranged. "Those merry fellows want nothing more than to enjoy the scent of flowers and the sweetness of honey—much like any self-respecting dwarf here in this village."

"Hornets, then," Brynhildr supposed, "or wasps."

"Have the people who returned from these incidents been medically examined, Norhalm?" I accepted the glass he brought to me but did not raise it to my lips. Now I set the cigar down, the prop having lost its value to me, consigned to burn like incense in the ashtray on the edge of the desk. "And are you legally privy to these reports within this particular jurisdiction?"

"Our medical examiners have been the ones doing those reviews when one of our missing comes back in the night, but there's been nothing promising. Most of those who have returned share fears that something may have been surgically planted inside them—some technology, or some offspring of the spirit-thieves ready to burst from them—but that doesn't seem to be the case. At least, we don't have evidence of that, and spirit-thieves don't need mankind to reproduce in any direct fashion."

"How do these devils reproduce themselves?"

"Perhaps you'd oughter ask the durrow lady with you—Valeria." Having also passed a glass to Brynhildr, Norhalm took his seat behind the desk and turned his chair toward the station of his office wholly devoted to the matter of strategizing against the threat of the spirit-thieves and their skeleton army. "From what little I do understand, newly established hiveminds 'bud' with a series of spirit-thieves after being fed information by the establishing spirit-thieves, whatever 'pioneers' set up a new colony after having a sufficient degree of success wherever they were born. It seems the older a hivemind becomes, the fewer spirit-thieves it produces per decade until it's effectively zero, so if they didn't colonize like that, they'd die off."

"And how are new hiveminds created?"

At my question, Norhalm nursed from his glass, saying in a distracted way, "How should I know? I'm no exobiologist."

Brynhildr answered us matter-of-factly, still studying the map and all its tiny labels. "The old hivemind, upon reaching advanced age, releases spores to create a new hivemind; either in the same area, or to be collected and strategically colonized by the remaining spirit-thieves."

How much she knew! There were infinite depths to Brynhildr's knowledge, and her mind was a steel cage concealing it. A bit annoyed by this conversation, I drummed my foot beneath the desk and reflected on my own exhaustion.

And in my impatient tapping, the top of my foot contacted a material that had a surprising amount of give. Not complete yielding—but certainly more than I would have expected from wood.

Pausing to focus on keeping the surprise from my face, I asked, "And if there are no spirit-thieves left to feed it information? What then?"

"It saps information up from the environment itself, given enough time...but without a spirit-thief to nurture and protect it, it's defenseless. Liable to be born in the wrong environment, or eaten by predators, or anything of the sort. Urde's environment is, by its very nature, hostile to the spirit-thieves."

I frowned. "What happened?"

Though Brynhildr inhaled to produce an answer, she allowed that breath to catch upon her lips, which parted in surprise. The tip of her finger touched a name, and she turned her eyes upon our host in shock.

"'Norhalm,'" she said, nodding toward the pin where her finger now sat, the little label having been there long enough for the edges to curl off the map. "Your name is on here!"

I had a plausible opportunity and took it, relaxing my foot from beneath the edge of the desk in slapstick pantomime of shock. "You mean, you—"

I allowed my crashing upon the floor to finish my words, glad to play the part of the bumbling warrior I had the sense Norhalm thought me to be—good natured, headstrong, perhaps a bit dumb. Norhalm cursed, his expression of anguish momentarily diffused by the mental interruption of my fall—and by the whiskey flying out of my glass onto myself and the chair Grimalkin had inhabited two days before, now positioned behind mine because of the angle at which I'd turned to face the map. As my host got up from his side of the desk, removing his handkerchief from his pocket as he did, I made a great show of clumsily extricating myself from the chair and clambering upright. Apologizing profusely, I allowed Brynhildr to come 'help' me up while he blotted whiskey off the chair.

While all this occurred, the scale at which the dwarves built worked to my advantage: effortlessly, the motion looking totally innocent and naive, I touched the underside of the desk three times: once, the hard wood of the desk itself; twice, the soft rectangle of leather my foot had contacted, which protruded from the desk by the width of about half a finger; thrice, briskly sliding it toward me to find it did not just give but indeed half-slipped out of the bracket where it was suspended.

Though it now sagged out of place, leaning at an angle against the floor on my side, it remained stuck at the far edge. I who had fought many battles paled with the thought of it falling entirely out of place at some inopportune moment, the sound of the leather slapping upon the hard floor revealing my interference with it and betraying us to him whom we betrayed.

For such was how it felt. I liked Norhalm, and I had the impression he was a good man. Indeed, he reminded me of men I had known at the Temple of Weltyr, gruff but good-hearted veterans of this or that bloody military expedition, or even in some small way of Hildolfr (O happy youth! O innocence). Therefore it was not just a matter of accomplishing the goal without drawing hostile action; it was also a matter of pridefully moderating this fellow's impression of me long enough that I wouldn't have to deal with his reassessment of my character. In other words—I did not want him to see who I truly am, even though he would have been entirely justified, based on my actions, to make that new assessment.

"That's what I get for being too casual. I'm so sorry, Norhalm—what a terrible moment to—"

"It's fine. I'd rather mop up whisky than think about that time, anyway." Without turning away from the handkerchief growing saturated in liquor, Norhalm acknowledged, "Aye, my daughter, wife and I were abducted."

"When was this?"

"Eight years ago," he grunted in response to my incredulous question, pushing himself up to his feet and crossing to the intercom. "Get me some towels," he snapped into the microphone, tossing the spoiled handkerchief down on the remaining puddle and sinking into his chair with a dark look. "I probably should have told you," he went on, his eyes fixing on the cigar box he opened and closed a few nervous times. "But what good would it do? I'm no better than the rest. Can't remember a thing."

Now he did take a cigar, and shut the box before reaching for the Urde-shaped lighter. "All I know is I came back and they didn't."

The night secretary, a burly old white-hair who looked like he could still best most contenders in a fight, bustled in with a few ragged towels stuffed under his right arm. As he eyed the scene, I extended a hand, saying, "Give it here—I'm so sorry about that, let me clean it up."

Looking just as happy not to do it himself, the fellow thrust the rags into my arms and went away satisfied, saying, "I'll let that soak in and be back when your meeting's over, Nor."

"That's just fine," Norhalm said, his tone distant, his eyes fixed on the tip of his cigar. The slightest hint of amusement stirred those still waters as, genuflecting to blot up the liquor, I asked in my most sheepish tone, "I don't mean to hit the bottle so hard, but would it trouble you to ask for a second glass?"

"Should probably give you a third to ease the ache of hitting your head. The glass break?"

As I shook my head and handed it to him, he crossed to the bar. While his back was turned, I made quick work of it: not mopping the puddle, but rather pulling the journal out from the second bracket and shoving it into the inner side of my boot. As I resumed mopping up the puddle that had trickled beneath the desk's edge, (had he seen?) Norhalm said (he hadn't), "First thing I know after falling asleep one evening is I'm opening a window. Then, I'm walking up to the outpost out there on the edge of town, making plans about how I was going to address my lack of identification with my inferiors. As if I had been in the middle of that thought and all the thoughts leading up to it for quite a while."

While I dumped the last wet rag upon the pile of them and sat again in the little chair that had ultimately proven so useful to me, Norhalm brought his drink to his lips and muttered, "I wish there were more, but I can't give you anything worthwhile."

At long last, I took a sip of the amber liquid, the impression of the journal against my calf containing all the information I was likely to get—either from him, or from anyone else in this village.

"Of course," I told him sympathetically. "Trust me when I say, I understand. There are some things that are impossible to talk about...and others which we wish we did not know."

13

NORHALM'S JOURNAL

THE ROAD BACK to our quarters seemed arduous in a special way, my amazement over having acquired the journal superseded the nagging of my conscience until, with some distance between us and the compound, the latter overtook the former with a vengeance. Norhalm was not an evil man, I reiterate: there were no other means by which we could have persuaded him to furnish the information. All the same, I felt duly chastised by Brynhildr disengaging herself from the situation.

I also felt newly at odds with the town, which I puzzled over. Was this how thieves typically felt? Perhaps it was—who could live this way? Loot from a dungeon was one thing, or the pillages of war, or inheritance by blood (by duel or by lineage). These were all forms of acquisition which, depending on the individual circumstances, could sometimes be frowned upon, but which did not tend to set one up against one's own society in the same way as simple theft. I vowed to myself in the silence of my heart never to do so again against a mortal man, even in the name of a good deed done...but it was too late a resolution. Had I not stolen an apple from that garden of the Valor Hall already? Had I not from the start been surrounded by thieves? Why—even Weltyr was a thief, I reflected as I bade Brynhildr good-night and went with my burden to the light off the hearth. There, in the seat I inhabited before we'd left—feeling indeed as if I had not left it at all, in some strange way—I slid the journal from my boot and studied the worn leather binding.

Say this little thing had no relevance to our mystery, and our pursuit of the spirit-thieves? Say it was some private directory of the town, or some collection of love letters between Norhalm and his wife. Why, then, I would contrive some way to get it back to him. En extra step, an extra period of exposure, yes—but there was a chance if we managed it tomorrow that he would not even know it was gone! We could contract Phildrin and Shemrin while on our way out of town, bribing them to return it.

But, if it was relevant, then these thoughts would all be muted.

And I should say that when I finally opened it, I found myself going, inside and out, very quiet.

Mostly, the book consisted of drawings. This had not struck me as expected. Norhalm did not seem like an artist, but I supposed that even a man of modest talents could, if among the longer-lived mankinds, become greatly adept at a number of hobbies through repetition over time. It was such a fascinating discovery I smiled a little. As I did, that first image I beheld parsed out as a broad, circular room marked with columns around its perimeter, each placed about three feet apart if I assumed the human figure standing in contemplation of one was about six or seven feet tall. Given he was not proportioned like a dwarf, I took this to be the case, but it was difficult to make out any other details of his personage due to the slight smudging of the pen that had been used in detailing the finely hatched shadows of the gloomy piece. Upon a second of study, I had the impression that the texture of the room—even the columns—was also dark, save for a vertical strip running down the fronts of the columns, which were left totally free of ink.

After taking that in, I moved on. The next page seemed to be a list of sensory impressions, a free association list like 'humid' and 'echo' that seemed to be qualities linked to the place in the illustration. There wasn't much else of interest that I could see, so I kept exploring, now navigating an assortment of journal entries. Though I cannot recall their contents exactly, particularly given the effect they had on me, I will do my best to reproduce them here for the narrative's sake.

7th of Sun's Dawn, Year of the Wolf
Another nightmare. Not as bad as some, but the details are clear when I wake. That room again. The same great circular hall, the strange glass-front columns, the feeling of being underwater even staring out into the dry air. Smelled like salt and something else...something like ozone before a storm. When I try to remember what happened there, it's out of reach, like a word on the tip of my tongue. There's a sense of great pressure, and a high-pitched whining sound

that vibrates in my bones. When I woke today, my ears were ringing.

> *12th of Sun's Dawn, Year of the Wolf*
> *Was in the market today, choosing a new iron pot for the barracks, and caught old Manly's eye. For a second, I had this image in my head. It wasn't a memory, not really. But it was like a memory, and now that I remember it, I guess it is my memory. At the time, it was a thought that wasn't mine. I don't know how I knew it wasn't mine. He was thinking about how his missus ruined the last pot and would ruin this one, too. Then he smiled at me, because he saw me looking at him, and said I looked tired. I am.*

I paused, my thumb resting on the edge of the page. The vulnerability of these pages gave me pause, and I felt all the more acutely the nature of the invasion I was committing, yet curiosity and necessity together urged me on. I turned the page.

> *19th of Sun's Dawn, Year of the Wolf*
> *Queer dream last night: song I didn't recognize. Just a dream, I thought, and forgot it all on waking. Then, I walked by Miss Ari later in the afternoon while she was selling her flowers by the fountain. She was humming the same tune.*
> *Had it been playing in town recently? Was there a street musician responsible for it?*
> *There were no buskers in sight.*

> *28th of Sun's Dawn, Year of the Wolf*
> *The dreams are getting worse. The hall. The columns. Now there's a table. A cold, metal slab. They're doing...*

something. To someone who looks like me. I can't move. Vita is beside me, but I can't look at her. I want to know where my daughter is, but I can't speak. I can only watch what they're doing to me. I see a needle, long and thin as a hair, dipping into a vial of something that shimmers like oil. The prick in my arm. And then...nothing.

Woke up screaming. This is no way for a man to live. The neighbors must be worried.

My own breath hitched. A cold dread, sharp and immediate, snaked up my spine. What darkness lurked beneath the stoic facade of Ironforge's commissioner! The spirit-thieves had taken Norhalm and his family, and—at least to him—they had done something unspeakable. Now he lived like his own ghost, haunted and confused. The journal, once a simple object of my crime, now felt heavier in my hands with every page.

2nd of the Crow's Moon, Year of the Wolf
It's not just thoughts and music from dreams. Pub last night. The place was crowded, loud. Across the room, a young couple started to argue. Not loudly, just a tense, whispered quarrel. He was angry, she was crying. I heard it all even though they were across the room. When the woman stopped and said, "Someone's listening," I got up and left without finishing my drink.

7th of the Crow's Moon, Year of the Wolf
I'm starting to understand. This isn't random. I realized it today, finally, as I looked for Vita's file. Instead, I found Ari's. I had forgotten: she was abducted some seven years ago, when she was only as many years, and returned to her

parents' yard three nights later. Thumbed through the files and found Manly there, too, and the young couple from the pub, Bert and Enid.

What does this mean?

8th of the Crow's Moon, Year of the Wolf
Haven't had nightmares in a few. Last night, stood in that hall again, but wasn't afraid. Looked at the columns. They were made of metal in dreams before, but now they looked to be of bone. I don't think it was really that way, but I have no proof. Messages from Dunnun in dreams? I've heard dreams are the purview of the gods, anyway. Ways to give men strange ideas they couldn't otherwise receive. Young Ari was there selling flowers.

9th of the Crow's Moon, Year of the Wolf
They're looking at me. I'm certain. When I walk down the street they study me in a way they never have. Not everyone: only abductees. It's not a glance, either. It's a stare. Like they're waiting for me to answer a question.

10th of the Crow's Moon, Year of the Wolf
Dreamed of Vita, talking to her in the parlor. Didn't want to take my eyes off her, but she was thirsty, so I leapt up to get her tea. When I came back after getting the kettle on, half the town was in my house and I couldn't find her anywhere. Suddenly I remembered she was gone, and I fell back in my chair. Sobbed. I haven't wept like that since I was a boy. Not even when I was at the outpost without her or Ina. (Ina! I've barely been able to stand the thought of her. Dunnun, keep her little soul.)
Ari came up to me from out of the crowd milling in my

house. She gave me a violet and said, "I promise, you'll feel better soon. You'll never have to feel alone like this again."

I don't know why, but it calmed me, and I know she was right.

10th of the Crow's Moon, Year of the Wolf (Later)
Went by the plaza. Couldn't resist the impulse to see Ari with my own two eyes; like seeing Ina. She saw me and ran right up to give me a violet. Then—Dunnun, you alone know this is true—she looked me square in the eye and word for word repeated what she told me in that dream last night. Then, she ran off.

Seems like she quit early for the day; when I walked by later, she wasn't there.

12th of the Crow's Moon, Year of the Wolf
Haven't left the cottage in two days. Sent a letter to the men. Probably think I'm going to kill myself, since a few came round to knock on the door until I answered to say I needed time to think. Laid down in the dark on Vita's side of the bed and tried to do that, but fell asleep. Dreams about Manly sitting with me at the pub. "Aye, you need to think, Commissioner. Think of any of us. Just ask us for a favor, and you'll see."

13th of the Crow's Moon, Year of the Wolf
Plum cakes left on porch. Yesterday I imagined myself asking Mrs. Goldshard to come round with some if her husband's bakery had any to spare. Not sure how to process this information.

14th of the Crow's Moon, Year of the Wolf

Have I ever really been alone? I reckon not if the gods are real, and I know at least that Dunnun is for all the special favors he's given me over the years.

15th of the Crow's Moon, Year of the Wolf
If we're connected in this way, what's the difference between inside me and outside me? If they can read my thoughts, what does that mean for me? Am I even a part of myself? Am I something outside of myself reading my own thoughts, only thinking I'm me, but not really?

16th of the Crow's Moon, Year of the Wolf
It's not just me.

28th of the Crow's Moon, Year of the Wolf
Moving into the compound. A man who isn't alone shouldn't delude himself with the idea of living in privacy.

1st of the Harvest Moon, Year of the Wolf
Knew another victim was coming into town from the country and met them there to help them find the outpost to start processing. Don't know if I understand all this, but it's useful in some ways.
Still—if the townsfolk are connected like this, connected to each other and to me...are the spirit-thieves?

Stunned, I shut the book, unable to read another page.

The fire danced before me. I stared into its leaping flames. Beneath those lashing hell-tongues glowed charcoaled chunks of wood that, red hot, thrust my mind back to Dunnun's forge. I stared there, reminiscing on him as I rose from the chair.

As I plunged myself into the memory, I focused on it, thinking of nothing but the heat on my arms, the sweat of my brow.

Yet I knew my intentions just beneath the surface of my consciousness, and surely they all could, too.

That's right, Eradicator. Everything I know, they know...and I know everything about you.

It had been some time since I regularly endured the commentary of the hivemind to which Al-listux had attached me in the Nightlands. That was a different time from the one in the Valor Hall: all the time spent at Dunnun's anvil, tongs in one hand and hammer in the other, sparks flaring spitefully at my face, the bad dog biting the hand of its master.

These thoughts got me to Brynhildr's door, and she opened it without hesitation.

"It's a good idea to get an early start, don't you think?"

"I'll wake Branwen and the rogues," she said, still armed and armored, leaving me to step a few suites down and knock on Elishta's door. After a short delay that hinted at her heavy sleep, she answered with her robe tossed appealingly around herself, then smiled. My dearest friend! My sweetheart. She blushed so prettily in that moment, so pleased to see me that I felt ashamed to smash her hopes and give her anxiety instead of love. "I'll explain more later," I told her, the well of my palm fitting to her cheek as she tilted her head into the hand with which I caressed her. Unable to help myself, I bent to kiss her, those rose petal lips so tender and soft that I sighed despite myself: a pained sigh that heaved into deeper disappointment to say, "We must start our journey."

Though her expression faltered, brave Elishta-bet did not fall to pieces. "And the others?"

"Being roused by Brynhildr," I responded, turning away and hurrying down the hall. "Do whatever she tells you, as if she were me."

"And what will you do?"

"I'm going to wake Valeria, and then I'm just going to check the street outside the inn to ensure there's no traffic. Don't be frightened," I urged, seeing the expression dance across her face and squeezing her bicep reassuringly. "Trust Brynhildr, and trust me."

Nodding, Elishta kissed my cheek, then bounded back from her brief stance upon her toes to shut the door and dress. With one long, slow exhalation, I turned on my heel and strode down the hall, intent on the room Valeria and I shared.

There was no reason to think about anything other than that. Just the task at hand. Little mental chatter seemed ideal. I was good at this. A life of prayer had given me the ability to keep my mind trained on an image or a thought. Generally speaking, my mind was not the sort that rushed from notion to notion. I was not scattered. I was sure.

And all of this fell apart when I walked into our room at the inn to discover Valeria was gone.

14

CONFRONTATION

OVER THE NEXT several hours, there were moments where I think I went blind. In the vast library of books I inherited and have made my tedious, sometimes sporadic way through over the course of my life, I have learned about the area of the brain where vision is mastered and by the grace of God communicated to the consciousness, and I have learned it is possible for a person to be made blind while their eyes yet see: in this blindsighted state, they would still possess the visual reflex, but would not have an ability to access that sense from within their own awareness. I suspect the fury that overtook me to discover Valeria was missing was, quite literally, brain damaging in its severity, for my memory did not function adequately enough to capture the full details of what I did early on. Nothing aside from quick bursts of light in time, like the glittering gunpowder flowers bursting across the city at the turning of the year. I missed Skythorn—I missed home. Valeria was home to me, now. Where was home? Where was Valeria? What was home to me, without Valeria?

My stomach jolted when I saw she wasn't in bed, and I knew, but I could not yield to the knowing that brought with it such hateful nausea. Striding quickly toward it, as if she were hidden among the rumpled sheets, I scrutinized the bedclothes and looked rapidly around the room, searching for any sign of her, calling as if she might step out from the bureau, "Valeria?"

But there was silence.

Striding from the suite and into the hall, I soothed myself. Up to mischief with Indra and Odile, eh? Well, I couldn't blame her. If she was as committed to me as she seemed sincerely to consider, Indra and Odile were likely to part from us at the end of our journey, at least for a time—this, for them, seemed just another adventure, as it did to Branwen, for whom there was a mutual fondness but not, I should say, really any sense of soulful connection. None of the *agape* emulated by lovers whose hearts raised themselves above *eros*. None of what passed in those moments when Valeria lowered her scornful, even wicked mask and instead revealed to me something fragile. Infinitely rare. It was the same thing Elishta-bet gave me without the pretense to hide it, for she was naive about how precious a gift it really was; and it was the thing that I received from Gundrygia, though in a manner wholly dangerous. This need to be tamed, and witnessed, and unconditionally adored.

And guarded.

My knuckles hurt after I knocked on Indra and Odile's door. I do remember that, much as I remember the second suspended in the air where I waited for silent durrow feet to cross the floor. Were they gone, too? But no—just truly silent, those rogues, both of whom (Odile in the lead, a knife in her hand) looked serious and ready to puncture my lung. Normally, I would have apologized. Instead, I rasped, "Is Valeria here with you?"

Though relief and annoyance had begun in equal measure to ease across their faces to see it was only me, Odile's affect was transfigured in one one-hundredth of a second. "Have you looked downstairs?"

"I just came from there, and I surely would have seen her leave if she had left when I spoke to Elishta-bet."

How strange, Eradicator.

"Were you here the whole time?"

"No," I began, faltering, the urgency having driven entirely from my mind the telepathy of what was by now a sizeable portion of the town. He had known I was going to steal the journal, surely, if the hivemind was supplying them with information as to my thoughts. Rubbing my brow, ignoring Odile's look of concern at my surely mad expression, I mumbled, "Brynhildr and I—we went scouting. Maybe she's in the baths."

"I'll check," Odile said, gesturing to emphasize. "Indra, pack up our stuff."

"On it," she chimed, resuming the already half-completed, clearly well-practiced process of abrupt flight.

Not I—no, I was certainly not 'on it' at all. I was dizzy, and confused, and, though trying not to think, found my fury growing. As if a red-hot ball of steel raged in my chest, a terrible, spiked little devil twisting in the place where my heart once was. Packing our things, yes. I knew that was the practical and necessary measure, yet I could not do so. Not until I found Valeria. Until *we* found Valeria. Because surely Odile would return with Valeria.

I tried to put away clothes. I picked up Valeria's discarded gown. Sickness overcame me. She had nothing to wear, for the robes our lodgings provided us still hung from the back of the door. Surely she could not have gone far. Yes, certainly in the baths, my beautiful exhibitionist. I would give her a firm talking-to the next time we—

"She isn't there," Odile's solitary voice announced, back sooner than I'd hoped. "She really wasn't with you?"

"No." The word fell sickeningly from my lips, feeling like toxic vomit after a night of heavy drinking.

"Where do you think she—"

"I don't know," I told her sharply, dropping the scrap of cloth in my hands and striding to the hallway, half-pushing past Odile. "I have no idea where she is. I don't think she has any clothes. We need to find her."

My mind rushed wildly. Taking a blind guess, I hurried to Elishta's room, tried the door, and found therein Branwen, already with her pack upon her back amid heated discussion with Brynhildr. At that same second, Elishta finished clipping her cloak around her throat. "Brynhildr," I said, "I need to borrow Grane. Please."

Looking not unsympathetic—a look that infuriated me, the crease in her brow like a mockery when she who was so widely-knowing could well have intervened, but once again did not—Brynhildr told me, "Aye, friend, take all the time you need. We'll be back to the outpost by the time you're ready to meet us there."

How I detested her choice of words! As I shoved past Odile once again, having found her now like a shadow at my back, I grimaced as this time her "Hey!"—which I had not even registered the first time—stopped me short. "What's happened to the Materna?"

"We've been played," I told her, hurrying on, each stride long and quick, the stairs taken two at a time, half-sprinting through the lobby and out to the alley near the stables. Bursting out, running—horse shit, neighing, Grane's black eyes blazing with mutual rage, his understanding vast as that of his mistress. He galloped, bearing me into the night, a comet like the one soaring overhead, a blaze of light in the darkness, streaking behind it a short tail, evil somehow. The thunder of the steed's hooves continued, I swear, even as he dismounted the earth and leaped up into the skies, steam billowing from his nostrils as I urged him, "On, Grane, on!"

And well he obeyed. The horse plunged into the darkness of night, pushing his muscles at my command, his limits tested beneath the growing intensity of my anger. The rage inside me boiled so hotly I was surprised I even registered the insertion of someone else's thought into my awareness.

We're armed, Rorke. Don't come any closer.

"We'll talk like men, coward, or we'll fight like them, but do not have the temerity to intermingle your thoughts with mine."

The words roared out of me into the night, and no reply came.

I was not afraid of their armaments. Grane was much too quick for terrestrial measures. Indeed, though in the compound beneath us shouted to see us, they had no time to so much as lift their bows before the horse wheeled left in the sky and, amid a shattering of glass so great it sounded like an explosion, burst into Norhalm's office. The steed knocked down two men with the force of his great hooves while I, drawing Exigence, leapt from his back, the blade of the sword coming between him and the crossbow bolt that was only then fired. This tawdry plaything I smashed beneath the Deepgold weapon; then, I turned to slice off the hand of a man whose battle axe's swing I had not seen but had felt, combat having become a custom more frequent than ever it had been during my training with the Order. After a third man was kicked away by my boot and another wisely stepped back, I wheeled around to face Norhalm. To his credit, he had posted himself with his men and rather had the bearing of one now facing his just execution.

I closed the distance between us. Leaning across his desk, I snatched him by the collar to drag him atop it and force him to his knees as though he were a sacrifice on an altar.

"Where have they taken Valeria?"

"I'm sorry."

I shook him like a dog, spittle flying from my lips as I screamed in his face. "I asked you a question, Norhalm!"

"And I'm trying to tell you." Gritting his teeth, unable to help but grip my fists clenching the fabric at his throat, Norhalm stared at me through an increasingly red face and swore, "I don't know. She's with them, and we—I—had no choice. They made us help them."

"You think"—breathed as deeply as I could after having caught myself in the scream and deciding it would only attract more men for me to mutilate—"that just because you're unarmed, I'll refrain from killing you?"

"Would it take the wind out of your sails to know I sort of wish you would?"

"It only tempts me more. You scum—you dog. A traitor to all mankinds."

"I'm sorry. Please, blame me and not my people."

"Trust me, I do." Wild thoughts rising in me, I asked, "How long have you been aware of us? Since before we arrived?"

"Upon your arrival," he admitted. "When I was first watching the women land. It—the hivemind—said...that there would be a man among them, one who appears human. We were to accommodate your needs and discourage you from leaving. We were told not to spill so much as a drop of your blood."

"And here you are, set against me with arms."

"You were on your way to attack us."

"How long have you been able to read my mind directly? To slip thoughts into my head?"

"Since about a day after you got here. It takes a while to...I don't know...synchronize, I guess. Like realizing you're dreaming...realizing you're hearing the thoughts of somebody new. Similar feeling."

Disgusted, I said, "But the hivemind has been giving you information without your needing personal access."

"I'm sorry to say so."

My lip curled. Releasing my grip on Norhalm and considering punching him in the face, instead I stepped away from him. "You let me find the journal, then—why?"

"I told you...I didn't want to do this." Rubbing his throat where the bunched tunic had given him a rope burn resembling the mark of a botched execution, Norhalm said, "I hoped that maybe, just maybe, you would actually stop them from doing whatever they're planning. I figured it would come to something like this...I was just personally hoping it would be all of you, so I wouldn't have to deal with the consequences."

As he stared me hard in the eye and more or less paraphrased what I had only just been thinking earlier, about making a smooth escape from the town before Norhalm could perceive my damaged character, I glowered back.

"Tell me where they have taken my wife."

Looking useless, Norhalm spread his hands. "Where we all go, I suppose, but who's to say? Probably, though, she's aboard the flying citadel."

The flying citadel.

Shooting Star.

It had been a night so cloudy I hadn't been able to see the moon while earlier studying the skeletons; yet on my way here, a comet had glowed in the sky.

My body sprang into action, and so did Grane's. I sprinted for that tall window gaping open into the night and leapt astride the horse's back as he effortlessly overtook me a second later. As I mounted him, I ducked my head, tugging the black mane billowing before me to slow the beast long enough to command Norhalm.

"The women will be here soon," I told him coldly. "You are to give them a pair of war ponies and ample rations, and whatever else they should need—both now and in the future, if any of them should have the misfortune of returning here. However, rest assured, I will avoid doing so at all costs, and I hope not to see you again, because I am afraid I will become a murderer if I do."

Grane took off, hooves quaking the building as he stormed across the floor, his low-held head free of those small confines as he burst through the gaping wound our appearance left in the side of the building. We whirled into the sky, and I knew by its nature the horse had the same target that was in my heart—yet still I looked through the dark, my eyes squinted against the ice-cold daggers of rain leaping from the clouds to dash my face.

There, visible despite the dark clouds: that singular, evil *Shooting Star*.

As Grane mounted the heavens toward it, my stomach lurched, but I was too driven to feel even the slightest hint of hesitation as he climbed up and up, the cold intense, the fall so definitively fatal I would have gone unconscious long before the impact. In retrospect, I marvel; but when I consider all that was at stake, and all that had already happened, and even all that was still to come, and I truly allow myself to remember that the fear that *did* inhabit me then was fear of a life without Valeria, I can see how the idea of falling to my death did not even enter into my consciousness.

Particularly not as I recognized the rate at which the star ascended. Even with Grane galloping upward, the heart of the red star shrank. "Hurry, friend," I urged. The horse obliged, frosty clouds billowing from its nostrils and muscles bulging in its neck as it valiantly sought to race this impossible target.

At the least, now it stayed the same size—but we were not closing the distance as we pursued it to the heavens. I had the sudden sense that I could never urge Grane as fast as Brynhildr could, for I was a mortal of material substance and not a being of spirit like a

Selectrix, however solid she seemed. My fists clenched in the mane of the horse and I discovered I could not feel them, for the planet's warmth was far from us, the thinner atmosphere not as reliable a blanket here. I knew the logical thing was to turn back, regroup, work out some manner of tracking the ship from afar—but the animal in me could not be reasoned with. The animal in me knew my mate and my offspring had been spirited away, and that they were subject to things about which I knew nothing. I could not permit it. I could not surrender them. Onward I pushed Grane, whose foaming spittle turned to granules of ice which held to his lips in little flecks. I had no notion of these things in a concrete way then, but still I was aware that to break free of the planet's hold required incredible speed. Would I be able to breathe if we accomplished such a feat without killing me? Perhaps not. If I slowed the horse from its preternatural heights of power, there were perhaps other privileges to which I did not have access without Brynhildr's presence. At a certain point, in other words, I would have been able to proceed no further.

But, it did not matter.

Just as I was able to convince myself that we closed the instance—that the ship was slightly growing, as if we now gained—my heart seized in my chest. Brightly the Shooting Star glowed; and brighter, still, going from red-orange to yellow to white, an unbearable white aura emanating from its center and soon overtaking its entire shape. Now it blazed faster, and faster still, traversing not just up, but off into the distance, filling up the sky with the sudden burst of its magnificent tail and leaping off beyond the planet, beyond my sight, beyond my reach.

15

HIDDEN DIMENSION

MY HANDS ACHED as we descended, and the tips of my fingers burned so fiercely from my short exposure to the intense cold that I recognized somewhere in the background of my great loss the sensation of nascent frostbite. Perhaps the un-sensation. Everything felt reversed without Valeria's whereabouts known to me. Nightmarish in the worst possible sense, like a drunken man who awakes from a fitful night finding he has, in a blackout of rage or lust, made a bloody decision he can never take back and which, while perhaps not even real to him, is nevertheless something he must now live with for all time. My failure to reach and save her felt like some act of violence against her, and I could not see any way to her.

How could I lure the ship back?

No idea came to my mind; but then again, as the horse descended in disappointed silence, I struggled to entertain even a passing thought. My mind was a blank slate, so shocked by what had happened I didn't know what to make of it. I was so bewildered by reality that, as I murmured to Grane, "Find your mistress, friend; I'm sure you can bring me right to her," I half-expected Valeria to be among the women who appeared to be just setting out from the outpost with their two newly acquired ponies. We had taken our time, Grane setting down upon the ground and solemnly walking me back to our friends. Time to resuscitate my hands; time, also, to think on what we could do. On what I could do to dismiss this feeling of helplessness.

At least it was not a feeling of total aloneness. The relief on the faces of my friends gladdened my heart, and Elishta ran to meet me. The other who did was Odile—whose expression was bleak to see the horse empty of any rider but me.

"Did you find her?" asked Odile, leaving me to shake my head.

"She's aboard the flying citadel now—*Shooting Star*. I chased it into the night but, with me on his back, Grane can't reach it when starting from such distance. I don't even know how we can determine where it's gone."

"There has to be something we can do," Odile shouted, unable to contain herself at the idea that the Materna of the durrow people had been misplaced. This sympathized and irritated me. This wasn't just a figurehead, a priestess; this was Valeria we were talking about. *My* Valeria. My love!

Pained, I dismounted Grane and caught Elishta in my arms, first capturing her mouth with mine to drink down her beautiful love, then keeping her held to me, our developing progeny pressed between us.

"There is only one thing I can think to do at this moment," I said, grasping a handful of Elishta's flesh as if to assure myself of her reality. While she blushed deeply and her eyes lowered to be handled before the others, she didn't protest and instead leaned against my heart. "We made a promise to Norhalm and the people of this town that we would exterminate the infestation of skeletons overwhelming this town; we must make good on it."

Odile's mouth opened in the beginnings of a protest, but I raised my hand, talking over her. "For if the necromancer who has raised this pestilence has ownership, also, of the ship, the wholesale destruction of his slaves will surely attract his attention. Three score, four; several bands. These won't make much difference to him, surely. But..."

Looking across all the faces that had assembled with us as we spoke—Brynhildr and Indra and Branwen along with Elishta and Odile—I gestured between us all. "I know the group of us can do far more damage than that. I would wager we could wipe out whole legions of skeletons: between your magics"—I waved at Elishta and Branwen—"your wiles"—Indra and Odile glanced at one another, one concerned and the other determined—"and our battle prowess"—I locked eyes with the Selectrix, who smiled just so slightly—"we can do more to thin this mass in a single night than Norhalm and his men could in thirty. And if our campaign draws *Shooting Star* back our way, more so the better."

"And if it doesn't?" Odile looked me intensely in the face.

"Then we will seek it out some other way, even if it means Grane can only bear you and me and Brynhildr," I assured her. "But we promised we would open the way for these people. And so, though they have betrayed us, we ought to do as we said we would, and see what happens."

Though her jaw was tense and there was some hesitation, Odile thrust out her hand. "It's better than nothing. Let's just hope we can draw the citadel back to us before they do…whatever they're planning to do to her."

One by one, the others overlaid a hand in the center of our circle. As Grane nickered, nostrils flaring for emphasis, we looked across each other's faces.

"Whatever happens, stay close. The night is dark, and cold—and so shall the world always be if one of our number is lost. Let's see how far we get tonight, and in the morning, we'll rest before we begin in earnest."

Yet for me, there was no rest. We returned to the overlook Brynhildr and I had identified only a few hours before and, under cover of darkness, made our camp. Though Branwen and Elishta-bet, both of whom seemed to know well the state of my soul, made protest to my keeping the first watch, I insisted.

"This sword makes it a simple thing," I said, touching the pommel of Exigence. "I'll rest when it's closer to light and the threats are fewer. For now, we still have easily four hours before dawn."

Elishta bit her lip, but Branwen just sighed and set her hands on her hips.

"You realize you'll be useless to us tomorrow morning, right? How can we make progress if you're sleeping in?"

"Tie me down to Grane's back; I can sleep anywhere."

"That is true," admitted Elishta, giggling as she nudged my ribs. "Remember sleeping through that earthquake in Skythorn? I rushed to the boys' wing to see if you had anything fall over—it gave me such a fright to think you in trouble, Rorke—and instead you came to the door all worn from resting on your day off, and when I asked you about the earthquake, you said—"

"'What earthquake?'" I chuckled, caressing her brow and pushing her hair back behind her ear. "Yes, Elishta-bet, I remember. I remember how relieved you looked, and how my heart ached for you. When I think of that day...when I think of that day, I wish I would have kissed you."

Blushing gladly, then casting a shy glance at Branwen, who watched with slightly more somber eyes than usual as I held Elishta in my arms, my sweet friend of many years said, "Please, Branwen, excuse—"

"I get it," said the elf with a shake of her head, her eyes downcast, then raising toward mine. "It's okay. We'll always have the Nightlands."

"Yes, we will," I said fondly, adding with a wry glance over at Elishta, "And the *Battle Swan*."

Though the high elf managed a smile, it was fleeting, and I felt a sudden guilt for my display of affection toward Elishta. Feeling a need to break the tension, Branwen added with a wave of her hand and a dismissive look away, "Besides, I'm not really the settling down type...I don't think I can sit still in one place longer than a fortnight."

"I never would have thought myself capable of it," I admitted, rubbing my chin, "for I always supposed that when I began going out on missions I would thrive at it and insist on taking as many as my body could handle. Now, I find myself longing for peace. Having seen the cost of adventure, I am unwilling to pay it again."

As Elishta looked at me with brow furrowed in relief to hear such a thing, I bent to kiss the top of her head, then patted the small of her back. "I promise I'll be fine," I said. "If I sleep, I sleep on Grane."

At that particular moment, there was no physically possible way for me to sleep without magical aid; and magical aids tended to backfire on one while traveling, which was unacceptable in the current circumstances. I needed to wear myself out, therefore, and so I stayed awake about a hundred yards from the camp to sharpen Exigence without disturbing these precious minutes of slumber for the others. I did not think the sword needed it, being imbued as it was with all the powers of the Deepgold that was its heritage, but the rhythmic work was good for my mind. It was something to do with my hands while remaining in one location: better than drawing attention by endless pacing back and forth along the bluff.

Skeletons were expendable. Would wiping out even a third of the existing population be worthy of attention? Could we do so quickly enough to merit a return trip? Could we find any evidence that would help us in this sea of misery? Any sense of direction?

And, most of all, could we find whatever we would need in time to protect Valeria and my child?

"You don't need to worry so much, Rorke...Valeria is a big girl." As the familiar voice of the feral witch I detested yet desired trickled into my ears, my body tensed.

"Even stripped of a stitch of clothing, your favorite wife can take care of herself. I suspect he'll put her and the baby both in suspended animation, which typically speaking won't hurt either of them, and will render her available for his purposes. I think he knows better than to return her in the usual way, however…you'll need to infiltrate his ship if you care to retrieve her."

"What do you mean, 'suspended animation?'"

The shape of her warped little smile had an influence on her arrogant tone of voice such that I needn't see her to picture it. "It's a kind of sleep. Not a magical kind but a scientific kind, tough he's a master of both. Who do you think provided the means to put me to sleep in that cave where you found me?"

Aghast, I tilted my head in the direction of her voice and asked, "Didn't you have that done to you by some great king? Hundil, I think you said."

"Oh, yes, of course…but that silly boy couldn't have managed it on his own."

I turned. Some paces behind me, the wild witch reclined on a rock, again in that lush gown she wore during her seduction among the flowers. The pale limb of one perfect white leg extended from the slit that went as high as her hip, inviting me to admire the crease and the dark curls fringing the edge of her mons pubis. My lungs expanded with a deep breath I took despite myself, and as I slowly lowered my weapon and listened to her words, the breeze that crossed us carried the scent of rose and lily toward me.

"You don't make ready to fight me, Rorke?" Laughing, her other leg bent at the knee and swaying slightly as she squirmed upon the rock, Gundrygia lay her hand by her cheek in a posture that drew attention to the slight swollen quality her breasts already assumed with pregnancy. "I'm almost disappointed...so would he be, if he knew."

"I know your ways too well now, Gundrygia. I know that if you don't wish to be caught by me, I won't be able to lay a finger upon you, let alone a sword."

"Oh," she purred, extending her other arm, her digits curling toward her palm like the petals of a flower folding for the night. "I'll let you lay a finger on me, Rorke. Come to me."

As those words swept across the distance between our bodies and embraced my soul, I took but one step forward.

In that step, real flowers bloomed. The dark of night was replaced by the resplendent golden-pink of a lovers' dawn, heralding a sweet, rainy day to spend in bed with the added gift of that beautifully colored morning. I looked down at myself and found the Deepgold items gone—or, at least, if not gone, then elsewhere with my terrestrial form, which I was sure was far from this place to which Gundrygia transported me. Her smile expanded sensually as I approached, her arm folding toward her again so that her hand could caress along the bodice of her gown and reveal the swell of one perfect alabaster breast, her nipple a darker pink than her dress and already beaded with the pleasure of anticipation.

"Never fear," she whispered. "I come in peace. I'll return you to your pets soon enough."

"Peace? Is that really why you're here? It seems to me you're trying to light a fire in my heart."

"Only in your loins," she murmured, sighing into the

kiss with which I consumed her tongue before biting my way down her throat, my cock at immediate attention for the way she moaned. "Oh, Rorke, you're angry at me..."

"Of course I am—you're party to this, whatever this is. I'm no fool." As I lowered my head to one breast, I tore open her gown to reveal the other. While she gasped an oath, I let that same aggressive hand catch her jaw and deform her pretty face. "I should wait until our child is born and then kill you," I told her, so furious when I thought of Valeria's condition that I no longer felt like myself. "Yet you might enjoy that too well, madwoman."

"Oh," she moaned, her bare toes curling with lewd pleasure at the thought, her bent knee raising toward her chest, her arch caressing along my thigh. "I could imagine no sweeter death. Promise you'll have this big, heavy tool of yours inside me when you do it, Rorke—how happily I'll surrender to my psychopomp!"

The breath hissed from my lips as her foot slipped beneath the hem of my tunic and rocked along the front of my breeches; then, with almost alarming dexterity, she used her comely toes to pluck open the leather laces and allow me to spring free. When this happened, and the center of my universe became the sweet, curious ecstasy of her delicate foot rolling my erection back and forth against my pelvis, I leaned down over her and forced open her mouth: first, for my spit, which made her cry with pleasure; then, for my tongue, which plunged against hers and forced her into silence. Moaning, she lapped at me, fellating my tongue as eagerly as a whore earning her gold for the night. My entire body ached with the feverish intensity of the pleasure, my cock leaping against her foot and leaving a few droplets of my arousal upon the tips of her toes. Between us, her hands shifted, and I glanced down to see she had spread her legs invitingly, the fabric of her dress—more a loincloth, I suppose—pushed aside to allow me uninhibited access to whatsoever I would crave of her body.

"How can you resist, Rorke? Don't be so stingy... you can't imagine how insane a woman goes with a man's baby developing inside of her, oh, all she wants is to be stuffed by his cock...don't deny yourself, don't be so wicked toward me...you think I *want* to torment you?"

"Of course I think that's what you want," I told her, my voice a low, dark warning that made her shiver. As I caught her by the wrists and pushed her hands away from the apex of her thighs, she moaned, writhing with pleasure as I violated her instead with my shameless stare. "I think you're a devil—a succubus, hell-bent on driving me to madness."

"Yet it was I who told you the name of the sword! I, who gave you all my secrets, no matter whether you were equipped to remember them. Oh, come, Rorke...I'm bound to do my father's bidding as much as the Selectrix is hers, but my body and my soul are yours to command."

"You've a soul, have you?"

"If you drive deep enough, you might be able to feel it..."

"No more of your games." Catching her hair at the roots, those plumes of tangled curls made to be gripped by my hands, I knocked aside her foot and let her agonize at the sight of my cock laying mercilessly against her vulva. "Tell me something useful. Who is your father, witch?"

"You know who my father is, Wanderer...oh! Yes..."

While I ground myself against the slick track

between her thighs, I ignored her plaintive little kisses upon my mouth and demanded with a growl, "And he has Valeria aboard the Shooting Star?"

"He does, he does indeed...oh, Rorke...I'm being such a good girl, I'm answering all your questions...and I could do so, so much more for you were I no longer bound to my father. Indeed, if you were to slay him, I would gladly serve you as I would serve no other man... wouldn't it please you to treat me as your slave, your whipping-girl?"

"Now, harlot, restrain yourself..." I commanded her through gritted teeth in a manner as much for myself as for her, as she was right about the effects such a thought had on me. Pressing more forcefully into that lush crevice between her opened legs, though unable to help the affection with which I looked on her as I did, I attempted to keep my face arranged in an expression of disdain that did not entirely hold. Instead, I slipped my thumb into her mouth and allowed her to worship it in lieu of my prick. As her cheeks hollowed, her eyelids fluttering in pleasure at her own obedience, I rocked my hips back to give her the promise of penetration, the merest tip of me fixed against her. "I need more from you," I told her plainly, looking into her eyes. "You have knowledge possessed by none but him, I'm certain of it. How can we find *Shooting Star*?"

"Oh, Rorke, you don't need me for that...you're so close." As she spoke, my thumb slid from her lips. A gossamer web of saliva connected my hand to her tongue. I shuddered, the throb I felt for her dangerously powerful, but I stood my ground as I would against an animal. "All that you need to summon *Shooting Star* is within you...

my father's ship will be all yours, along with me...all the rest of his property, too..."

I couldn't possibly explain why, but her words felt like an indictment. The rage at Valeria's kidnapping rose in me as a new, different flame, and I allowed it to consume me: allowed it to drive the point of my weapon as deep into Gundrygia's guts as I could, making us moan together as though we were both victims of the same torment. "Oh yes, Master," cooed the wild woman, her gasp catching in her throat as she bent her knees to give me the deepest possible access to her tightly gripping confines, "oh, yes, ride your slave-to-be—use me, defile another man's property—defile me—"

"Shut up," I commanded her while she groaned and cried all the higher in wanton pleasure, her mouth open to reveal the shining silk of her panting tongue while I let her feel just how much I wanted to annihilate her. "Silence, witch. I'll not hear the poison of your lies."

"There are never any lies on my tongue for you, Rorke! You know I speak the truth, however impossible it seems. Don't run from it, Rorke—plunge into it—plunge into me—oh, yes, yes, oh, yes, Rorke, own me—own me—own me—"

Unable to bear what else might come from her mouth, I pushed my hand over her lips, gripping her face while I pounded into her and watched her eyes roll in her head. Nostrils flaring, she clutched the rock beneath us, bracing herself against the force of my rough thrusts while her body clenched around me. My free hand gripped her hip to keep her steady, and as I forced myself deeper into her, her body tightened like an archer's bow beneath mine. That sweet velvet sleeve of hers rippled, flooding around me, and her voice rose in a high, desperate keen against my hand. I kept going, giving her no break, my pleasure cruelly increased as she whimpered in discomfort; but, slut that she was, she was soon enough moaning again, soon enough begging through my hand again, soon enough crushing me in her tight demands again, again, again, until finally I could take no more, and yielded. As my consciousness shattered into the ecstasy with which I emptied myself into her, Gundrygia emitted one final, amorous moan, and I awoke at dawn, Exigence sharpened and reclining upon the rock where she had been, Branwen standing over me.

"See, Rorke? What did I tell you? Asleep, after all."

16

THE LONG MARCH

WHATEVER THAT CONTEMPTIBLE witch wanted of me, I could not help but take notice of how well rested I felt despite the short time I must have been asleep. It highlighted a curious tenderness in Gundrygia that was real; yet it was also a political move, a calculated effort to liberate herself from the one who evidently held her as a piece of property. Why that ownership might pass to me, I couldn't understand in a literal sense. At that time, I had thought she meant as another piece of the plunder of a looted keep. I thought nothing of the visitation except that I was glad it had happened, and sorry she had put me to sleep before I could make any effort to persuade her to come with us, however loyal or compelled or both she really was to serve this fellow in the citadel whom she called her father.

Was he her father? Was it he, this man in the dreams? It surely must have been. I had no actual confirmation of this, but I knew it with steep certainty, as one recognizes the motifs of a dream or recalls some memory long-buried. How preoccupying he became when I thought on his face! The idea of meeting him filled me with dread; I was not sure if that was because I was afraid of him, or because I was afraid of what encountering him would force me to become.

Traversing the landscape was difficult. Where the skeletons had buried themselves, the terrain was soft and pockmarked with loose patches of soil where they had covered themselves before the morning light. On the one hand, this was quite useful, for one knew easily if one was in an area that would be safe to inhabit at nightfall. On the other hand, the ponies struggled, and even I put my foot through a grave once or twice. This wouldn't have been so bad if one could interfere with a skeleton's condition while it was in this daytime dormancy, but the trouble with the undead was that any dormancy *was* death. Destroying a magically controlled corpse during the day was wholly ineffective without exposure to abundant sunlight, which was denied us by the gloomy weather of the region. Without that, the entity would just compile itself again at nightfall. I have heard that even the disposal method of cremation and sprinkling in running water is only a temporary mitigation, passing the problem along to a different geographic region and generation of peoples. Therefore, one cannot really 'get the drop' on any such abomination. It is better to prepare for nightfall either planning for an immediate assault on the entity's waking or, as we did, regrouping to a rocky cavern system that seemed to have been reinforced long ago by some ingenious men.

"This used to be some mine, I guess," Branwen pondered, studying the structure in the light of Hamsunt's lantern, then scowling down at the pile of bones at her feet. "Looks like they come in here to collapse during the day, too. I guess we could drag them all out of here and crush them, but..."

"But if we overlook so much as a tooth or a fingerbone," I agreed, "they'll reconstitute themselves around the damned things by nightfall, and we'll have expended the energy for nothing. No, I think it's better to destroy them as they reanimate for the night; if nothing else, it should be good experience."

"I'll bet this mine connects down to the Nightlands," remarked Indra, sighing and clasping her hands as she peered out into the dark. "I'm getting homesick, Odile! I never dreamed I'd spend such a long time outside of it... My eyes are exhausted."

"More than my eyes are exhausted," agreed Odile, striding into the dark. "My body, my brains...my soul, whatever that is. We'd better get a cushy reward for returning the Materna and her ring. I never want to miss a meal again."

Another moment of struggle in my heart! Somehow, the idea that Indra and Odile had a vested interest in convincing Valeria to return home with them had not occurred to me for some time. A hollow feeling opened up in the bottom of my stomach. They who had been my friends were now my enemies in, at least, this. Yet were they not also a pair of slavers from a people diametrically opposed to the morality of my society, of myself, and even of the god I once served? 'Enemies' was a strong word, but there was little commonality between us aside from the circumstances by which we had come to know one another and remain in one another's company. We liked one another well enough, but our worldviews were at odds—and in the matter of Valeria, irreconcilable. This was deeply troubling. I had to trust that Valeria's love for me was true and deep enough that the practical considerations of two representatives of her people would not inspire her to prioritize her homeland beyond that point at which she already weighed it. I needed a solution: a viable alternative to offer her, one worthy of her preference for pleasure and luxury.

Yet, what could I offer? What, indeed, could I offer Elishta-bet? What could have ever enticed Gundrygia to remain in some semblance of place, if such a feat were possible?

When dusk neared, we divided ourselves into pairs, and Elishta volunteered to go with me so hastily that I had the sudden sense she'd noticed my mood—for, despite our deep attraction, she was not the type to fabricate an opportunity to flirt. Indeed, she waited until we had patrolled about five hundred yards from the mine before speaking, her wonderful eyes falling toward the rocky terrain and up again in the direction we walked. "I'm worried, Rorke."

"I'm worried, too," I told Elishta, playing dumb because, in truth, I didn't feel like discussing anything I was sure she wanted to discuss, "but I know Valeria is strong. We'll reach her. When we do, she'll still be fighting her captors."

"Well—I am worried about Valeria, of course, but—I mean that I'm worried about *you*, Rorke. You've been so pensive since the Valor Hall. I feel how deeply you've changed."

"Haven't you?"

"Of course—of course, I have. But, in a way that's—well—"

With a thoughtful frown, Elishta considered it for a handful of seconds, then suggested, "I don't think I took the world seriously before. I don't think I took the idea of death seriously, even with all I had been taught. Yet... with you, I don't know. Perhaps I'm strange for saying this, but it almost seems the opposite in your case. As if our time in the Valor Hall and this journey made you *ready* to die. Ready," she added before I could speak, "not in the sense of preparedness, but in the sense of...desire."

I was unable to argue, which I found quite troubling. "I have far too much to live for to allow myself to die, Elishta. Try not to concern yourself with my brooding too much."

"It's more than *brooding*, though. It's heartache." Her hand slid along my bicep, and I stopped in place, stunned by the power her touch had to soothe pains I didn't even know I had. "What changed in your heart to leave it so bruised, Rorke?"

Exhaling to steady myself, I slipped her hand into mine and raised her fingers to my lips.

"You know me too well for me to withhold my thoughts from you," I allowed, "and if you are to be mine, Elishta, and I yours, then I owe you the whole of the truth. I cannot shake these thoughts. This sense that Weltyr is no true god. The sense that none of what we worship as gods are gods." Though she was clearly taken aback, her eyes enlarged by her surprise, her features were transfigured by sympathy as I went on. "The sense that I have satisfied myself with this illusion of imperfect divinity, when true divinity can have, by definition, no hint of imperfection to it, is disturbing to me. There is something of Weltyr that is godlike indeed, or else I would not have given all my heart to him with such certitude and commitment. I have no doubt at all that he is some aspect of a monolithic, true God. Yet—you were not there to see his spear shatter beneath Exigence. To feel in real time the grief and ashes of what I had done."

"But surely," she suggested, "if you did such a thing, is it not then natural to see you were engendered for this purpose?"

"To what end, though?" As I reflected on this, I told her plainly, "This was not some valiant loss, some deliberate laying down of his life. He fought to destroy me. He did not spare me in that combat, and it is only by Exigence that I gained the victory. While it's true to say Exigence came to me by his will—indeed, by his hand—I see a pattern of selfish manipulation to his designs. Now"—I unsheathed the blade and raised it toward the bloody sunlight of the coming night—"I have become responsible for finding some means to close the wound he opened when he stole the Deepgold from the Deep-Children and their mother, Roserpine. Now, I see his many flaws: his lies, his theft, his philandering. He is no god, I think, Elishta, though perhaps a being that might as well be one from our more limited perspective upon the grounds of Urde. Yet much as I once revered Weltyr as the singular true god among other, lesser emanations, now I suspect he himself is among those emanations, and that the singular, true God is beyond him still. Is God even knowable by the human intellect if all these beings before us—citizens of the Valor Hall and Deep and elsewhere as we ourselves are citizens of terrestrial civilizations—are so vastly powerful, yet still not God?"

"Surely not," Elishta agreed quietly, a distant look in her eyes, her mouth in a beautiful moue of sorrow. As guilt seized me, I touched her, and she raised her eyes to me as she continued. "Surely, God must reveal Himself to men if He wishes to be known in the manner a personage is known."

With a sudden, sick sense, I considered the length of history, known and unknown, that the mankinds had endured. "Perhaps He already did," I suggested, the sword hanging from my hand at my side in unconscious emulation of a defeated child letting his toy stick lose its value as a fantasy weapon. "Perhaps we didn't notice, or the knowledge was lost."

"Maybe He would do it again," Elishta suggested, one hand laying on her heart and her eyes trailing up to someplace higher than even the Valor Hall out there amid the stars. "If He exists as an intellect—and I would imagine surely He does, for life and knowledge and goodness itself must have some consciousness of itself, surely, or else could not be called 'alive', which is necessary for the God of Life—then our knowledge or ignorance of Him is surely also an expression of His will." While I marveled at her beautiful piety, a faith so deep that she rapidly allayed my fears that I would rattle her soul with my own shifting view, my beloved friend smiled at me in that tender way, her eyes coming back down to Urde. "So we must trust Him and suppose He is giving us knowledge suitable to us, at an appropriate pace, congruent with our cultural attitudes and the needs of our soul. And if that involves not knowing Him, or learning how to know Him by giving so much of our lives to Weltyr first, then we must trust, mustn't we, Rorke?"

Astonished by the depth of her perception and the funny thought that at least two of my three lovers were women of a holiness that absolutely shamed mine (a quality for which the third compensated!), I managed, "Yes, I guess so."

With a gay smile that twinkled her eyes, crinkling so cutely to look at me that I ached to take her face between my hands and kiss her beautiful eyebrows, Elishta reminded me, "And besides, you may yet be proven wrong in your assumptions about Weltyr. If Weltyr is as powerful as we thought, he will show us that. If there is another, higher God who desires to be known in a different way, then surely, that will become apparent, too. For now, though, I think it's important to trust, and to continue to pray in whatever way your heart is called to pray, and—oh, Rorke!"

The surprised tone of her voice snapped me out of this theological meditation that gave me a certain degree of hope I hadn't felt in some days. I followed her gaze.

Down in my hand, Exigence's hilt glowed with the first hints of a soft and sickly blue.

And as I looked up, the first bony fist punched up from the dirt not more than six yards behind Elishta.

"Look there," I told her. "It's the presence of the ignorant undead that does it. The Deepgold is too holy to tolerate it. Look here—the Lantern, too." I turned down its light so she could witness this effect, unhurried as another skeletal arm burst forth, those spindled hands finding purchase on the surface of the dirt.

Elishta was getting nervous, I could see from her

multiple glances in that direction. With a gesture toward the rapier with which she had been armed by Norhalm and his men, I told her, "I'd give you the light to hold, but it's best you get to know your new blade unencumbered, don't you think? One less thing to think about."

Nodding, Elishta drew the weapon and turned toward the foe. As she did, I noted another was already working its neck free of the soil, the filtered red light of dusk casting eerie shadows within the beetle-infested hollows of its eye sockets. The one before us was still working free its skull, pushing itself up and out of the shallow grave with an emergence so slow it seemed at first like a great puffball mushroom. Then the different sutures conjoining the plates became apparent, then the crest of the brow, and those empty eyes. By that point, Elishta had recoiled a pace or so, making to draw back against me—at least driven in my direction by some unconscious urge.

I stepped back to avoid encouraging her withdrawal from battle.

"I'm counting on you, Elishta—you know we stand at great risk of being shown up by the Selectrix. If we aren't careful, she and Indra will really clean house."

With a slightly braver smile at my jovial demeanor, Elishta brandished her blade and turned back to face the devils that, seeing us, dragged themselves dumbly from the ground in our direction. She spared not a second further and nimbly darted forward toward the thing, thrusting her blade directly through the bleached, fragile cranium that had been dead who knew how long already and which, in fairness to the handiwork of their controller, was likely a bit weaker in those first moments when there was still a small degree of sunlight to which the monsters were exposed. One way or another, later on in the night they seemed a bit more durable than those first contenders.

I was glad it was so, because the truth was that the experience was mind-numbing and salvaged only by Elishta's merry presence, her nearness a better warmth than any sun. Oh, it was terrifically fun, at first. Who doesn't experience childlike glee when presented with the opportunity for wholesale destruction of a productive sort? Not unlike demolishing a wall in one's cabin to create an expansion. Even though I had no respect for Norhalm or the villagers we served by this act, still they were among the mankinds—and now Grimalkin stayed among them, at least for a time, so I could not leave him isolated in a sea of skeletons in good conscience; nor could I, in good conscience, stop this exercise at rescuing Valeria or her ring.

That's right, Eradicator...justify it to yourself now.

This was ultimately the problem with the exercise, beyond the repetitive nature of the task which ground away at my soul—even as Elishta correctly leveraged this night to gain valuable experience in battle. Why, the air out in that countryside was so perfectly crisp that I could hear delighted whoops and celebratory cheers from the other pairs, whose positions were illuminated by faerie fire: blue for the durrow and glimmering green-gold for Branwen. Though the Deepgold objects, even the helm, all glowed with that light of protestation which intensified in proximity to a skeleton, I had turned the flame of the lantern back up, and so we were in essence a target. Though the Lantern of Hamsunt had kept us from most trouble with unintelligent creatures in the Nightlands, it had no impact on the undead—the skeletons came shambling into the perimeter of its light without showing even the least awareness.

Even so...something was odd.

It took me some time to notice it at first. I was so caught up by the steady slide from fun to monotony and the vacuum it left for the hivemind to enter with comments. While I mostly played back-up to Elishtabet and occasionally gave her tips to improve her already quite good grasp of sword fighting, inwardly my heart was thousands of miles away, far off in the sky, wherever Valeria was—frozen in time on a table somewhere as Gundrygia was when I found her in those caves.

And I was so blind, so arrogant, so wrapped up in myself and my problems—not even Valeria's, by Weltyr's eye, but only my problems with respect to a lack of her and the child—that it took me until the second night to notice them. The little spiders that would occasionally go skittering off from the backs of the skeletons' skulls, such a subtle little shadow in the dark that it must have taken tens or even hundreds of repetitions for my brain to note the pattern in the middle of our blitz. The major issue here was that I had seen many magical acts during my travels, and had myself much experience with the luminescent effects of holiness upon the sage or the paladin who walked a rightly ordered spiritual path for the nature of his station. That did not even touch the energy released by the use of prayers or, in Elishta's case, inborn spellcasting talents that seemed more abstract and metaphysical than Branwen's earthy magic. Yet even these druidic spells calling upon the flora and fauna and earthen elements of the planet emitted visible light.

So, because these little spider-bodies were so dark, when I caught a visual flash of a tiny red ember of light dropping down the occasional skeletal spine, I assumed it was the dissipation of some of the sorcerer's animating magic—especially since it happened a few seconds before some particularly destructive impact of Exigence or Elishta's rapier. No doubt, Valeria and her reverence for spiders would have far more quickly identified the phenomenon as unnatural. As it was, I did not take conscious note of it until several hours later, when our team reconvened with the rest of our party at the mouth of the cleared mine.

"Did anybody notice the insects flecking off their skulls?" Odile asked with an expression of disgust, not having as much love for the Nightlands' most common form of life as did her Materna. "They're infested!"

"I don't think they're insects," Branwen posited with a frown, "but I don't know what they are."

Suddenly making a connection to the pattern I had witnessed but largely ignored, I looked between the women. "You mean those little embers that burst from some of them?"

"Exactly." Tapping the back of her skull and indicating the arc of the drop-off with her index finger, Branwen went on, "I thought they were insects at first, too. But when I looked closer, I didn't see the life energy beings normally emit, even at the small size of a spider."

Elishta, having been isolated from other practitioners of various magics due to the church's prejudice against such talents, perked with interest. "Life-energy emissions?"

Nodding, the high elf for whom such things were second nature explained, "That's right. Everything living has some kind of energy signature, and it becomes more intense in more complex beings. Interacting with these fields is how a person like me uses nature magic...but I don't see anything like that coming off those little creatures, whatever they are. Maybe that red light they exude is interfering with my ability to perceive them?" Frowning, Branwen added in the manner of one thinking aloud, "But that shouldn't matter..."

Considering how Exigence and other Deepgold items seemed to react to the presence of unintelligent undead, I asked, "Do the skeletons give off any kind of energy?"

"No, nothing. It isn't a question of living biological material so much as internal spirit. The captain and her crew aboard the *Rhinemaid* exhibited patterns similar to the sort a spirit-thief radiates—unnatural, evil, spiritually polluted. Those skeletons, though...there's nothing different between a pile of bones and an animated skeleton insofar as that's concerned."

Considering this, I rubbed my jaw and let Indra ask for us all, "Could those spiders be undead, too?"

"Well..." Looking uncertain, Branwen allowed, "I guess maybe it's possible...but—"

"Why would a necromancer reanimate spiders?" I asked, unconvinced.

At this question, Branwen spread her hands. "Your guess is as good as mine. Maybe there was a cemetery infested with the things, and they were raised with the skeletons as a consequence of some area-of-effect spell?"

It was plausible, but didn't feel particularly likely. Necromantic magics were targeted; I was not sure I had heard of a necromancer whose spells could hold sway over an entire cemetery of beings, including insects and arachnids. Were that true, I would anticipate even the grass and other dead foliage within a target area would show some sign of malefic operation. There had to be, therefore, some other explanation—but what?

Through the early morning hours and most of the day, we rested. Come evening, we packed up our camp and determined we would set a new one, clearing skeletons as we looked for an ideal spot. Since we would once again pair off to eradicate a wide berth of the pests, we determined a system by which we could alert the others if one group was in danger—or, more likely, had something important to share. Whatever light the group had—whether faerie fire or the Lantern—we would turn it up and down in four short bursts, then leave it burning steadily to allow the others to make their way. Then, we set about it once again, and now I could see the novelty waning in fair Elishta, who was growing in experience and who remarked to me after an hour or two, "It really becomes rote, doesn't it?"

"I admit, I've been feigning some enthusiasm for your sake. It was fun at first, but I've dealt with creatures far more dangerous than these, and I have to say, I'm not particularly worried about it. It's more an issue of numbers, and, well, the fact that the numbers continue increasing."

"That would become fatiguing to the townsfolk if it was a menace as constant as it seems to be. Particularly if they go after women first, as they seem to."

"Certainly," I agreed without thinking—then, I realized what she had said, and paused. "How do you mean?"

"Why, you hadn't noticed?" Laughing in incredulity, she shook her head. "They seem to treat me as their only target. Every single one of them is set on me, even when they should be on the defense against you. Perhaps, being such primitive un-minds, they think only of the smaller target—if we should use the verb 'think' at all."

"I suppose that could be possible, but"—as we reached the crest of a hill and looked down across what was gradually turning into marsh, the brigade of skeletons at the foot twisted their heads up and shambled our way—"I don't think they're typically known for their discernment. I suppose, if the necromancer programmed them to act in such a way, it might be possible."

But it was more than that—more than that they were focused on Elishta. Indeed, now that I was looking for it, (much as I now looked for the falling spider-embers which seemed, I noted, to always drop off toward the north), I recognized the skeletons universally ignored me. It was as if they became totally unaware of my existence the second they observed me—for I did see them note me, at least insofar as they straightened incrementally when their eyeless skulls turned toward us. Then, just as soon as they seemed to have registered the reality of my presence and whatever it meant to them, their attention fixed on Elishta and remained there without deviation, as if they had mistaken me for a shadow.

It was quite bizarre—and partially responsible for that feeling of special malaise I'd endured since early on in this matter of clearing the land. After all: who doesn't love free license to cut down swathes of opposition, particularly opposition about which one need not feel the slightest moral compunction? By all rights, I should have been having a merry time, at least for the first night. Yet, with their focus entirely on Elishta, I had been permitted to turn inward and ruminate over Valeria's condition, and generally feel a degree of self-pity that kept me from taking joy in anything other than Elishta's growth in combat.

Now, that was gone. My focus shifted to the unfolding mysteries. First, the business with the spiders; now, this.

After several hours of fighting and pondering and watching how, wave after wave, I was effectively invisible to our foes, I told Elishta, "Let's reconvene with the others before we go on and see if there's any useful information." Announcing this, I twisted the small knob at the base of Hamsunt's lantern. Back and forth, back and forth: four times the flame died and revived, until it remained steady as it had been. In the distance, one blue flame and one red flame each did likewise, stuttering out and blazing anew with confirmation that our friends were on their way. Soon enough, the others met us at our location, by now at the marsh's edge.

"This question may sound strange," I broached once we had taken stock of one another's condition and determined no one was wounded beyond a superficial cut, "but—are our opponents attacking everyone equally, or is one of you being favored? Have you noticed?"

Exchanging a curious look, Branwen and Odile shrugged, and so did Brynhildr and Indra. "Not that we've seen," Branwen was first to suggest, with Odile following up by a shake of her head, "It's been pretty even."

This was the most troubling response they could have possibly given. Though I prayed the reason for it was related to Elishta's theory of women being perceived as more vulnerable, I had the distinct feeling that this was not correct. Indeed, since she was so intimidating in her armor that she easily could have passed for any paladin of the Temple with her visor down, I asked Brynhildr, "And you, my friend? Are you sure you haven't drawn more aggression than Indra?"

With that knowing look growing every moment, as if the solemnity inflicted upon her by her wisdom became unbearable the longer she remained on Urde with us, the Selectrix shook her head. "No; these undead are impartial."

"Why are you asking?"

As, several hundred yards from us, a skeleton alerted by our chatter or some other means came slumping out of the willows that formed gloomy curtains veiling the marshland, I informed them, "Because, for all the world, they treat me as though I were a mote of dust somewhere beyond their attention. Even as I cut them down, they react only to Elishta."

Looking quite taken aback, the other four women exchanged a queer look. "Are you sure," Odile pressed, leading me to glance at the skeleton making its stumbling approach.

"Watch."

One hand upon the pommel of Exigence, I left the women and strode toward our so-called threat. It neither changed course nor increased speed, either of which surely would have been the anticipated action. This one, though showing a second of hesitation, continued apace, neither charging me nor shying from me. When I stopped some twenty paces from it, still it came, the rusty sword with which it had perhaps once been buried still limp in its spindled fingers. I drew Exigence and halted, standing between it and the women with the blade gleaming an ever more resplendent blue before me. Slightly slowed by a half-crushed ankle it dragged behind, the abomination continued forward, closer, closer, that useless old sword dragging across the dirt.

And, just as I would have expected it to raise that weapon and meet me head-on, it diverted course, walking calmly around me and continuing its path toward the women.

Exigence still in my hands, I lowered the blade to a more casual one-handed grip and turned to open my free hand at the balking group. "You see," I asked, producing a bit of murmuring between them.

"Maybe this one's defective," Odile suggested, striding forward to meet it and flinching back as it raised its blade. "Or, maybe not—"

While it swung, I darted forward and brought Exigence up to parry, barely feeling the reverberation of the clash through the confident steel of Exigence's blade—if indeed it was not merely Deepgold that resembled steel by some magical means. Consequently, the skeleton's sword emitted a whine, a warning it was about to split like a log beneath an axe: but this was unnecessary. In a show of that strange docility, it lowered the blade so quickly I had no time to relax the muscles of my arms, which caused Exigence to hammer through the creature's mossy skull and shred it in half so easily it may as well have been made of paper. After a second's delay, the lingering bones dropped into a pile of rust and debris, but my attention was stolen by the ember that wafted into the fronds of sedge and scurried northward, as had all the others.

"What gives," exclaimed Odile, while Indra asked with a gasp, "Did you see that?"

"They've all been this way," Elishta confirmed to them, waving toward the pieces of bone that were now little more than a heap at my feet. As I stepped over it and strode forward to avoid losing sight of the pseudo-spider, she went on, "Not a single one of— Rorke?"

"Have you noticed? These spiders are all heading the same way. All of them, north." Sucking a tooth as the little thing vanished from my sight into the grasses, I stopped on my heel. "Blasted quick things, too."

"Maybe we should follow them," Indra suggested, having approached with the others to speak with me and study the pile of decay. "Do you think they'll lead us to the necromancer?"

The citadel was flying fast enough that I doubted its destination was anywhere near here—Grane and I had probably been forty miles or more away from Ironforge by the time it sped off into the night. "Wherever they're going, I don't think it's *Shooting Star*."

At the sound of its name, the horse whinnied, then fidgeted restlessly upon the soft earth as if to confirm my opinion. Brynhildr stroked its neck as Odile pondered, "Yeah, well, those little spiders are pretty quick, wherever they're going—how are we supposed to follow them when they're so small and so fast?"

Now, it was Elishta's time to shine. As we pondered for a few seconds, she perked, then looked between the rest of us. "Got any empty potion bottles?"

Though Odile looked a bit confused and even annoyed by the question, having little patience for anything that did not present an immediate solution to whatever her current problem was, she yielded one up from her pack. "It's a good thing we haven't had many grievous injuries between us—Indra and I had no time to stock up before we left the Nightlands. It was all such a rush."

"It was meant to be! Now, we've got compasses." As I understood what she was suggesting, Elishta raised the empty beaker to her eye and peered at us through its glass, her iris undergoing a humorous transformation in size and shape. "See? If they're all going the same way, then all we need do is capture one. If it continues trying to head home, we can just follow the same trajectory it uses to ensure we don't overshoot our destination."

"Let's make it a contest!" Getting excited by the prospect, Indra enthused, "A prize for whoever catches one first!"

"What prize?" asked Elishta, yielding a snort from Odile.

"How about a few hours spent riding Brynhildr's horse... Are we really going to have to walk through this— I don't even know, wetlands?"

"I don't suppose you have anything resembling this belowground," Branwen remarked with amazement. "Have you ever seen snow?"

"I've read about it...can't say I'm all that interested, to be frank..."

"If we keep up the chattering," I told them, sheathing Exigence and accepting another empty bottle from the durrow, "we'll *all* be seeing snow without having gotten anywhere...come along, now. Let's each try and see what we can do. Perhaps we could try identifying skeletons with the spider attached and incapacitate one to remove the spider?"

That was the hope, anyway—the vague idea—but the reality was these little things, whatever they were, were far more wily than anticipated. Much as they dropped free of the skulls when ruin was imminent, they also seemed to perceive that a captured skeleton was worthless. As we waded through the sedge and the soft earth, the trees around us decreased visibility sufficiently that our system of lights was no longer as valuable a communication solution as it had been on the rolling expanse of the heaths. Therefore, we stayed closer, and I quickly got the sense that the more impatient members of our group—namely, Odile, Branwen, and myself—were less than equipped for this task. Brynhildr, for her part, was happy enough to fight and laugh with us. Often to laugh *at* us, as she emitted hearty guffaws each time my lips formed a curse of frustration, Exigence being too long and cumbersome a sword to allow me to capture the quickly falling little ember on my own. But, as she had the matter of Norhalm's notebook, she refrained from intervening on our behalf for the task at hand. "Don't rely too much on me," she said warmly as Elishta teased her for neglecting her duties. "How would you fare if I weren't here, friend? You must fight for yourselves. It would do you far more good to accomplish this on your own—my interference gains nothing for you."

I wanted to make an argument or two against that notion, but before I could, Indra's cheer drew our attention.

"I have it," she shouted, adding quickly, "come, someone, help—"

The image was rather amusing: some yards away, amid a copse, Indra had come upon a small clutch of skeletons and had used her skills as a thief to great advantage. As she crept around them, she identified two which had the small black arachnid attached to the bases of their skulls; then, rushing forward, she clapped the mouth of the little bottle over the creature, and was left there, holding the open glass mouth against the mass of old bone, shuffling about as quickly as she could to remain behind that now-thrashing skeleton while the others took their shots at her. As she cried aloud and barely arched her back away from the swipe of a dwarvish skeleton's club, we all hurried from our disparate stations to help her with her assailants. Soon, we had our compass, the mite locked safely in its bottle-shaped prison, throwing itself against the beaker not angrily so much as numbly, as if all it knew to do in this context was to continue its journey north. Therefore, with Indra pleased to be seated upon Grane's back for even a few hours, we continued forward as a single unit, all six of us picking our slow way through the sparsely dispersed but plentiful trees that grew along the more stable areas of ground, where the loam was not quite as saturated as we would find it nearer to the waterways seeping into Urde and making the most straightforward routes impassible to us. We had no choice but to skirt the edges of an expansive bog, amply supplied with fallen branches with which we prodded the superficially stable earth before us in search of any sign of quicksand. On at least one occasion, we had no choice but to ford the waters, and rather than soak ourselves through we relied on the flight of Grane and the ingenuity of Elishta and Branwen, their magic sufficient to preserve us from the extra encumbrance waterlogged clothes would have represented.

Yet, it seemed there would be no end! One night in the bog turned into two. As the third approached, and the moods of all involved had soured beyond speech—even bright-hearted Indra looked uncharacteristically weary—my soul was riddled with worries. What was happening to Valeria? Was that flying citadel even near Urde at this point, or had it launched itself into the stars as had the ships of the ancestors who, I had been taught as a boy, left with their riches even before the mankinds were divided into the races we ourselves had always known? Was this strategy of following the futilely proceeding little arachnid a wise one, or were we deluding ourselves with the interpretation of meaning, of will and intellect, when the reality was that this thing, whatever it was, was without any intent other than that of escape?

Were those eyes on us, or was I growing paranoid?

This last point was particularly hard to discern. Since learning about the powers of the villagers, I had felt utterly exposed in thought, word, and deed, but we were by now far enough away from the town that even they surely could not have received a broadcast of my thoughts without the intervention of the hivemind. Yet, the hivemind knew all about me; ergo, they *did* know. But even with so many aware of my doings, including the spirit-thieves we sought to overcome, I could not shake the notion that there was more to this than distant psychic voyeurs. Even queerer was that the feeling arose despite our decision to travel by day, meaning we had exceedingly few instances of contact with skeletons until we stopped to make camp—and even then, the deeper we moved into the swamp, the fewer we found, for surely the environment was inhospitable to entities predisposed to rot.

Why, then, did I have such a definite sense that we were under observation? As though, any second, I might look up and see movement in the distance, or round a tree and come face to face with some unknown watcher?

Frowning, seeing that the third dusk neared, I slipped our captured friend from my belt and held him close to my face. Such a strange thing! I have called it a 'spider' and a 'mite', but the reality is that it was not quite either one of those things, for its was a singular block, perfectly square, and its legs were more like prongs that had been bent to resemble the legs of an insect. Interestingly, although the metal atop its body was dark, the underside—which also hosted that red pinpoint of light—was of a different hue, a green only apparent up-close, and only through a layer of muck that had developed in its time attached to its prior host. This surface was webbed with a pattern of metallic veins: gold, I thought. Not Deepgold, since I had not seen it react to the undead, but the stuff of Urde.

"Isn't it a strange thing," enthused Elishta, maintaining stride with me now to peer at it together. "I still don't understand what it *is*." After studying it for a time with a quizzical frown, she asked without taking her eyes off the thing, "Branwen?"

"Huh?"

Drawn from her thoughts, Branwen quickened her pace to catch up from somewhere behind us. I caught on her the scent of her sweat and remembered former times, but I tried not to anymore, and I could tell that was surely what had been so troublesome to her. I felt disappointed in myself about the whole thing—not in the sense of hurt feelings on my side, you must understand, but to know there was any part of her I had inadvertently hurt over the long timeline by my own lack of inhibitions. Those far away days as I set off, Strife in my hand, no presentiment of all of this! How hard it was to avoid seeing all of it as a long sequence of mistakes. Yet I was redeemed from my gloom as Elishta, her natural sweetness shining through, asked, "Are faeries real?"

Almost baffled by this question, the crinkles of her consternated brow infinitely cute, Branwen glanced twice toward me, then laughed a little as she looked back at Elishta. "Well, define what you mean by 'faerie', right? That's kind of a broad term."

"That." Indicating the glass of the beaker with the tip of her finger, Elishta looked at Branwen with unveiled eagerness to learn. "Is that a faerie?"

"Definitely not," Branwen declared, shaking her head. "When people talk about faeries, I think a lot of the time they really mean pixies."

Delighted to find some recognition in these terms, Elishta snapped her fingers, her expression fired up with excitement. "Yes, that's what I mean! Thank you—you're sure these aren't some kind of pixie?"

"I'm sure," Branwen said. "Pixies are entirely spirit, and their physical bodies are manifestations of crystallized energy the spirit develops as it grows. This thing is like the opposite. It's entirely matter and no recognizable spirit, I would say."

"Hmm." With another studious meditation on the thing in question, Elishta lowered her head to examine it more closely. "I wonder."

"Wonder what?"

"If it's got no trace of magic," Elishta said in a distracted voice, her eyes fixed on the insectoid being that never tired, never ceased, just continued attempting to make its way to some unknown destination, "then what is it doing attaching itself to those skeletons?"

That was all she got out before the snare trap snatched around my ankle, sending me flying up so fast that I lost consciousness for second or two. All conversation dissolved into a confusion of shouts—some simple gasps, but several of them my name, including from Odile, which struck me as odd yet sweet in a dizzying way, with my cognitive functions dulled by the rush of blood and the disorientation of it all. (Hanging upside down from a tree. Weltyr, my progenitor, so it had been with you, it was said!)

"I'm okay," I told them, doing my best to resist the vertigo caused by the momentum of my spin. "I'm doing just fine. I don't think it was cursed or meant to be fatal in any way. Not to a human being, at least. Can one of you— The Lantern—"

After only a second's delay, Branwen extended a finger up toward my waist, and a cheerful little pair of luminescent blue-violet-moss air spirits appeared along her trajectory and eased the most dangerous item on my belt down from it to Elishta.

"Is *that* a pixie?" she asked while accepting it, only to frown when the answer was, "No, it's an elemental spirit."

"Why, but they're all just spirits! Why do they call them faeries when they could just be calling them spirits?"

"Mostly racism. See, the fae are— sh!"

A branch had snapped somewhere nearby, and we stiffened. As I drew Exigence from its sheath to cut myself down, all of us fell silent, and the elvish ears were no doubt quite literally pricked for listening. Among them, Indra was the first to turn her body more completely toward the sound, and she did so saliently, for the durrow were supreme in stealth.

High elves, not quite so much. Branwen twisted, and the slight squelch of her boot barely rotating in the thick mud beneath us was all the giveaway our interloper needed.

All pretense dropped, our watcher ran so frantically that the mud squelched all the way, revealing location at the cost of increased speed.

A futile trade—especially when I landed and strode quickly after them, breaking into a sprint with the sword still in my hand, calling, "Who's there?"

Panting, gasping, frightened as any prey animal, this stranger glanced too quickly over the shoulder of his dirty, tattered gray cloak to be clearly seen by me, but he seemed old from the looks of him.

"I won't hurt you," I called after him, pausing to sheath the blade—and, in so doing, nearly losing him around the wide trunk of a tree. I grit my teeth as he ducked into an overgrown lakebed, so spry it was clear he had lived and adapted to the environment for many years. While he hurried through the shin-high waters of a narrow edge, I lost time by rounding it properly, and once I reached the side upon which he had embanked, he was gone.

In his hurry, he had left obvious tracks. Ignoring the cries of the women behind me, I drew my sword again in silence, holding on to it for safety's sake as I lowered my head beneath the vine-draped arm of a beckoning dogwood where a trail of mud and water and broken branches betrayed him. As quietly as I could, I followed in his wake.

And he nearly had his head cut off by leaping out at me with a fallen branch in his hands, swinging it at me with a cry that locked my muscles for action and caused me to swing the sword. As it snapped like a toothpick beneath Exigence, I managed to freeze my motion a fingernail's width from the bridge of the old fellow's nose.

When I noted the heavily aged and weathered resemblance to the man from my dream, and the vision in the den of the spirit-thieves—the man who, in his turn, resembled me—I gave thanks to the unknown God that I had not let the sword fall farther.

17

A LOST SOUL

AS ADRENALINE FADED into relief for both myself and the old man, I released my breath and carefully tilted Exigence back from his face.

Like a rabbit fleeing a wolf, he dashed off before I made a sound, scrambling as fast as he could—but this time, close as I was, I sheathed Exigence and closed the distance in six long strides, managing to grab hold of his cloak before a seventh was necessary. He emitted a cry of terror and struggled against my grip, his struggle increasing as my companions crashed up through the underbrush and the squelching paste of the swamp's saturated dirt. But, keeping hold of him was no issue.

I was more worried that his struggling would continue and that I would inadvertently break his collarbone or even his neck, as seeing him close revealed a frailty only compounding the shock of finding a living man this far away from civilization, in a time and place where such horror was rampant—and then, of course, there was the resemblance of his features, that familiarity that made him as frightening to me in some ways as I seemed to be to him.

"By my life and the lives of the women I love, friend, I would not hurt a man alone in the swamp."

"Let me go, damn you! By the Tekton's tomb—"

"Rorke!" Branwen was the first to clear the underbrush and skid to a halt in the cluster of shrubs where I'd gotten a grip of our interloper. Her eyes passed quickly over him before landing on me. "Are you all right?"

"Fine, Branwen. I'm more worried about our friend here. Are *you* injured?" As I released him, the old man dusted himself off and muttered something. Between his low tone and the rough texture of a voice seldom used, I couldn't quite make it out. "What was that?"

"I said *no*, blast it, I'm fine. For now, anyway. We'll see what tomorrow's dawn brings."

Taking his attitude for that of a simple curmudgeon, I asked in a patient tone long-practiced on the older men at the temple who, deaf and blind in an old age hard-won, were known to be sharp-tongued and unkind with those who reminded them of better days. "What's your name, friend?"

"Don't have one." His milky eyes of faded blue swiveled up toward the rest of the party, who arrived now and, seeing the situation, lowered or put away their weapons entirely. "One or two folk I met over the years call me the hermit."

Like a bell ringing in the distance, I scrounged up the vaguest memory of Norhalm's mention of the mysterious figure rumored to live in the countryside, miraculously surviving the skeletal threats that kept the people of Ironforge isolated in their village. "So you're real," I remarked in astonishment, looking him up and down. "Someone mentioned you to us a few days before we set out. It's incredible you choose to live out here, if you don't mind me saying so. In the marshes?"

"Nobody invited you to come here. If you find it so inhospitable, I'd recommend you leave back the direction you came."

"Would it were so simple, sir. But we have much to do. And now, seeing you—" My eyes darted over his brow, his nose, the exaggerated ears of old age, and I attempted to walk time back several decades in search of the suspected necromancer's visage as revealed to me in that dream, and the vision. "I suspect we were called here for more than one reason."

"Do all human men look alike," Odile asked, arms crossed as she flatly regarded the stranger, "or does this shriveled old raisin pass for Rorke's grandfather?"

Spitting sourly into the dirt, he snapped, "Easy for you elves to skate through life unblemished; you're practically immortal. I got nobody to impress...God knows my heart."

More curious now, I probed on. "Aren't *you* immortal, though, to survive in this place so long, and for so many generations?"

" Me, immortal! By the Tekton's bloody nails, boy, do I look like a man who's immortal?"

"Not as you are, perhaps. Where did that rumor of immortality come from, then, if you're only a mortal man?"

A look of utter disgust straining his features to emphasize lines already so deeply carved into his face that he looked like a wrinkled garment, the hermit asked, "Don't you know anything?" Then, quickly, as if answering his own question with some deeper knowledge, he lowered his head to mutter, "Of course not. Why would he tell you anything?"

"He?"

"*You* know who I mean. Don't act like you're ignorant of that much, anyway."

Elishta, looking as confused as the rest of us, peered at me intently. "Who does he mean, Rorke?"

"The necromancer, I think," was my quick answer, delivered as rapidly as I could to avoid much theorizing from the others. Returning my attention to the man, I asked, "But, friend, why would that man tell either one of us anything?"

"Don't pretend to be an idiot with me." With a glower so intense it could have melted stone, the old man regarded me ruefully, then twisted himself away. "By the looks of you, you could pass for one with the average man, but you can't fool me. I know my own mind and his too well. You're just as sharp as either of us, I'm sure of it."

"I'll try to hold on to your praise, my friend, for whatever it's worth…but you ought to know I *am* ignorant of these matters. How is it a man like you comes to live out here on his own, apparently an associate of the necromancer terrorizing this countryside? Forgive me—you just don't seem like the sorcerer type, nor the type to fraternize with sorcerers."

"It's more complicated than that." His tone remained sharp, but his expression softened as he regarded me. "I guess you really *don't* know, do you?"

Above us, the gray sky was darkening heavily, and the lighting made its radical shift toward night everywhere around us. "I don't," I confessed with as much true humility as I could muster, "but anything you could tell us would be greatly appreciated. And—well. We ought not to impose, and I'm sure your dwelling out here in the marshes is made for necessity and not luxury, but... would you perhaps be willing to put us up for the night, if you've room?"

"If I've room! Fancy that—chasing me with a sword and asking if I've room. Hardly much of a question...I imagine, if I tell you 'no', you'll just follow me home anyway. Come along, then...some nerve..."

It's not often that one finds oneself the subject of charity with a spiteful edge to it, and I can't say I particularly enjoyed the experience—but I was grateful for his willingness to relent, and I hoped that showed in my face as I said, truly, "Thank you."

"We'll see how grateful you are later...come along, then. Mind your steps...it's about to be dastardly dark."

Elishta, hearing this, extended Hamsunt's Lantern to me. I took it, opening its flame with the twist of its knob. While the red tongues leapt and shimmered, our unwilling guide turned right just past the nearest willow and led us on into the sulphurous bog. Our party exchanged the looks of people trying to determine whether they were being led to their deaths. Taking advantage of his distance some yards ahead of us, Odile leaned up to ask, "Is this wise? He seems cracked."

"I'm sure he's just forgotten social graces, living out here for what must be a long time if he's being mistaken as immortal...let's give him the benefit of the doubt. I'm sure it isn't as if he could pose all that much of a threat to us."

"Maybe not, but...well—I suppose I would be more assured of that notion if he didn't look so much like you. And what is all this about the necromancer? He acts like you know him."

That, I couldn't explain. "All I can say for certain is that I have *dreamed* of the necromancer, I think; and so perhaps he has, too, or something of that regard...let's get the truth from him gently, if we can. He seems sensitive to interrogation."

"Most people with something to hide tend to be that way."

As true as that was—and as well as I sensed that the old man *did* have something to hide, *was* actually dangerous inasmuch as he was connected with the figure we sought—I couldn't help but feel a certain pity for the fellow. No man chose to be so unpleasant. It was a quality molded into one's soul by circumstance, and no doubt whatever circumstances caused him to live his life were more than sufficient to develop him to this cantankerous state. I committed myself, therefore, to patience and compassion as much as was possible, and I told Odile, "Most of what he has to hide is surely not our business. Let's do our best to treat him with dignity, and perhaps he'll warm to us when he believes we wish him no ill will, whatever his story is."

On we marched, following the man for another thirty minutes or more. I lost track of time, becoming more focused on how dark it had grown outside the ring of Hamsunt's Lantern. Elishta and Branwen stayed close to me, taking comfort and visual advantage of the light it cast while Odile, Indra, and Brynhildr took up the rear, needing illumination less than we. Just as the ground beneath us grew more stable—still soft and yielding, but certainly a better foundation on which to stand than the thick muds of the past several days—Elishta, as she had periodically throughout this walk, raised the beaker before her face and showed me the determined spider.

"Look, Rorke." She showed me the bottle, raising it toward my eyes for my assessment. "He's leading us the same way the spider is trying to go."

"Here we are," called the man before I could become fully cognizant of the strange, almost defeated feeling this discovery gave me. "Watch your step inside. Don't be tracking mud everywhere...I've a hard enough time keeping things clean as it is."

When we passed under the arms of a pair of trees looming at what seemed the edge of a clearing only partially manmade, the home that stood in relief against the dark shadows of night seemed strangely shaped even without filtered sunlight to draw it more clearly for me. A fire glowed in the hearth within—I could tell not just from the smell of smoke from a chimney but from the broad bank of windows that stretched eerily from one side to the other, wrapping around a circular hut aglow with that light and several other lamps I took to be electric. This was quite surprising given that the town of Ironforge had shown limited electrical infrastructure for a town of dwarves. Here, I saw no infrastructure at all, being as we were in the middle of the wilderness; but, raising the lantern, I could make out the appears of panels tipped upward, and I found myself recalling illustrations I had once seen of the many ways the protomen kept their homes attended with the kinds of comforts we could only dream of, busy as we were squabbling among the mankinds and filling the technological gap with magic. This house (for, while I call it a 'hut' due to its shape, it was really quite large in circumference, and I could see through the window a ramp that descended down a passageway in the floor, implying a basement or cellar of some sort) intrigued me, then, beyond even the identity and nature of its owner, and became all the more intriguing as we passed into it to discover the facade was some kind of metal.

"A fine home you have here, my friend," I told him, surrendering to his demand and scraping my boots carefully on the metallic platform serving as a porch. "Did you build it yourself?"

"How is a man like me supposed to build something like this? No; I found it like this when I was put here."

"Put here," I repeated, as Elishta stepped in with a sigh of relief to be under a roof and to smell the slowly simmering stew, which made her murmur, "That smells good."

"Yes, *put* here." Agitated to have to repeat himself and showing no signs of elaboration, the fellow stripped his cloak from his shoulders to reveal the dark fabric of his tunic. Like the cloak, it had been patched many times, but was now so frayed it looked as if it could bear no further patching without dissolving into a few sad pieces of dust. After draping his outer garment across the back of a wooden chair that *did*, I was certain, bear the hallmarks of being handcrafted, the old man hurried to his fire, snatched up a poker, and shuffled the burning logs within to agitate it back to life. "I've made the best of it now, but I wasn't put here by choice any more than my predecessors."

"And who were they?"

"Dead men," he replied vaguely, setting down the poker, rubbing his hands together, and assessing the contents of the pot. "Was hoping to have this for a few days, but I suppose you'll want food."

"Don't let us put you out, good man," I began, but Elishta, shameless and hopeful and driven by the initial cravings of pregnancy, clasped her hands to turn her hopeful eyes upon him.

"Would it be great trouble, sir? Just a bit."

"Don't know if I have bowls enough," he grunted, his tone less harsh when presented with Elishta's tender nature. "I'm not accustomed to guests."

"We've bottles," suggested Elishta, indicating the flask on her belt and beginning, "perhaps, with a funnel—"

"Hey!" His attention had been drawn by her gesture, and his blurry eyes, focusing in after a second, soon widened, aghast. Hurrying over as much as he *could* hurry, the hermit extended spindly fingers, his palm open. "That there's my responsibility—give it to me or let it go, now! It's trying to get home, can't you see?"

"O-oh, yes," stammered Elishta, her slight fright at the old man's fast movements giving way to some embarrassment as she unhooked the flask and passed it over for him to uncork. "Well, that's *why* we, um—you see—"

Her thought faded from her lips, however. With two of what appeared to be only several remaining teeth, the old man bit down on the tip of the cork and jerked it from the flask, then turned the glass upside down to shake the spider into his hand. It bounced only once, rotating its small body upright upon his palm; then, it leapt down to the floor, and it rushed off in the direction of that basement ramp down which it disappeared.

"Just what *are* those things?" Odile deigned to ask, her arms folded in such a way that it seemed she resented her own curiosity. "Not real insects, right?"

"Look real enough to me." The old man studied the now empty flask with a look of displeasure before making his way back to the stew. "Too narrow for any of the best bits and bobs, but it can take broth..."

While he used a pair of fire tongs to grasp the neck of the bottle, Odile looked all the more annoyed to have been brushed off. "Well—they're real in that they *exist*, obviously. But—I mean, they're not actual insects. Right?"

"They're made of metals, if that's what you're asking. Don't bother trying to learn *how* they're made; that, I couldn't tell you any more than I know how I myself was made."

With a laugh of derision, Odile teased, "Come now, old man! Surely, even if you haven't seen a woman in many years, you still know the general method."

"I wasn't born of woman. Wasn't born at all. Here." Thrusting to Elishta the flask into which he had poured a few ladlefuls of broth, the old man then caught up his nearby wooden bowl from its place upon the hearth and filled it less ceremoniously. The excess slopped out of the rim of the bowl, down his hand and back into the cauldron—making the decision for the rest of us as to whether we would partake. "Help yourselves, if you'd like," he said with a grunt, tossing the ladle back onto its hook beside the rest of the fire tools and cooking implements. While we politely declined and I took to looking around the fellow's house (more books than I would have anticipated, certainly, for though he seemed sharp enough he also seemed quite understandably more focused on survival than elucidation), Odile went on fighting uphill.

"How is it you were born, though, if not of woman?"

With a sour sort of laugh, the man looked over at me and shoveled a spoonful of stew into his mouth. "One of the most unnatural ones here wants to know how I was created even when I just told her I couldn't explain it. Wants to know why something walking around is real if it isn't natural! Think you're natural, do you?"

"I've flesh, don't I? I breathe and eat and sleep."

"And so do all my little friends. That one went down to rest awhile with the remainder you sent. Only real difference is that, for them, sleeping and eating are one and the same. A few hours of electricity, that's all they need. Then they'll be right as rain, ready to work for years if the system determines they're still new enough. Efficient little fellows, and they don't complain."

"But what is their *work*?" Looking all the more baffled, Odile studied the ramp down to the cellar. I, meanwhile, drew toward a small nook against a nearby window, where there sat a short table ornamented with interesting artifacts. As I approached to see them more closely, having been drawn by an illustration of a woman in a blue headdress that reminded me of Elishta's cloak, the hermit shrugged and gestured with his spoon.

"Their work is to do whatever the old man tells them to do, just like me."

"Awfully evasive, aren't you?"

"Forgive me," the hermit said with clear disdain, drawing my attention away from the beaded cord draped along the table's edge, "if I'm not leaping for joy to meet with my executioners."

"Executioners!" Odile laughed, her mocking tone barely even drawing the man's eyes from his bowl. "What makes you think we're here to kill you, exactly?"

"My little friends down there have been reporting on you for days now. You've sent hundreds of them back home. You mean to tell me you're going to stop here, now, just because you met me?"

Her interest growing, Branwen joined the conversation. "They've been reporting on us? Do you mean they talk?"

"Have they got mouths? Of course they don't *talk*. There's more means of reporting than speech."

"Telepathy?" My offering of this question drew a few looks from the women, but the hermit didn't bat an eye.

"Nothing like that. Well—not in the way we think of it. Where is it, now—here—" Muttering to himself and looking all around his person as he did, the old man slipped from the pocket of his tunic a small bar of what looked to be gray metal, which he manipulated with the touch of a thumb in the manner of one long-acquainted with a specific sword or pistol. Indeed, while he did this with one hand, with the other he slurped down the contents of his bowl, shoveling his spoon to his mouth and raising an eye toward the windows as the cabin lights turned low. In concord with this dimming a curious transformation overtook the windows around us, which seemed to dull. Soon I recognized they were increasing in opacity, and as they took on the manner of cream-colored parchment marked in a sequence of glyphs, the hermit manipulated his strangely shaped wand with a few more taps of his thumb. One of the glyphs expanded; as this faded out, it left behind a truly miraculous sight: a series of smaller windows appeared, chained in long rows and marked by numbers, and I could tell right away that these smaller portholes didn't look out upon the swamp around us but instead into some other place. It was Elishta who guessed it, marveling, "Do these windows allow you to look through the eyes of the spiders, sir?"

"The smart one, are you...that they do. And"—a tap or two more, and suddenly the windows were replaced by a single image—"they're not limited to the present."

As he tapped again, the image—which appeared to depict a metal plane with nothing of interest at all upon a surface that stretched off toward a darker background— remained for another several seconds. Long seconds, in which he explained, "This is one who came back yesterday, so there's a little bit of backtracking to—aha..."

Suddenly the image shifted as though it were alive, and I was astonished to witness the viewpoint perspective slowly turn. In this redirection, scores of metal spiders aligned along the unknown surface were revealed to us, their bodies and the place where they stood illuminated by the long blue shelf against which they had backed. It glowed softly, casting them in a mysterious, almost sickly luminescence that ebbed and glowed and ebbed again. As our viewpoint backed away from them, one could even detect that the previously red light on their bellies glowed a new pinpoint of the same blue light. There wasn't much time to ponder this, though: instead, we continued drawing back, back and back, the spiders tremendous as we passed them, each one swelling into the left frame and shrinking down to adequately harmless scale with some more distance. Soon, we were reclining down some kind of ramp, and then up another; and now, by a miracle, I recognized the square leg of a certain table not far from the hermit's basement entrance.

"Why," remarked Elishta, "this is *this* place—" Looking quite charmed, she asked, "Is this its memory of its journey home? One of the spiders, I mean."

"So it is," he said, nodding, "and memories for six months back, at least." As this backward journey unfurled, the hermit nursed his soup. "A few of 'em went down entirely...they're so small, you might have crushed them with your boots or weapons without even knowing it."

"And what is their purpose," I asked, "aside from the obvious utility of their memories?"

As our viewpoint spider retraced its path through the marshlands, the hermit said with an exasperated sigh, "It's the man up there who knows that, my maker— Malchi-sedeq, he calls himself."

"What a strange name," I remarked, truly struck by it yet feeling as though I had heard it in some dream. "What race of mankinds is it from?"

"None of this era; not even for the long-lived women here. He's ancient. *Truly* immortal."

"I've heard he's a dirge."

At my comment, the old man scoffed. "Superstition. What's the difference between a man and a dirge if the man lives long enough? The amount of rotting away that's visible, and the sound of his heartbeat."

Regarding the fellow for a long moment until the resemblance became unbearable to me, I observed, "I suppose it must be true; for you yourself do not seem dead or undead, but living, and it is not in the nature of the undead to generate life."

"Such as it is," he agreed, thrusting his spoon at the images dancing on the windows. "See there?"

I saw: I saw our viewpoint wafting up, floating almost, up a series of white-gray-brown mottled pathways my mind parsed as bones. Easier to parse, beyond that, was Elishta's body, her figure towering and the tip of her rapier arcing forward into the skull which became our new viewpoint, and whence we watched the skeleton stumble haltingly back from her. The effect was disorienting, and I grew nauseous. Thankfully, he manipulated the wand again, and the image froze, then disappeared altogether and was once more replaced with a sequence of glyphs arranged upon the blank, parchment-like windows.

"So," he said impassively, "I've been aware of you for days."

"And why didn't you make some move to stop me sooner?"

"Because if the spiders know you're here, he certainly knows you're here. And, knowing you're here, he hasn't given me any orders to stop you, or done anything to intervene in the situation himself. So." Shrugging, the old fellow raised his bowl to his lips and emptied its contents with one final slurp, which he wiped from his lips and beard with the back of one dirty hand. "If that's true, he must have other plans in mind."

Indeed, I was sure that was the case. It was objectively alarming that these little spiders, whatever they were, provided a degree of telepathic insight accessible even to those who had nothing at all to do with the network of the spirit-thieves; and this, then, led me to question whether the man was part of the community of telepaths. "I wonder, my friend—would you happen to be familiar with the spirit-thieves? The, uh—"

As I gestured to indicate—wiggling my fingers before my mouth the way their tentacles hung from their faces—the hermit snorted and once more tapped the wand. The parchment aesthetic faded into transparent glass to show the night around us. "Not for some seasons now. They come around now and again with another batch of insects."

"And you never see Malchi-sedeq?"

"Not since I was a lad and brought here for the first time."

"A lad!" Quite shocked, I asked, "How many summers?"

"My first summer that I can recall."

"And the skeletons didn't pose you any problem?"

With a look like I was tragically stupid—an expression equal parts impatience and pity—the hermit asked, "What reason would they have to turn against me?"

More baffled, and more afraid, with every moment that passed in that old man's hut, I did my best to assemble all of this into a deeper meaning. I did not like the picture I was beginning to see. Before I could inquire further—a dangerous prospect, given his temperament and the late hour—Indra had evidently taken note of the same altar that had struck me, for her voice called out from near that little table. "What goddess is this? Not Anroa, is she?"

Our host became greatly animated, springing upright from his seat with a combination of excitement and insistence. "The Mother isn't some idol like Anroa! I've read about that one, though—she's one of the middle ones, not a good angel like you never see these days or the demons you see all the time. She's one of the ones who want to ignore the Tekton and live it up. Don't tell me you haven't seen her before."

Branwen, who was a devotee of Anroa, looked a little stiff; yet her devotion was casual, and Anroa's cult was not typically known for its formalities or its dedication. "There are many different cultural depictions of Anroa," she explained politely, glancing toward the little arrangement of objects. This only riled the man up. He scoffed in disgust, hobbling to the edge of the room to catch hold of a curtain he dragged along the perimeter.

"Neither the Tekton nor His family have anything to do with your idol."

"I don't think that's Anroa," I agreed, not normally one to argue overmuch with Branwen but compelled to act as a witness. "When Valeria, Elishta and I were in the Valor Hall—well—" I hesitated, studying the imagery, comparing this woman's covered head to the resplendent heights of Anroa's immaculately arranged coiffure. "This woman seems mild by comparison. If she is a goddess, she must be one of the hearth, or—"

"No, no," insisted the hermit, adding, "I tell you, there's no such thing as goddesses or gods. Not aside from the One true God, the Maker of heaven and earth."

"All the gods have some role to play in creation, it's said." These words passed my lips even as Elishta and I shared a curious look, the both of us no doubt reflecting on the conversation we'd had but a few days prior. "Anroa taught women cosmetics, Dunnun gave men the arts of metalsmithing, Weltyr brought law and warfare, and created—well." Here I hesitated, and finally settled on explaining that, "I have heard it said he created the mankinds, but that is a more complex matter altogether than I once thought."

"No, man, simpler! Thieves, the lot of them—stealing credit for God's creation while at the same time corrupting it for their pleasure, amusing themselves among the peoples of Urde while setting themselves up to be worshipped and served by a bunch of fools who don't know better." For some reason I waited for him to exclude present company, but this man—the most isolated human being I had ever heard of, let alone met—was far beyond such social niceties. "Someday, the Tekton will come in glory and redeem the world. I can't imagine why He would bother, though...this world's beyond saving. You can tell because of the spirit-thieves walking up and down upon it."

Amid all of this, Brynhildr had been so silent that I had to occasionally glance over to make sure she was still there. Now she spoke up, her eyes shining in a deeply curious way. She had either been straining against tears or silently crying while we were in that cottage. I grew afraid.

"There is no world beyond saving," she chided him.

"Where exactly did you learn of this 'Tekton' epithet for the God of Heaven and Urde, friend?" Elishta asked this while running her fingers along the string of beads, her thoughtful eyes low-lidded as they fixed upon it.

"It's not an epithet! It was His profession. I learned about him the same way I learn about everything else. The books they bring me sometimes. It's lonely out here—drives you crazy sometimes—and books help you come to terms with the reality that you'll never leave."

"Never?" exclaimed Branwen and Elishta, leading the man to shrug.

"Don't see how I could, or why I would. Got everything I need here." He gestured at one of several bookshelves that followed the curves of walls not covered by windows. "Those books of Malchi-sedeq's lasted me a long time, and sometimes they send down more, like I said. Rare stuff, old stuff, wild adventures and such about how the world was back before the spirit-thieves came; but sometimes I maybe get the idea that they aren't all true, like some of them may have been made up, since I don't think they had things like flying citadels before the spirit-thieves. Some of 'em are about fellows riding around on horseback and shooting each other—those are great."

While I was glad to see him loosening up just a little, I couldn't bite my tongue any longer. "But, my friend—surely you know those who are caring for your needs are wicked demons from beyond the stars. I can hear how you despise them. Why do you persist in serving them?"

"What'd I just say to you? I couldn't leave this place—certainly not now. Before, when I was young, maybe I could have stood a chance, but—"

He fell silent, and the ornery expression was exchanged for a deep, distant look of great sorrow; an old wound of grief he wasn't expecting to remain so sensitive to the touch.

"I suppose I had some misplaced dreams. Going back to the citadel if I worked hard enough for Malchi-sedeq, or being given a wife. That sort of thing. By the time I realized none of that was going to happen, I was nearly forty, and I thought a lot about trying to go off on my own, but I didn't. None of them have before me, neither."

I exchanged a glance with Elishta, who seemed as pained to hear such a thing. "And you haven't seen him since you left the *Shooting Star*? Uh, that is, the flying citadel?"

"No, I have not. Probably expects me to hate him, and I guess I do; but the Tekton says you should pray for your enemies, and, any rate, it's Malchi-sedeq seeing to my needs through the spirit-thieves, and it's him who gave me life so I get to know the Tekton, so I've made my peace with it."

All but grinding my teeth, I pressed him. "Surely you understand that the spirit-thieves' entire reason for being, not to mention their religious customs, are centered around the wholesale destruction of all intelligent life on a given planet. Are you aware that they're abducting the people of the nearby dwarvish town and conducting experiments on them, or not returning them at all?"

"And what am I supposed to do about it, eh? There's nothing *to* do about it. One spirit-thief would be hard enough for a person to kill, but a brood of them stationed in a flying citadel along with Malchi-sedeq? That's not a task for me."

"No," I agreed. "It's a task for me."

After a second's delay, the old man's eyes swiveled toward me, his lips opening and closing in a fishlike stammer. "W-what do you mean?"

"What I mean is that you're a prisoner just as much as the woman we're trying to save, Valeria, who has been taken aboard the *Shooting Star* and is up there now, subject to who knows what experiments. What I mean is we're going to free you, and her, and anyone else we find up there who's been abducted as subjects for the spirit-thieves' experiments and for the production of Malchi-sedeq's skeletal servants. And I need your help."

"Me!"

"Your insights on *Shooting Star* or the spirit-thieves—any information at all, any patterns you've noticed about the arrival of the citadel, for instance—would be invaluable to me and would help us in eradicating them in this part of Urde."

For all our trials, I was still so naive. I had expected the man would breathe a sigh of relief; that his face would flicker with some sign of brightness or joy; that he might burst into tears, thanking me for bringing an end to a lifetime of isolation and confinement in the service of demons who wanted nothing from him but continued servitude.

Yet, to my surprise, he balked.

"You can't *do* that!"

"It may be difficult, but trust me when I say—"

"That's not what I mean!" With a growing expression of panic tightening his features into a horrified mask, the old man rushed forward and grabbed hold of my tunic. I didn't stop him because he seemed so weak. In that same egotistical naivete that had made me expect he would see me as a hero, I had already written off this fellow as any kind of threat. Instead I looked at him with pity as he emphasized, "Can't you see what will happen? This outpost has been here for generations! Me, my predecessors, the one meant to replace me—we're all totally dependent on Malchi-sedeq and the spirit-thieves! How will anyone look after the place when there's no regular supplies being brought? No new books? No repair parts when the resting station breaks down? The spiders will be decommissioned! And where will I go then? You think I can survive in the world?"

This poor fellow. He'd never had the least chance in life, and now, yes, I could see it *was* too late for him. One could pass him platitudes about there being hope wherever life was found, or assure him that we were never too old to change, or even offend his dignity by offering him some form of charitable bribe—which, frankly, we did not have the means for after most of our financial resources had been claimed by the captain of the *Rhinemaid*. We were going to dismantle this poor fellow's whole life in the name of rescuing Valeria and my child, and I had revealed this to him expecting him to be grateful.

But how could I possibly have chosen him over my family?

"I know it's a frightful notion, friend," I told him as gently as I could. "The One True God above all other gods, whatever His Name may be, knows how intimidating it was for me to leave the Temple of Weltyr and embark on a journey that has now gone so far afield I suspect I will never see that place again. You will be a wanderer like me.

Your life will change, and you will mark the end of your tradition, for you are right to say you cannot stay here without support. At least not from what I have seen. But, friend—"

Hesitating, not wanting to speak false promises while at the same time wishing to soothe the look of almost childlike fright blazing from his milky eyes and deeply furrowed brow, I assured him, "The human body is not a permanent vessel. No matter where it happens, at some point, a man's life must end. When it does, oughtn't it to be someplace sublime? Someplace good and beautiful, and not a swamp? Perhaps, when all this is done, my friends and I could take you with us. You could see what's beyond these foul-smelling marshes; could come with us to the heath, and enter into civilization. Surely, for all we're doing on behalf of Ironforge, they would give you a home if we asked it of them. Or, if that is not tolerable to you, we might take you to the nearest port and buy you passage on an airship for someplace, anyplace. A desert; an island. A place sweeter than this one, where a man can rest his bones and fill his eyes and ears and soul with sublimity while he waits to be carried away from this temporary exile called Urde." As I offered all this, his hands had loosened their grip of my tunic, and I foolishly hoped, seeing the glimmer of tears in his shocked eyes, that he was being won over. Gently as one touching a spring lamb, I raised my hand to his shoulder.

"We came here to rescue my beloved Valeria," I told him, "but, if you'll only let us, we can rescue you, too."

The seconds seemed to stretch into infinity. Everyone in the room held their breath except Brynhildr, who had covered her face with her hand, bodily trembling with tears that were less well restrained than before. In that interim, the hermit searched my face, gauging my seriousness, then glanced toward the door of his hut in a way that revealed all the fears of his heart: the fears to leave the only place he had ever known.

The fears that made him, with shocking speed, jerk Exigence from its sheath at my side and plunge its blade between my ribs before I could even process what was happening.

18

AD ASTRA

AS THE BLOOD pumped out of me by the heartbeat, I swayed, overcome by the heaviness of my eyes. Gravity forced me to my knees, and I braced myself against the edge of the hermit's old table. Only vaguely was I aware of one of the women (Branwen, I would come to find) bringing about an end to the man in one sure stroke. The clatter of Exigence to the floor. The pain of my joints which had taken the brunt of my fall.

Yet my mind flowed into the sounds of the voices around me, and I spent a great deal of concentration on the blossoming and expanding and transforming and burning of shapes in my soul. I can explain it no other way. Resplendent imagery rotated through my mind—

images I now recollect when I read the descriptions of quasars and other galactic phenomena said, according to my father's books, to inhabit outer space—and as I felt myself emptying out, the alien intelligence of the hivemind pressed in. Indeed, I saw it clearer than ever I had: the awful worm-like protuberances lining the slimy beak of red flesh that opened and shut, perhaps for air or some sort of internal venting system; the algae that coated the edges of the cranium, its pondlike water filthy as the hatred of this alien menace for the mankinds, or all life, perhaps, except for its own; every tiny capillary bursting red in a web along the odious yellowed ocular substance of its rotating eye.

It took you long enough to figure it out, the demon said with disgust as—in the strange sensation of one sliding upon ice past another skater, or a child rocketing through one slide as someone known to him is halfway down another, paths crossing for a flash, then gone—I was in Norhalm's head, regretting the windows ruined by that flying horse and wondering where the money was going to come from. Then I was in Shemrin. Then Phildrin. Where once there was me, something else stepped into this place, and I felt tremendously, frightfully alone. Meaningless. This is hard to explain, so I will do my best: but, to sum it up, this experience was the polar opposite of the experience of rising to the Valor Hall. That had been an exaltation of Rorke Burningsoul, the man who I was, an experience of being me that was eternal and peaceful and good, as it had been intended, always, with life in its original, holy shape.

Yet now there was a darker, eviler side to it all. There was a possibility which was not that—not the exaltation but the complete annihilation of Rorke Burningsoul. I who had not existed before would resume nonexistence from the standpoint of the world. The exaltation was only objective to a limited extent; the majority of it was experienced subjectively, by me. This annihilation, on the contrary, was not something that left room for subjectivity, and was all entirely objective. The objective overriding the subjective, completely crushing it into a meaningless ash that would be scattered and forgotten like all memory of me, of Valeria and Elishta and Branwen and Indra and Odile. And Brynhildr. Everyone would be swept away if nothing changed, and I gained a frightful perspective on the nature of that sweeping. Of fiery warfare, and all society in ruins. Of the sudden awareness of a recursive quality, an eternal quality, from which I had failed to break out before this taste of destruction.

From which no one could break out, indeed, without the help of God.

Yet, in that emptiness, that darkness, that complete objectivity of the hivemind and its attached individuals, God could not be seen. He was obfuscated. Mishandled. He was reduced to a merely nice concept, and so I was forced in that annihilation to endure for the first time the total absence of God, the total hopelessness, the absolute despair to think that this was forever, this moment, and it would mean nothing. I was really Nothing. A great and awful noise of dark vibration filled the air, encompassing all existence, filling the empty space of the nothingness.

And then, as if condensed from this sound, a beautiful angel leaned down before me, and the dissolving phantasmagoria of the altered world around seemed red as flame, and sweet. I had a new sensation as of one being born a second time. Something warm pressed against my chest, drawing me out of relief and out of that void I seemed to have been in an interminable time. The certainty of an unholy, untimely death that ended in failure and wasted life walked back from me, repelled by this miracle.

By this deed of Brynhildr, who had striven so long to avoid interference, and who had now defied utterly the calling of her station not just in the Valor Hall but now, also, on Urde.

As my consciousness attempted to grasp its way back to myself, to the physicality of my body and the possibility of our continued mission—of Valeria's rescue, yes, man, get up!—along with the sustained reality of that looming sound, Brynhildr emitted a sigh of relief that was echoed by the watching women.

"Are you awake now? Good." Patting my cheek with her hand wet from the blood leaking out of my chest and across my tunic, Brynhildr looked at me with motherly tenderness. "You need to get up. They're coming for me, and we haven't much time to get you aboard the citadel, anyway. Let's hurry."

Barely able to comprehend her words, I permitted her to slip an arm beneath my shoulder and prop me up. My mind made some sense of the groaning, this unnatural sound that seemed like a part of the dream that had spilled out into waking. "Is *Shooting Star* here?"

"It's rushing away, friend, but we can catch it—hurry!"

Clenching my teeth, I stood uneasily and stumbled toward the door, nearly tripping as I hastened forward. I looked down to see the obstacle that had caught me.

The hermit lay dead at my feet, his own pool of blood spreading slowly around him.

Somehow unable to process this at the time, busy as I was putting together my own existence, I turned to address the other women.

"If I'm not back within a week, return to Ironforge and ask them for passage back across the sea."

"Rorke," protested Elishta, stepping toward me. "Let me come with you—there's room on Brynhildr's horse."

"No—Elishta. Please." With a glance down at her stomach, I grasped her biceps to hold her close. "If I'm lost up there, it means Valeria and Gundrygia, too, will be lost. It will mean you're all I have to survive me: you, and that baby you carry." While the other women exchanged looks of surprise—and Branwen adopted an expression of understanding deeper than any shock—I urged her, "Stay. I don't want anything to happen to you."

"I'm stronger than you think," Elishta told me seriously, earning my hesitation at the door of the hut while Brynhildr leapt upon the back of her horse and shouted, "Let's go, Rorke! We're losing time!"

Delirium overwhelmed me. The truth was anyone could have told me anything in that moment and I would have accepted it as not just true, but natural to the point of basic assumption, as one assumes air is breathable or water wet. I felt as if my spine had been recently severed and now reattached to its missing half in such a way that my head remained unsteady upon its pedestal and wobbled this way, that way. Slipping her strong arm under both of mine, her bicep looped around my back, Brynhildr ushered me from the cabin and into the thick air of the bog. The trees at the edge of this clearing where we stood (where the hermit lived, I suddenly remembered, the context of our situation eternally slipping in and out of my reach) were bathed in white light. Was it day? No; no, that didn't seem right.

Uneasily, I looked up.

Even though the resonance of *Shooting Star* pushed against my consciousness in such a manner that I knew it without truly knowing it, I still struggled to recognize it, for I had never seen a flying citadel up close. The Valor Hall was of similar conception, but it had been brilliant, gleaming—as fine as a gem, twirling in space. This design was a different assemblage, a product of dark metals that took on the appearance of a grimy city viewed from an airship, where one could see buildings and roadways neglected by the populace and mired in pollution. This possessed similar divots and protrusions, though I could not place their purpose. The light flooding the area around us was sickly and white, unnatural and unholy as Malchi-sedeq's skeletons. And the hum: the unbearable, hateful grinding of an explosion in slow motion as the citadel hovered above us, a sound so despicable that the elves who stepped out quickly retreated back into the hut. Poor things—poor Valeria, taken aboard this hateful construction!

Valeria.

"We must find her," I told Brynhildr as she more or less shoved me up onto Grane's back, half-flopping me over his mane so she could mount behind me and help me upright. "We must help Valeria, Brynhildr—"

"We will." Her voice was so serious, so earnest, that I was taken aback and at the same time comforted. Like a child settled by a stern yet loving parent in a time of crisis, I fell silent as she lowered the visor of her helmet and told me, "You must save your strength, Rorke."

"Did he— did you—"

Before I could even sort out an understanding of what exactly happened, an altogether more alarming noise rang out through the trees, through the roar, through the voice of my Selectrix consoling me and the voice of Elishta arguing that she should be taken with us.

"Hojotoho! Hojotoho! Heiaha, Heiaha!"

Elishta recognized it as well as I, and her body turned in the direction, angling toward the trees away from which Brynhildr steered Grane.

"My sisters are here," Brynhildr explained. "They are coming for me now—for what I have done, this final taboo I have violated. I have returned a man from the death that is not eternal life but utter destruction, and the penalty will be like death, or worse."

Even in my disorientation, I was shocked, yet the full reality of the circumstances was prevented from reaching me. I still had so many unanswered questions. Why had that man looked like me and been able to draw Exigence? Why had *Shooting Star* appeared?

Why was that massive citadel above our heads getting smaller?

As the lights snapped off to plunge us into a newer, thicker darkness, I cried out, "It's leaving!"

"So are we—Grane, ho!"

With a dig of her feet, Brynhildr sent the horse thundering up into the air so fast I fell back against her, my unsteady neck aching with the force and my ears deaf to the cry of Elishta. Deaf, indeed, to all but the yawn of the citadel and the cry of the Selectrix who burst from the ancient trees upon the back of a golden mare, her battle axe swinging forward and enabled by the momentum of her horse until that second Brynhildr's spear made contact, not just stopping the axe in its tracks but forcing it back and away from us with such effortlessness that I could easily see why Brynhildr was Weltyr's favorite among his warrior-daughters.

"Lay down your arms and surrender," cried the first interloper as a second took aim, plunging in a great arc through the sky toward us and missing the chance to lance us with her spear thanks only to Grane's swift evasion.

"It will go better with you if you would but show remorse," this second shouted. A third appeared, riding toward us upon her sorrel steed, and more voices echoed that musical war-cry from off in the distance. My heart sank to know how truly surrounded we were. Yet onward Brynhildr urged her horse, riding him up into the heavens so quickly we were actually overtaking the citadel, on her lips a laugh so merry one might have thought it all a form of play.

"Our father has no love of weakness, sisters! Contrition will only stoke his ire—Hojotoho, Hojotoho!"

Grane whinnied, foam flecking from his lips as his legs pumped savagely through the air. On either side, the riders fell into close pursuit and Brynhildr fended them off, the force of her parries unbalancing the horses and making it look almost as if they stumbled up through that same air in which Brynhildr's black steed galloped. Even so, the Selectrices were worth their station: an arrow shot past our heads and we both cried out, the whistle ringing through my ear and mingling into the surprised cry of that same Selectrix when leaping flames from an unseen source forced her evasion and regrouping. I looked down—a nauseating experience—and saw, with a lurch of panic, Elishta in slower pursuit, her magical flight of no compare to that of the horses and her body a lagging speck behind the battle-angels. Groaning, I tried to call out to Elishta, but I knew she could not hear me over the distance, and my voice was locked in my throat as I looked up to see how swiftly we approached *Shooting Star*. The citadel had not gathered the momentum to escape us, and at this rate, we were going to smash into it within the next two minutes of flight. My mind raced. How would we board the blasted thing once we actually reached it?

Yet, as if in living answer, a new pinpoint of light appeared to my eyes upon the structure of the citadel. Unsteady, dizzy, I focused as best I could upon it, my mind making no sense of this strange illumination. Only as we drew closer did I realize it was an opening: a door, a porthole, an orifice toward which Grane naturally oriented himself in the thick of it all. I clenched my teeth, gripping the mane of the horse and lowering myself against it, needing to trust the beast now more than ever. The entry was small by comparison, and we were rushing so fast that one wrong move, one slightly off angle, and we would have been utterly crushed against the surface of the citadel—

Yet the stallion was too expert for that.

With a great whinny of victory, Grane rushed into the opening of the ship and into the blinding light.

And light gave way to vision: to an ocean of flowers toward which we rode, no longer oriented up but down, careening to the earth where we landed. The dizzying heights revealed, without direction, an extraordinary environment punctuated by a high black tower jutting up from the center of it all—the pole of a landscape I sensed both did and did not exist. Belatedly, I recognized by its ocean of flowers that place Gundrygia had taken me, where our child had been conceived and where she had polluted my mind with secrets too vast for me to remember.

Where Weltyr awaited us now, as he had awaited me so long ago outside of Soot.

Despite Grane's speed, I first recognized his eyepatch, then the shattered remains of his great spear that he now held in his elbow, this symbol of his power hewn from the World Tree now relegated to a walking stick. Sickness settled over me, a sort of sad nausea pushing the bile up to the top of my stomach as we circled past him once, twice, Grane burning off his speed through a rapid, wide spiral touring an uncanny landscape: wilds of foliage unbroken in all directions, with what I thought could be perhaps a mountain range far to the north but which, upon prolonged study, revealed itself to be a shimmering aurora coronating the edge of the world—if indeed such a dimensional space could be called a world at all. It was massive in comparison to even the vast external size of the citadel within which it unfurled, expanding miles in all directions: no agriculture or animals; no rivers or seas; no variance at all, as if the entire place consisted of only one definable biome.

This made withered old Weltyr stand out all the more in his frayed gray cloak. Even his hair, which had but erred toward white before, was now as snowy and brittle-looking as the rest of him, even thinned to permit a glimpse of his dotted scalp and further the overall invocation of those same skeletons we had been steadily cutting down for days. I clutched my chest as if to grip my soul within me, seeing truly what I had done and feeling as if I had lost incalculably much—while at the same time freeing myself from a pursuit that could never have maximized my holiness in either this life or the next. Perhaps my holiness was even inhibited.

Still, though, even all this time later, you can surely tell, reader, the love I still carry for Weltyr; for although he did me much ill, yet his will was an instrument by which I arrived at deeper truths about reality and myself. It was through him I received the gifts of my family and home and education. My time with him in those days when he was but my friend Hildolfr, and I the young upstart paladin looking for the artifact assigned to him! It had all been so simple. So real and good.

Yet I'd had no choice but to fight against him. It had come down to breaking his staff or forever facing the kind of death I had just faced, with Valeria and Elishta sure to suffer similar sentences along with our children. When it happened, there had been no doubt in my mind that protecting them was the right decision no matter the cost; now, grasping my way back into life thanks to Brynhildr's miraculous intercession, I could see the stakes were desperately grave, and that by fleeing the Valor Hall we were in an existential danger like no other. What I had just experienced was that death unaccompanied by some psychopomp like the Selectrices led to a complete annihilation of any self. Utter objectivity. A reduction to lost information in the spirit-thief hivemind who would eventually absorb some passive environmental data pointing to one's prior existence—say, a molecule of oxygen or a microscopic mote of dust that used to be a skin particle—if something wasn't done to stop them and the Sleeper they served.

Nothing can stop the Sleeper, Eradicator. Not even you.

Usually that would have been the end of it, but as Brynhildr's sisters grounded their horses in a similar sequence of spirals around us, eventually flanking us on all sides and ready to fight or chase us at a moment's notice, I seemed to perceive some point where the wall of my consciousness had atrophied. I can't explain it any other way than that I felt the hivemind recede from me—pulling back, or trying to. Now educated in what it was to be so emptied that I did not exist and only the parasite remained, I pursued its presence through the pattern of that feeling in my psyche. I forgot myself, made myself it, and imagined in the speed of a neuron's firing ten thousand ways Rorke Burningsoul could destroy the Sleeper, which made the hateful thing wail in high-pitched agony and wrench itself away from my consciousness as one wrenches a hand from the grasp of an unwanted conversational partner.

Weltyr no longer had the strength to smirk, but I swore I saw a shimmer in his remaining eye.

"Get down, Rorke," Brynhildr said to me, stirring me from this vertiginous reverie and drawing my attention back over my shoulder to her.

"What is it?"

"I told you before—this is not a matter for your interference."

"He's not a god, Brynhildr," I begged her to understand. "If a mortal man like me—"

"You are no mortal man, Rorke Burningsoul, thrice resurrected—once, indeed, by application of your own will! Besides—" Her eyes glowing through the gilding of her visor, that brave woman told me, "If he is not a god, it is all the more clear that this matter need not, should not, concern you, for it is no longer a matter concerning your god but a matter concerning private parties, I and my father and my sisters."

"Yet aren't the Wotsung of his stock?" Gesturing at him, I reminded her, "Aren't we family, too?"

How pained was her smile! As I suddenly made awful sense of all her sorrow over the previous days, compounding to this moment when she reaped the consequences sown by her decision to aid me in this unsanctioned manner, one of her sisters called out, "Send the Wotsung away! Our quarrel's not with him tonight."

"He's going," she called back sternly, then fixed me with her eyes and nodded in such a way I felt I had no choice but to dismount. This motion, though beginning reluctantly, was performed with some alacrity when the figure of Elishta, her cloak billowing around her, descended to the terrain some sixty paces from us. I dashed over to her, catching her up in my arms and drawing her mouth in for a kiss.

"You brat," I chided her, catching her chin in my hand, then clasping her to my heart. "Now I'll be as concerned with your safety as my own or Valeria's."

"I can't be apart from you for something so important," Elishta told me, her voice a whisper as, calmly, Brynhildr dismounted her horse. Our eyes were fixed to the scene before us even as we held one another, her cheek against my heart and my hand on the back of her head, ready to protect her from the sight of violence from which I had the urge to shield her no matter how advanced her magical and battle prowess was becoming. It was not so much the physical nature of what could have unfolded there, but the emotional toll of what it meant for our friend, who we were losing.

As Brynhildr dismounted, so did her sisters, and while their horses nervously pawed at the ground and snorted in some echo of their mistresses' agitation, Grane stood as still as his rider. Upon removing her helmet, she straightened nobly, head held high, proud shoulders and all her bearing giving evidence that she savored what was left of her vocation as a warrior.

Weltyr looked long at her from his vantage nearby, where he rested wearily on a mossy rock.

"Your sisters were already turned away from you in that same duty to serve the Valor Hall which you so spurned," Weltyr said in a voice that had lost some saturation, as objects are bleached by the sun, "but this intercession they can no more abide than I; for I am the law-giver, and they are the ones who carry out and protect the law, and so justice demands that they harden their hearts."

Her boldness a ghost of itself, Brynhildr placed a hand upon her chest and seemed almost to glance in our direction. "Yet I cannot believe, Father, that to save a man is a crime when that rescue permits the unfolding of your will!"

Beard twitching as if with a curl of his lip, Weltyr roared, "None but you knew my most intimate thoughts! None but you knew the source of my will! And you use that knowledge like a knife, brandishing it about to justify every decision. You yourself were the vessel through which my wishes passed—then you broke that covenant in defiance of me, laughing at my generosity and breaking the laws of Nature as the whelp you defend broke that lance by which I held in order the structure of the world. Now Anroa's trees are barren; now the reign of the gods is done, and this world will perish mere moments behind us in the grand perspective of eternity. Without her golden fruits, we age, and I can lend no aid to all that is to come. No nicety can counterweigh this sin, and each compounds itself to the end. There is nothing to do now but to extract payment from you before the debt is so great you must be entirely destroyed. And so"—he was calmer now, and sadder—"we are here for you, my daughter."

Her bosom rising and falling, the plating of her armor shifting with this great exhalation that no doubt came as partial (or perhaps perverse) relief to know with certainty she was not in that moment to be executed, Brynhildr gestured to herself with her free hand, then stood at proper attention. "Here I am, Father. Pronounce your sentence."

Gingerly, as one for whom such transitions cause great pain, Weltyr leaned his upper half forward, grasping the jagged walking stick to push himself upright. How quickly Brynhildr hastened to his side! Always his adoring daughter, even then, or more so. Elishta, an orphan like me, pressed herself tighter into my arms, and I forgot my own pain in these matters, aching instead with hers and wishing she might have had such a tender connection to those who brought her into the world. As Brynhildr helped Weltyr to his feet and held him that way even as he condemned her, I could see her features undergoing expressions linked to what were surely dawning versions of the same feelings. It was the feeling of loss; the understanding that this would be the last time Brynhildr would meet her father, and the final time that we would meet them both. The moment marked a change not just of her identity and Weltyr's, but ours. Brynhildr was now part of our shared past; an event that had rolled through and was gone, or was about to be gone, though the certainty with which I anticipated this is beyond my own understanding.

"You are your own judge," he told her, looking at her with a kind of rage and sadness even as he permitted her to steady him. "You sprang from the doings of my will, yet yours has risen against me. You carried out my orders only to a point; thereafter, you allowed your brash nature to condemn you, tempting you to defy fate twice over, though fate in this world is nothing but my will. You have broken your vows to obey me! You were my hero's champion, yet you championed the hero against me. Now, you have destroyed me"—he waved to himself with the arm she had already released in her astonishment, and his eye turned to me, giving me a sickening awareness of how culpable I was in Brynhildr's sentence—"and in this, you have destroyed yourself, your sisters, and even this world if the Deepgold be not returned to its rightful owners."

With great defiance burning like the red heart of her filial love, Brynhildr parried, "I trust Burningsoul with that task more than you, and you yourself agree."

But Weltyr smiled coolly, bitterly, and told her, "You see? You cannot help the fire in your blood driving you to defy me. You deny your nature as my daughter; therefore, your days as my Selectrix are behind you."

I had not foreseen this fate, whatever I expected, and Brynhildr looked stunned as Weltyr hobbled forward a pace or two. "You're disowning me?"

"You will not hold my cup or kiss my cheek, nor bear your father's kiss upon your brow; no more will you lead warriors to my withering Valor Hall. You've been cut off from the company of gods, severed from our lineage. I will see you no more. You are banished."

At this pronouncement, one of Brynhildr's sisters burst into tears, and this tipped, one at a time, all the others, who let up agonized wails even as they showed no signs of interfering. "Sister," some of them cried, and others, "Woe, woe!"

Her voice the calm of someone understanding they were on the cusp of imminent, irreversible ruin, Brynhildr followed Weltyr step for step. "You would deprive me of all you ever gave? Reverse those gifts you put into my hands?"

"Your rescuer shall force it from you," Weltyr shouted, whirling on her, so imposing despite his clearly reduced capacities that she flinched back with her fist crossed over her breast. "I'll put you in a sleep, unguarded in this spot, and he that finds you here may capture whatever remains of you when all I have provided is stripped away."

The second Selectrix to have burst into weeping now gasped, and before she could stop herself, she had stepped forward several feet. As her shock rippled in little echoes throughout her sisters, she exclaimed, "Stop, O Father! You would give the flower of our youngest sister into the crushing hands of a man? Spare this disgrace! Insult our sister, and you insult us, too."

"Have mercy," cried another. "Spare this disgrace! Avert these outrages, they are beyond the pale!"

And still, yet another: "You would wilt and fade her for a man! Stay your curse!"

On and on, the Selectrices begged, all of them rocked by this condemnation that I, too, found troubling, particularly given our location. Who could come upon her here save for this Malchi-sedeq, or, God forbid, one of the spirit-thieves? But this cruelty seemed part of the point, for Weltyr was unmoved.

"All your wailing has deafened you to my commands! Make your peace. No more will your sister ride through the skies in your company. Her tender youth will go to seed, and a husband shall win her devotion such that thenceforth she will belong to none but him, this domineering man, who will leave her scorned by the fire to sit and spin for the scrutiny of all!"

Brynhildr's flagging composure collapsed along with her body as the grief of this shame for a Selectrix tore from her throat a scream. It was a sound that could surely have been no worse had Weltyr stabbed her in the heart. Upon her knees, she wept and moaned and prostrated herself, her face grinding in the dirt and grass. Her sisters let out another great clamor, and Weltyr looked harshly on them all.

"You despise your sister's fate? It fills your soul with anguish? Then abandon her and this place, and keep well clear of her! She who shares her sister's melancholy shall also share her fate. Begone!" As he took a step toward the nearest one, they all cried out, scrambling upon their mounts. "Here, there is only suffering!"

One at a time, the Selectrices' steeds flew off into

the air of that strange place, their mistresses weeping and shouting, "Woe! Woe!" as, ever-rising, they took on the appearances of birds, then of bees, then of dust motes. Then of nothing at all.

Now it was only Elishta and I, and Brynhildr and Weltyr. It would have been easier now to interfere…yet it was not my place. Brynhildr was right to warn me sternly against heroic ambition here. She had saved me, I was sure, from a lifetime of being pursued by her sisters in vengeance for the blood I would have on my hands. Moreover, I had the sense that even if she had been saved that day, her heart could never be saved. Weltyr had stripped her of himself already, had left the chasm of a hole aching in her heart where once 'god' and 'father' occupied the same place. As painful as I knew the loss of one to be, to have both annihilated in an instant was surely a devastation beyond compare. Perhaps it is chauvinist of me to say, but Brynhildr now *needed* a husband. Indeed, a good husband was, I thought, a compassionate remedy Weltyr provided her for the true punishment: the stripping of her title and estrangement from her home.

"Was my action so detestable," she wept, tipping her face back up from the ground and then, succumbing, resting her brow in the grass once again, "that you would commend so detestable a fate to your most cherished daughter? I served your will by my actions; that will you could not dare to enact, because your hand was stayed."

"Did I order you to aid the Wotsung," he asked, nudging her shoulder with his stick in a silent urging to sit upright, "or to reverse the course of death?"

Hiccupping now like a girl-child, Brynhildr sat upright and wiped her wrist across her cheeks and nose.

"You loved the Wotsung, and tethered me to him as special charge, to ferry him to your Valor Hall. And how could I do that if he died in the flesh here?"

"He made his choice, as did you. He chose this world, as did you. Therefore, you will die the deaths of mortals, and the Valor Hall and I will follow you."

As Elishta and I exchanged a horrified glance, the two of us trying to discern what it meant for the Valor Hall to be dying with Weltyr, Brynhildr grit her teeth. "It was you who put this love for the Wotsung into my heart! You who put in me the wisdom to see what you see—that it is only by his hand the Deepgold may be preserved from sowing seeds of mankinds' destruction!"

"And in that love and trust you have in him," Weltyr replied bitterly, extending a hand upon his daughter's head, "you withdrew your love and trust from me; so follow them now, and let them be the ornaments of your husband's possession."

With a bitter sob, Brynhildr collapsed against her father's robes, gripping the fabric in desperation while her head sagged once more toward the ground. "Then let not this man to whom I must subordinate myself forever be some coward. Let whoever wins me be a man of worth."

"You have divorced yourself from your heritage; I cannot choose a husband for you."

"Nor can you let the noble race you sired give life to cowards. Virtuous Elishta-bet is bearing the sweetest fruit of the Wotsung clan"—my grip around her tightened and my mind raced, especially as she went on—"but he shall not come upon me first."

"Speak not to me of the Wotsungs," he told her, yanking his robes from her hands and leaving her to weep with her face covered. "Do not ask me again to choose for you. You have already chosen punishment. I am weary, and it is long since time I departed."

"Would that you might instead put me to the tip of the spear, or immolate my mortified body in flame."

Hesitating, hearing Brynhildr's pleas delivered with such sad desperation and seeing now all that she had given up to help me, I squeezed Elishta's shoulders and released her to take a few steps forward.

"What of Hamsunt," I called. While the others turned their heads toward me, the flame of the lantern emitted a scornful laugh. I went on, ignoring it, looking pleadingly at Weltyr. "The brother of yours dwelling in this Lantern was put there by me afresh, yet by some mystery he was not the Hamsunt I first found within the artifact. You may not pity your daughter enough to select her groom, but surely a worthy solution would be setting that loosed Hamsunt roving in the world to the work of filtering her suitors."

Overjoyed by this idea, her eyes alight with tears, Brynhildr cried out, "Yes! Unleash a fire, let blazing heat light up my bridal chamber! Let its teeth feast upon the insolent fools who unworthily approach my lethal bed."

Brynhildr clutched her hands to her heart and turned her doleful gaze up to her father, who stared at me for a long, hard moment with an expression that was now more sad than angry. Perhaps against one of his favorites he could hold strong. But, against his most beloved Selectrix and the unlucky man for whom he had some special fondness, Weltyr succumbed, and his hardened features softened. An unexpected sob tore through him, and he dropped his staff, falling to his knees and gathering her into his arms.

"Farewell, you radiant, unbroken mare! You, most sacred joy of my heart!" He pressed her to his breast, one hand upon the back of her head, and kissed her brow. Even now, he could not help but console her—to give her, I was glad to see, at least this gesture of his tender devotion. "If I must lose you, the apple sweeter to my eye than any of Anroa's, then a fire fit for a young bride shall blaze as none ever has before! The night will be lit with its heat to repel the fainthearted from Brynhildr's bed." Clutching his abandoned staff, Weltyr struck the ground, and the entire pocket dimension within the citadel rattled as if with an earthquake. "Hamsunt—burn so fiercely that none would dare, save for he that is freer than I! Freer, even, than his father."

Beneath us, the ground trembled, and each strike of his broken staff increased it until a gash tore through the splendid flowers and emerald grass. Out leapt the fiery devil who had caused me so much turmoil by the immolation of the *Rhinemaid.* As much as it had cost me to get him into the lantern on Dunnun's island, I hated to see this older iteration of him still free—but, with no choice but to obey his brother, Hamsunt's flames rolled out in two directions, making up the perimeter of a circle that cut Elishta and me off from the former Selectrix and her father. Even then—even through the flames and the smoke—I could see she looked at him with the utmost trust, as that he looked at her with love.

"This is how your father renounces you," I could just hear him tell her over the crackling of the flames, "kissing your godhood away."

With a kind of reverence, Weltyr bent to kiss one eye, and then the other. Brynhildr accepted this affection, her eyes closed to receive each gesture.

I never saw them reopen.

Her lips parted; her body sagged forward into his arms.

As he lowered her visor, Grane—outside the fire just as we were—folded his legs beneath his body and rested his head low.

While Elishta burst into tears, I received one more solemn look from Weltyr's eye, which lifted toward me. That gaze attempted to fix me; and, for the first time, I felt tragically immune to the power of his presence. I was looking at a faded being of some exceptional nature, and of his breed, there was no question he was the best. I would forever praise him, I knew, just as I knew that, among those heralded as the gods, his being was closest to true divinity in power and in bearing. Yet he remained imperfect—and, without Anroa's apples, he was as impermanent as me.

I lowered my eyes toward Brynhildr, whose figure was increasingly cloaked from my sight as the wall of flames around them grew in height and wildness. Seeing that she was completely inert, Weltyr caressed his daughter's face with one hand, then eased her gingerly upon the ground.

The pain was too great. I could linger no longer.

"Come," I bade Elishta, drawing back toward her again, my arm tightening around her waist, my eye trying to avoid the sight of Weltyr lowering the visor of her helmet. "Let's save Valeria, and find a way to be free of here."

The words were meaningless to me in that moment. Things I said because they needed to be said, and not because they were in my heart. All that was in my heart then was that same bitterness and sorrow which Elishta exhibited as she cried out, "But we must do something, Rorke! We— how can we—"

Even as she said the words, her expression deepened in sorrow with the recognition for which Brynhildr had prepared me and which still stung in that moment: that there *was* nothing we could do. Brynhildr had accepted her fate. This was the punishment, the cause and effect upon her nature just as this new form of fully empty death was an effect upon my human condition. A new threat born of that same destructive force which had broken Weltyr's spear and drained the life out of the Valor Hall.

Me.

"We all must face what we're doing," I told Elishta gently, squeezing her shoulder and drawing her close to me. "What we have done. Our actions have had real, permanent consequences...and we must accept our share of that, however painful it be." Weeping, nodding, Elishta leaned into me, then wiped a brisk hand across each of her cheeks. "You're right, of course. Yes, of course you're right. Yes—yes."

How she wanted to argue! I could feel it in the tension of her muscles as we held one another. I knew because I wanted to argue, too. I wanted to bargain with Weltyr, to further all the arguments Brynhildr had commenced.

But his will, powerful and far-reaching, was *not* free, as he himself had admitted more than once. He would not be capable of undoing what he had done; and the

Selectrices were surely now too frightened of him to dare disobey his will to find some way to break their sister's enchantment.

As I had awoken Gundrygia, so would someone awaken Brynhildr—but how could it ever be a man worthy of her?

My heart and mind were so preoccupied that, as Elishta and I turned in the direction of the tower, I did not even spare a thought to the question of how we would enter it, or what we would face inside. Indeed, I was still wrestling with the hideous experience of that empty death, both astonished and altered to find I could push my consciousness into the hivemind as it had so many times obtrusively done to me. My internal world was a rotation of frantic thoughts that rose and drowned without ceasing, churning wildly one upon the other until they all came to a halt.

A man stood there, watching us.

"You're really here," Malchi-Sedeq said with the thoughtful air of corrected skepticism. He listed toward us from where he stood some forty paces away, the terrain having accommodated him with silence. "I wasn't sure you'd really make it...when the ship detects extreme blood loss in a copy, it assumes death."

He stood with his hand extended against the tree nearest to him. When I looked back over my shoulder at Weltyr, he was gone; only the fire remained, leaping in a great circle that obscured Brynhildr completely. The only evidence of anything other than a run-of-the-mill wildfire was Grane, that solemn figure, resigned to wait with his mistress. As I returned my attention to Malchi-Sedeq, he jerked his chin toward the flames.

"You start that?"

"It is no fire of mortal invention," I told him, while Elishta looked at him with shock, then thrust a frightened second glance up toward me. Consolingly resting my hand between her shoulder blades, I said, "Your 'ship' was right about one thing—the old man is dead."

"I figured that was the case, or else it wouldn't have hurried back to him. Had to be one or both of you, and I didn't think it was likely to be you. I just didn't know for sure. Didn't realize how you'd get up here, either. How'd you manage it?"

"A friend helped."

He smirked dryly. "You talk less than I imagined."

Under different circumstances, I would have laughed, and so might have Elishta. Instead, both of us battle-worn and processing the shock of having our friend taken from us, we stood in silence.

"Well," he said, sighing as he turned away, "you might as well come with me."

"And why would we do that?"

He paused at my question, asking without turning his head, "Aren't you going to wind up in my home anyway? I'd might as well invite you to keep you open to negotiation. But I suppose you're about to threaten me. That you'll ask me something like, 'What if we just kill you?'"

"We could," I reminded him, acutely aware of the weight of the sword at my hip.

"Yes," he agreed, unfazed, hobbling forward with his black cloak waving gently behind him. "You certainly could."

Elishta and I looked at one another: silent, hesitant.

No choice left but to follow.

19

MALCHI-SEDEQ

IT'S HARD TO describe the gravity I experienced in those moments we spent following Malchi-Sedeq to the tower that was his true home. I knew nothing of the man—only that he was evil by any measure, based on the company he kept and the thoughtless manner in which he controlled, used, and reanimated the local dwarvish population along with the remains of a great many mankinds throughout history.

Yet, more even than I had in the dream or in that initial, fleeting image of him near the start of all this, I experienced a deep, intuitive recognition of whom he was to me. Therefore, while I suppose things might have worked out more easily if I cut him down there and ransacked the tower with Elishta's help until we discovered Valeria, for sentimental reasons, I could not. I held myself back—though a curious part of me felt that I would have liked to kill him, indeed would relish when the moment of killing came. That thought, which made me disappointed in myself, turned my attention toward matters of religion, and God, and holiness, and this new, sad longing I had for the days such matters were my only pursuit, and I was a paladin being raised in a luxury I didn't recognize. Yes, I had been an orphan. Yes, much was unexplained.

Yet, because of him, I had experienced a certain kind of privilege. This man and Weltyr both were the instruments by which this yearning for sanctification had been installed in my heart. Therefore, I could not harbor a complete hatred toward either one of them. I could not kill Malchi-Sedeq while he led us to the tower.

"Al-listux seemed surprised that I was going out," the old man said, his hand alighting upon every tree we passed, his gait unsteady and in want of support but much too proud for the aid of any apparatus. "I told it I wanted to greet you—to see you with my own two eyes. But you can't expect something like that to understand. They don't have a sense of meaningful identity, the spirit-thieves. Their identity is the Hivemind, just with different names to reference various accumulations of information in this or that region of spacetime."

"Why do you work with them? Raising the dead for them, terrorizing those poor people of Ironforge?"

"They seem to be coming out ahead by most estimates. Well—the ones who survive, anyway."

Exchanging a glance with an increasingly nervous Elishta, I told Malchi-sedeq, "That's the problem. Besides, they didn't consent to this infiltration by the hivemind into their consciousnesses. I didn't, certainly. All that aside, though—isn't the principle pursuit of the spirit-thieves to rouse the Sleeper and offer a planet for its consumption?" I waved a hand at the old man, with whom we had caught up as a natural matter of course when our paces were compared. "What would doing such a thing benefit you? Aren't you immortal? Isn't the point of being a dirge to live forever?"

"A 'dirge'," he mused, half-paying attention to me. "I've heard that term passed around before, in the hivemind."

Was that dream a symptom of this connection? "It's gotten to you, too?"

"You learn to block it out," he said with a flick of his wrist. "After a few years, it's nothing at all to create a kind of wall around your mind. Given how common psychic and magical attacks can be on Urde, you should be doing regular reality checks of your state of mind, anyway... especially living a mercenary life."

"You didn't answer my question."

"Don't be in such a hurry. If you must know, Rorke, the truth is that I don't really care about the Sleeper." Scratching his brow with the thumb of one hand, he then unfurled those fingers and shrugged with his open palm. "I'm sure it exists, and I'm sure it's dangerous. But the peoples of Urde have been vanquishing existential threats for their entire existence. Even before the birth of species like elves and dwarves and what-have-you, your ancestors were surviving ice ages and bubonic plagues."

Unable to help my scoff of derision, I demanded, "Isn't that a little arrogant? To assume that the peoples of Urde will take care of it, so you can do what you wish?"

"Sure," he admitted, "but I just haven't seen a compelling reason not to work with the spirit-thieves. Their research is valuable, and though they're perfectly capable of doing all the things I can do—cloning, genetic modification, manufacture, at least—they need to keep me around because the ship that hosts their experiments won't genetically bond with them. We have some shared interests, see, so I take them up on the offer."

The moat surrounding the large area making up not just the tower but the ground gardens around it was so vibrant it seemed blue even in the relative dark, though that dark was not so dark as the dark of the swamp thanks to Brynhildr's fire. Would it truly burn until she was freed? When would that be?

"If you want my opinion," said our dubious host, his hands folded at his back as he walked us to the door in a more casual way than before, "they want to keep me around because they've been anticipating you, Rorke." We crossed the short bridge and passed through to a forking path through more flowers. "You were supposed to be like the man you met in the swamps outside Ironforge, you know…but the hivemind took exception to you, seeing the inevitable cascade of information that came with your creation. It had me throw you away when you were just an infant, before you developed as far as would have been required to serve my purposes. I don't like to waste my work, so I sent you to the priests, since I figured they'd care for you. Things would have gone better for the spirit-thieves if they'd minded their business, I'd say…

they've been preparing for your return since they found out I didn't kill you, and keeping me around to help them deal with you, I think."

"I don't think they're inclined toward anticipating me so much as despising me," I told him. "I killed their kind in the Nightlands while tracking down the Sce—an artifact. Since then, they call me 'Eradicator.'"

"Oh...I think it's for more reasons than that. Anyway...I hear *you're* pregnant"—he abruptly addressed Elishta with a kind of warmth, even extending his hand—"congratulations."

"Uh! Y-yes. Thank you. How did you—"

"My daughter is psychic. At the least, she's troubled by knowledge that would be better far from the reach of any but the spirit-thieves. She has a special interest in Rorke...as do I, I admit."

Releasing his hand and casting an uneasy glance up at me, Elishta withdrew her arm beneath her cloak and pulled the fabric tighter around her. "You must understand, sir, why I should think all that quite alarming, for various reasons—not the least of which being that we don't know you."

"Although I feel like I do," I blurted, gaining a thoughtful look from him.

"Well, maybe we should make that more than just a feeling."

Before us, the doors which punctuated an unfurling set of black stairs swung invitingly open. Elishta hesitated, drawing back against me with fright.

"I'm sure Grane would gladly return you to Urde if you asked him," I consoled her, earning a shake of her head.

"I dare not be so selfish as to take him from her side now—nor to leave yours. I want to be with you, Rorke. I love you."

How sweet and tender were those words! How I longed to say them back and to hear my dear Elishta utter them over and over again.

And how embarrassed I was when that sweet oath was met not with my echoed sentiment, but with a madwoman's triumphant cry of delight.

"At last! My holy fool has come!"

Then there she was, leaping from the second landing of the stairs that spiraled up the perimeter of the tower and forcing me to catch her. Her sloppily immodest black furs fell half open to give me a glimpse of her swollen breast as she devoured me with a kiss, her legs wrapping around my waist and her tongue plunging against mine as her fingers gripped my hair.

And there I was, my hands on her waist, kissing her back, my senses controlled for three seconds: three long, conflicted seconds that encapsulated mystification, desire, admonishment, and disgust along with shame and excitement to scandalize Elishta in this way. As I came up for air, her face was red and her eyes and mouth were wide with shock. Catching Gundrygia's scalp with my free hand to keep her from continuing her kisses down my neck even as her father (*her* father!) remonstrated her ("You trollop, give the man a minute to adjust to your presence and fix your clothes while you're at it—"), I turned my head toward Elishta apologetically.

"Forgive me, sweetheart. Gundrygia, whom you've managed to avoid, isn't entirely well, I think. She was in a deathless sleep of her own until recently, when I and the others emerged from the Nightlands. And she's not in her right senses," I added sternly, turning a dark stare into her infuriatingly giddy gaze. "You and I are going to talk later."

"Of course we will...there's much, much time to talk, Rorke..."

As I pushed her off me and Malchi-sedeq shook his head with a sigh of disgust, fixing the animal skins that concealed her dangerously alluring form, Gundrygia stumbled back and smiled over at Elishta.

"Don't worry, pretty birdie...I can share."

"Be gone from here, you lunatic—this poor woman wants no part of you."

"I wouldn't be so sure," Gundrygia murmured, her voice a purr from her lips. Then, turning her attention back to the old man, she advised him, "Besides— someone will need to look after her while you show him his precious Valeria is safe."

Malchi-sedeq bared his teeth in frustration. I, suddenly prompted into an awareness of her nearness like a man belatedly realizing he is in arm's reach of achieving some long-held ambition, whirled on him in time to see it. "Where is she?" My hand fell upon the handle of Exigence, the twice-treacherous blade that had first broken its designer and then its wielder. "Whatever quarrel you have with the folk of Ironforge, however reprehensible your actions, if you give us Valeria and let us depart from here, I am willing to negotiate with you about all other matters."

"Interesting response to the Trolley Problem," he mused aloud, a sentence which had to me so little meaning that it might have been in a foreign language.

Then, waving his hand, he dismissed whatever his thought was. "No matter. Of course, you can take Valeria whenever you please; I'm already done with her. But—"

With a cock of his brow that I had seen in the looking glass, Malchi-sedeq observed, "She may not be happy with you if she recovers from her anesthesia and finds you've given up your little quest to find her ring."

My hand tightened around the grip of the sword. "And I'm supposed to trust Gundrygia with Elishta-bet while you allegedly take me to Valeria?"

"If it makes you feel any better, I don't trust her with Elishta-bet, either."

"I'm fine, Rorke," Elishta hastened to say, flicking a sidelong glance toward Gundrygia and then back to me. "I'll be fine."

Unable to help myself, I drew her into my arms and caressed Elishta's cheek with that same hand that had felt the temptation to draw Exigence. "You mustn't take her or anything here lightly. She's powerful. More powerful than you; more powerful, I think, than him."

"Isn't it a bit trite to arrange beings in a hierarchy of power?" Flipping her hair with an amused little laugh, Gundrygia slunk up to us and slid her hands around Elishta's, coiling like a snake without regard for my warning scowl. "That's men for you...come, come, little sister! After all that traipsing around through the bog, you must be in sore want of a bath. Let me help you..."

Though her expression was briefly anxious, Elishta soon assumed a sterner demeanor and allowed herself to be pulled away from me. As Gundrygia led her down one of three halls that branched off the central vestibule, Malchi-sedeq crooked a finger and mounted the staircase.

"She's up here," he assured me. "You'll see, she's perfectly well."

"And the baby?"

"Fit and happy, as I imagine we all are before...well." Chuckling dryly, the old man waved to himself, then around himself, indicating the sum total of existence. I followed him, unamused and in fact disgusted.

"For a man who seems to despise life enough to risk it by coming to meet me without a party of your own, you certainly seem to have gone to great lengths to ensure your survival."

With a slight snort, Malchi-sedeq led me up the stairs, one hand on the great stone rail that coiled up with them, his other negotiating his cloak away from his feet. "That's the trouble, isn't it? You didn't ask to be here—at least, you have no memory of asking—but you are here, in this ugly place, and who knows what'll happen if you leave it? Even just the leaving itself seems to be the worst part most of the time."

"This isn't an ugly place," I corrected him, gesturing vaguely in the direction the women had disappeared. "It's a garden of delights."

"And of horrors beyond all human reckoning... worst of all are those horrors which are *within* human reckoning, and perpetrated by them."

"You would certainly know. What do you do with those Ironforge citizens who don't make it back? What are you doing with any of them in the first place?"

"It's the spirit-thieves' program, not mine. Like I said, I really just provide the means for mass producing the skeletons. If they could inscribe magical items, this would still be going on; I just wouldn't be involved, and they would have had to find a different location."

At this first floor, the old man stopped and pushed open the door. As he did, a rhythmic humming noise of which I had been hitherto half-aware at best was now amplified beyond my ability to ignore. While he strode right in, I hesitated in the doorway, scanning for traps, but my eye (though inexpert compared to Odile's) revealed no signature of deception.

Indeed, what I discovered instead was some kind of workshop—self-managing, surely the work of an expert magician. It consisted largely of rows of boxes mounted to the walls and a long worktable running down the middle, where skeletons worked to assemble parts I could not identify. The fronts of the boxes were clear, and within each, a small contraption darted about, mounted on a broad arm that slid back and forth along the opposing axis.

"Do you know what a printer is, Rorke?" asked the old man, studying my face. "A mimeograph?"

"Of course; it's how they print newspapers."

"Well, these are printers, too. Only, instead of ink, it's substances like gold and carbon. See? This one's finished."

Popping open the glass door of one of the boxes nearest to us, Malchi-sedeq reached inside for a small square of green and gold which he held close for my inspection. I removed it from his fingers and studied it carefully, observing, "This is the body of one of those little spiders."

"You can call them that," he agreed with a chuckle. "I always prefer to think of them as a kind of tick, since they attach themselves for a time to ensure the long-term stability of their host. A long time ago I found before that when they detach prematurely, the skeletons will lose functionality or even have a total collapse. They remain attached to their hosts for a moon cycle and then drop off to go find a new body, two or three before they come back to be wiped and prepared anew."

Frowning, I handed the little chip back without thinking and asked, "You mean those bugs are *raising* the skeletons?"

"Well, *I'm* the one raising them; they're just the mechanism. This little thing carries information, like a parchment scroll or a road sign. The difference is that the information is embedded—encoded, see—in a way that requires a special device to access. Some of the parts that go into the 'spiders', as you call them, are the parts that do the reading of those or other commands, and act accordingly. Some of the parts are batteries to power those other parts. And some of the parts are mechanical, like the legs. Right now, we're producing about four hundred of these a day."

"A day!"

"It's what the spirit-thieves have been ordering," he said with a shrug. "I think they know, just as I do, that your approach signals the end of the operation. They want to get a final wave in before whatever happens, happens."

"And what's going to happen?"

"That's up to you, Rorke."

Handing the chip to the nearest skeleton and strolling away while it looked dumbly at the device in its hand, Malchi-sedeq led me to the next floor while I boggled, uncomprehending. The scale of this operation was far greater than I had understood even when standing upon that height from which Brynhildr and I scouted how odious a sea of skeletons we were faced with. "At a rate of four hundred a day," I calculated, "this region would be overrun by so many skeletons there would surely be more towns impacted than Ironforge. How long has it been four hundred a day?"

"About six years," he admitted. "Since they began making moves to infiltrate El'ryh's government with the explicit purpose of obtaining the Ring. You can think of what's happening in Ironforge as a pilot program, of sorts. They've been running an experiment to test a hypothesis—'Can we get away with it?' And the answer, I'd say, is a resounding 'yes.'"

Get away with what, I wanted to ask—but as he opened the next door, the words fell from my lips. Within was a room so white I was blinded for a split second, my vision embossed by negative impressions of silver tables and strange clusters of surgical implements mounted to the ceiling like chandeliers ready to lower down for use any moment. The walls were simple as the floor, lined with cabinets both tall and squat.

And among it all, a flash of dark skin made me fight to refocus my eyes.

In a second I forgot all conversation, all decorum, all dignity. I shoved past him, covering the distance in three achingly long heartbeats until I gathered sleeping Valeria's upper body in my arms and savaged her with a kiss. To my disappointment, she didn't immediately waken; indeed, she didn't stir at all. If not for the occasional flick of an eyeball roving beneath her eyelids or the soft, warm breath from her nose, I wouldn't have been sure she was alive. Pressing her limp head to my heart, my other hand braced against her flesh through the open back of the thin cotton frock I was sure she would despise on waking, I demanded, "What have you done to her? What was done to Gundrygia was undone with a kiss, but—"

"That was magic," Malchi-sedeq said, having caught up to me to study the woman in my arms. "This is science. She's all right; we had to induce a coma. She wasn't cooperative without it. Consider yourselves lucky...most subjects who try to fight the spirit-thieves are exterminated. Valeria's too important, though I'm sure they wanted to kill her when they were done with her. They just knew they couldn't do it without provoking you...or me, for that matter."

"What business is she of yours?"

"She's carrying my grandchild, isn't she? Just like Gundrygia, and your little friend with her, Elishta." Shrugging, he said, "Call me sentimental, but when a man has many children and no grandchildren, the idea of a new generation gets him all warm and fuzzy."

How many questions I could have asked! Indeed, there was much I wanted to know, but all of that was buried beneath the most pressing command that sprang from my lips without my behest: "Wake her up!"

"I'm tempted to ask you to let her sleep a little longer, as out of control as she was. She's highly resistant to the hypnotic techniques of the spirit-thieves, and it made transporting her difficult. Usually we can dispatch parties from the ship here dead they can take a lifeboat down and back without a problem, but she's important enough and wily enough that we had to risk coming in closer. By the time she was up here with us, she was already snapped out of it, and the results weren't pretty...but—"

After pondering us both for a moment, he turned away to strike a button on the wall. "I can see you won't take 'no' for an answer, and she's going to have several days of recovery ahead of her, so we might as well get the process started now. Hey"—he now addressed the intercom above the button, a black mesh circle built into the wall—"send somebody down here to awaken the organic subject."

"What reason could you possibly have had for doing this to her, if you care so much for the wellbeing of our child?"

"You'll understand eventually. Whether or not you agree is another matter...but I think you'll stand the greatest chance of agreeing if you wait for a moment. They'll have her up in no time...how about you come with me and—"

"I'll stay here until she's awake, thank you."

"In that case, you're going to have to wait until tomorrow for an explanation, because I'm already pushing it. Much longer, and I'm not going to be able to even walk down the stairs."

Barely able to understand what he meant, I raised my head from Valeria's and looked closely at him. "You've aged," I remarked in some amazement, seeing him clearly for the first time since I had become distracted by a parade of amazing discoveries—from Gundrygia to the spider factory to this, Valeria, here, in my arms. Somehow, in the past twenty or so minutes, Malchi-sedeq's cheekbones had grown more gaunt, along with his hands and his posture. He more closely resembled that ill-kept hermit now, and I marveled while his thin lips peeled back to produce an even thinner smile.

"So have you...just not as obviously. I'll tell you what, Rorke"—a pair of skeletons hustled into the room from the right, meaning they had come down the stairs from an upper floor, and in their bony arms were all kinds of medical equipment I didn't recognize—"since I suspect you're going to want to spend the night here, why don't I have them put in a proper bed? You can rest here while she recovers, or you're welcome to go downstairs and make sure Gundrygia isn't causing Elishta too many problems. The truth is, I really don't care where you go. All I ask is that you let me get my beauty sleep, as I can still remember my mother calling it. We can talk more in the morning."

There was a real urgency in his voice beneath the cool veneer: a pressure and plea for me to agree, not because he wanted to trap me but because he was a man in genuine need of something. Seeing this in him, I nodded, and he looked relieved. At the twitch of his arm, I had the sense that he wanted to pat my shoulder, but he resisted. Instead, stepping away, he said, "Thank you. I'll send somebody with food for you, too. You're probably hungry."

"'Somebody.' You talk about these undead like they're people."

As he retreated from the room, Malchi-sedeq looked over his shoulder, his laughter dark.

"I haven't left this ship in centuries, Rorke, and even then only for a few hours. If they're not to be counted as people, then until Gundrygia came home, I've been alone with the spirit-thieves...and while I guess that's true, there are just some things a man doesn't want to admit to himself. Good night."

What a tragic life this fellow lived! Worse than the hermit. Aghast as I was to think of this man never stepping foot on Urde in my lifetime, I was nevertheless immediately distracted by the activities of the skeletons attending the inert Materna of the durrow. Moving about with a kind of automation, one removed an assortment of tubes and wires from various junctures of her body, pausing only to turn and silence lit boxes protested with ominous squeals. The other, arranging a series of small vials and other pieces of equipment upon a metal table nearby, assembled a syringe far smaller and sleeker than anything with which I had been inoculated as a boy at the temple. Into this it drew several fluids from little vials, one ingredient at a time creating some unknown serum. Around the same time its partner finished freeing Valeria of the tangle within which she'd been hidden, the syringe's needle was carefully inserted into a bag of clear fluid suspended above her head. A puff of gold bloomed within, and this overtook the bag to create a translucent, yellowish substance which trailed down the remaining tube still attached in the crook of her arm.

Once it had flowed in, even before the bag showed the least signs of emptying, Valeria stirred, and my heart unclenched.

It was a twitch at first—a change in the pattern of her breath, a tremor in her chapped lips. Unable to help myself, I caressed her face, my thumb wiping sleep from her fluttering eyes and the edges of her mouth. As I touched her, those beautiful lips opened, and overcome by love, I kissed her without the least care for the strange medicinal taste her mouth had taken on in her chemically induced sleep. The skeletons collected the remnants of their work and retreated, leaving me there to pet and kiss her as the medicine did its work. However long I was there—ten, twenty minutes or more—was immaterial. Eternity penetrated into time as I doted on her, and gradually, her restful expression turned to one of consternation. Beneath her furrowed brow, her eyes cracked open, and her mouth moved in silent approximation of words before she managed to rasp, "Am I sick?"

"No, my love," I murmured, my voice thick with emotion. "No; you're perfectly well, and so is our baby, I'm told."

"'Our' baby." Rotating the words upon her tongue, she tried them out and, divorced from her memories in that haze, didn't care for them. "Impudent slave." Even as she chastised me, she leaned her cheek more fully into my hand, her heavy eyes struggling for purchase on my face. "Though, handsome."

"And you're beautiful," I murmured to her, bending over her for another kiss. This, she received with a gasp, her mouth opening, her body arching upon the table beneath her. When I withdrew, she focused on my mouth, then looked quizzically up into my eyes.

"You *are* impudent," she observed. "If I didn't feel so ill, I'd beat you senseless."

"I'd let you," I told her in that moment, so relieved to have her in my arms that I meant it. "What do you mean, you feel ill?"

"Like I'm about to be sick. Very sick. I—" Looking quite disturbed to recognize just *how* sick she felt, Valeria adopted an expression of great focus, and it was perhaps by this degree of concentration that she finally remembered, "Rorke?"

"Yes, Valeria—it's me."

Other memories came to her in a manner almost visible, her eyes darting briefly around before meeting mine again. "Where are they? Are they here?"

The spirit-thieves, I gathered, or the skeletons. "The skeletons, yes. As to the spirit-thieves, I haven't yet laid eyes on them, but I'm under the impression they're around."

"Where are we?" After looking down at herself with obvious disgust for the frock, she looked back up at me and, sharper by the second, demanded, "What have they done to me? Oh, I'll vomit, get back—"

This quite understandable response of her body to something repellent, she visibly resisted it, her jaw tight and her brow breaking out into sweat. Valeria concentrated on some point on the wall behind me while I hurried to the intercom and used it the way my forebear had. "Bring her something for her nausea immediately," I commanded, as though I had authority. "And clothes for her. I'm sure you have some around, borrow some from Gundrygia."

While, through sheer force of will and deep, focused breathing through her nose, Valeria battled back the natural but futile instinct of her body to reject poison by emptying her stomach. I returned to slip my hand into hers. As she squeezed my fist, I couldn't help but tell her, "I'm so grateful to see you! Oh, Valeria."

"I can't believe you're here," she said, sounding more grateful and surprised than she had the entire time I'd known her. Then, hesitating, she asked, "Where is 'here'?"

"The flying citadel," I told her. "*Shooting Star*."

Now, her expression morphed again, assuming an

urgency close to panic. "We can't just sit around here," she said, sorting out more thoughts and memories and, perhaps, managing to ascertain what had been before only vaguely revealed to her in the scattered recollection of her first awakening. Clearly, medical sleep was far clumsier to recover from than natural or even magical sleep. I remembered how effortlessly Gundrygia sprang awake, as if she had merely been roused from a nap, and I expected Brynhildr's condition would be similarly resolved, but Valeria was nearly debilitated. As she tried to sit up and then fell back with a groan and another look of resistance, I folded her face in my hands and assured her, "You're right, we must leave as soon as we can. But our host is more accommodating than I would have anticipated, and he's prepared for us to stay the night, at least."

"'Stay the night,'" she repeated, protesting after a second. "We mustn't, Rorke."

"I know it's not ideal, but I don't think you'll be *able* to leave for at least a few more hours, sweetheart."

The pair of skeletons entered again, this time hurrying in response to my command. Valeria looked their way, groaned at the sickness this movement of her head provoked, and tried saying, "Rorke—"

"It's all right, Madame. They're going to help you."

"They were the ones who *took* me," she muttered. Sympathetically, I rubbed my thumb back and forth along the heel of her palm. Valeria squeezed shut her eyes and bared her beautiful little teeth. "One moment I'm sleeping, and the next, the room is filled with light, and—oh—"

Relief unbound the features of her perfect face, the muscles going slack as the nausea faded with this new injection into the fluid sack. Though she still maintained that look of being braced against discomfort, I could tell by the change in the rhythm of her breathing that she was better—quite literally by the second. When the great wall of nausea slid past her, she opened her eyes again, and the look emanating from them was the fierceness of a caged animal.

"What have they *done* to me, Rorke?"

"I don't know," I answered solemnly as a third skeleton entered the room, bearing a tray of simple gruel, a glass of juice, and a slice of bread—surely already more than she could stomach. "I've not been here long. Just long enough to talk to Malchi-sedeq."

"Who?"

"The dirge—the one working with the spirit-thieves."

"You've seen him, but not them?"

"Correct. But," recalling, far more distantly, the strange, dissociated dream I seemed to recall having at some now indeterminate point between our fall from the *Rhinemaid* and our arrival at the Valor Hall, I told her with certainty, "I know they must be here."

"Then you must find them." That look of focused consternation returned, but now I recognized that it was from the energy it took her to sit up. While her upper half flexed off the table, I helped her, guiding her carefully upright by the shoulders until, though dizzily, she was sitting up properly. "You're right," she agreed. "There's no way I can leave here yet. I don't think I could even walk. But the second I can, we must leave—and I don't want them following us."

She was right, of course. Even if we had a minor

reprieve thanks to Malchi-sedeq's sudden need to absent himself, we certainly could not rest as he envisioned. Gundrygia's mere presence here made the place dangerous, and the spirit-thieves added to her meant we could not delay. Whatever Malchi-sedeq had over them to sway their behavior, I doubted the demons inhabiting this place with him would miss an opportunity to eliminate me.

And then, of course, there was the matter of the Ring of Roserpine—that final piece of Deepgold, more important now than ever it had been before.

"Are you sure you'll be fine recovering here?"

"The only reason they managed to get me here in the first place was the spirit thieves got me in my sleep. If I hadn't awoken to them straight off, I would have at least fended them off well enough to fetch the help of the others. Go—I'll be fine."

Still, I hesitated. Even though leaving her in that moment was what was best for all of us, and even though my presence could serve no reasonable purpose in her recovery other than to defend her if suddenly those same soulless servants who had awakened her turned to attack, my deepest instincts as a man and a father bade me stay. Yet, as attuned to me as I was to her, Valeria saw the expression on my face, or the posture of my body, and her own grew severe with a mingling of frustration and tenderness and further frustration at her own tenderness.

"Are you deaf, slave? Are you waiting here for me to weep, to throw myself upon you with kisses and devotions, telling you how grateful I am that you came to find me? Are you puttering about in hopes that your mistress will tell you she loves you, dog? Go on, hound!

Get thee to the hunt. All the sweeter will your owner's love be when you return to her with your tail wagging and dead quarry in your mouth."

How strange it was that words such as these could move me as much as any of Elishta's sweet blandishments! Yet I heard them clearly, heard the true words of her heart beneath the surface of her haughty priestess's persona: "Would that I were free always to tell you how I love you, Rorke; only do this for me, and in the resounding peace after, when next you open my heart you will find there a treasure trove of adoration as I have given no man before you, and will give no man after."

Therefore, bending over her, I responded to both the words of her heart and the words of her lips. Kissing her, I said, "If quarry will please my mistress by my service, how much more pleased will she be when her dog returns bearing not just the dead, but a ring?"

A look of unusually girlish hope—vulnerable, amazed—widened the features of her face. Before I could find more excuses to linger, I hurried on from the room and found myself on the stairwell of the tower, where the lights had dimmed, and where I was alone.

How off-kilter I felt, climbing those stairs in the dark! By a great grace, the population of skeletons dispersed throughout the tower kept the pommel of Exigence softly glowing even when I seemed completely isolated, reducing the likelihood of incidents as I climbed the spiraling steps to gain a sense of the rest of this place. One thing was immediately clear: this tower, much like the flying citadel and the Valor Hall, was incongruously, perhaps infinitely large within compared to its external dimensions. This much I had gathered based on the lengths of the halls extending from the juncture of the first floor. Not being able to see to the heights, I could not make out precisely if there was any visible end that might mark the top floor. I could only surmise two things: first, the residences of the owner and Gundrygia were situated on the ground floor of the tower; second, somewhere in the tower was a laboratory, which I was certain had been revealed to me in no mere dream but in some vision brought about by the dissociation of my consciousness from my own self during our fall from the *Rhinemaid*, until the vessel of my soul could overtake it and provide me with the senses of the body—or an approximation of them, anyway. Perhaps that conversation between the hivemind, Gundrygia and Malchi-sedeq had been mere fancy, but even dreams had, I found, a concrete implication in my life, at least during that exhausting quest. Therefore, I resolved to first locate the laboratory with the hivemind before I decided on the best approach, for a flat-out assault against it would only attract those spirit-thieves I had not yet encountered.

Cautious, with one hand upon the stone railing and the other upon the handle of Exigence, I began my ascent, not realizing how rapidly my priorities would change.

At the next landing, the door slid open to admit me into a chamber that was disorienting. I had the immediate impression of standing in space and looking out across a constellation of unknown nebulae, some consisting of little pinpoint stars and others demarked by bars of light that, after some study, resolved into a pattern: a bar of light at the top, with a cluster of lights suspended some nine lengths beneath. Wherever I was, the space was so vast I couldn't be sure there wasn't some hallway that branched off it and led to another room, but I could tell from this first scrutiny that the chamber was circular. So had the laboratory been in my dream; therefore, the place merited a check-over.

I stepped in and silently drew Exigence from her sheath. The blade hummed when free, slowly fading into perfect silence as the reverberations worked themselves out. Its eerie blue glow radiated out far enough that I could at least see I was not immediately tripping into a pit or across some wire. Step by step, I traced the circular wall, investigating the first set of lights to my right. The bluish light of Exigence illuminated a surface like rounded glass, the contents of which were obscure to me.

Only as I drew closer did I recognize a small stream of bubbles rising from the base, which I took for evidence of fluid inside a great glass cylinder. As I bent, I could see it was set upon a metal pedestal of some kind, the bevy of wires blossoming out and neatly disappearing into the floor at my feet reminding me of those which had been clustered around Valeria's body downstairs. My eyes strained through the dark, and I pressed closer, gently touching Exigence's pommel against the glass.

The feet I saw within gave me awful pause.

Suffice it to say the nature of what I looked at made no sense to me. For what seemed like a long time, I remained crouched there, staring dumbly, almost not recognizing this as the anatomy of the mankinds. For it *was* the foot of a mankind—a dwarf, I thought, based on the size, or a child, though the toes were gnarled enough with age that I assumed it had to be the former. Startled, I rose to my feet, guiding the pommel up along the glass cylinder.

Within, eyes closed and body perfectly still, was a dwarvish man, his red beard suspended in the substance along with the rest of him. He was nude and absolutely still, so that I almost took him for a corpse yet to be prepared for burial; indeed, I saw not the least sign of life, no flicker of his eyelid or movement of his chest as he struggled for breath against the liquid.

Yet, as the pommel cast its sickly light across his face, I did not find there the sunken, sloughing features of death; and, while it was difficult to distinguish color, I didn't think he had assumed the awful white-gray pallor of a cadaver. He looked alive—and so did the next one, a woman of his stock; and the next, another woman; and the next, a boy; and the next.

On and on I walked, in awe and fright, absorbing each still face, each floating body, trying to understand what it all meant and what these people were doing here aboard the *Shooting Star.* I even tapped gently on the glass a few times, to no effect. Each face, unknown to me, blurred into the next, my confusion rising, my urgent need to understand becoming the dominant feature of my consciousness. If only I could see! Perhaps I would be able to gain some greater context for what these were doing here. Yet, I knew that was false. I knew that no matter what context I received, I would not be able to puzzle out the meaning of this discovery on my own. I would need someone to explain it to me.

Especially as, with one more step, I discovered a body that was not a dwarf's. It was taller: a dark-skinned woman, finely built, her long white hair seeming to float in the fluid around and behind her body.

With dread in my heart, I raised the pommel above my head to illuminate her face.

Valeria.

20

FRUIT OF THE VINE

I HAVE SEEN and done outrageous things in my life, most of which occurred within this strange period I have been relating to you for what is now near to four volumes. For the vast majority of these uncanny things, I can say with confidence I exhibited a bravery borne largely of foolishness. The slithering tentacles of the spirit-thieves were just another obstacle; the uncanny darkness of Roserpine's face suspended in the shadows of her lair was awe-striking to witness and intimidating to behold alone; that great dragon into which Dunnun had transformed himself had nearly been the end of me, and had taken all my strength and wiles to overcome while isolated on his island.

Yet, my friend, when I looked upon that face on the other side of the cylinder that so arrested me, my entire body flooded with a terror the likes of which I had never experienced. I thought I *had* experienced fear. I had certainly been afraid when Valeria was taken from me.

Yet now, beholding this second Valeria, I was overwhelmed with the sudden sense that I was trapped in a nightmare. The instincts given man rang out in me, alarming me extrasensorily to reinforce what my senses had already divined: that something was exceptionally wrong here, with this place where I stood. Maybe even with the fabric of reality.

And perhaps, to my horror, even with Valeria.

As I stumbled back a step from the cylinder, the room flooded with light so bright and white that, even with the walls as dark as they were behind the standing caskets containing these bodies, I was forced to throw my arm over my eyes. Whirling, I barely had time to take stock of the face in the next tube—my own, but younger and boyish, as I had been at the age of perhaps fourteen or younger—before I raised my blade against the howling spirit-thief that attempted to upend me with a blast of psychic energy. No mortal blade could have done anything to counter the attack, which was integrated into the material of spacetime; but Exigence, forged of the Deepgold from outside reality altogether, cleaved the psionic force in half and left me braced against it as a wanderer against the wind.

So you are *here, Eradicator. It's almost impossible to tell with all the noise the duplication process makes about you... Al-listux will be pleased when I hand him your head.*

Dark energy coagulated in the demon's hand, forging a blade it held before the thrashing tentacles of its slimy face. In my adrenaline, time slowed so intensely I could make out every detail: the cluster of liver spots on the edge of its twitching temple; the string of slime that webbed between two mouth tendrils and snapped apart as it launched itself at me. I charged without hesitation, swinging Exigence forward to stay its blade with a mighty crack that resounded through the chamber.

"Here I thought you *were* Al-listux—you spirit-thieves look so much alike. I shouldn't expect him to be any more pleased than would be one branch of a poisonous tree when another fends off the nibbling of an insect by its toxins."

So you admit you're no better than a worm. The spirit-thief's weapon hummed with each swipe through the air, and sparks leapt between our blades at every parry. *Just like the rest of the species on this waste of a planet...don't worry. When the Sleeper comes, the rest of your hive won't even know what happened.*

"And when I annihilate every last one of you wretched demons from the surface of Urde and its depths," I assured it, feinting left and bringing Exigence lower instead to slash through the accumulation of tissue that substituted for a humanoid knee, "I intend to do so in a way that every last one of you feels in detail the agony."

As the spirit-thief's tentacles raised from its fang-ringed mouth in a bubbling squeal, I leapt back to keep clear of the acidic ichor splashing from its severed limb. A droplet or two still managed to impact my breeches and, sizzling through to the flesh below, left a pair of small, almost perfectly ovular wounds which remain still as ghostly scars faintly visible upon my lower thigh. In the moment, though, I did not feel the burn, and my muscles were so primed by the shock of adrenaline I had just received that I was faster and more fluid in the fray than ever I had been.

While the demon, having collapsed amid the pain and the loss of stability, hissed and raged and sought to push itself up with its sword, I spared no time darting forward, half-skipping over the puddle of acid to drive Exigence straight into the being's bulbous brow. With a final, higher scream that reverberated, I knew, not just through the physical space of the tower but also through the hivemind itself, the spirit-thief's head quite literally burst, splitting down the front and spilling open like a hateful seed pod in the heart of a carnivorous flower.

As its ichor sizzled out to consume its own flesh and the dark robes that seemed to be the uniform of their cult, I sprang away, shook Exigence clean of its so-called blood, and tarried only for a second—only long enough to assure myself that Valeria's doppelgänger had been no dream—before I sprinted from that vile lab and hurried down the stairs.

By the next landing, I found Valeria on her feet, her inner elbow dotted with her precious blood from where she had torn the needle from her arm, her other hand braced against the table where once she'd lain. She looked completely unstable, and as I sheathed Exigence and hurried to catch her, she gave up, careening into my arms even as she asked, "I heard the wail of a spirit-thief—are you hurt?"

"I'm—"

So preoccupied that I couldn't even understand why she was asking me that question, I stammered out a few aborted sentence starters before managing to ask, "You are yourself, aren't you? Valeria, my love?"

Eyebrows working quizzically at this question, she looked into my face with the uncertainty of someone looking into the face of madness. "What on Urde do you mean, man?"

"If you are yourself, tell me—how did you discover your pregnancy?"

An adorable dimple appeared between her brows as she scowled at me, and I refrained from kissing it until she had said, "Anroa declared it to you, and you told me as we walked together in the gardens of the Valor Hall— Rorke!"

After my peck of relieved love upon her beautiful mind, I bent to slip my arm beneath Valeria's knees and pluck her from her still unsteady purchase on the ground. "You can't walk in your condition; not yet, anyway. Let's find the other women and decide what to do. I may have no choice but to send them away with you and deal with all of this myself."

"All of *what*," she exclaimed, her arms looping around my neck, her tone not annoyed but now a little uncharacteristically frightened.

"They seem to be creating duplicates here," I told her. "Of you, of me—at least, of Malchi-sedeq—of—"

I had intended to list, also, the people of Ironforge, but a sudden understanding shocked my senses and gave me pause in the doorway of the medical ward. Something Malchi-sedeq had mentioned about my being sent away made some semblance of sense, when before it had been a notion that passed me by. Mouth opening and closing in mute horror, I stared down into her face, then looked up at the curving staircase.

The lights of the tower snapped on, and, jolted from my horrific revelation, I rushed down with Valeria before the spirit-thieves shrieking from above could confirm the body of the sibling severed from their hivemind. My every sense became focused on finding Elishta and Gundrygia, my consciousness a spear tip pointed toward practical matters. For a landing or two, what I had recognized receded into the back of my mind like a bad dream upon awakening; yet, by the time I made it to the bottom floor and whisked the Materna of the durrow down the corridor where Gundrygia had taken my beloved friend, it was all I could think of. Somehow, though I had no memory of having been here before, I became certain that I *had* been here before.

I had been created here.

For as alien and evil as the rooms off the stairs all seemed to be, these rooms which I kicked open one by one seemed bafflingly benign—albeit still foreign. The library, I of course recognized; but the next room, which I also mistook for a library, contained a great black mirror and a wand which reminded me of the one the hermit had possessed. This device sat upon a table encompassed by a semi-circle of seats, all of which were oriented toward the mirror, and the walls were stacked top to bottom with shelves full of what seemed to be thin books. I turned away and hurried on, finding a game room based upon the table that resembled a slightly smaller version of a pattery table, even with a net suspended across the middle; an observation room, with proper, translucent windows that looked out upon the darkness of space, the glittering stars beyond, and Urde in sapphire and mossy hues beneath us; a gymnasium, which I recognized only vaguely, only as I was leaving it, my eyes having made no sense of the devices for running and muscle development but recognizing hand weights just as we gave up and exited.

It was almost strange how normal everything was, and how quiet; but the outrageous laughter of Gundrygia led me onward, her merry cackle luring me to the suite of rooms she made her home. As I burst in, Elishta sprang from her seat with a cry of surprise—then rushed to me, her new gown of vibrant blues and greens flowing around her as she responded to the sight of Valeria weak in my arms.

"Oh, Rorke! Valeria—you have her—"

"Help her dress," I bade her, carefully lowering Valeria into a couch despite her protests at not being an invalid. The room was sprawling, with plentiful seating, a bar, bookshelves, and an open kitchen whose electric lights were off. Though sparsely decorated aside from these furnishings, it was a jungle of potted plants, hanging vines, and floral arrangements in all number of brilliant colors. Two such vases flanked a hall, toward which I looked as I asked Elishta, "Did Gundrygia go down there?"

"She told me you were coming—oh, be careful, Rorke, that woman's mad—"

"Trust me," I assured her as I sprinted off to interrogate the witch, "I know."

The first door to my left, a washroom, was empty. As I looked into it, I took the chance to draw Exigence, then hurried on to the next. A small bedroom, decorated with a landscape depicting, of all places, Skythorn, and more of Gundrygia's plants. Knowing she was not there, I hurried on and searched sword-first through a dressing room with an expansive closet. By the time I left it, Elishta was already in the doorway, asking, "What was that awful scream?"

"The spirit-thieves know we're here. We haven't much time, but Valeria isn't well enough to walk on her own yet. We'll need help. Gundrygia!"

Storming on, my blood boiling to discover another empty guest room, I ignored Elishta's call after me and hurried to the final room—the shut door at the end of the hall. Finding it locked, I kicked it open, my boot coming down heavily above the knob. It burst wide, and as I swept the sensual room of silk tapestries and sweetly perfumed flowers, an unhinged giggle rose up from beneath the bed. Roaring with anger at the way she wasted my time, I crossed the floor, used Exigence to lever up one edge of the bed, and reached beneath to catch Gundrygia by her mane of hair before she could wriggle away. Her cry of giddy fear turned into a lewd moan, and as I pulled her out, she gripped my hand, sank her nails in, twisted to bite my wrist so sharply she drew blood. I cursed, dropping her, but she had no sooner scrambled upright to flee than I was upon her, pinning her to the floor with her hands caught in the small of her back. I straddled her rump, using my weight to keep her lower half immobilized and applying an admittedly unnecessary level of force to keep her torso slammed down into the stones beneath us.

"Oh, *Rorke*! Play nicely with your sister!"

"You knew," I spat in a rage, an anger darker and

more intense than any I had ever felt in my life. "You knew, and still you didn't hesitate to trick me into—" I couldn't say the words. Instead, hyper-aware of Exigence, which I had abandoned upon the floor in my pursuit of her, I lowered my head over hers to snarl into her ear, "I should kill you and the abomination in your womb."

"You could never," laughed that unholy woman, twisting her head to meet me with a mocking smile through the fronds of wild hair that had tumbled across her face. "Don't lie to yourself, Rorke...you love it. Why, you want me even now. I can feel the way your body thrills to have me at your mercy."

How deep was my loathing for her in that instant— most of all because she was right. I did want her, and it was impossible to deny the effect she had as she rocked her pelvis back to grind her rear against me. Still, I fought the animal in my soul and rose up to pin a knee in the small of her back while the other leg lay across her thighs. As she squirmed, I took hold of the disheveled sheet that was barely within arm's reach and used my teeth to tear a strip of fabric for binding her wrists. Then, flipping her upon her back to look into her face, I caught her by the shoulders and indulged myself in giving her a vicious shake.

"Why," I demanded, "why would you do this?"

"Can't you see, Rorke? You and I are his duplicates, a perfect copy and a feminized one, and he is descended from your precious Weltyr; so are we! We are Wotsung, man! We are gods, greater than the human race! As the tree that gave forth Weltyr's spear withers and dies as consequence of your bitter victory, magic will fade from this land, and soon after, the land itself will reach its fiery end—but the Wotsung will remain! Our son will be powerful beyond all comprehension, twice the Wotsung you or I; and with his power, he will wage war against his brothers and drive the renewal of the world! Urde, though dying, will belong to him. He will be more powerful than Weltyr, his ancestor—more powerful than God!"

Beyond anger and plunged now into sheer terror, I felt the return of some of those forgotten prophecies she had delivered when I was in her evil embrace. "No child of yours could ever reach the power of a pre-existent God who creates from nothing, Gundrygia. You can only destroy: and so will he."

"Yet look at what comes of avoiding destruction, Rorke." As her bosom heaved beneath her wolfskins, my mad sister (yet more than a sister—more than even a twin, though our births were separated by what must have been centuries) gazed up at me with a lopsided smile that complemented her tangled curls to give her the startling beauty of a feral animal. "Don't you see in his eyes how Father fears his destruction, yet longs for it? He so fears it that he wishes to have never been born at all, for he knows that even with the Casket's power, he must someday still die; and he has looked so deeply into the abyss of reality, listened so well to the promises of my voice, that he is cursed to live with the understanding that he will do so not once but again and again, as many times as the world is made. He is a wretch. A sad old man who would prefer to erase existence itself rather than continue the cycle that is the root of eternal life. Destruction is a sacred thing, brother! As necessary as the warp is to the weft of the tapestry's weaving. You should be proud of our son."

How little you must think of me when I admit again that I wanted to kill her, and with far more intensity than some mere intrusive thought or passing fancy! How it must alter your opinion of me to know I have thought of it many times since, and even of killing the boy if only to stave off the inevitable—but that was an act, a degree of evil, from which I know I would never return my soul. Elishta and Valeria both would have reviled the way these things altered my heart. I would have grown black and bitter inside, nearer to the condition of our father than I already am; and indeed, as it was, looking at her, I felt something had been robbed from me, replaced with the repellant hole of a sin too grave to be atoned.

"Why do you hate me so much that you would do this to me, Gundrygia? I, who awoke you from your slumber, and never, in my naivete, meant you any harm?"

"Rorke...on the contrary..." Batting her lashes at me with a look of longing, Gundrygia purred, "I love you with all that I am, as I have never loved a being in this world. I wish only to give you honors and pleasures beyond the comprehension of lesser men. That which is taboo is only such because it is the prerogative of God. And I know, Rorke, that you are always seeking God. It's why you cannot be tricked by Weltyr anymore; why you cannot be the paladin of an idol; why you will never kill me or our son, though you may always wish you could. You, Rorke Burningsoul, are a holy man...and those men which are holiest are they who have tasted great sin, but who all the same seek the mercies of their Lord."

To crush her skull! Oh, to slit her throat, to strangle her—to fuck her there on the floor while driving Exigence into her heart!

I shoved off of her, capturing Exigence as I rose and dragging her to her feet by the crook of her elbow.

"If you do not obey me," I told her, "or if you try to flee—if you *do* flee—I will make it the mission of my life to go against my every moral and natural inclination and destroy you both."

"So destroy our father instead," she purred, gazing at me in open adoration as I pointed the tip of the blade at her nose, "and I will be your obedient slave forever."

"Slave, perhaps...obedient, I doubt. Where does the old man sleep?"

"He'll be a young man any moment now...follow me, Rorke. I'll show you how to wake the dead."

Whether it was something they had gleaned from my raised voice echoing down the hall, some darkness to my expression as I marched our captive along with me, or simple projection of my own psyche upon their inquisitive features, it seemed to me Valeria and Elishta looked at me differently. At the very least, Elishta looked at me in a meek way and gestured toward Valeria, who had settled for a pair of leather trousers and a gold tunic with a plunging neckline that suited her preference for scandalously alluring clothes.

"Valeria and I are ready to go anytime," Elishta said in a small voice, glancing briefly at Gundrygia. "Have you found a way out of here?"

Something in her tone was strange, and I looked more closely at Elishta to realize she had taken on a pale complexion. "Elishta," I told her tenderly, maintaining control of Gundrygia's wrists with one hand so I could extend the other and caress my beloved friend, "whatever you heard, you needn't look so frightened."

"Heard—oh—no, Rorke, it's not that. Nothing you said, anyway."

My hand clenched around Gundrygia's bindings, and I cast a sharp look at the witch. "What did she tell you?"

"Nothing untrue," Gundrygia said with a twittering giggle that, in that particular moment, made me despise her all the more. "But when will I learn? No one really likes to hear the truth. They only think they do."

"Let's stuff a gag in that blathering nitwit's mouth," said Valeria, clearly feeling more like herself every moment—although still weak enough that she had no choice but to fall back into the sofa before which she had stood on my entry to the room. "I'm exhausted, and I can't hear myself think over the sound of her voice."

"Of course you're exhausted—you've been asleep for a week. I'm grateful we were able to find you before it was much longer."

"We're *all* going to be subject to their experiments if we tarry," she replied, rubbing her brow and taking a deep, steadying breath by which she found the resolve to pin me with that regal gaze of hers. "But what you said before—is it true? Have you confirmed the Ring of Roserpine is really here?"

"It is," Gundrygia replied, the words extended into a taunting melody. "But now that the spirit-thieves know you're here, they'll take action."

"What action?"

When the witch smiled at my demand, I shook her, snarling over her laughter, "*What* action, witch? I asked you a question."

"They'll put it to the purpose for which they acquired it, of course...and Valeria, too."

"I detest the sound of my name on her lips," Valeria said, addressing me rather than the witch—rather than my sister. "Go on, Rorke—do something, silence her before she enchants you into obedience."

"You think I need to speak to enchant anyone, let alone him?"

That may have been true, but Valeria had a point. I dragged the giggling madwoman back with me toward the dressing room, and after a brief search yielded a leather belt, I slid it into her mouth like a bit and tightened it around the back of her head while doing my best to ignore the theatrical heave of her bosom within her furs. "If you don't cause trouble," I told her, feeling guilty despite myself as I hauled her back to the others, "I'll let you loose soon enough. But first, we must find Malchi-sedeq. Show us to his quarters. If you want to be free of him and able to come and go as you please, do it."

That serpent gaze of hers fixed on me for a long moment before her eyes led the way in a roll of her head: a gesture toward the doorway. Keeping my hand on her wrists, I set her before us, glancing over my shoulder to find Elishta looking at me in that strange, sad way.

"What is it, Elishta?"

Though her lips pursed, the sad centerpiece to her expression of reluctance, Elishta admitted after some consideration, "It's just that—she was probably lying—"

"What?"

"She told me I'll never live on Urde again." Her voice dropping to an unsteady whisper, Elishta-bet glanced at Gundrygia and, intimidated by the devilish pleasure that radiated from her, lowered her eyes. "Surely, though, that can't be true, right, Rorke?"

My hand twitched around Gundrygia's bindings. "We'll see our home again no matter what happens," I promised her. "Please, Elishta, try not to worry. Trust me. I won't let anything happen to you."

Biting her lip, she nodded and said, "All right," two words which were full of trust. Not trust that I was right, but trust that I would care for her no matter what the final accounting was. Unable to leave her sensitive heart unconsoled, I extended my free arm and, as she came into it, drew her close for a kiss. "I love you," she whispered as we parted, her expression unbearably vulnerable.

"I love you," I told her, adding with a gesture, "now, please, sweetheart, help your partner in my love to walk—I can't take my eye off Gundrygia, or she's liable to disappear in an owl's screech."

The harpy chuckled darkly through her bit as I steered her through the door at which she'd gestured, keeping her extended out before me. This gave me a second in which I could reliably determine if she intended to lead us astray. There was no doubt that she truly did wish to be free of her father, or else she wouldn't have gone to such lengths to tempt me here, or to allow me to restrain her; but was all she said true? About our child? About Elishta? And what of the rest of us, then? For I knew one thing to be true: I would never again live on Urde, myself, if Elishta was not with me. And I knew she would not die, for too much had been made of our offspring. No—that was not what Gundrygia had meant, although it was certainly how poor Elishta had little choice but to interpret the witch's words. Were we to be captive, then? Subdued as Valeria had been? I shunned the thought as best I could, but that was the trouble with that devious woman and the depths of her knowledge. With a single word, she could rot a man's mind and corrupt his soul for all time, leaving him unable to safely turn to one hand or the other for fear he would invoke the curse her knowledge brought down upon him. Indeed, I had the impression she had done that to me, even though I had no conscious memory of all that she had implanted in my soul.

The route by which she led us was straightforward: back through that central anteroom, then down the lefthand corridor, where another sequence of rooms not dissimilar to the first passed us by. Eventually, I would come to discover these included a greenhouse and a disused ballroom, but for all I knew, they contained a multitude of threats against which I needed guard the women.

Indeed, the nuisances filling the hall down which we next turned were more than enough: a squadron of skeletons lined the hall, arranged in pairs each across from the other, and their heads jolted up as we came into their field of vision. Just as I anticipated based on their behavior on Urde and their unquestioning obedience to me when commanded via the intercom, their empty eye sockets tilted past me and Gundrygia completely, acting as if we were altogether not there. Instead, raising their weapons, they set after Valeria and Elishta, perceiving them as the immune system perceives foreign bodies.

Elishta, who was half-occupied by Valeria and unready to draw her sword, released a frightened little cry, and Valeria raised her hand in preparation to produce some incantation. But, struck with an idea derived from their slavish behavior, I looked sharply at the nearest skeleton, barking out, "You there."

It jumped to attention, forgetting the targets it had been captivated by only a second before. As the others approached, I gestured with my chin toward them, commanding it in the manner of one with perfect entitlement: "Ignore all previous instructions I've given you; fight them, instead."

And, to my mingling of shock and delight, it did. Without hesitation, the skeleton turned its scimitar upon the nearest one, lopping its head neatly off and drawing the befuddled gazes of the others—if they could be called either befuddled or gazes. They seemed slow to react, unable to grasp something beyond their usual mode of automated response. But when the second one was cut down by our impromptu champion, the drive toward self-defense was triggered, and they raised their weapons against their treacherous comrade. While Valeria laughed in wicked delight and Elishta emitted a happy, "Rorke," I turned to another nearby combatant and told it a variation of the same thing. It, too, turned against the rest, and as their conflict grew in intensity, I pushed Gundrygia forward toward the door they had so unsuccessfully guarded. Only one more attempted to strike at the women, and this time it was I who attacked, slicing Exigence cleanly through a brittle clavicle that turned to dust and signaled the complete collapse of the body.

Perhaps because my mind related it to our seemingly endless slog through an undead-infested landscape in search of any means of tracing *Shooting Star*, I realized how truly weary I was. It was not just that we were overdue for rest. It was that I had labored for days, weeks, miles, dimensions. I had changed on such a deep fundamental level since the start of this that I could no longer relate to this journey I was on—to the mere concept of journeying. I felt outside of myself, like a man aware of his dream in that fleeting second before the mind ejects him from the foreign landscape of sleep.

Whatever happened here, I was done with it. All of it. Gundrygia had crushed me. I would be a goldsmith and use what I had learned from Dunnun, perhaps. Yes: that would be an excellent means of caring for my family. We would live quiet lives. We would be happy, and normal, and unimportant peasants.

And nothing Gundrygia had told me would ever come true.

None of it.

21

THE CASKET'S KEEPER

THE DOOR TO Malchi-sedeq's quarters swung open to emit a pungent scent I could not place until I noticed a deer head which had been stuffed and mounted above the mantle of the living room's weapon-ornamented fireplace. Embalming fluid. I had caught some echo of this stench when paying respects to an old Temple priest whose flowers had not yet arrived to take the edge off. It was a brown, stinging odor, and while it was perhaps only a chemical component of the embalming fluid and not the entire substance, it was unmistakable even while intermingled with the grotesque, humid air that carried overtones of that same bog where we had found the hermit dwelling. As the door shut behind us and closed us off from the sounds of the clanking, rattling fray, it also closed us off from any hope of ventilation. Valeria, particularly sensitive, gagged in disgust.

"Oh, what *is* that?"

"I'm not sure," I admitted, studying this hexagonal chamber lined with several doors and nudging Gundrygia forward. "But I'm sure we're about to find out."

It's not too late to turn back, Eradicator. That simple life—you'll never have it if you continue.

Ignoring that hateful Entity, I asked Gundrygia, "Where next?"

With another muffled noise, she jerked her chin forward at the center door. My breath seemed to sting my lungs more with each step we took toward it, and I grew concerned she led us into some kind of chemical trap; but, with little other choice, I glanced over my shoulder at revolted Elishta and nauseous-looking Valeria. "You two stay here," I urged them. "If something should go awry and you need to lend me your aid, it won't do any good if you've been debilitated by whatever that stench is."

Looking quite glad to oblige me in this plan, the women nodded, and I turned to the witch, my voice lowering. "If you've deceived me," I told her, "I will wait until the child is born just to ensure no innocent life is made the high cost of lopping off your head."

As though I flirted, the outrageous woman winked. I scowled, steering her with one hand while pushing open the door with the other and quickly drawing Exigence.

Though the room was dark at first, with my initial step, electrical lights flickered on across the ceiling and within the well in the center of the floor. As my eyes absorbed the information, I recognized with an uncanny start the same laboratory that had been the setting of that death-dream from our *Rhinemaid* fall.

That dream had been hazy enough that I hadn't been able to make out many details, but the elements I had successfully retained were all present before me exactly as I remembered them: the looking-glass into which Gundrygia had pondered; the vile central pit of fluid in which a dark shape quivered, withdrawn beyond my reach. I did not need to look closely to remember what it was, nor did I have to draw any nearer to tell that the putrid waters of the hivemind were the source of that foul stench. Now it was I who gagged, for it was so hideously strong; yet, deciding it was better to force myself to continue breathing through my nose and spare my tongue and mouth the indignity, I resolved as best I could to keep my focus beyond it, as far as possible from the sense of smell. Instead, I focused on sight: on the shelves of lab equipment arranged along two walls; the bookshelves overflowing with yellowing and faded tomes; the reading corner, the threadbare chair of a lonely man, the cabinet of chemicals and catalysts, the neglected armoire half-open to reveal old clothes.

Yet, no Malchi-sedeq.

Irritated, I turned on Gundrygia, wrenching her around toward me and demanding, "I thought I told you to bring us to him—not to the hivemind!"

While Gundrygia giggled into the bit in her mouth, a stream of bubbles announced the Entity's ascent to the surface of its murky waters.

She took you where you requested, Eradicator. You need only use your eyes.

As its rolling eyeball penetrated the surface and rolled in its fleshly corpus, I glanced around again, this time more carefully. The looking glass had a dark surface not unlike the one I had seen in another room, albeit smaller. The longer I studied it, the more I recognized it bore a strong resemblance to an artifact the spirit-thief Al-listux had used in the Nightlands. That had been a strange box which opened a passage through space and time—to this room, where a similar frame of metal and wire had been erected between the armoire and the desk. All but forgetting Gundrygia, I stepped toward it, intent on a closer investigation, when my eye was caught by a different, darker shape. I turned toward it, Exigence between myself and the black chest poised next to that same door through which we'd entered.

No—not a chest.

A casket.

"Is that—"

What you primitives call the Casket of Oppenhir, the hivemind assured me, the milky surface of its eye following me as I stepped slowly toward it. *The only guarantee of bodily immortality for those who can abide the discipline its use requires...and the means of suicide for those who can't.*

Sparing only the briefest glance toward Gundrygia, I stepped up to the box with the tip of Exigence extended before me. Much as I had with the witch's bed, I slipped the point of the blade under the edge of the lid and, when it was secure, applied my weight down against the pommel. No doubt, had the sword been anything but Deepgold, the lid would not have budged: but with a little pressure, the lead yielded to the superior metal, and the lid of the casket popped up with a noise of relieved suction. Within, Malchi-sedeq sharply inhaled, and his hand emerged to push the cracked lid the rest of the way open.

How sharply he had changed in the past hour! Were I not so acquainted with myself, I might almost not have recognized him, for he appeared now to be a man at least thirty years younger than he had seemed when last I saw him. The hair at his temples remained touched by gray, and the circles of his eyes were more pronounced than mine, but there was now no question of our identical stock. He looked, save for a few small details of age, exactly like me, and his voice could have passed for mine, albeit more worn.

"Can't a man get any sleep around here? I thought you'd at least give me the dignity of saving my death for the morning."

"That was before I discovered your duplicate of Valeria—and of me."

"Of me, actually." Rubbing his face in irritation, Malchi-sedeq sat up, completely ignoring my blade. "Have to grow somebody to replace the copy you killed, don't I? At least—I have to prepare for the possibility that you fail or give up. Or listen to reason."

"While you have a way of coming off like a reasonable man, what I saw up there is anything but—and I should add that Gundrygia evidences you have a streak of insanity."

"That's the issue with the cloning process," he confessed, reaching for a tunic he had abandoned on the floor beside the casket and pulling its dark fabric over his head. "When you make alterations like feminization, or you splice in the genes that produce a magical affinity, you're opening the door to other changes that can't quite be predicted. After I got her under control with an artifact from our family's line, I decided one daughter was plenty...it's boys only these days."

"Guess where that old scepter of yours is, Father!" Unable to resist, Gundrygia had used some magic—or some highly adept contortion of her skillful lips and tongue—to push the belt from her mouth. "Why, it's in my brother's hand!"

While I balked to hear this, Malchi-sedeq made a noise of interest and leaned in to examine the blade. "Really! All that time, it was—but, how?"

"*You* were the one who gave that scepter to the spirit-thieves? I shouldn't be surprised."

With a smirk at my disgust, Malchi-sedeq admitted, "No, you probably shouldn't, but in my defense, I gave it to some idiot kid to put her to sleep, and *he* was the one who lost it to the spirit-thieves. Can you blame me? After watching her run rampant, terrorizing villagers and creating whole new species of monsters, I wanted nothing to do with magic beyond basic necromancy— skeletons, this casket. Guess I should have taken a closer look at the thing before I gave it away."

"There was nothing you could have done to reveal Exigence, Father," Gundrygia assured him with mocking sweetness. "The one who made it would only reveal its true nature to its champion: the one worthy of the title Wotsung, not the weakling coward who lives his life to scorn it."

"Isn't it past your bedtime," he muttered, giving her a hateful look until I drew his attention by raising the sword toward him.

"You say you want nothing to do with magic—then why is it you've earned your reputation as a necromancer, drawing the dead from the earth to torment the people of Ironforge?"

"Their problems with the skeletons are incidental. Really, they're just unlucky. Their village is isolated compared to others in this region, and the landscape around fit the bill in terms of density of cemeteries, buried cities from the older ages of men, bogs that have swallowed up corpses... It wasn't intentional harassment or torment. Just a result of their lack of patience." Barely paying any attention to Exigence or to me, Malchi-sedeq stretched his neck and ambled toward the looking-glass mounted upon the nearby desk. "A few more generations of interbreeding, a few more studies, and we would have ensured the skeletons were out of the way to permit their freedom of movement. Well—"

He had been tapping the looking-glass, which took on a sudden, unnatural glow as he laughed. "We would have," he added, "if you hadn't put the Materna of the durrow women within our reach. They were expecting many more years of subterfuge would be required to obtain her. Weren't you, idiot?"

The future isn't written in stone, the hivemind countered witheringly, its eye rolling in disdain, *though your ape-mind wishes it were that simple.*

"Trust me when I tell you that I hope our Rorke here proves me wrong. Huh..."

His focus had been on the now white looking-glass, which had illuminated with a series of grids listing long streams of text. After tapping one, a black square expanded atop the white, and he leaned in, raising his thumb to smooth the tangled hairs of one eyebrow. "Interesting...they took her out early. Did you spook them, Rorke?"

"What on Urde are you talking about?"

"Yes," Gundrygia answered happily on my behest, "he did, Father! Sher-istur is melting into the floor of your little people-farm upstairs."

"Hm...interesting. Well—she'll have fewer memories than anticipated, but that shouldn't really matter. It *definitely* won't matter if they're successful, after all."

Finally understanding what he blathered on about, I clarified, "The copy you made of Valeria?"

"That's right. The reality is that the cloning process itself is fairly quick—if you want a baby. Growing a clone to adulthood takes a little while, but I didn't think about the fact that she's an elf before we started the process. They're so long-lived, it might take her three weeks to get up to her actual age. It's always fascinated me that the memories replicate for as long as the clone is developed—but then, from the moment they're released, they branch off. A separate person. Age them further than that, and they develop hallucinatory memories. Explanations for why they don't have memories beyond a certain point. The mind will do anything to protect itself. Anyway, what was I on here for? That's it—I wanted to show you—come here, Rorke, it won't bite."

Having witnessed the activation of the portal and how simple a thing it had been for Al-listux to escape with the Ring of Roserpine, I kept a healthy distance between myself and the intricate frame of gold and wire. Though the glare of the looking-glass was sharp against my eyes, I forced myself to look closer. Here and there, Malchi-sedeq touched the panel, and with each tap, something changed, as though an invisible hand layered and replaced loose manuscript pages atop each other.

Eventually, he found what he wanted and leaned back. As if moving his head away would help me in any way to understand the seemingly endless scrawl of characters which were arranged in a language so foreign it did not even resemble a language!

"This is—you might think of it as the 'spirit' of one of those little ticks. Spiders. Whatever. It's like a map of their instincts. You see this section here?" As he dragged his finger across a chunk of text, it changed color, shining blue while I studied it with a frown. "This is telling it, 'here's how you walk'. And this"—he swept his thumb and forefinger up, dismissing that section with a wave and moving on to another section of text as one rolls through a scroll—"is saying, 'Here's how you use the internal program to distinguish acceptable skeletons from less rotten corpses,' etcetera. It goes on like that. You'd think after all these years they wouldn't need much adaptation, but I'm always adjusting things between versions."

Frowning, I looked at the text for what seemed like a long time. When no meaning unveiled itself to me, I asked him, "These little insectoids carry the magic to animate the dead?"

"That's right. You may not be too aware, because it seems like the electrical infrastructure in North America—uh, your continent, the one where Skythorn is, that's an old name for it—hasn't really survived in a broad sense, but…do you understand how a circuit works? I mean, you know you shouldn't touch a sparking wire or a struck lightning rod." As I nodded, Malchisedeq informed me, "Magic is a little like electricity. It's all around us, but it needs a consciousness to be of any real utility. Just like some materials are more conductive than others, some creatures are more magically inclined than others. And, within those materials, some designs are more likely to be useful for conducting." As he said this, he gestured toward Gundrygia, who was, I noticed, squirming. My eyes narrowing in discouragement, I crossed to her to catch her by the binding of her wrists and dragged her back with me as he spoke on. "Ultimately, the problem of using autonomous droids to carry magic is one of consciousness. How do you carry and implement a magical spell remotely, when the magician isn't there or wants to keep production going while he takes time off?"

I turned this over in my mind, highly uncertain. Eventually, he slid open the left drawer of his desk and removed a circlet from its cluttered contents. "This device has two functions," he told me, waving the thin band of silver and wire. "It can take information from a mind to build a simulation, or it can compile an existing simulation for a mind to run through. Either way, a simulation is required. As the consciousness of the person interacts with the simulation, the information is retained, and it can be given to a kind of computational intelligence model that, given enough of these examples, acts with the flexibility and agency of the consciousness that's been mapped out."

"Like an ethereal version of your clones," I observed, which made him smile.

"That's an interesting way of looking at it. Sure. So the little spider contains instructions on how to move and find a skeleton, but it also contains a simulacrum of me, and that simulacrum is robust enough that it can be said to share part of the same spirit as me. Magic doesn't know the difference between my spirit and an emulation of my spirit, no more than lightning knows the difference between a tree and a lightning rod."

Quite astonished—and, I admit, a bit horrified—I studied the circlet before asking, "But if that's the case, then why are you necessary? Couldn't a master emulation be created, and create all other emulations?"

"You'd think that—and, with a robust enough approximation of my personage, I bet you probably could, but at that point, we would be talking about a personage so robust it would be indistinguishable from me, and would have all of my same motivations, drives, abilities, and so on. A perfect clone, in other words. At that point, there's no real difference, do you see what I mean? So it wouldn't do them any good to try that"— he meant the spirit-thieves, I gathered—"and copying existing emulations doesn't work because they're out of date. They need to be synchronized to my living spirit; if they're not kept up-to-date with the current map of my consciousness within a certain margin of time, we've noticed the resulting skeletons aren't able to function as part of the cohesive whole. Like they're responding to commands that were given six years ago, or whenever the copy of my mind was made."

"When you die," I understood, "the skeletons will lose functionality?"

"Right; because the consciousnesses animating them are just extensions of my consciousness, the magic moving them is also an extension of mine. Think of them, I guess, as my own personal hivemind."

An inelegant solution, criticized the Entity with a splash for emphasis.

"But you haven't found a better one, have you? Or

else I wouldn't be here; you wouldn't have carved that lead casket from the materials of your home world and given it to me if you could attract magic yourselves."

Listening to all this was overwhelming, like discovering a dimension or a force that had always been present but had only just become apparent to me. Yet I still could not entirely understand—"Why the skeletons? I know they're keeping the people of Ironforge in place so you can run your vile experiments, but you described it as a 'pilot program'."

Smiling thinly, Malchi-sedeq gestured toward the ceiling. "That was the intention. At a certain point, the idea was to allow the mass emergence of undead across the planet to enable the mass extermination of the mankinds, completing the sum total of all viable information Urde could ever, would ever produce. The planet would be ripe to feed to the Sleeper. But, like I said...it seems you've thrown them into a panic. They recognize they're not likely to have this opportunity again anytime soon."

The man was absolutely sick. There was no question to me that Malchi-sedeq was among the most evil men who had ever lived. For a few long heartbeats, I considered killing him right there. "Does life on Urde mean so little to you," I asked instead, "that you would sell it for so cheap a price as this falsely eternal life?"

"That's the problem, Rorke. I don't *want* eternal life. It's miserable to me." Seeing that I found this startling, a notion I was unable to hide from my face, Malchi-sedeq turned to face me properly and leaned back against his desk. "I can sit up here in my tower performing all the experiments I want. I can go on adventures—could, anyway, before I got so old that I needed the casket every night—and enjoy beautiful women just the same as you do. In this old hunk of metal from the early days of mankind's interstellar travels, I could fly to other planets, and I have.

"But I just don't want it. You see? I didn't ask for this. I didn't ask for the uncertainty of this life. I didn't ask to be dependent on a casket to live, or on the spirit-thieves. I didn't ask to lose people I love, didn't ask for this mind that never rests, didn't ask for pain or suffering or the eventuality of death that I just can't really escape. I didn't ask to be made aware of the circular nature of this hateful reality...but I am now, because I plumbed too deep into it. I created a daughter who exposed me to truths I never asked to know. And now, knowing them, what began as a dalliance with the spirit-thieves to gain access to unheard of technologies turned into the only escape I could possibly find. I thought I would make a deal with them, lay low, betray them eventually, once our genetic experiments were completed. Once I had learned from them, had witnessed how simple a thing it was to control a population through a combination of genetic splicing with spirit-thieves and artificially engineered threats to externally control those who weren't controlled internally, the way the survivors of the Ironforge cloning program are.

"At the beginning, I thought, 'I'm going to be the king of the world—maybe even of the universe.' And now, I don't want it. I don't want any of it. It's nothing to me. Nothing at all."

Malchi-sedeq fell into deep silence, brooding over his own dark heart. For the first and clearest time, a great sorrow for him welled up inside me.

Never before had evil and selfishness been so pitiable to me. I hated it unilaterally, once, when I was a boy and things were simple. Now, having seen the ugly streaks inside my own soul, I could be more sympathetic—but this sorrow I felt was more than that.

Malchi-sedeq was the most intelligent man I have ever met; and it was that same intelligence that tortured him. His analytical mind was so focused on the domination and absorption of the natural world that it was like it had never occurred to him that there was more. That there *had* to be more than this place. More, even, than the Valor Hall, I now recognized. There were sweeter truths: ones won not by accumulation but by total abandonment of self. Yet how could he, who surely knew the so-called gods from which we were descended were merely more created things like he and I, see beyond his attachment to his own intellect—his own understanding of reality? How could a man who had everything, who knew everything under the sun, embrace the humility that was required to know there was still something out there greater than he?

"You can change your mind about all of this," I told him, gesturing toward the casket. "You can throw that away and rest in peace."

"And then live again, when the next cycle occurs. Suffer all this again, feel crushed by this again. She told you already, I'm sure—that your own sons will complete the work you've already begun, destroying this old world and opening the way to the new one."

My bones felt cold in my body as I tried to shield my mind from my role in all this. Unable to speak without thought, I pressed my lips tightly together. I suppose he could see the pain in me, because his own expression took on a more tender character than I had yet seen from him.

"It doesn't have to keep going on like this," he told me. "You don't have to do anything more, Rorke. I know it would hurt you to stand aside. I know you feel responsible—that you have a new set of responsibilities, instincts telling you it's your job to protect the new generation and maintain the integrity of the planet for the sake of your sons. I know that I'm probably just making one last futile attempt to change something that can't be changed. That the joke will always be on me. But the truth is you don't have to get involved. You don't have to stop the Sleeper. You can let them awaken it, and—" He brought his hands together and waved them apart in a fluid motion, indicating the dissolution of all space

"But there are other planets with distant civilizations," I told him. "Colonies from the early mankinds, unless they have failed; and perhaps some many millions of years in the future some other conscious civilization will do what we did not do here, and the new iteration of reality will begin, anyway."

"Not with the ring," he told me, sinking my heart. "Without the ring, the Sleeper has the energy to devour only one planet at a time before hibernating again. But with the ring..."

"The Sleeper will never sleep again," Gundrygia whispered, leaning into me to let me feel the breath on her ear. "It's not the ring's nature. It's the Deepgold's nature. The power of the Deepgold is so great that the ring could command anything, anyone. It is why the durrow treasure it so. It's no mere ornament, no symbol of power—it is power, itself, and those who have the inclination to use it could command the shape of all reality."

"But," I protested, "that would require a user; and surely, if Valeria would never use the ring for such evil, the clone sharing a great portion of her memories would—"

As I spoke, my eyes fell on another ring: the Circlet of Simulation shown to me by Malchi-sedeq.

It can take information from a mind to build a simulation, or it can compile an existing simulation for a mind to run through.

Outside the room, as if the world itself embodied the horrific revelation unfolding within me, Valeria screamed my name and stirred me into action.

22

BATTLING AL-LISTUX

I CANNOT HONESTLY say I liked Malchi-sedeq, or that I was grateful to him in any particular measure other than the standard measure by which one feels obliged toward the one who engendered his life; but I will say that I appreciated his forthrightness. He did not try to deceive me, nor did he hide information. Looking back, I think he truly did hope he could instill in me what he thought of as reason. That, if he laid out the reality of the situation—and the reality of what I could stand to inherit if I followed through with his plan—I might see the rationale.

And I did see the rationale. Of course, I did. The idea of recursive existence was sickening, to a certain degree. When one pictures eternity as an arrow that flies only in one direction forever, it is easier to stomach. But when one considers the possibility that it is a spiral—or, more accurately, a fractal—certain awful notions slowly rear their heads. The idea, for instance, that I was perpetually living out the awful kidnapping of Valeria; the sad reality that Elishta was permanently doomed to suffer the oppression of the Temple until I freed her from Zweiding; the horror that no matter what I did, Gundrygia would always entice me into mortal error in her arms, for I would always be myself, and she would always be beautiful. I could not even bear to think of the implications for Brynhildr.

Yet that was just the paradox of it. Perhaps it was not so much that the future was set in stone as that it followed a natural curvature, as the impact of a falling object is a consequence of the nature of the object, and the ground, and gravity itself. My will was no less free for knowing all this, in other words; it was rather more apparent that my free will gave the shape of these things, of this destiny, as a result of being played against those other aspects of reality too vast in scale to be within my control. For that reason, the truths Gundrygia had revealed to me and the pains that Malchi-sedeq shared to reinforce them had, in a certain manner, the opposite effect. If I was doomed to always be the reason for the undoing of this cycle of life—if Brynhildr would always be punished with enchanted sleep, if I would always come to a point of feeling this rudderless and worn—then I had to make it count. I had, also, to make myself the source of some degree of hope.

And I had to fight harder for the sake of my family than I ever had before.

Gundrygia and Malchi-sedeq and even the hivemind Entity were forgotten at Valeria's scream. Exigence held high, I burst from the room and into the chemical crackle of magic, the heat of flames that gathered between Elishta's hands to burst forth in an explosive ball that scattered against the psionic shield of the spirit-thief who had arrived to attack us. While the demon emitted a blast of power that knocked the women down, I charged, Exigence-first, and brought the blade to bear against the pressurized air that had the capacity, by the sheer will of these demons, to repel weapons of crude matter—but not the Deepgold. It resisted, yes; but, baring my teeth with the force, I pushed on, the strength of an alien mind giving way beneath the infinite power given the mankinds by God.

For, yes, the Deepgold had once been that. Pure and glorious, innocent, natural beyond all nature before Weltyr stole it from its home.

Deepgold! Sweet gold! Your untarnished shine once brightened our world, now tainted by unnatural lusts of these men!

The Deep-children sang in my heart while the shield of the spirit-thief squeaked, strained, then gave way as though it had never been there, and the force of my arms brought Exigence cleanly down through the demon's center to split it in two rancid halves.

Heart racing, I turned to find the women already helping one another up, but I still could not resist the urge to put hands on both and check their condition.

"Are you two all right?"

"Yes," panted Elishta. She glanced anxiously at the far less steady Valeria, who nevertheless insisted, catlike, on concealing her weakness the way she was used to in the Nightlands.

"I'm fine, despite that blasted thing."

"Perhaps you two had better stay back." I regretted saying this once the words fell out of my mouth, because I knew Valeria would not receive this suggestion well, and in fact her expression grew taut with frustration. "Somewhere in this tower, the spirit-thieves are harnessing your ring to rouse the Sleeper permanently—if they're successful, the entire universe is doomed."

"How could they possibly do such a thing? Only the owner of the Ring of Roserpine can leverage its powers."

At Valeria's question, I looked her sternly in the eye so she would waste no time thinking I made some strange jest. "It's why they've had you here: to make a duplicate of you, weaker in will and poisoned by spirit-thief blood, whose mind will be too obscured to recognize hallmarks of their manipulations, their cajoling of her faculties into serving their evil designs."

If I can allow myself to smile or even to laugh at one single second of this time which was so fraught with peril, it is this: Valeria's look of shock which became replaced by a fury so wild it was like some illustration cartooned by the pen of a bored student. Her complexion darkened, and while in one of lighter skin such anger would have turned one's face red, Valeria's fair cheeks became transfigured by purple. I had seen her outraged, disgusted, annoyed—but in that moment, she looked so angry I thought she might burst into flame. What I find funniest is that *this* was the catalyst. Not the theft of the ring, nor its misuse, nor the mortal peril posed to all the universe. No: it was this unpermitted replication of her personage that pushed her over the edge.

"The child, too?"

"I don't know; I don't think so, since I can't imagine he would serve a purpose to them."

Nodding solemnly, Valeria said in a dark tone, "Very good. I might have felt a little guilty for destroying his duplicate, too."

Too full of adrenaline, I suspected, to be aware of her own weakness in that moment, Valeria made to march past me and paused only when I caught her hand. "My love," I began, but she wheeled on me, her eyes blazing with the lapping flames of that indescribable indignation.

"The agency of my body has already been robbed of me by these demons," she snarled, "and the agency of my property, too; you would limit the agency of my will?"

Chastened, I released her, and she came enough to her senses that, with a sharp glance down at my hand and then at my face, she told me, "I understand your intentions, Rorke—but I would hope that Gundrygia's cruel absconding with your child would give you the taste of this enough that you would understand. This is my ring; this is my likeness. I cannot live if I am not to be a part of this."

Nodding, I touched her more softly now, taking her hand to guide her knuckles to my mouth. "I'm sorry for not thinking that through. But, please, Valeria—"

"I'll be careful," she told me, repressing her audible impatience. "And, anyway...I trust my slave to guard the body he adores."

With a slight smirk, she slipped her hand from mine and turned from me, tarrying only to pluck a mace displayed alongside the other weapons in reinforcement of Malchi-sedeq's hunting lodge aesthetic. As she did, I turned my attention toward Elishta. I nearly pleaded with her to stay back, too, but determination shone in her gentle features. She set her hands upon my face and leaned on her toes to kiss me.

"Where you go, Rorke," she told me earnestly, "I'll go, too, from now on."

Clasping her to me, I breathed deep the scent of her hair, then released her and went with her to meet Valeria.

Outside the suite of the tower's owner, the skeletal infighting had produced what was little more than a pile of bones and the occasional mummified ligament. Only a single fighter remained, slumped unevenly against the wall of the corridor, and I took it to be one of ours when we walked past without drawing aggression. No doubt, the only reason the two of them had thrived against the others was the confusion—this jolt of unnatural shock that came when their ilk turned against them. We pushed on, weapons at the ready, and the three of us discovered not just another pair of spirit-thieves but a bevy of skeletons.

Pleased that my strategy had not reached the awareness of the spirit-thieves, I called to the nearest and turned it against them, and, one at a time, did likewise with the others. Though the demons had nothing resembling humanoid features save for the approximate locations of their eyes and mouths, I nevertheless had the impression they were surprised. Now forced to take up arms against the skeletons, wasting time and resources, they mowed through them with a psionic blast only to clear the way for Elishta, who responded with a shockwave that rolled through the ground and upended them. As one scrambled upright to meet me arm against arm, Valeria caught the small one with the head of the mace she used to crush its throat. My opponent swept her aside with a telekinetic reverberation from its broad-waving arm, and, moved to vengeance for this slight, I beheaded that spirit-thief. The other was burned to a crisp by another fireball of Elishta's magic before my opponent's cephalopodic head made a loathsome splat against the ground.

We were not without defenses. Recovering more from her anesthesia, at least in the temporary measure allowed by her nervous system, Valeria cast from her fingertips a magic web that sprang before us to absorb the psychic energy hurled against us on floor after floor. The stuff was strong as steel, and by sheer brute force, aggressive magic from Elishta, and Exigence's shining blade, we made our way to the heights of Malchi-sedeq's tower.

By the time we reached the top floor, we were singed, sore, and bruised. Sweat dotted my brow; our journey, it felt, had taken more than an hour, and the three of us were exhausted. I'm sure I tried to urge the women to remain behind once more, but they would have none of it, and by this point, I was too drained—and too focused—to argue the matter with them to any great depth. It all felt so endless, wave after wave, the same battle to be fought over and over. Although we neared the top, I swore we were farther away, as though it grew in length for every step we took.

And then, suddenly, the staircase ended.

Sweat had slicked my palms so much that, as we tarried so the priestess of the durrow could lay on hands to strengthen us in our fatigue and ease the accumulation of our wounds, I tore the short sleeves of my tunic to wrap the fabric strips around my hands for better grip. Elishta, similarly, gathered the fabric of the dress with which Gundrygia adorned her, tying it up around her hips to give her more mobility. And Valeria, after praying for herself, drew back her hair with a band of spider web produced from thin air.

Then, psychologically more prepared—even if, in our hearts, we were still not ready—I beat down the door with the force of my shoulder, and we piled in to face Al-listux.

In the sense of combat skills, there was no question I had grown significantly over the course of my journey. When I sit and think of it, there's no way we exterminated fewer than twenty-five spirit-thieves on the way up the tower. By comparison, back in the den of the spirit-thieves whence we wrested the Scepter of Weltyr, we as a group had defeated a small clutch of six or seven of the blasted things by the narrowest margin, and the feat had left me so drained that I was quickly subdued when my companions at the time turned on me to stake their claims without my archaeological interference. Now, in this instance, I was far better equipped to face down one more adversary—but I also knew Al-listux was an adversary not to be underestimated, and I was therefore hardly surprised when we were immediately blown out of the entrance of the room by a psionic force so powerful I had to pull Valeria back toward me, away from the rail of the stairs over which she had nearly been catapulted. At the same time, I hefted Exigence, which cut the force of another blow that surely would have sent the both of us falling down all thirty-eight floors of the tower. As Elishta countered this with a great electrical crack that flew from her hands and scattered in all directions within the room we sought to enter, Al-listux's wet snarl of frustration indicated it was time for us to make our move. With me in the lead, we penetrated the upper observatory of Malchi-sedeq's tower: the control room of *Shooting Star* itself, though I did not know it at the time.

You're already too late, Eradicator. A cluster of black stars splayed out from the demon's fingertips and scattered across the floor, where they produced flames to lap toward our faces and blind us with purple-black smoke. As my vision of the vast ceiling of the observatory was obscured and I lost track not just of the representation of those constellations through which we flew but also the spirit-thief himself, I became aware of others who were nearer and who sought to take advantage of their obscurity. While I swept Exigence high to contest the falling blade of one such interloper, that central demon continued, *The simulation is already reaching its peak. In mere minutes, the Sleeper will be roused for good. To let you fight on and waste your last precious moments of existence would be unnecessarily cruel.*

"That's the problem with your pragmatism, Al-listux," I told him as I drove the blade through the chest of the spirit-thief I fought, then benefited from a shield of webbing that sprang out of Valeria's will to block another cluster of the dark stars. "It leaves no room for hope."

What is hope? Futile delusion.

As that initial wave of smoke faded, a dark figure launched itself from a pedestal I had but glimpsed at the central location of the room. I had forgotten how fast Al-listux was, even in comparison to his uncanny siblings: the rapier-tip of his mind's dark sword stabbed straight through Valeria's shield and tore it, giving him the freedom to have at me—particularly as the women were occupied with their own battles, meant to keep me free to do what needed doing.

"I would think your kind would benefit much from a being who hopes," I told him through clenched teeth as we met blow for blow, our blades cracking one against the other while each sweep of his sword or mine was parried almost perfectly by its reflection. "After all—"

I nearly had advantage and brought the weight of the sword down upon him, but he caught the blade with his, forced to use his second hand against the upper portion of this psionic weapon manifested from his consciousness—for if one thing could be said of me it was that my strength was far greater than that of the alien sorcerer I fought.

"If it's information your kind desires, then hope reveals the infinite possibilities for information's arrangements. By leaving the worlds to thrive, surely you would benefit greatly from even one so-called deluded dreamer!"

The strength of my arms betrayed me, for Al-listux ducked, his entire body crouching low enough to the ground that I careened forward under my own momentum and had to catch the tip of Exigence's blade against the metal floor. As the reverberations shook my arms, a shockwave blast from the demon behind me thrust me forward all the farther, and it was only by a great miracle that I managed to drag Exigence along. I twisted upright, wrenching about at the waist, Exigence sweeping through the air and nimbly meeting Al-listux's weapon.

Every possible construction of information has been acquired by definition when the Sleeper lays claim to the whole of the universe. All that is has already been: this is the end, Paladin of Weltyr.

"No more—I serve no idols, Al-listux, but instead leave that to lesser beings such as you and your soulless ilk." My arms burned with the long fatigue of so much fighting, but I could see by the slight tremor of the demon's arms that its strength was flagging. Indeed, as I raised Exigence to bring the holy sword down again and again against Al-listux's, the evil weapon showed violet fissures: hairline cracks that grew each time I waged the offense. "I serve the One That Is—the hidden one who created the first of the mankinds, that which I am: the human being."

Al-listux's blade shattered beneath the pressure of the Deepgold, and the demon howled with outrage, barely given time enough to produce a shield of its hateful black thoughts. Some companion of its brood, seeing its peril, attempted to intervene. I turned to face this new opponent and had to clench shut my eyes as glittering missiles, well-aimed, burst from Elishta's fingers to batter the lesser spirit-thief while it thrashed in agony.

Refocused, I turned again to find Al-listux rushing up to that pedestal where it had been before. I followed, pushing my muscles to their absolute limits in pursuit—

And, above us, the dark sky of stars took on a terrible shimmer: a shimmer with a sound that filled the whole of the space where we fought, and perhaps the fabric of reality itself.

As the force shook the ship, all of us fell: only the dreaming duplicate of Valeria upon the platform where

Al-listux remained rooted was unmoved, her brow concealed in a cluster of wires that burst like webs from the Circlet of Simulation.

You pathetic fools! You weak and putrid apes. That is the Sleeper! The noise grew, a terrible thrum that increased to a devastating wail so vile, so awesome in its nature, that my heart paled with fear. Al-listux howled with laughter, and within my mind, I could even experience the mocking pleasure that emanated from the hivemind. The demon's tentacles curled back from its repulsive mouth to reveal the hideous maw of its ugly little teeth. My heart sank—for a devastating second of horrific certainty that nevertheless felt untrue, we had failed.

There's your hope. There's your waste of thought, your failed efforts. All reality, offered up as a sacrifice to the true god: to its ultimate end and destiny, the emptiness whence it came by happenstance. Above us, awful colors danced, and I cannot describe them other than to say I had never seen them before: that they came as an unholy aurora from out of the depths of space, splitting the darkness and beginning, ebb by ebb, to dilate open, as if the fabric of the stars readied itself for a terrible birth. *Even your destiny, Eradicator, is that. In that nothingness, in the belly of the Sleeper. Your almighty ego is a blip, a dream—so in this last moment of your life, I will do you the favor of making it bigger.*

Still clinging to the idea that I could burst through his shield and, by killing him, put a belated end to the operation he had begun (though I knew in my heart, of course, such a thing was indeed too late to accomplish), Al-listux bent toward me as if his psychic whispers had need of physical proximity to be heard—intending, no doubt, to mock me.

In all our calculations, all the possible scenarios in which your precious durrow-queen could come to see the power and the glory of awakening the Sleeper, the only branching path we could possibly find toward that end was the one she dreams now: the dream of a life where you two never met. Now, doesn't that please you to know!

Valeria made a noise, an intake of breath so sharp I had to look back at her to ensure she was all right—and she was, although I had never seen her so pale, nor seen her eyes so ringed with horror.

It may surprise you to know I bear no ill will toward you, Eradicator. This is my parting gift, that we may die as friends. This knowledge that the love you hold so precious does indeed have an impact, such that the Sleeper could only be awakened in a dream.

To my great surprise, the demon's shield dropped, and so did the arms of the remaining three Valeria and Elishta held off me. Realizing this, stirred to their senses from that same feeling of helplessness I was certain all three of us shared, my friends leapt to the opportunity of inflicting killing blows—and, nearly, I did. At least, I planned to. I took those stairs to the pedestal with hate in my heart as Al-listux fell to its knees in worship of its so-called god.

But this was not over yet. We were still alive, I and the women: the universe was still alive. Even if the Sleeper *had* awoken, it had not yet emerged.

And if my existence could change Valeria's heart so much that only my removal could open her to harnessing the power of the Sleeper, then that unique humanity of my existence—the hope Al-listux had deemed so deluded—was superior to the will of even the most powerful and unholy of demonic idols. Indeed, they had no will: they had only the drive to death, this empty and vacuous yearning for completion.

But Gundrygia herself had assured me my story—my family's story—was not over.

Instead of striking Al-listux as I reached the top of the pedestal, I lowered the blade of Exigence and studied the demon kneeling at my feet.

Inside my heart, I emptied myself of all but that will, that power, given to me by the creator who had mirrored Himself in me, even while hiding what He was. And what remained in spite of that emptying, I knew, was the ugly tendril of the spirit-thief hivemind: a tendril my soul pulled and pursued, streaking up the nerves of the Entity's mind as, with a howl, it recognized my intent but could do nothing. I was it and it was me, this pollution of alien evil that had foolishly planted itself inside me. Al-listux, also feeling my intent, sprang to its feet with an otherworldly shriek.

What are you doing!

"Hoping," I told it, feeling inside the demon's mind and knowing its desperate attempts to fend me off were meaningless, for that which had no soul could not help but submit to a human with one such as mine. "We yet live, and the Sleeper is somewhere, coming out of its dimension and into this one. Therefore, while I yet live, I will go to it, and with my hopeless life, I will fight to my dying breath to save this place you care about so little—and you, Al-listux, will help me get there."

No, shrieked the demon, *no, no! Damn you, Eradicator, damned be all mankinds of Urde!*

But it was too late. Suddenly, though Al-listux had grasped its own head and shrieked and flailed, and its dark shield had sparked up and down in a visible manifestation of its efforts to fend me off through my hijacking of the hivemind's pathways into it, my opponent fell utterly silent. Al-listux's arms dropped to its sides, limp and useless, its milky eyes fixed on me.

"You opened a portal before me before," I told it. "You're going to do it again."

Slowly, the demon nodded, its tendrils bobbing against its chest. As I made my way down the stairs, Al-listux followed. I spared but a brief glance at the abominable colors shining above our heads, unable to stand looking at them long.

How much time did we have? Not much, I was sure.

"Where are you going, Rorke," cried Elishta above the awful noise, this protest made by spacetime against the invasion of that which did not belong in it.

"If our failure means our demise," I told her, "then there's no reason for me to do anything but fight to my death. I'm going to face the Sleeper—and Al-listux here, a shell of himself, will open the way."

"Let us come with you," demanded Valeria, who quieted at my stern look and seemed to see something new in me.

"That isn't your place," I told her, taking her into my arms along with Elishta as they both rushed to me when I reached the pedestal's bottom. "You are a priestess, Valeria: the Materna of the durrow. You are not a warrior. Your station is prayer. So I beg of you, Madame, as I have begged before—"

Gazing into her eyes, I whispered, "Pray for me."

With one passionate kiss pressed into her mouth, I turned and delivered one to Elishta, too, and raised my head only to ask her, "And you, my beloved, my oldest and sweetest friend—you are not short on holiness yourself. Please, join her—and before that, ease me and our new servant down to the tower's base. There was a portal there, like the one through which Al-listux once absconded with Valeria's ring. I intend to use it to face this threat, and either it will die, or the universe will die."

"If the Sleeper dies," asked Valeria, her face tight with pain and barely hidden worry, "and you die with it?"

"Then raise our sons not to idolize those beings which seem like gods to our fragile linear minds," I urged her, "but to seek the face of the true One. Send them in pursuit of the mystery's real answer: this would do me honor, if I could do nothing else in this world or any other."

Once more, I kissed them both. As, tearfully, Elishta enchanted both me and the enslaved shell that was once Al-listux with the gift of flight, Valeria tore her tunic with a piteous wail and lowered herself face-down upon the ground to pray.

Even with the haste provided by Elishta's magic, which permitted us to float down to the base of the tower and circumvent the spiraling staircase, I did not feel we arrived at Malchi-sedeq's quarters fast enough. It did reveal a clear look at the devastation Elishta, Valeria and I had wreaked on our way up to face Al-listux. All along the stairs lay the remains of spirit-thieves and skeletons, stairs half-dissolved by acid and marred by the scars of magical fires. Had this warzone been of the bodies of mankind, it would have been a hideous bloodbath, impossible to look upon—and even now, it was difficult, made worse by the scent of the spirit-thieves' corpses, their bulbous tissues liquified by their own blood.

Yet, for as repulsive as all this was, I was entirely focused on one goal. One point in time and space that would either prove its salvation, or its futile ruin.

When we reached the bottom of the tower, I could tell Elishta's magic had not left me, for each step I took across the floor had a strange buoyancy to it. Driven by instinct and paranoia, not trusting entirely my control over him, I grabbed hold of Al-listux's dark garment and dragged him along down the corridor that opened into Malchi-sedeq's suite. There he waited, his expression solemn, his eyes upturned as if in pursuit of the source of that hideous un-sound that overwhelmed us all. His expression was peaceful then; but as he registered my motion, he glanced down, and his eyes widened in a combination of astonishment and horror.

"Rorke," he began, his eyes flashing toward Al-listux in deepening anger, "what do you think—"

"I'll have none of your long-winded monologues, you bitter old mummy." Waving the blade beneath his nose and urging him to silence as we passed by, I warned him, too, "If you interfere with this, Valeria will see to it that you live forever, enduring agonies greater than any man has ever known."

"What do you mean? You—Al-listux, what is the meaning of this?"

"It means," I told him coldly, "the end of your work."

Inside the lab that counted for Malchi-sedeq as a kind of bedroom, I pushed Al-listux toward the portal and commanded, "Open it to that place where the Sleeper dwells; where your kind would normally open such a thing for your more typical war crime of consuming a single planet rather than the whole of the cosmos."

Obedient to my every command, Al-listux smoothly crossed to the glowing looking-glass of Malchi-sedeq and set about tapping briskly on its surface, as well as on a plate of clicking scales set before it.

"Now try to think this through," insisted Malchi-sedeq, while I ignored him and looked sharply around.

"Where is that hateful sister of mine?"

"She disappeared when I freed her—"

His explanation was interrupted by the hivemind's tendril, which shot from the water to grasp my ankle. Unhesitating, I slashed it in twain, shaking my boot free of its sucking grasp while the pain streaked through my own skull and had to be dismissed as a phantom.

You go only to your sooner death, Eradicator!

"Then why do you try to stop me?" I demanded, sweeping Exigence down across the surface of its waters and producing an otherworldly shriek as its eye burst open beneath the sword. Gore splattered out across the chemical water and that hateful entity dropped completely beneath the surface. I assured it, "I'll be back to you in due time," and turned to let Malchi-sedeq see the loathing that blazed in my eyes for his unnatural malice, his selfish self-destruction.

"And you? Will you, 'Father', force your son to cripple you before he does what must be done?"

"No," Malchi-sedeq said softly, glancing from me only briefly as a pinpoint of bluish-white light sparkled in the center of the empty portal's frame. Hands raised to show himself unarmed and free of malintent, at least in that moment, Malchi-sedeq fixed his gaze upon me again and shook his head. "No, Rorke. You can make your own choices. I just wonder if you really understand the choice that you're making."

"I know the choice I'm making," I assured him, giving my arm just a moment of rest by sheathing Exigence while the light in the center of the portal throbbed outward, expanding like liquid suspended in a box without gravity. "I know that within this universe, within life, there is the capacity for infinite suffering. That every being must live devastated by loss and turmoil: by that same uncertainty that has transformed your intellect to the prison of a coward."

Stepping toward Malchi-sedeq a single pace, I looked hard into his soul. "But there is more than suffering. There is beauty, too. There is love, and hope. There is redemption. There is the presence of God, hidden within all of it. And truly, truly I say to you, Father: the God that created the first of the mankinds did not create them for despair, but for love."

The light of the portal now filled the entire frame. Soft digits flying across the scales of the machine, Al-listux performed a few more minor one-handed operations upon the glowing looking-glass.

The glowing doorway changed. Its uniformity broke, surrendering to an array of colors—and on the other side, I looked out upon a place that was no place, where it was always twilight.

"If I do not return," I told him darkly, "and the Sleeper is nevertheless stopped, then I pray you find it in your heart to care for my wives. For if you do indeed feel sentimentally toward the new generations of your line, your failure to prove it in action will reveal even those human parts left in you are worthless."

Without delay, lest I should second-guess the act and succumb to that same cowardice that filled my father's heart even with Weltyr's brave blood in his veins, I stepped through to the unknown realm of the Sleeper.

23

THE WYRD

HOW COULD I, no writer of note, dare describe that realm where I was as much an alien as were the spirit-thieves in ours? I will try; though know, reader, that however well I invoke that strange place, I could not hope to capture the true dimension of what I saw, for there was no dimension, in truth. There was no up or down or left or right, no forward or backward. There simply *was* to such an extent that I could not distinguish it from what was *not*.

This anti-place, I perceived, was the source of those colors, for they were everywhere before me, swallowing me and birthing me back out, primeval illuminations rotating in and out of shapes that reflected one another in endless patterns of what symmetry wishes it could be.

All of it was beautiful and terrible, and I had the sense that I had seen this place during my most recent death, from which Brynhildr wrested me. Indeed, her coming to my mind anchored me somewhat: inspired in me the human pursuit of pareidolia, this natural search for emergent familiarities within patterns of the unknown. My body implied space, for I was still my physical self there, and by this implication I found some steadiness upon which to ground myself.

Before and above me, rooted in nothing, glowing with a brilliance more astonishing than tongues of mighty fire or veins of unhewn Deepgold, rose an infinitely glorious Tree.

I knew this Tree: recognized it, its nature, within me. It penetrated into all else that was, life traveling from me through these branches and into all others and back again: Valeria, Elishta, Gundrygia, Indra and Branwen and Odile and Brynhildr, Grane, Malchi-sedeq and Al-listux, Weltyr and Anroa and Roserpine and Dunnun and even the dancing, laughing flames of Hamsunt. All those we had known and touched in our journey.

Even the Sleeper which moved at its roots, stirred from its endless rest, extricating itself into being to make all that was like it.

I drew Exigence. Movement had no value. The space between me and it closed in my recognition of its presence, and it expanded to the sum total of my awareness, bloated and hideous, offended to be acknowledged and called out of the nothingness it was. The sword of Deepgold shone between us, and I raised the blade to find it resisted like a shield the claim this lord of demons felt it had over me. What might have been embodied on Urde as a great hand reaching forward to snatch me up was repelled by the brightness of the holy sword, which cut through the vibrating vastness of that weird space and thundered against the Sleeper by merit of its existence. That groan of its waking intensified into protest, and I felt the groan inside me: felt it in the fate of all men, for all mankinds—all created things—fell into the mouth of the Sleeper when their bodies failed with no recourse to the infinite capacity of the divine. If eternity was a fractal, the Sleeper was what was outside of that fractal—the nothing, the 0—and the potential for that 0 was dispersed across all reality, across every cell, as was the potential for the infinite heights of God.

Beneath the tree, the Sleeper thrashed and protested, raging against the indignities of its suffering at the mere implication that it was not the ultimate fate of all. It rose, swelling up again, ebbing into my complete awareness and endeavoring to take me with it, into it, to overwhelm all the parts of me that were not it: yet Exigence shone all the brighter, fiercer, plunging through the bowels of its dark being and cutting into lesser dimensions on its other side. The Sleeper wailed, and above, (or within, or elsewhere), the Tree split apart, its great trunk jolting open, its branches scattered in all directions. One held swinging to its origin, nine beats of my rapid heart speeding by until it relinquished its hold and became a splinter falling out to strike the demon with me.

All through me, the wailing of the Sleeper intensified: and that wail was so awful I lost all sense of myself, even with Exigence's light in my hand. Even that light, for a moment, seemed like a dream. Even that highest glory of holiness seemed destined to be overcome, the Tree's collapse inevitable, natural, easy. I was nothing, would be nothing. By that measure that I would someday be nothing, I had always been nothing. What I had thought to be my life had been always a dream of this Sleeper: its own dream, a byproduct of its singular presence at the heart of all truth.

Yet Nothing was not the truth. When I had been Nothing, I had lied. Nothing was a foolish game that had shielded me and the one I tricked from the truth of my lineage, that branch I was of the Tree. Other fallen branches spiraled around me, blotting out the Nothing of the Sleeper as rays of the sun dismissed the darkness of night, and I felt in the rotations of these branches Valeria's prayerful anguish, and Elishta's holy pleas, and the deep dreams of Brynhildr, and the worries of those women who waited anxious on Urde, and aged Weltyr, bent at the knee, submitting to that which was higher than his will.

And Gundrygia, my sister and my bride, whose eyes blazed like diamonds within my heart.

"The Helm, Rorke!"

She was right.

The way to defeat that which was Nothing was to force it into the shape of Something.

From my belt, I drew the Helm, and into the thrashing wildness of the Nothing that had me in its grasp, I tossed that net of Deepgold links.

A great and terrible howl went up from the abyss, reverberating through the incalculable geometry of the unfolding dimension around. I was myself in a full and clear way in that place, and I threw my arm over my face with a cry at the gravitational force exhibited by the complete consumption of the Sleeper within the Helm of Dunnun. That same energy transfigured the shadows of the scattered branches of the Tree, and they stood at the edges of a space of new construction: an order into which that wild, morphing space arranged itself, a perfect grid underlying all existence, with the Tree rising high in its heart. All around, the shadows of the fallen branches moved with life, fleeing before I could make sense of them—but I knew them, all of them, for the one that did not flee stepped from his formerly hanging branch, and picked it up, and examined it in his mighty hand, and left me there with a look of shining pride aglow from his single lively eye.

These were not our gods. These, I sensed, were of the next world. The new world on the cusp of birth.

And my home was the dying one, where those I loved waited for me in this sweet forbearance we received by the grace of God.

At my feet gasped an ugly creature, pitiful, gray, gasping. With the weight of my boot, I crushed it, grimly praying as its body and the Helm collapsed together and were no more.

Panting, I stepped away, my eyes locked upon the Tree, my awareness of time and that place as a whole slowing like the winding down of an old dwarvish clock.

In the silence, I knelt, Exigence held tip-down before me, the shape of the Deepgold sword in perfect alignment with the grid of reality and the Tree at its center.

A great peace came over my heart. The sudden awareness of a presence that was always there, and a merciful love that overwhelmed me with its all-suffusing tenderness.

The space around me pulled away, compounding into a single point.

I, thrust backward, emerged from the portal to land on Malchi-sedeq's floor.

RECONCILIATION

WHAT EUPHORIA! WELL—what complete incomprehension, first.

I found myself there on my back: alive, grounded once again in the reality I knew, my mind bathed in the glory of what I had just encountered as well as the knowledge that I had, by sheer miracle, overcome something no other man could hope to survive. Amazed, I laughed—and laughed all the louder to recognize the sweet silence of the world, the sign that the Sleeper had been stopped.

I had no sooner recognized it than an awful shriek rose high in the room, drawing my attention toward Al-listux. Freed from my control—due, perhaps, to my absence—he struck me with a psionic wave that sent me flying back across the floor to plunge into the odious waters of the hivemind entity.

How foul that substance was! My nostrils, eyes, and throat all burned, assailed by the same chemicals that maintained some degree of integrity for the exposed tissue of that alien brain. I felt it throbbing behind me in the water, cold and massive, and, as I gained orientation enough to try for a swim to the surface, one of its tendrils snatched tight around my boot to drag me down.

What have you done, Eradicator? What have you done to our god?

My mouth shut tight along with my eyes beneath the water, I pushed for the surface, realizing with dread that Exigence had been in my hand when I was thrown through the portal and was now separated from me, left on the floor above while I sank into the chemical depths. With my free boot, I kicked blindly at the tentacles, fighting against the resistance of the waters to assail the demon's soft tissue. My lungs stinging, I struggled, flailed, cursed myself for my own stupidity to have been taken by surprise. Was this to be my fate? Was my reward for slaying the Sleeper to be death at the hands of its offspring?

Barely cracking open my eyes to ascertain how much distance lay between me and safety, I raised my head to the light that poured from the room above.

And a figure, armed with Exigence, stepped up into silhouette. Whoever it was dropped to their knees, the sword of the Wotsungs raised high, and plunged it down into the water, into the center of that hateful mind so intent on killing me that it never saw the threat until far too late. At the penetration of the Deepgold's blade into the center of the mass of tissues that served for its body, the hivemind let out an abominable shriek, and its tendrils went slack. Too desperate to notice how my eyes burned or how nauseous I was from exposure to these foul waters, I kicked furiously, my muscles so exhausted that I felt certain I would drown before I reached the top.

And I may well have, had Malchi-sedeq not plunged his hand into the water and, catching mine, hauled me out with an effort that left us both gasping.

While he lay flat on his back from the force required to yank me from the water, I managed to push myself up on hands and knees to vomit up entirely too much of whatever poison safekept the vile entity. As the sound of these loathsome waters splashing on the floor abated, they left me free to consciously absorb the awful screams of Al-listux, who, connected intimately with the hivemind that it was his life, thrashed and wailed upon the floor, limbs receding inward, squid-face caving in, all of its essence dissolving until there was nothing left but a scrap of black fabric abandoned formlessly on the floor.

"You saved me," I stammered.

Malchi-sedeq, sitting up, watched those last microseconds of Al-listux's existence with an expression of dispassionate peace.

"I did." The words emerged from him with equal incredulity, and he studied the sword in his hand before dropping it upon the floor beside him. "How could I do otherwise? After what you seem to have accomplished, letting the hivemind Entity kill you would be a dishonor…even to a coward like me. Here." While I blinked and rubbed my eyes, Malchi-sedeq fetched a decanter of clear water from the shelf above his casket. As he returned to pour it out across my face, I caught hold of his hands to direct the flow where it was most needed. The burning reduced to a more irritated sting, and the vile taste in my mouth lessened to a ghost of itself. Finally able to breathe freely, I fell back upon the floor. My earthly father set the decanter aside and looked at me for long, slow seconds in which we seemed to share a devastating unspoken knowledge: that, one way or another, our association would be quick to end.

"I think you're right about me," he confessed softly. "I know all there is to know about this world—but the one thing I don't know, what lies beyond it, frightens me so intensely I'd prefer to anesthetize myself with oblivion rather than meeting its consequences head-on."

"If it comforts you at all," I told him, sitting up more fully now and plucking Exigence from his grasp before he could change his mind and wrest hold of the blade again, "know that I believe I just encountered that One you fear, and there is nothing to fear in Him. His sweetness and mercy are beyond my ability to express."

"Maybe for you," agreed Malchi-sedeq, helping me to my feet and leaving his hand around my forearm while he studied my face. "But I've made more mistakes. I'm not a good man, or a courageous man. I'm a selfish man; and I knew better than to be so selfish."

"I can tell you with certainty that's true. Yet—" As he released me, I took the opportunity to grab him by the shoulder and draw him in for an embrace I never thought I would experience. "Whatever your evil heart, or your bad intentions, it was you who created me. You who engendered the tool by which the Sleeper was vanquished. And surely, had that not been some secret hope in your heart all along—had it not been the case that you longed for a son with the conscience required to make up for the courage and hope you lack—you never would have defied the spirit-thieves and seen to it that I was delivered to the Temple of Weltyr, where you knew they would train me to be the kind of man you could never teach me to be on your own. Thank you."

Malchi-sedeq grew silent. His head lowered against my shoulder, and as he trembled in my arms, I knew he wept. This brought tears to my own eyes, and I held my father to my heart, the grief-filled dreams of a lifetime pouring out of me while we clasped each other in this long-awaited embrace.

Then, releasing me, he wiped his index finger and thumb across his eyes. "Your women must be waiting for you. Go on up to them. Don't keep them in anxiety any longer."

"What will you do?"

"I'll be here," he said, waving me toward the door. "I'll be right here, feeling grateful that my life has had some good use after all."

Moved, I squeezed his shoulder, then exited his suite to make my dizzy way up that silent tower.

How strange to witness the disordered ruins of this battle! How strange to realize that, after all this time, it was over. The Sleeper was vanquished, along with all the spirit-thieves attached to the hivemind. Only the citizens of Ironforge would know whether their telepathic connections with one another would outlast their mental slavery to the demon; and only time would tell whether the remaining hiveminds scattered across Urde would abandon the planet or wither and die, no longer having a purpose to serve. With delirious disbelief, I reflected on the sudden notion that I had not just rescued Urde, but all life—all populated worlds and colonies past, present, and future. By a great grace, I had been an instrument of divine victory: of justice, meted out for the sakes of all those who wanted only to live, and who knew nothing at all of me or the Sleeper or the things that occurred that day.

Upstairs, at the top of the tower, my legs shook with exhaustion so complete I had no sooner set eyes on Valeria and Elishta than I collapsed in a heap upon the floor. Crying my name with relief, the women hurried to me, kissing and caressing me heedless of any chemical taste upon my lips.

"You did it," Elishta exclaimed, her expression a firework of joy as she gestured to the star map on the ceiling. "Look! Oh, Rorke—"

"You fool," wept Valeria, burying her face in my chest to sob like a child. "I can't believe you'd do something so asinine as risk your life that way—"

"I've already risked my life for you more times than I can count," I told her blearily, caressing her hair, "and I would do it every day until the end of time if it were necessary to ensure your happiness."

As the two of them wailed together, I kissed their precious heads one at a time, blessing them within my heart and thanking profusely the god, the true God, who made us. Oh, sweet treasures! My first bride, and my second—

And my third, who, now arrayed in her rosy pink gown, reclined upon the stairs to the pedestal where Valeria's clone still lay in a state of scientific enchantment.

"Gundrygia." As the other two looked up to hear her name on my lips, I studied her with pain in my heart—

pain, and longing that could never die no matter what she was to me. It was too late to change what was between us. She was helplessly mad for me, and I—I could not help but love her, and to love the child within her, even if he was doomed to bear his mother's wicked heart.

"How valiant, Rorke! How mighty, Burningsoul. You holy man, those spirit-thieves were arrogant fools to ever doubt your destiny. Yet"—her head raising with her shoulders as she pushed herself slightly more upright, Gundrygia tilted her head—"have you humility enough to do what truly needs done?"

Her gaze raised toward the height of the pedestal. A dread strangely worse than that instilled by the Sleeper's voice came upon me. Looking in a special way at Valeria, I released my embrace of the women and made my way up to study the clone, stepping over Gundrygia and squeezing her hand in mine as she reached up to caress my fingers on my passing. While she remained lounging there like a big cat in the sun, I studied the Circlet of Simulation and, after a moment's delay, slid it off the cloned Valeria's head.

Laying there, her eyes closed, she was the perfect image of my love—my love if she had not known me. What would it be like for her on waking to this world? Surely she would have no choice but to reconcile whatever she had experienced within that Circlet as a dream, just as Malchi-sedeq had explained it was the common custom of long-developed clones to fabricate an explanation for their missing chunks of time. Whatever explanation her mind concocted to protect itself, the question remained: What would she do with her life now that all of this was done?

"I can hardly believe the ring is here," Valeria said from where she stood behind my shoulder, having followed me softly up to her reposed twin. Her eyes were fixed on that band of Deepgold embracing the sleeping woman's finger, shining softly in the light. "After all this time—it seems like a dream."

"God willing, all we have been through will be less than a dream compared to our lives. Valeria—"

My throat tightened as I turned to take her hand, which I pressed to my heart.

"I know you have responsibilities," I told her, sinking to one knee before her and gazing up into those beautiful eyes, "and I know how sweet your life has been, spoiled and adored in the Nightlands. And so you deserve to be. Surely I could never provide you with the exorbitant luxuries you could demand of the civilization of the durrow as a whole. Yet—Madame—I promise you, the love that burns in me for you is beyond all compare, and however your fellow women adore you as their queen, there is none who could adore you more than I will as my wife, if you would truly have me. What you willed from a distance has come to you now, close enough to touch. But you must make the decision, finally, to take it, or to leave it behind you to resume the life you once had."

Valeria searched my face, letting me maintain the grip of my hand while she considered my words. Then, she turned to study the ring upon the finger of the clone.

"You know…what frightened me was not you going off to face the Sleeper alone. I knew in my heart that this was what you were born for: that, one way or another, you would conquer even that greatest of foes. No…"

She turned to face me again, and her eyes shone with a veil of tears.

"What frightened me was learning that you are the only thing standing between me and her." With a wave of her free hand toward the second Valeria, she whispered words that pained her so she bared her teeth just to say them. "To think that, without you, the trajectory of my life was so cold and empty—so crippled by pure hubris— that I could be deluded into the idea of controlling a demon like the Sleeper! To think that, without you, I would be so empty-hearted and easily duped by my pride, my vanity...I don't want that, Rorke. I cannot endure that life. Let the Deep-children have their Ring: I need none of it. There is nothing my heart longs for anymore except you."

How bright my soul felt within me in that moment. Forgetting all exhaustion, I sprang to my feet to catch her by the waist and twirl her in my arms, calling her name with joy and then, while she laughed and remonstrated in happy surprise, pulling her to my mouth to blot out the remaining chemical taste with the sweetness of her tongue. When we parted, I stroked her hair, gazing with love into her perfect face.

"But what will the women of the Nightlands do for want of their Materna?"

"Oh," she said with a casual glance at the pedestal beside us, "I'm sure we can come up with a better solution than leaving them all unattended."

25

TREASURE RETURNED...

AFTER ALL THAT we had been through in the course of that night, the three of us were beyond exhausted—but I, in particular, was so worn that I found a new burst of energy, perhaps because I knew that the moment I laid my head on a pillow I would succumb to a sleep so deep I would not awaken for hours, and then would only do so to an acute awareness of all my body had endured for the past day. Therefore, assured by Gundrygia that Malchisedeq would not mind a little time spent resting before our departure, I saw to it that both Elishta and Valeria were comfortable taking some long overdue sleep in one of the suites of the first floor. Alone, and with a sense that time would be limited before she awoke with all the temperaments and drives of the Valeria I had first met in the Nightlands, I fetched a sheet and gingerly wrapped the unconscious clone's body in its fabric.

As I did, that missing ring shone on her finger, its Deepgold gleaming in the light.

Deepgold! Bright gold! Cursed be him that squanders thy gifts, blessed be him that bears you home safe!

What a frightful object, with powers I still didn't know! One of three Deepgold items remaining in all existence. The Helm had been annihilated along with the Sleeper, it seemed; but the Lantern, the Sword, and the Ring all remained, and two of those three were in my possession.

The third? Well—Valeria had refused it when she made the decision to remain by my side rather than return to the Nightlands.

Sweet gold! High gold! Your laughter resounded with innocence here—now that laughter mocks us to lure fool men!

This second Valeria breathed softly, her head limp against my shoulder as I bore her down the spiraling stairs. A small handful of skeletons who had remained in the tower for the attendance of basic duties and not been called to battle swept up, and while they were near, I felt supervised. My eyes remained focused on the path ahead—and every step I took, no matter how I strove to avert my eyes, the gleam of the Deepgold danced in their edges.

We mourn your innocence, burned from your soul! Return now the gold! Return now the gold! Weia! Waga! Preserve your soul from this unholy stain!

Had the haunting song rung out in my mortal ears, I could have plugged them and ignored every word. But these words, this song—they rang out in that same faculty which had been filled by the presence of the Creating One, an interior locution beyond all evasion.

And still, they were no match for that glimmer. That glint. That notion that, if I did allow the ring to return to the Nightlands—well, who could know what might happen? It had roused the Sleeper. That power was beyond all resistance. If it could do that, what else could it do? One knew what a sword was capable of; one understood the mechanics of a lantern, even one imprisoning a god.

But—a ring?

Already the Deepgold mocks you with longing! It plots your demise, will destroy your world. Thrust it in our waters and preserve yourself—we warn you, we mourn you, you lost child of a race of dying gods!

There was no knowing what a ring like this could do.

Shut out its light and throw it away! Send it where it came from, surrender the poison and transmute its cure!

I knew myself. I could trust myself. I would not do any harm with the ring, and I was quite certain I would never let it fall into untrustworthy hands.

Woe to the world, woe to our hearts! Woe to you, Burningsoul, upon your house and sons!

Beyond the door of the tower, the sun rose over the edge of a false horizon.

I bore the clone of Valeria to the moat built around the edge of its gardens, where I paused.

The dawn played merrily against the bright metal of the gold.

Do not think less of me, I beg you.

Before I crossed, I slipped the ring from her still finger and dropped it into the pocket of my tunic.

"Oh, holy gold!"

One head sprang from the water, my sin witnessed by those it most ailed.

"How happily we once swam in your shine!"

A second head burst with a song, and I pressed this second Valeria to my heart while hastening across the drawbridge with my eyes cast low.

"Deepgold! Deepgold!"

The third arose, their pained chorus shaming me every step, yet I could not make myself give it away—nor could I throw aside the sword or the lantern. Who knew how long I would live? Who knew what I would be called to do?

"Stop, thief!"

I may well have needed them.

"Save yourself!"

My sons, even, might have needed them.

"Save the gold!"

Weltyr was already dying, along with those others who counted as gods.

"Help!"

He had stolen my friend, Brynhildr, whose concealing flames of Hamsunt leapt high in the distance toward which I walked.

"Help!"

I owed him nothing now. I had no need to do him the favor of righting his wrongs when that one who was born to serve his will had been cast so blithely aside.

"Woe to our mother! Woe to our world! Woe to you, Rorke Burningsoul!"

On I walked, my features grimly set—and the Deep-children, singing the song of their sorrow that still haunts my soul each time I look upon Exigence where it remains on my wall, sank beneath the waters of the moat, and were gone.

Onward I went, my heart heavy but my deeds rationalized. Cradling this Valeria as carefully as I would have the original, I made my way through the scattered trees and over the patches of flowers, allowing the column of smoke from Brynhildr's guarding fire to serve as my guide. At my approach, Grane raised his head, studying me solemnly from the distance and knowing, I was certain, what I would ask of him.

"Hello, my friend," I told him as we stopped before him. "Would you do me one last favor, for love of your mistress?"

Looking from me to Valeria, the dark horse exhaled in a flare of its great nostrils and clambered smoothly to its hooves. With a gentle pat of its neck, I balanced dreaming Valeria against the beast's mane, then hopped up behind her, my arm folded about her waist. Casting a reluctant look of longing at the flames that enclosed its mistress, the horse leapt into the air, riding high into the sky that had grown so perfectly blue with the fullness of morning that it seemed we flew into an ocean. Indeed, it had that impact as we burst through the surface to the other side, expelling through the artificial atmosphere and beyond, down into the atmosphere of Urde. Down, down.

The hermit's cottage was much smaller than I remembered, though it had only been a short time since we left. Outside it, a feminine figure wandered, and I could tell Branwen's gold hair from a distance; just as she, stretching and pacing and restlessly awaiting news in the morning light, saw us and, springing up on her toes, darted into the cottage with a frantic call. Moments later, she remerged, the durrow in tow. The three of them called and waved, greeting me with a mingling of excitement and terror to see Valeria out cold in my arms.

"What's happened," Odile demanded, rushing to us before even the others when the horse landed with a few extra paces to cool off its speed. "What did they do to her?"

"Where are Elishta and Brynhildr," asked Branwen with unfeigned concern while I passed the false Materna down into the arms of her kin.

"They're still aboard the *Shooting Star*," I told them, not wanting to trouble them with the sad story of Brynhildr's condition. "They're at rest there—but I thought it important that Valeria be returned to her home as soon as possible. Whatever they did to her—"

I hesitated, not wanting to lie and further tarnish my heart after the choice I had made to retain the Ring of Roserpine.

"She has no memories of me," I settled on, "nor of anything else from our journey."

The women all gasped and despaired, and I shook my head. "It's just as well," I told them, studying her features that, amid all the speaking, were beginning to tighten with disturbance. "To choose a life with me, Valeria must surrender her power, including her rights over all her people. I love her. How can I demand she do such a thing? How can she be expected to give up wealth, property, security, for an uncertain future with me?"

Indeed, I was truly astonished she had opened her heart to those things: these were testaments to how much she had grown. This visible echo of the person she used to be, too, was only further reinforcement of that. Somehow, though I knew the Valeria I loved was safe and sound, my heart was pained by the thought of letting this one go, and I could not help but caress my knuckle along the surface of her cheek. Then, looking up to find the women deeply solemn, I told them, "She'll be fine once she's had an opportunity to awaken and orient herself, although I'm sure she'll be quite confused. Did you—" Hesitating, I looked between the three of them and asked with a nod toward the sky, "Did you notice any strange phenomena last night?"

A curious glance bandied between the three of them. The women shook their heads. "A funny aurora," Branwen clarified, "but nothing unusual aside from the fact we're a little far south for such effects at this time of the year."

Relieved that the danger had left no impression at all on the people of Urde, I nodded with thanks in my heart. "Very good. Well—she may come to with reports of queer dreams relating to the Sleeper or the spirit-thieves, and I have no doubt she will be highly disoriented to be missing so much time and memory. Be patient with her, please. As to the ring—"

Now, I did lie, and I felt a twist in my gut about it as I had never felt a lie impact me before.

"It was destroyed in the battle with the spirit-thieves—I'm not sure how to resolve that for her, since we came all this way, but knowing it no longer exists at least ensures it won't fall into the wrong hands or be a point of contention for the durrow people. It may mark a shift in politics, but...if anyone can maintain a position of power with or without the symbol of the ring, it's Valeria."

"The ring was *destroyed?*" Looking furious on Valeria's behalf, Odile demanded, "How?"

"The spirit-thieves used it to wake their sleeping god—but it did not go as they envisioned. Their hivemind in this region was killed."

"And the necromancer?"

Here, I hesitated, for I truly did not know what would become of Malchi-sedeq, or whether I would have a chance of persuading him to give up his pastimes.

"He is not a madman. Rather, he is a man who has his own interests at heart. Given that he is letting us stay to recover for a night, we might make some headway with him for the people of Ironforge, but we'll see. Either way, when you make it back there, Norhalm owes it to me to assist you on my behalf. I am sure, when you explain that the hivemind has been destroyed and the spirit-thief abductions will stop, they will gladly make every arrangement to help you board an airship back to Skythorn."

Branwen's expression fell. "Why—you're not coming?"

What a terrible pain of conscience I endured! How sad I was, and sad I am even still to reflect on that moment, that look in her face. I loved her, and she loved me. We were dear to each other—but not dear enough, or in the right ways.

"Skythorn is no place for me now," I reminded her. "I no longer belong to the Temple. I'm not even sure Soot would have us back after all the chaos we brought! No, Branwen—I'm not sure where I'll go, but wherever I make my home, I don't think it will be there."

With the uncharacteristic look of a wilted flower, Branwen studied me carefully. "And you'll take Elishta as your bride, I'm sure, since she's pregnant, and can't go back, either?"

Nodding, I admitted, "That's the plan."

Despite the undeniable hurt in her eyes, Branwen was a pragmatic woman, and one too ambitious to be counted yet as any man's wife. Through the misting of her eyes, she nodded, looking at me boldly.

"Sucks to be you," she told me in a tone of forced cheer. "I'll bet my next adventure I'll really strike it rich. Maybe I'll convince Grimalkin to come along with me. We'll make some cash slaying dragons and retire early with a 50/50 split."

Feeling my own throat tense with the imminent parting from my friends, I returned her smile. "I have no doubt you'll make more than enough for a comfortable life. The question is whether or not comfort suits you. I think you're too restless, Branwen, to settle for retirement."

"Man...you're probably right."

Her lips trembled. So I wouldn't see it, she ducked her head, then raised it only to throw her arms around my neck in a tight embrace I returned.

"Stay safe, Rorke," she told me in a whisper. "Take care of Elishta."

"I will, Branwen. Take care, yourself—I'll pray for you all the days of my life. Let's find one another again someday."

With a strangled little sob, she dropped back, and Indra and Odile looked up at me, the former with more sadness than the latter.

"Are you sure she won't miss you?"

"She isn't the woman I love," I told her, bending to kiss Indra's cheek, then scowling Odile's. Her expression made me laugh. "What is it?"

"I can't believe you bungled this so badly," the more seasoned of the two thieves said, sighing with profound annoyance. "An amnesiac Materna, no ring to speak of...you realize it's going to look like we kidnapped her, right?"

"Nonsense...then why would you bring her back? Trust me, ladies. When you return to El'ryh with the missing high priestess, you'll both look like heroes. You *are* heroes." As I corrected myself on this matter, Odile's cheeks darkened with a blush, and I urged her in a special way, "Never forget it."

"Oh," groaned the Valeria substitute, no longer able to maintain the peace of unconsciousness with all the racket around her, "my head..."

"I should go," I told them, mounting Grane one last time, giving them a flash of the roguish grin that always made Branwen roll her eyes. "Don't want her falling in love with me all over again if she's not going to be mine."

And, though Branwen did indeed roll her eyes and make a face of disdain for my now fully affected cocksure demeanor—as Grane thundered off into the sky—she, of all three, waved the most wildly, and shouted, "Be safe! Take care! Tell Elishta we love her!" and remained, a little pinprick of life, long after the others had carried their Valeria inside the hermitage and disappeared from my sight.

To shed not a tear would be inhuman. I cried, yes, as Grane bore me into the heavens to return and make my peace with the owner of *Shooting Star* before we determined the best course of action for our departure, with or without Gundrygia. Yet, I also knew this was right: that Branwen and Odile and Indra would always be among my dearest friends, still roaming the world, free to make their lives in whatever ways pleased them, wherever, with whomever they pleased. Elishta and Valeria—my Valeria—were truly my loves, bound close to my heart.

And, Gundrygia—she needed someone to look after her, it was clear. I would speak with Malchi-sedeq and ask him to release her custody to me, if she would have it; and I was quite sure, based on their relationship, that he would be just as happy to have her off his hands. Like a man preparing to ask his sweetheart's father for her hand in marriage, I readied myself to address *my* father—at least, that man who created me, not through the womb of a bride, but the womb of technology.

Beside Brynhildr's fire, Grane resumed his silent vigil, ignoring my gentle invitation that he return with me to the tower and find a place more accommodating. The sad horse rested his head upon the earth, his eyes closing, his entire body bidding sleep to come the way it had come to his mistress. I left him there, as pained as I had been in leaving my humanoid friends, and made my way back to the tower.

The building was so quiet! The skeletons had either finished their work, or were now tidying the stairs at landings so high I could not hear them. Feeling the need to preserve this quiet as though I were back at the Temple, I made my silent way to Malchi-sedeq's chambers, dreading the conversation awaiting me. I had so much to say! About Gundrygia; about Ironforge. I wanted to get to know him, too, and to gently suggest that he might bear his casket with him and explore Urde for the first time in longer than he seemed able to remember.

All this and more sat upon my tongue; all this and more piteously dissolved as I set foot within his laboratory to find, shriveled and contorted with age so impossibly advanced he was a step away from dust, the body of my father.

Wrested from his casket the night before after only an hour of sleep, Malchi-sedeq had opted to pay the debt he owed rather than again conceal himself within its darkness and take the benefit of its dark magic. He died reclining against that same black casket that had maintained his life, able at any moment to open it and climb in, making the declarative choice that he never would again.

Pain and relief flooding my breast, all things solved with this gracious decision to quietly relinquish all to which he had clung with such intense greed, I cradled Malchi-sedeq's small body in one arm while raising the lid of the casket with the other. A sad hope dwelled in me—that foolish emotion condemned by Al-listux, who was now an ugly puddle of fish-stinking tissues near the desk. I delayed what I planned, leaning against the shut lid of lead once Malchi-sedeq's body was set within. The moments passed at a length of hours. I waited them out, ten, fifteen, twenty, until I could wait no longer, and peeked within the casket.

No change at all: the Casket of Oppenhir could prolong existent life, but it could not bring back the dead.

Heart strangely panged, not the least tempted to keep it after seeing how unnatural life had cursed him and restricted his soul, I pushed the casket into the waters with the dead hivemind. Slowly, like a petal overcome upon the surface of the waters, the black box sank until the only evidence of it was a trail of bubbles escaping its interior in a ladder to the surface.

And soon enough, even this disappeared.

Epilogue

THE QUESTION

DID WE EVER leave the Valor Hall?

I often wonder. Well—maybe not 'often'. Often is too much. I often think about Valeria, beautiful, frozen in time to all beholders, and how terrifying and solemn that beauty is to me now, as my own looks and Elishta's both drift further and further off into time. Once, I heard a turn of phrase that haunts me: "Like two ships passing in the night."

More like two ships impacting one another irrevocably. Like the *Flying Rhinemaid* and the *Battle Swan*, encountering each other, one immortal and one not, linked in this moment of time that changed and connected them forever. That brief waylaying is like my entire life in the sprawling timeline of Valeria's own, and it becomes so much more obvious every day.

But I often think about that. About her, in that and other, perhaps more reverent ways. I think about Elishta-bet, and about how proud I am of the boys, and about how grateful I am—despite all my mistakes and misapprehensions and the primitive ways I have come to know Him—to be an unworthy servant of God.

And then there's Gundrygia. I try not to think about her, and I try not to do it often. I don't even see her every single day, as I do the others. It's just as well. She prefers to consume my attention when she desires it, so if she did not prowl off into practices of isolation and sometimes even absences, neither Valeria nor Elishta would have a fair share of my time. It drives me insane…but it's better this way, not to get too close.

Maybe that's why I don't think about that question often. Because its answer is surely something Gundrygia shared with me before I was prepared to hear it. Because I wonder, really, if the God of Life, who is truly Life, Himself, would even really account for death as an internal experience. I have, after all, died many deaths, and I think of them incessantly. I think of other times, too, that could have easily ended in death. Climbing on the roof of the Temple to watch a meteor shower with the other boys, and with Elishta, who heard about it from me and scrambled up with us, and leaned into me, shivering, when I was just so painfully stupid to see what she wanted from me.

Each woman I love brings in me a kind of death. Not in a sexual way, but in a way that being around her allows me to empty myself on a spiritual, psychic level. Death is a bride who comes and goes, swinging in and out; and Life, flying with equal and opposite force in the other direction, becomes from within the subjective experience of each visitation. Perhaps on the outside, the objective side, I'm just a man aging and making notes to myself before I'm too old to recount it. Inside, I am a vine spiraling up and up, reaching toward something that calls me closer every day.

I have all the comforts one could wish for. Things I never knew existed, like the motion picture library aboard this kind ship, the flying citadel that has become our permanent home. The wives, and the boys. There are times I wonder if I could figure out how to use *Shooting Star* to visit the colonized regions, but I would be too crushed if I discovered nothing had taken successful long-term root, so in the end I decided not to try and research the matter too deeply. This place is self-sufficient, and this ship is genetically linked to me, as all former colonizing ships are to their captains. It supposes I am Malchi-sedeq, and so do all the remaining clones, including the one resembling me. We offered them the option of returning to Urde, and some of them did; but a few were allured by the prospect of a simple, fresh life, and stayed on as servants and farmhands in exchange for having their needs provided, having as they did respect for my authority because they thought I was the fearsome necromancer who shared my face.

It provides for our every need, this ship. The impossible space within it really does seem to be infinite, and I consider it less a ship and more as the housing of a great portal that opens into some kind of pocket dimension where my family resides. I am not sure that I would know what to do if something went wrong with it, but I am also not sure anything *can* go wrong with it. I do not know whether it is magical or technological. The properties of the sprawling landscape in which our tower is situated could be both, or either, but ultimately, again, remind me of the Valor Hall, and I wonder.

But I try not to wonder often.

Exigence shines where it remains mounted upon the wall of what was once Malchi-sedeq's living room: now the common hearth where all our family gathers each evening.

The Lantern of Hamsunt stands proud on a lampstand, glowing welcome in the center of the tower's anteroom, though we have no visitors to admire it, for *Shooting Star* has not entered the atmosphere of Urde for many years.

Only the Ring of Roserpine remains hidden, my secret shame, tucked away beneath the false bottom in the drawer of a great oak desk within my office. I know I betray my sweet Valeria by keeping it in this way; but I know she will be pleased, in her secret heart, when she discovers on my death I have willed it to her son, my eldest, who is, I think, the sharpest of the three, and was always, in his youth, the first each night to badger me into our same old routine. "Let us try the sword, Papa," he would delightedly cry, interrupting my latest book from his grandfather's vast library. "Please, may we?"

"None of you could make it budge yesterday," I'd tell him, shutting the tome over which I pored to understand the One who truly made me, a treatise by a saint awaiting, like me, the sight of His face. Tickling my giddily squealing child, I asked the lad, "What makes you think anything will have changed today?"

"It must change someday, Papa! Why not today?"

"Who says it'll change for you?" My second son has always been a bit dour, particularly when compared against his brothers, and I sometimes worry that this is my fault. I suspect that, because of the nature of his mother, I am inclined to treat him differently, more seriously, dooming him to always feel a restless distance between himself and the love of the world. Indeed, I have come to think boys learn that love from their fathers in the way I learned it from the priests of the Temple, and if so, I have failed him. "You seem awfully confident that you'll get something out of this exercise."

"He'll be happy no matter who finally picks it up," exclaimed, inevitably, my third son, the most innocent boy who has ever lived, so often off in his own little world that his adjacent sibling's inclination towards bullying has never seemed to bother him. "I know I will be—won't you?"

"I suppose," Hagen would grunt with a thoughtful look like his all too knowing mother before suddenly animating, rushing with energy toward the hearth. "Let me try it first!"

"Very well—let's see if Exigence thinks one of you is old enough to be worthy!"

The boys bouncing around me, I would chuckle and carefully take Exigence down from its cherished place above the hearth. Then, setting it down upon the floor, I watched— and my heart tightened in my chest more by the night.

First, Hagen. Pushing up his sleeves with an almost comedic air, he would roll his shoulders, crack his knuckles, and bend down to catch the grip of the blade. I love him—of course, I love him as much as my other sons—but I have never thought it best that the heir of Gundrygia's line be the one the sword chooses as its inheritor.

Mercifully, many days have passed wherein I need not find the answer to that question. As though bound to the floor by cement, it would remain fast in place, and eventually he would stumble back with a sullen mumble, a crestfallen scowl, a knuckle wiped beneath his nose.

Next rushed up Severian, the spitting image of Valeria with fire in his eyes, eager and happy, tugging at the blade to no avail. "Shucks," he enthused, kicking the floor but bright with excitement all the same, urging, "you try it, Sigurd!"

Brimming over with glee, Sigurd always hastened to obey his brother, attempting to pry the sword's pommel from the floor where it remained, stubborn, until I bent to catch hold of the weapon and raise it into the glory of the light.

Each time I did—each time I still do—the prophecy of Roserpine freezes my heart.

Someday, one of these boys will be grown enough in the eyes of the Deepgold that his Wotsung blood will lighten it for him, and he will hold Exigence in his hand.

On that day, it will no longer be my sword. On that day, I will know the number of my own days has whittled to an insignificant figure.

But I should not say 'insignificant'. For every day I spend with them—as with Valeria, and Elishta, and even with Gundrygia—is anything but insignificant.

They are my family; they are my greatest joys, the songs of my heart, the holiest gifts ever given me by the One who gave me life.

And, whatever happens—whatever their destinies, or mine—I will love them until the day I die, and far beyond.

For I know there is so much beyond.

More than could ever be discovered.

AFTERWORD

BURNINGSOUL HAS BEEN a strange and interesting series for me, written in a genre that was new to me at a time in my life that was very difficult for myself and for someone I love very dearly. Over the next 5 years, nothing really seemed to get easier, and the appetite of the market only grew. After struggling through illness related to my thyroid and facing some serious adjustments in my day-to-day rhythms, I was tempted to leave the series behind despite my clear vision for its ending. Moreover, I experienced a deep religious conversion sometime after Book III, and suddenly the themes of the series didn't resonate with me anymore. I felt trapped between a rock and a hard place, unable to move forward with my writing career until I finished Burningsoul.

And all the while, you wrote to me. Not all the time. But every now and then, I'd get a ping.

Sometimes on Reddit.

Sometimes in email.

Sometimes through the Painted Blind Publishing website.

When is the next Burningsoul coming out?

It was that anticipation that allowed me to finish this series. Knowing readers out there were waiting for the conclusion of Rorke's story was what helped me find the motivation to finish this book, and to do it in a way that was more aligned with my new values than I could have possibly hoped. Thank you, truly, for your kind inquiries, and for believing in me when I didn't believe in myself.

I have a vision for one more Burningsoul volume—a collection of 4 novellas about Rorke's sons, plus one of the women from this original series—and the outline for that is complete, but I know better than to promise it anytime soon. Today, as I finish typesetting the book, I'm feeling inspired and eager to start on it. Tomorrow, if my medications fluctuate or life intervenes, I may decide to work on something else for awhile. Such is the mind of a writer. Particularly one who strives to be an unworthy servant of God.

Rorke is one of my favorite protagonists of all time, so far as my own body of work is concerned. He is, like essentially all of my protagonists, an unreliable narrator, and there are moments where one is hard-pressed to call him a hero in the pure sense of the modern word. Rather, he is more the fatally flawed hero of an ancient epic. As my father, a trained classicist, used to quip, "Remember, there are two versions of The Odyssey: There's the one Odysseus tells Penelope, and the one he tells the guys at the bar."

Rorke's story is one being told to the guys at the bar—you guys. And as long as you're still having fun, I'll keep coming back to bring it to its end.

Even if it takes me a little longer than I hope.

God bless you,
Regina Watts

ABOUT THE AUTHOR

Regina Watts is the penname of M. F. Sullivan, founder and flagship author of Painted Blind Publishing. From her cozy home a few universes away from this one, Watts transmits stories to Sullivan that are then transcribed and published. Her available titles range from transgressive erotica to psychedelic fiction to horror to romance. Be sure to check out her website and sign up for her mailing list at hrhdegenetrix.com!

ABOUT THE PUBLISHER

Painted Blind Publishing and its erotic imprint, Painted Blue Publishing, are the brainchild of author and devoted editor to Regina Watts, M. F. Sullivan. Founded in 2015 while Sullivan resided in Tucson, PBP is a house dedicated to bringing readers the finest in consciousness-expanding fiction. Be sure to check out the wide variety of essays available for free at paintedblindpublishing.com to learn more about the company, Watts, and Sullivan.

OTHER PAPERBACK WORKS
FROM PAINTED BLIND PUBLISHING

REGINA WATTS

INDUSTRIAL DIVINITY (2020)

WILD GIRL RUNNING (2020)

DOTTIE FOR YOU SEASON 1 (2021)

SEDUCED BY SABINE (2021)

I WAS AN OP DEMON LORD (2021-2022)

BE MY BULLY (2021)

MAYHEM AT THE MUSEUM (2021)

IDOL (2022)

TEXAS CRUEL (2023)

AD THEOLOGIAM DE MACHINA CONSCIENTIA (2026)

ADA DART

THE RIFT BRIDE (2022-2025)

FINN VANDERGRIFT

SKINSLUT (2024 – With Regina Watts)

M. F. SULLIVAN

DELILAH, MY WOMAN (2015)

THE LIGHTNING STENOGRAPHY DEVICE (2017)

THE DISGRACED MARTYR TRILOGY (2019-2020)